COLLIDED

DIRTY AIR SERIES BOOK TWO

LAUREN ASHER

Copyright © 2020 by Lauren Asher.

All rights reserved.

No part of this book may be reproduced in any form or by any electronic or mechanical means, including information storage and retrieval systems, without written permission from the author, except for the use of brief quotations in a book review.

This book is a work of fiction. Names, characters, organizations, places, events, and incidents are either products of the author's imagination or are used fictitiously.

COLLIDED

Editing: Erica Russikoff

Cover Designer: Books and Moods

Interior Formatting: Books and Moods

To the Sophie Mitchells out there—
Be different. Be genuine. Be you.

PLAYLIST

COLLIDED - LAUREN ASHER

Break Free — Ariana Grande ft. Zedd	3:34	+
I Just Wanna Shine — Fitz and The Tantrums	3:26	+
Can I Kiss You? — Dahl	3:27	+
Greenlight — Jonas Brothers	3:00	+
Butterflies — Kacey Musgraves	3:38	+
Trying My Best — Anson Seabra	3:42	+
What I Like About You — Jonas Blue	3:55	+
There's No Way — Lauv ft. Julia Michaels	2:54	+
All To Myself — Dan & Shay	2:49	+
Break My Heart — Dua Lipa	3:41	+
Symphony — Clean Bandit ft. Zara Larson	3:32	+
Yellow — Coldplay	4:26	+
Fight Song (Acoustic) — Rachel Platten	3:23	+
What Have I Done — Dermot Kennedy	3:36	+
Cross Me — Ed Sheeran ft. Chance the Rapper	3:26	+
Falling like the Stars — James Arthur	3:32	+

PROLOGUE

Sophie

Three Years Ago

D o you know what happens when people turn eighteen? They have nights filled with freedom, exploration, and boxed wine.

For me, eighteen doesn't look the same—at least not yet.

James Mitchell smells trouble a mile away with his exposure to Formula 1's bad-boy racers teaching him a thing or two about handling a daughter. Ever since we moved from California to Italy when I was five years old, I get the same treatment as the Bandini drivers he manages. In his house, I adhere to his three Rs: respect, rules, and responsibilities.

My dad let me join him for one Grand Prix this summer before starting my university classes. A rare occasion, seeing how he has kept me away from the race scene ever since I grew boobs and learned what clothes flatter my body shape.

This morning, I trudged my feet through our hotel room, arms crossed over my chest, and bottom lip fully displayed in a pout. My dad kept his face neutral with not a single gray hair out of place, unblinking and unwavering as I protested his plan.

Guess who won that battle? Not me, in case you were wondering, but thanks for the moral support.

Instead of hanging out in Bandini's pit garage, my dad volunteered me to dress like a princess for a kid's birthday party while I paint kids' faces. Don't let looks deceive you, I may be the same height as the eight-year-olds running around, but my brains, wit, and sass make up for my small stature.

I'm kind of like a lemon Starburst—sweet but packs a punch.

I run my hands down my ridiculous Rapunzel costume my dad bought. Joke's on him this time because he didn't realize he grabbed me a kid's size. Velvet material barely contains my breasts, suggesting I want to offer way more than candy and face painting to unsuspecting partygoers. The skirt rests above my mid-thigh, revealing tan legs and white Converse because this princess wears comfortable shoes. Screw heels and being a royal pain in the ass who needs to be protected by a pretty prince.

No thank you. I'd rather save the day in sneakers.

I ditch the sour attitude once I arrive at the party. Face painting can be a cool gig, letting me show off artistic talents I tamper down into nothing nowadays.

See, I've loved art ever since I picked up a paintbrush at two years old and decided to paint all over the canvas stools in our kitchen while under the influence of too many *Bob Ross* episodes. My dad wasn't amused when he sat on wet paint and rocked an imprint of a sunflower on his ass. I'd love to say an artist was born that day, but my dad didn't support my creativity as anything more than a hobby.

So now, instead of pursuing a degree in anything art related, I'm forced to attend a college tailored toward business degrees.

I almost fall asleep thinking about it.

But I want to make my dad happy because he never lets me down. Blame the daddy's girl in me. He does so much, playing both a mother and father, no matter how awkward or uncomfortable it makes him.

At least I can create mini masterpieces on everyone's faces today. I choose different themes for each person because I'm not a basic bitch. I've never been wired that way, ever since my dad bought me a *Star Wars* backpack instead of a princess one because no daughter of his believes in fairy tales.

I scroll through my phone to pass the time. Kids move on to the bounce houses, no longer amused with the clown or me. Said party entertainment sends me sly grins across the lawn, weirdly making phallic motions with his balloon animals while mouthing for me to call him.

Someone leans against the table where I spread out my art supplies. My eyes trail his jean-clad legs before they land on golden arms crossed over a firm torso. Tense muscles pull against the black fabric. I hold my breath as my eyes meet two icy blue ones, the color of melting glaciers in the Arctic.

I'm an artist, not a poet.

"Blink twice if they're holding you against your will." He smirks at me. His voice has a hint of an accent I can't place, the English smooth yet different at the same time.

My mouth opens before closing again. Because *holy shit*.

This guy looks like he belongs surfing on the beach somewhere, all blonde hair and skin with a summer glow. I look around to make sure I'm at a kid's birthday rather than daydreaming. The bounce house bumps up and down, roars of screaming children a reminder of how this is all very real.

"Oh, shit. I knew there was something weird about Evan. Who knew he liked holding beautiful girls hostage, dressed up like fucked-up Disney porno characters?" The stranger's eyes roam up and down my body.

My cheeks uncontrollably flush under his gaze, new reactions sparking inside of me around this man. "Oh my God. *No*. Evan has been nothing but nice to me. And he's very married. I'm here for the kids' face painting and stuff. His daughter thinks I'm Rapunzel." I fumble with paint tubes while I ramble, knocking a few to the ground.

I bend over to grab the tubes. The stranger beats me to it, our fingers brushing against each other, warmth radiating from his touch. My heart jolts at the contact.

Um. Okay.

The stranger gets a look at my chest when I pull myself back up along with the paints. My blonde hair whips to the side as I turn toward the table, wanting to hide my flustered state. This whole meeting is going terribly wrong, making me look like I don't know how to act around someone unfairly attractive.

Can I blame the fact that I went to an all-girls Catholic school my whole life? Sounds plausible.

"Ah, she has a voice." He lets out a rough laugh, his chest shaking before he controls himself.

"Duh."

He points at the different brushes I set up in a perfect line, his thick fingers lingering over a paint tube. "You like painting?"

"I love it like a sordid affair. It's a hidden secret, only known by a select few."

"I love a good secret." He pulls a finger to his lips, drawing my eyes to the fullness of them.

"You and everyone else. Care to share one of your own and make it even?" My mouth runs quicker than my brain, not caring enough to filter my words.

"I'm shit at secrets." He shrugs.

"Then, I'm shit at talking." My arms cross over my chest, making my boobs hike up an inch. *Whoops.*

His eyes lower as I uncross my arms. "You have a bite to you. Fine. I like to read at least a chapter of a book every night before going to bed. It's a tradition I've had since childhood that I still keep, despite a busy schedule." He says his admission like a dirty secret, something contrasting against his athletic image. Somehow it makes him sexier.

"What's your favorite book?" Doubt colors my voice.

"If you have a favorite, I don't trust you. Any book lover has at least five they can name off the top of their head." His blue eyes hold mine.

Oh, wow. This guy actually likes reading. He grins when I roll my eyes with little effort, not putting much sass behind it.

"All right. Name your top author then since you're such a scholar." My voice rasps. I imagine him in bed, blonde hair ruffled while he rocks reading glasses and a thick paperback because he'd rather be practical than carry a heavy hardcover.

Sigh. Damn him and his nerdy secret.

"Brandon Sanderson. No questions asked." His voice drops.

"A man who prefers to live in a fantasy. How cute."

"I'd be your best fantasy, no book needed."

A kid comes to my paint station and plops himself into the seat in front of me.

"*Ciao, amico. Che cosa vuoi—*" I turn toward the child.

"Shit. You're hot and speak Italian." He smiles wide at me before he turns toward the child. "Twenty euros. Leave." The blonde-haired, blue-eyed man holds out a crisp euro straight from a designer wallet. The kid gets the meaning of his words as he grabs it and runs, leaving us alone yet again.

I laugh at the ridiculousness of the exchange. My new acquaintance catches me off guard by sitting and crossing his arms.

"Do your absolute dirtiest." His wicked grin fills my chest with warmth. It's a new sensation I can't pin down, heat searing its way up toward my cheeks.

"If you say so. But I don't think you can handle it, or me for that matter." I offer him a playful grin of my own. If my heart wasn't hammering in my chest, I'd gloat at my flirtatiousness.

"Please. Don't insult my talents." He presses a large hand against his heart while his lip wobbles on command. I like the way he drags out his vowels and emphasizes his *T*s, his accent unplaceable yet distinct from my fused American-Italian one.

"All two of them?" I shake my head at him.

He drops his head back and lets out a deep laugh, not giving a damn about the staring parents around us.

"And what two talents do you think I have? Do tell." He smiles at me, revealing straight white teeth. An idea pops into my head about mucking up his perfect face, wanting to take away his prettiness and remove some of his appeal.

I tap my chin with a paintbrush. "Bribing people and not taking a hint. Two very undesirable traits if I do say so myself."

He shakes his head at me, his lips fighting a smile. I squeeze black paint out onto the palette and swirl my brush in the dark color.

My fingers raise his chin, revealing bright eyes and thick, dirty blonde lashes. "Now keep still. I don't want to ruin the look before it starts."

The stranger shudders when my fingers press against his face, my brush sweeping across his skin, black paint replacing tan skin. He smells clean and expensive, a mix of freshly showered with some fancy cologne. His blue eyes remain on my face the entire time except when I ask him to close them for me to paint his eyelids.

His obvious perusal surprises me. I center myself, wary of my desire toward him, from the way my cheeks flush to the feeling of my skin heating up as it touches his.

I concentrate on my task while ignoring his glances. He looks young, but still too old for me. I'd guess he's probably in his mid-twenties from the looks of him, showing the smallest smile lines when he laughs. Our faces remain mere inches apart as I paint his face, familiarizing myself with every divot and scar that mars his skin. Black paint contrasts against sharp cheekbones.

I trace the curve of his neck with the end of my paintbrush, eliciting the slightest shiver from him—one so subtle, I almost miss it. "Do you care if I paint your neck?"

His heavy-lidded eyes capture mine. "Do I get to kiss yours

after?"

"I'm going to ignore you because you're way too old for me."
I wish I could take the words back the instant they leave my
mouth.

"Says who?"

"Says the fact that you look like you have a decent savings
account and a stable job."

His lit-up eyes hold me in a trance. "What an observant
princess. What about me screams that I have a big bank account?"

"I rock Converse on a first-year uni student's budget while
you wear Gucci sneakers and corrupt kids with a Louis Vuitton
wallet."

"Ah, how perceptive. Eighteen is definitely too young." His
eyes dart to the side.

"Yup. But lucky you, I'm not too young to blow your mind."
My brush taps on his face, hinting at my artwork.

He laughs, and for some reason, I like making him smile. I
grab the mirror off the table and reveal how he looks.

"Holy shit. You seriously have some talent with a brush. I
look like someone's worst nightmare."

That's because you are.

He shoots me a smile that makes me feel all sorts of things,
both good and bad. I find it difficult to ignore the tug of desire I
have toward him despite our age difference.

I grin at the skull face painting I did. Spinal cord bones trail
down his neck, intermingled with black and white faux muscle
tissue, disappearing beneath his black T-shirt. Blue eyes starkly
contrast against the black paint. His smile dims, revealing a row
of teeth I created. The design is hauntingly beautiful, just like

him, a man too old and too wicked for someone like me.

"Whoa. Liam, I didn't even notice you with that sick makeup. Sophie's talented, eh?" Evan, the man who asked me to do this ridiculous task in the first place, interrupts my moment with *Liam*.

Liam lifts out of the chair. His long legs make the task ridiculously easy, drawing my attention toward his body. His firm sculpted-to-perfection body.

Evan nudges Liam in the ribs. "Sophie, you did an awesome job. It matches how dead Liam's going to be after he doesn't land on the podium this Sunday."

"That's what you always say, except I kick your ass almost every time." Liam's voice has a hint of edge to it.

Dots connect because F1 has only one driver named Liam.

Liam freaking Zander. Germany's most revered and F1's up-and-coming star, wreaking havoc with Noah Slade and Jax Kingston since their young karting days. The racer who's on track to win his first World Championship this year. The same man who's almost seven years older than me.

Fuck me. I've been flirting with an F1 driver. My dad would kill me if he found out, never letting me off Bandini's property.

Evan takes a photo of Liam's face. "Seriously, this makeup is kick-ass. Great work. My daughter has loved Sophie ever since she saw her in the Bandini pit area. James Mitchell keeps this one hidden away, but I borrowed her talents for the day." Evan looks over at me. "Don't forget to remind me to pay you for your time."

I brush him off, focusing on regulating my breathing instead of anything Evan says to Liam. Evan tells us a rushed goodbye after claiming he needs to check on the kids.

"So, you're a racer." My teeth grind together, my annoyance poorly hidden by the clenching and unclenching of my hands. I hate how much I like his eyes raking over me. He looks like he wants to memorize the way my stupid costume presses against my body, committing the whole day to memory. And worse, I love the way his attention makes me feel.

"Mm, that's what they tell me. And you're Sophie, a princess?"

My name rolls off his tongue like he wants to test it out, his German accent drawing out the *e* sound.

I stand taller. "You can say that. Except in this story, I don't need rescuing."

"No, you don't. Maybe you're the one who does the saving." His lips twitch.

His charm covers up the weird sense of foreboding his words give. They sit heavy on my chest, along with curiosity to ask what he means.

He brushes his knuckles across my cheek, the rough texture setting off every nerve ending. A spark the equivalent of a blown-out fuse box. "But you're too young and naïve. And it's not the right moment. Maybe if we meet again under different circumstances, at another time."

Liam laughs to himself as his eyes roam down my body, not giving me time to respond, let alone process his words. "You're no princess. You're a motherfucking queen. Don't let anyone forget it, not even yourself. People think the king matters, but the queen brings down all the other pieces. Good luck in uni and chug a beer in my honor."

He reads books and uses chess references. Liam Zander is a closet nerd, and knowing this secret pulls a smile from me.

He tugs his hand away and stares at his knuckles. Confusion crosses his face before he covers it up and flashes me a smirk, the wicked paint covering up his perfect image. He winks at me over his shoulder as he walks away, leaving the party and me behind.

Damn. I think I just got mindfucked.

CHAPTER ONE

Liam

Two Years and Five Months Ago

My ringing phone pulls me out of my sleep. Sheets rustle as my hand fumbles for my phone in the dark. I press the green button without checking because few people would call me at this hour without an important reason.

"You need to get your ass over here now. Johanna woke up from a contraction, but we aren't sure if it's the real deal, gas, or a Braxton Hicks one. She's too far along so I don't want to risk it." My brother's statement wipes the grogginess from my eyes.

"You went to med school. How can you not tell the difference?"

"Asshole, I'm into neuro, not OB-GYN stuff. Just in case, I need you to grab Elyse and take her to Ma and Pa's."

I hop out of bed, nearly dropping my phone. "See you in ten."

Lukas ends our call without a goodbye.

Thankfully, I decided to stay in Germany for the holiday season since Johanna's about to give birth. I ignore the way my balls ache at the thought of labor.

I make quick time of getting ready, adrenaline coursing through my body. Within a few minutes, I hop into my SUV and make my way toward my brother's neighborhood. He had this all planned out months ago to make sure I was in town for the delivery. With Johanna being due any day now, Lukas is on high alert. Really. He's almost convinced Jo to go to the hospital once already for these "false alarms."

I pull into their driveway, park my car, and get out. Lights shine from every window of their two-story house. My brother opens the front door as I walk toward the covered entryway, the chandelier casting Lukas in a golden glow. He runs an agitated hand through his blonde hair, wrinkles etching the skin near his baby blue eyes as he shoots me a nervous smile.

I pull him in for a hug, standing head-to-head with him. "If it isn't the man of the hour. Tell me, how does it feel to see your handiwork coming to full fruition?"

"About as good as Johanna yelling at me to grab everything we need as a precaution. She's worried this is it."

"Her water hasn't broken yet?"

"No, but it's better safe than sorry."

Johanna, all beautiful with brown hair and doe eyes, pushes past my brother. Her flushed cheeks expand as she deeply breathes in and out, her lips pursing at me. "Men should be like seahorses. They can get pregnant *and* give birth. I read they're amazing fathers while the moms are dead-beat sea animals."

I shake my head at her. "You need to relax. You're getting all red and shit."

Johanna hasn't changed in the ten years I've known her, always one to get flustered during tense situations. She was the type who ripped me a new asshole for turning in our lab report at the end of class rather than at the beginning. While other high-school girls chased my dick for an all-access pass, Johanna ran after me to complete my homework and study for tests. Unlike others, she didn't let me slide by because of my Formula driving. I have her to thank for graduating from school in the first place.

She shakes a finger at me, her brown eyes shining. "You can tell me to relax when you have to shove a baby the size of a watermelon out of your body."

My brother looks at me with a face of horror. I could live a happy life without that visual ever again because I happen to like watermelon.

"Don't give me that face. This is all your fault." She stares at Lukas while pointing at her belly with two index fingers.

"I didn't hear you complaining during the act." He smiles at her.

She waves him off. "I forgot the repercussions of our actions."

I offer Lukas a telling grin. "You are the one who got her pregnant three months after having your first kid. Territorial much?"

"I love how she glows from pregnancy." Lukas tugs Johanna into him before planting a kiss on her head. He inherited his preference for gross displays of affection from our parents, the king and queen of too much groping.

"I hope you like the post-pregnancy paleness because the

only glow you'll get is from the fridge at 2 a.m. when you feed Kaia," Johanna mumbles into his chest.

I, for one, can't wait to meet Kaia, Johanna's watermelon and the future addition to our crazy family.

"Doesn't she have a way with words?" Lukas's arms tighten around Johanna before letting her go.

I fake-gag. "You both make me nauseous."

"When you get married, you'll understand. Until then, I can shower you with appreciation for picking me as your lab partner. Turns out the hottest guy in bio had a brother to match." Johanna winks at Lukas.

"Leave it to Lukas to stake a claim before I could try."

"You never had a chance. One look at me and she was a goner. We only had to wait until she was no longer jailbait," my brother says over his shoulder as he runs upstairs.

Johanna sends me a wobbly smile. "Sorry you got friend-zoned hard all those years ago. Who could resist the team captain of the hockey team?"

"I was hoping that you, the President of the United Nations Club, could, but now you're pregnant with my brother's spawn. I thought you'd want me for my wit rather than Lukas for his brawn."

"Seeing as I'm a neurosurgeon resident..." Lukas cautiously comes down the stairs, a sleeping Elyse in one arm and a weekend bag in the other.

"I really dislike how you two gang up on me now. It used to be the other way around before Jo turned eighteen." I cross my arms against my chest.

"Don't be that way. Look at you, a big bad Formula 1 racer

who recently won his first World Championship. You traded books for brawn after all." Johanna pulls me in for a hug. Her bulging stomach makes it difficult, but she wraps herself around me, hitting me with her rose scent.

"I never traded the books," I scoff. "The only thing that's changed is how girls don't meet me at the library anymore."

"I really hope you settle down sometime soon. You don't want those types of grid girls long-term because they prefer you for your name rather than your heart. Plus I can't be your one friend of the female variety. You're kind of needy." She sticks her tongue out at me before she waddles toward the front door.

"What? Since when? This is the first time I'm hearing about this."

"Since always, man. Just a few months ago, you drunkenly texted Johanna at 3 a.m. asking her to sing you a lullaby so you could fall asleep. Not that I'm complaining because your calls wake us both up." He shoots her a smirk I can live without seeing ever again.

"Okay, gross. Save your bedroom eyes for the next time you want to get her pregnant. I hope you're both aware of how those lullabies are the best thing I hear on the road. Even better than the pit lane on a race day."

Johanna has the voice of an angel and the singing to match. I can't help how lonely my drunk ass gets at night while spending most of my year on the road with my F1 team.

"You *really* need a girlfriend. I can't be your only best friend forever." Johanna laughs before she winces, rubbing her stomach.

"All right. You two need to go." I grab Elyse from Lukas's arms.

"Did you buy the car seat I told you about?" My brother eyes Elyse as I rock her body gently.

"Yes, Mother. I even made sure to drive my SUV because you hate my convertible."

Johanna smiles at my brother. "I wish you had a convertible sometimes."

"They're not safe," Lukas grumbles as he helps Johanna into his Land Rover. Somehow, in a few years, he went from a carefree guy to a new member of the safety patrol. It all began after he married Johanna, bought a house, and got her pregnant. Who knew picking the hot, quiet girl for a lab partner would lead to this? Lukas should thank me for thinking with my hormones and my need to pass biology.

I walk to my SUV, opening the door with one arm before placing Elyse in her car seat. The pink contraption looks out of place against the black leather interior. I fumble with the straps before getting her settled in, her pudgy face and blonde hair looking fucking adorable.

I place a soft kiss on Elyse's forehead before closing the door.

I turn toward the two beaming parents. "I'll meet you at the hospital once the sitter gets set up at Mama and Papa's."

"You fucking better. See ya." Lukas waves before pulling out of his driveway. Johanna smiles at me from the passenger seat, a vision of calm despite the potential hours of pain she will go through.

I drop Elyse off with the sitter before rushing to the hospital with my parents. My dad relaxes in a waiting room chair while my mom paces the ten-by-eight space. Her boots click against the floor as she alternates between staring at the clock and grimacing at the door.

My parents look like a Barbie and Ken duo set, all blonde hair and light tan skin. My mother gazes at me with stormy gray eyes, panic evident in her rigid posture. Her blonde hair bobs as she walks back and forth in a motion that does nothing to calm her while my dad does the exact opposite, leaning his head against the wall.

"Why don't you have a seat?" I point at the empty chair next to me.

"I don't want to. I hate this waiting part because I want to hold Kaia and breathe in that fresh baby smell already." She closes her eyes and smiles.

"You sound like a serial killer." My comment makes her eyes snap open. Pa laughs to the point of coughing.

My mom glares at my dad. "Don't encourage his jokes. You're the one to blame for how he talks to me."

"Someone had to teach him how to have a sense of humor." My dad grins at me, his blue eyes shining under the fluorescent lights.

My mom fights a smile. After a few more minutes of pacing, she sits by my side, pulling my hand onto her lap like I'm a toddler instead of a recently turned twenty-six-year-old. "Remember when we tried to set Johanna and you up for prom?"

"How can I forget. Lukas nearly kicked my ass into tomorrow."

My parents' front lawn has some fond memories, including Lukas proposing in the same spot where he decked me in the face years prior.

"That was the moment I knew they would fall in love. They

were like a movie, with the smart jock and the shy girl. He was only biding his time."

"You watch too many romance movies." I shake my head.

My mom looks for fairy-tale endings in everything because she's a hopeless romantic who found the love of her life at twenty-two. Lukas followed her love advice to the letter while I float around, not exactly pursuing anything more at the moment.

Johanna's words from earlier hang around me. Am I clingy because I don't have someone to share my moments with? I don't want to be seen as a needy guy. What are a few drunk calls in the grand scheme of things? Some people text exes while I call my friends, which isn't exactly a character flaw.

The skin around her gray eyes wrinkles as she smiles at me. "If it weren't for those movies, I may have never given your dad a chance."

This time I really do gag. "You guys should pay for my therapy because a psychologist would have a field day with this shit."

We sit around for what feels like hours. Unlike Elyse's debut, Lukas doesn't have time to come out and give us updates. I fool around on my phone to pass the time. Minute by minute goes by with no nurse coming out, giving us absolutely nothing to go off of as we wait around. Curiosity makes us all edgy as we await our new family member.

A nurse rushes into the waiting room, confirming we're the Zander family. "There's been a change of plans. Johanna's been rushed into the operating room due to some medical complications. We don't have a lot of information to report, but someone will return as soon as we have more news."

"Oh God. I hope it's nothing serious." My mom resumes her

pacing, abandoning her book on the chair.

"I'm sure the doctors know what they're doing." My dad's flitting eyes don't match the calming tone of his voice.

"Elyse was a natural birth. Why a C-section for this one?" My mom stops, pressing a hand against her chest as if the motion can calm her racing heart.

I place my phone back in my pocket, no longer in the mood to play a stupid game. "The doctor will let us know."

A few minutes later, the door creaks open, revealing a pale Lukas, his fists clenched in front of him. His eyes lack any sign of life. He appears devoid of emotion, like someone sucked his soul right out of him, leaving behind a husk of a man.

A cold feeling creeps up my spine as his eyes land on mine.

A tear escapes his eye. One single tear makes my chest tighten and my lungs burn. The room feels like someone closed off our air supply, the heaviness choking the four of us. We remain silent, watching Lukas as his chest heaves, his dark eyes landing on each of us.

I lift myself out of my chair, my legs wobbling as I attempt to regain my composure. "What happened?"

His empty, expressionless eyes find mine. "Johanna didn't make it."

Tears run down his face, my stomach dropping as his lip trembles. My mom chokes back a sob as she runs to my brother and pulls him in for a hug. My dad and I stare at each other, no words passing our lips, a lack of understanding among us both.

What the fuck is happening?

My brother shakes, his legs giving out as my mother kneels on the floor with him. My heart rapidly beats in my chest while my stomach threatens to dump its contents on the beige tile.

My brother whispers his next words like saying his statement with strength makes it too real. "The baby was stuck." Lukas's voice cracks. "Jo's blood pressure dropped during an emergency C-section, and she—" He sobs.

I don't feel like someone ripped the rug out from under me. That would be too simple, too sweet to describe the nightmare occurring in front of me. It feels like someone ripped my goddamn legs from my body, leaving me in a bloody heap, so fucking helpless as my brother breaks down in some shitty hospital.

This can't be happening.

Lukas's body trembles as he curls into my mom's, his soundless cries making my heart shrivel up. "She didn't make it. She… She asked to see me hold our baby girl. That's all she wanted. My fucking wife. Gone." His heavy breathing becomes panicky and shallow.

Holy motherfucking shit.

My best friend is gone. The same woman who was smiling at me hours ago, calling me needy. Johanna, the best part of high school and one of my favorite people in the world. My friend who rolled her eyes at girls wanting me for my racing talents rather than for my hidden geekiness. The woman who stole my brother's heart while making mine whole, branding herself onto each member of my family.

I don't fight nausea as I run to the nearby trash can, my stomach revolting, acid coating my tongue while unfamiliar tears stream down my face. My pale fingers tremble as I clutch onto the plastic rim, using the trash can as a support for my shaking legs.

"And the baby?" My mom's voice carries over the sound of my retching.

"Kaia's okay." My brother, the reserved one who taught me how to keep my cool, cries in her arms. Hoarse words pass his lips as he whispers to my mom. I can't take seeing him broken, his outward appearance matching the way I feel inside.

I grip the trash can, afraid of letting go as my dad runs a shaky hand down my back.

I hate the sound of Lukas crying. I hate this whole fucking day, the thought of losing my best friend while gaining a niece too fucking much. Why the fuck would God play such a cruel joke, snuffing out one life while saving another?

I escape the room, leaving my family behind as I run toward the hospital's entrance. Darkness greets me, matching the churning emotions inside of me, the bright moon mocking me as I lose my shit in the empty quad. My legs give out as I kneel onto the grass, the dewy blades hiding the tears escaping my eyes.

I throw my head back as I let out a hoarse cry, the pained sound drowned out by an approaching ambulance's sirens. The chilly air burns my lungs as I take in a sharp breath.

My dad shows up out of nowhere and kneels next to me, tugging me into his side as he holds me.

I can't hide the way my body trembles. "I don't understand. How can something like this happen? It's the twenty-first fucking century. People don't just die in childbirth anymore."

"I'm sorry, son. There's nothing that could've been done." My dad chokes.

"So what? How the fuck am I supposed to look at Kaia without thinking of *her*?" I hate how weak my voice sounds to my own ears.

"You can look at her and see the last beautiful thing her mother created. She needs an uncle now more than ever."

I clench my fist around blades of grass, tugging on the pieces, ripping them out to ease the edginess. "I don't want her. I want Johanna back."

"You don't mean that."

"Of course I fucking do. I want to turn back the clock and erase this shitty day from history." I don't feel the slightest bit guilty about my confession. My tightening chest reminds me of the pain burrowing itself in my heart, testing my sanity.

"We can't. But think of your brother and what he's going through. Be strong for him."

How can I be strong for him when my heart is going through a fucking paper shredder?

"I can't." I choke on the words, my voice a croaky whisper as my tears return, flooding my eyes as I think of Johanna. Of us getting in a paint fight while setting up Kaia's nursery. The image fills me with dread and nausea all over again.

I don't know how to cope with any of this shit. I'm unequipped to handle the brewing feelings, the painful memories, and the dull ache making itself at home inside of my chest.

My dad holds on to me, sitting in silence as pained breaths escape our mouths.

December 30th isn't only the day of Johanna's death. It's the day I let go of myself, shoving my broken heart so deep inside of my body I wouldn't be able to identify the tattered remains if I tried.

CHAPTER TWO

Sophie

Present Day

Not to be dramatic, but I just experienced the worst sex of my life.

No, I'm not joking, but I wish I was. It's the whole reason I hide in my bathroom, whispering to myself while the object of my frustration lies on my dorm bed.

Andre Bianchi: math whiz, business fraternity vice president, and voted *most likely to leave you unsatisfied* two rounds in a row.

"I should have taken the flavored condoms as a warning sign. No self-respecting male who has an inkling of a woman's body would have flavored condoms. Stupidest purchase ever. Also, who invented those because no woman in their right mind wants to lick a condom!" I whisper to myself, brushing down my barely ruffled blonde hair. It's further evidence supporting my sucky sex life. My hair looks as good as it did this morning when I brushed it. My makeup is barely smeared, and there are zero signs of rosy cheeks or post-coital glow. Green eyes blink back at me, looking as lackluster as my sex life right about now.

My chest squeezes to the point of difficulty breathing, reminding me of my disappointment yet again.

Clearly, I'm getting more A's than orgasms at my university. I don't know why the thought bothers me, but it really does. I don't sleep around, and I can count my sexual encounters on one hand. Worse, none of those include a happily ever after for me. I'm starting to consider myself broken because how can this keep happening to me? The guys get off fine while I blink up at the ceiling, wondering what I experienced.

No endorphins released. No post-sex bliss. Nothing. *Niente. Nada.*

This recent encounter hits me hard. What's the point of attending university if I'm going to live in my dorm, barely associating with others, experiencing sex once a year with a fellow bumbling accounting major? It ends with me asking them to go with a smile, pretending they rocked my world when I really sucked their dick while mentally listing off my pending assignments.

"Oh God. I thought about my accounting professor while giving a blowjob. This is the lowest of lows," I mumble to myself, barely withholding a groan.

I can't allow this to happen to me anymore. My type A personality is biting me in the ass, and not exactly in the *Hi, my name is Anastasia Steele and Christian Grey is my daddy* kind of way.

"Sophie, you're going to march out there and tell him to hit the road. It's past your bedtime, and you need to sleep off this terrible mood." I sigh as I gather the courage needed to face the poor guy outside.

Andre was nice and polite, even offering to pay for dinner before. I don't mean to be rude, but I struggle to understand my feelings right now. To be honest, I feel more disappointed in myself for not letting go, both mentally and physically. It's a genuine struggle between fighting for control while attempting to take a mental vacation from my brain.

I grip the handle of my bathroom door and whip it open. "Hi, sorry about that. I think it's—"

I let out a breath of relief as I check out my empty bed. Maybe tonight isn't a total bust after all. My eyes catch a piece of paper on top of my pillow.

Thanks for a good time. Let's do this again next weekend?

Nope. Absolutely not. I'd rather leave the country than see him again.

Wait. Now that's an idea.

I grab a recently opened bottle of white wine from my mini fridge as I turn on my laptop. Forgoing the glass, I take a big swig straight from the bottle as I open up my dad's Formula 1 calendar. He already booked next month's flight to Melbourne.

I open up Pinterest, wondering how Melbourne looks. As I scroll through some posts while intermittently taking sips of wine, I click on one labeled *Bucket List*.

I end up getting sucked further into the land of lost time and pins, scrolling through multiple travel bucket lists. Blame my burning sense of curiosity at what people come up with. I love a good list, but I've never considered half these crazy items. My head grows foggier as I continue sipping wine and searching.

My eyebrows shoot up to my hairline as another *Naughty Bucket List* crosses my feed. Interest eats away at me as I open up the list. *Naughty* is a word I've never associated myself with. At least not since I was five and my dad threatened to tell Santa I deserved coal for Christmas after I spilled a milkshake all over the interior of his McCoy Illusion.

Holy shit. People are mighty creative. I spend too much time going through multiple naughty lists. I could be studying, or sleeping, or finding a new beau on a dating app. But no. Buzzed me enjoys pinning my favorite sexy items. Where was this nonchalance two hours ago?

I don't know if it's my lonely evening or the wine I've consumed that inspires me to open my expertly tabbed agenda to one of the extra hidden pages in the back.

I work on a list of items I've never done but have always wanted to try. An hour later, I somehow have the coordination to type up the entire thing and color-code it. Before I press the print button, a name for the list comes to mind, and I type the words *Fuck It List* at the top.

I stare at the piece of printed paper, wondering why the hell I created this. Can I really convince my dad to let me join his F1 schedule? Better yet, can I really go through doing half these items? Ignoring my doubts, I pull out my personal laminator because, *yes*, I'm one of those people. I get the paper to fold after a few failed origami attempts and growls of frustration.

The Fuck It List shines in all its laminated glory. I smile at the twenty items I boldly, yet semi drunkenly, chose.

Fuck It List

Go skinny-dipping.

Buy a vibrator.

Try foreplay with ice.

Kiss a foreigner.

Do karaoke while drinking.

Try new food.

Go skydiving.

Watch porn.

Play strip poker.

Get tied up.

Be blindfolded.

Come from oral sex.

Try mirror sex.

Have sex in public.

Have sex against a wall.

Get high.

Have a quickie.

Have outdoor sex.

Kiss someone in front of the Eiffel Tower.

Experience multiple orgasms in one night.

Now I only need to do one last thing, probably one of the hardest tasks before I can start crossing items off my list.

Convince my dad to let me join him.

"I have a few rules before you join the tour. If you break them, I'll book you a seat on the next flight back to Italy." My dad taps away on his iPad, taking up his usual spot on our living room couch.

"I know you're a celebrity with the engineers, but when you call it a tour, you make it seem like you're a rock star."

"Famous among the nerds, I love it." He does a rock symbol with his hands that should never be reproduced again. "Anyway, the first rule is that I want you to try your best to stay away from the racers. I mean it, because they tend to have questionable intentions. Two: you need to check in with me daily so I can be sure you're not dead in a ditch somewhere. And last but not least, stay out of trouble. Say them back to me."

"You're getting old, needing all this repetition."

"Just because I have gray hair doesn't mean I'm old." He runs a hand through his thick strands.

My dad can be described as anything but old and frumpy, unfortunately for me because he's single, and the ladies do sure try to mingle. Women flock toward him like his aura says money and good times.

"No, but the fact that you have more rules than a private school handbook kills your young silver fox vibe."

"Please follow the rules. That's all I ask of you this summer."

My dad loves rules because he fears I'll end up like my mom. We don't talk about her much since she left us soon after she had me, deciding she wanted to save under-developed countries. The idea of diapers and baby bottles weighed her down and cramped the carefree lifestyle she loves. Nowadays, my mom lives her best life in Africa with her new boyfriend, who is five years older than me.

I'd say my dad has undisclosed abandonment issues. Every time I talk to my mom—a rare occasion as it is—he checks that I don't want to book my next flight away from him.

"If I weren't about to turn 22 this year, you'd probably make me wear one of those leash backpacks to keep me within a five-foot radius."

He looks up at the ceiling. "Don't tempt me because that idea sounds pretty good right now."

His vigilance worsened once I started college, with him being unable to control the desires of horny boys and F1 racers alike. The situation got to the point where he conveniently paid for me to go away every single summer—all coinciding with his F1 traveling.

I shoot him a glare that could melt steel. "Can you please relax? You're not going to be able to protect me from every male who crosses my path."

"I can sure try." My dad's teeth run against his lower lip as he goes through our itinerary. He can't suck the fun out of this summer. I want to meet new people, explore different cities, and make a few mistakes because Lord knows I need to. People underestimate how tough it is to be the perfect daughter for my dad, always striving for greatness to appease him. I'm talking straight A's, honor societies, and the equestrian club—all very uppity of me.

"Remember you need to finish the semester with all A's for me to fulfill my end of the bargain. I'll be checking your GPA before you get on the plane."

"Would you also like me to sync my study calendar to your phone? That way you can log all my hours?"

He fights a smile. "I don't know why I raised you to be such a smartass, but it comes out at the most inconvenient times. I only want to make sure you'll graduate on time."

I have one year before I walk across the big stage with an accounting degree in hand and a fake smile plastered across my face. My dad claims numbers are safe. They scream independent financial stability, except the only one genuinely screaming is me. But I chose the degree for my dad's peace of mind because he's endlessly supported me through the years. He sacrificed part of himself to be everything I needed and more, never adding a new woman to our duo.

"But I've always dreamed of being like other F1 principal's daughters with a limitless credit card and more Chanel purses than Coco herself." I bat my lashes at him.

"I better lock up my wallet at night."

"Oh, Dad. Everything's digital nowadays, so I already have your Amex added to my Apple Wallet."

He fake shudders. "Hopefully you don't run up my bill with all that European shopping."

"I hope you know I have other plans besides shopping."

"I can't wait to hear about them."

I recoil at the thought of my dad getting a hold of my list. My

Fuck It list is sexy, daring, and risky for a rule-follower like me, with some items that would make the nuns in the local convent blush. They'd probably throw a bottle of holy water at my head, hoping it knocks me out and saves me from a life of impurity and eternal damnation.

He shoots me a soft smile. "You know why I do this all, right? The rules and stuff?"

"Because you enjoy less messy versions of torture?" I drop onto a chair.

My dad offers a dramatic eye roll, similar to my own. "*No*. Because you don't understand the F1 world. You're pure-hearted while others aren't. I raised you away from it all, and sometimes I worry that I protected you too much, hoping to save you from being hurt."

The sincerity of his words hits me in the chest like a one-two punch. It'll be a disappointing day for my dad when he realizes his baby girl is not exactly a baby anymore. Honestly, it won't hit him until I have a baby of my own because women crush their parents' abstinence dreams once they give birth.

"I'm not going to get eaten alive out in the real world. You raised me better than that. If I survived an all-girls school and three years at uni, I think I can make it out there. Honestly, we're lucky the plaid skirts and mean girls didn't cause any psychological damage."

"You'll always be my little girl. The same one who put pigtails in my hair to match yours or drew fake tattoos with pens all over my arms."

"Speaking of tattoos, I was prepping myself for the real deal by testing out designs. That reminds me of my full sleeve idea.

Thoughts?"

His eyes narrow, and his smile turns into a frown.

"I'll take that as a no. Darn." I snap my finger in mock frustration.

"Show up with a tattoo, and you won't be on the next plane to Italy. Oh, no. You'll be off to Antarctica attending a once in a lifetime trip to see penguins and melting icebergs."

"I wonder if Leonardo DiCaprio would be down to assess climate change damage with me. I heard he likes to visit the South Pole too." I flash him a mischievous smile.

"Get out of here before I revoke your plane ticket and all-access pass."

I scoff in fake horror. He gets up from his chair and pulls me in for a quick hug, squeezing the air straight from my lungs.

I'm grateful for his leniency on the F1 issue. I get to trade virgin cocktails for champagne, bounce houses for gala events, and my princess costume for evening gowns. Finally, I'll live the life my lavish tastes deserve.

Men should be the least of his worries because, excuse my language, but I'm ready to fuck shit up.

CHAPTER THREE

Liam

I exit my Twitter app, wishing I could erase another article detailing me as some F1 fuck-up after my hookup with Claudia. My dick really got me in trouble this time. Usually, we work together because two heads are better than one.

My recent indiscretion threatens my contract renewal with McCoy, my dream team, the one I worked hard to join. No pressure at all. Either I perform well, or I'm demoted to a lesser team after two years of racing with them.

My team gives me the opportunity to compete against two of my friends who happen to be some of F1's best. Jax, Noah, and I make up a trio destined for trouble and trophies. To us, driving feels as fundamental as breathing, eating, and fucking.

The adrenaline high I experience when I sit behind the wheel beats nothing else—except I'll come down hard from my high like a lousy hit if I don't land a new contract with McCoy. So, I need to work my ass off double-time to prove my worth because being a past two-time World Champion means nothing when I fuck the wrong girl.

Don't get me wrong, I know my agent will receive multiple contract deals from opposing teams, but I love my spot in McCoy. I have enough fight left in me to give a nail-biter show to the fans, the team, and Peter McCoy himself.

I wrap up getting dressed and lock up my Monaco flat. My shoes click against the cobbled steps as I walk toward my car, breathing in the salty air from the Mediterranean Sea.

I drive down the roads of Monaco, the engine of my blue McCoy convertible revving as I shift gears. Tall buildings and coastal waters soar past me. The ringing of my Bluetooth speaker interrupts my thoughts.

"Hey, Pa, what's up?"

"Hi, what are you up to? Do you have a second?" My dad's German accent carries through the speakers.

"Sure. I'm driving to a meeting I have with McCoy."

"Good because we need to talk. Your mom and I saw the latest story. Please tell me it isn't true."

I grind my teeth together as I think of what to say. "Which part? The fact that I fucked Claudia? Or how I kicked her out of my apartment without a kiss goodbye?"

My dad lets out a deep sigh. "This isn't a joke."

"I know, but what can I do? Yes, I had sex with her, but we never were a couple in any other sense of the word. We were more like fuck buddies. She knew the deal—hell, she practically came up with half of it herself."

"What made you think hooking up with your boss's niece was a good idea? That's a new low, even for you."

"She fell into my lap at the F1 end of the year gala. She's beautiful, but I've since learned how desperation smells an awful lot like Chanel Number Five." I should have taken her ambitiousness as a warning sign, but fame makes people arrogant and complacent.

"When are you going to grow up and stop acting like sex and women are transactional? I thought you'd stop once you turned twenty-six, for fuck's sake. But here we are, almost three years later, and you're still screwing around." The speakers vibrate from his grumbling.

Guilt churns inside of me. "Maybe when I hit thirty-five? Retirement age, perhaps?"

"You keep messing around as you do, with women related to powerful men no less, then retirement will be a hell of a lot sooner than thirty-five. I can tell you that."

Shit. Someone call a doctor because my dad gave me a third-degree burn.

I resist the urge to snap at my dad. "I get it. I fucked up big time, messing with the man who signs my paychecks. But I plan on making smarter choices this year."

Thanks to my stupidity, I put a target on my back in a sport where there are only twenty spots with hundreds of eager drivers. No math needed to show what a fucking idiot I am because this one is easier than two plus two.

"I sure hope so. Look at Noah, now having to share Bandini with a younger driver. There's always someone eyeing your position."

I bite the inside of my cheek. "Santiago Alatorre is talented, I'll give you that. But he's a total psycho behind the wheel, so Noah having his hands full with him can work in my favor."

"Not if you keep messing up. You know, I'd hate for the day to come when you meet the right girl, but you're too blinded by your ignorance to see it. Your reputation will get you in trouble if you don't fix it because no worthy woman wants to date a guy who acts like you do."

"What woman wouldn't want to date a successful F1 driver?" My knuckles blanch as I grip my steering wheel, my nails biting into the leather.

"The same type who wouldn't want to date a has-been manwhore because she has enough self-respect for the two of you." His clipped tone echoes through the speakers as I pass ocean-lined streets.

I take in a few deep breaths before responding. "I appreciate how much you care. Truly I do. But I'm going to fix it with McCoy, avoid drama, and stick to racing. No more stories about my dick in the papers. I promise."

"If I had been half the idiot you tend to be lately, I wouldn't have snagged your mom."

My parents have a perfect marriage with arguments that end in a hug, a schedule for who takes out the trash and does the dishes each day, and displays of affection that no child should see. Thank God I have a brother because I would've been traumatized if it weren't for him. Lukas taught me why we don't go into our parents' room when they close the door, no matter how loud they scream.

"Not everyone gets to have a happy ending," I mutter into the

Bluetooth microphone. The usual tightness in my chest occurs at the memory of Johanna not getting hers.

Fuck. Leave it to my dad to stir up old feelings that have no place in my life right now.

"Listen…I know what happened with Lukas and Johanna affected you more than you let on. We all loved her, and you both were especially close. But you can't let fear drive your life. What happened was tragic, but that doesn't mean you need to live guardedly because you're afraid."

A bitter laugh makes its way out of my throat by its own accord. "I'm not talking about this with you."

"You *never* talk about it. Not with me, not with anyone. Her passing away was hard on us all. But you shut down, and now look at you. It's been almost three years, and you're still making these foolish mistakes. Every December, it's the same with you, holing up somewhere as soon as the season ends, making self-destructive decisions. You avoid us right after the holidays for Kaia's birthday. This time you ended up with the wrong girl at the wrong time. So, you can pretend to be fine in front of everyone else, but we know."

"Just because I'm having fun and hooking up with women doesn't mean I'm hung up on Johanna's death or anything. I get I messed up, but don't be ridiculous trying to connect it to shit from the past. I happen to get busy after Christmas." I bite on my tongue.

My dad sighs. "Save your lies for people who believe them… Really, it's okay to let someone in. To let them know you for more than the image you put out there."

The thing about being the nice guy is how no one sees how

corroded my heart is—how it leaks acid like an old car battery.

"I'm not looking for that right now." *Or ever.* Not since I experienced firsthand what happens to people who love hard.

Johanna's death changed me. A few months after she passed, I zipped up my race suit, signed a contract with McCoy, and won my second World Championship. I accepted the life I was meant to live while shunning the bitter memories. Passivity became my defense mechanism over the past few years.

My dad pauses. "That's what people always think."

I tap my agitated fingers against the steering wheel. "For a good reason, no doubt."

He lets out a deep sigh, probably rubbing his eyes. "No. The dumbasses who say that usually get hit the hardest."

"Hopefully, you mean fucked the hardest."

My dad's a good sport who laughs along with me while ditching his bad mood. He thinks I'm afraid, but I'm just indifferent.

"Liam...be careful, okay? There's no reason to make stupid decisions when you can have anyone you want. You only need to be willing to try."

It's selfish as fuck for me to still be affected by Johanna's death. I get it and despise it. Screw my brother for falling in love with my best friend. Part of me resents Lukas for making Johanna part of our family before she was ripped away, leaving me hollow and aching at her memory. Maybe if he kept to himself instead of pursuing her, I wouldn't be in this very position, screwing my boss's niece as some stupid distraction.

After chatting with my dad for another ten minutes, I park my car and situate myself inside of McCoy's waiting room. Rick, my agent, and Peter go back and forth, exchanging inaudible words with one another in a conference room surrounded by glass. Functionally stupid since I can see everything happening.

My agent looks at me a couple of times with a scowl. His slicked-back hair, cobalt suit, and tapping Ferragamo shoe mean business. My eyes stay glued to their discussion as I sit around like a little kid waiting outside the principal's office.

They call me into the room after five minutes. The sleek conference room feels small enough to make Peter look intimidating. His bald head gleams under the bright lights, highlighting his dark eyes and beard—a scary-looking motherfucker. Anger rolls off him, his eyes following me as I walk around the large table, my stomach turning at his frown. I give him a tight smile before taking a seat in one of the black rolling chairs, feigning comfort despite the edginess creeping into my veins.

Hopefully, my casual stance gives off a submissive vibe. I don't want to appear overly cocky because Peter looks like he wants to kick my balls hard enough to ensure my future offspring learn from my stupidity.

"As I was saying, Liam feels extremely apologetic about the situation with your niece. He never wanted the breakup to become public, especially when things ended amicably between the two. We have no idea where these negative reports are coming from." Rick's American drawl carries through the room. He does his job well, especially since he kisses Peter's ass enough to make it chafe.

Rick coughs, getting my attention.

I snap back into the conversation. "I'm sorry. I never meant to hurt Claudia's feelings, honestly. I shouldn't have pursued anything with her, out of respect for you and the team. We're not a good fit. But it won't affect my skills on the road or my professionalism because I love McCoy. I'm ready to land on every podium this season with no more drama."

"Drama seems to be following you around lately. Your name comes up way too often in the media." Peter's dark brow rises.

No one in McCoy is supposed to talk to gossip rags. Conveniently, Claudia doesn't need to sign an NDA like the rest of us because of her family name. McCoy didn't have a reason to believe she'd want negative press for a company that pays for her exclusive trips to Saint Tropez and her monthly shopping bills.

I lace my fingers together. "I'll do everything I can to fix my image and repair the public's perception of me."

Peter's narrowed eyes hold mine. "It would be best for you to remember you're replaceable. You're one of the best drivers in the whole sport, but nonetheless replaceable. I don't want to read any more nasty gossip articles about you. Chris picked you for this team, knowing you're one the greatest, up there with Noah. So, show us you're worth every million we pay you."

Chris, our team principal, manages the McCoy crew, including Jax and me. Peter bringing him up adds to my embarrassment, knowing I pissed off a man who has always believed in me.

I swallow back the lump in my throat. "I'll make sure to drive my best, and I'll keep my dick out of the papers this season while making McCoy proud. No question about it."

Peter stands. "You've got a tough season ahead of you, with Santiago joining Bandini and Noah having a fire lit under him from new competition. James Mitchell wants another win. I expect nothing but the best work from you and Jax, especially with the new lineup of cars we have for you. Now get out of here and go test the car out. I want to hear positive reports from the team."

Peter doesn't have to tell me twice. I say goodbye and leave like my ass is on fire. Somehow, I dodged a bullet. I'm shocked at how Peter seemed a lot more relaxed than I anticipated, but I can't help worrying about it all being a false sense of security—a trap to see if I fail again. But this time I'll stay aware and think before I act.

There's no need to harp on the conversation because this shit needs to be put behind me, including the crap my dad brought up today about Johanna. I don't race in F1 for the drama. No, I race for trophies, titles, and titties—except the latter now remains off the table for an unforeseeable future thanks to my recent blunders.

I want to keep the past in the past, right where those fucking bad memories belong.

CHAPTER FOUR

Sophie

Whoever came up with the statement B.F.E. clearly hasn't been to China. It's far, like probably the farthest I'll ever travel in my lifetime. Hence the reason my carry-on backpack looks about one second away from exploding because I take my snacks seriously.

Earlier, I didn't blink when the security man ruffled through my stash, pulling out my bag of cereal like it insulted him. Yes, I still eat Fruity Pebbles. *Sue me.* I'm a twenty-one-year-old with a dietary range of a child. But my list includes *try new food*, right next to *do karaoke while drinking* and *go skydiving*. Baby steps, right?

The airport bursts with activity. My hand clutches the handles of my luggage while I evade the countless bodies funneling through the baggage terminal. I smile at the older Chinese man who holds up a sign that reads *Sophie "Biggest Pain in My Ass" Mitchell.*

Dad, always a charmer. The driver grabs my bags and gives me a respectful nod, not letting me lift a finger. I get into the backseat of the waiting town car. My nose gets a whiff of fresh citrus and leather while I listen to the hum of Shanghai pass us by, the rumbling of the car calming my post-travel nerves.

I drop off my luggage at the hotel and take a quick shower before I visit the motorhome suite area. Team members hang out at the motorhomes before, during, and after the races. They're known as the ultimate relaxation spot where each team has their space to discuss logistics, eat, and take breaks.

I enter the Bandini motorhome and smile at the familiar colors of scarlet red and yellow. It fills me with warmth and fond memories, thinking back to my childhood where I ran through these halls with my dad chasing after me.

I patrol the food bar, hoping to find something to hold me over until dinnertime when I run into someone. We both let out an oomph as we catch our footing.

I stare into a pair of honey-brown eyes framed by thick lashes. My eyes roam over a woman who looks like a Spanish model, taking in long brown hair, brown eyes, and olive skin.

My cheeks heat. "Oh, sorry about that. I'm such a clumsy person." No doorjamb, chair, or bedpost leaves my big toe unstubbed.

"It's no problem. I run into things all the time too. I haven't seen you around here before." She shoots me a genuine smile.

"I'm Sophie. You probably haven't because I just got here."

"Maya. I haven't seen anyone my age except my brother. Glad

I ran into you—literally."

I let out a laugh. "It's my first time joining the race. I wrapped up my classes early for the year to spend time with my dad while he tours. Can't say no to a free vacation."

"I graduated in December! And who's your dad? I guess he's with Bandini then?" She waves around the busy lobby.

I tug on my gold star necklace. "My dad is the team principal. He's the one who runs the show around here."

Her eyes widen. "Oh, wow. And you're going to be here for the rest of the season?"

"I'm going to try to convince my dad to let me take my fall classes online so I can stick around for the whole Prix schedule. It's my first time around since I was younger, so I have to take advantage." Not that she needs to know, but I already have my speech prepared and everything.

"Nice, we can hang out since I'm going to be here for the whole season. It'll be awesome to have someone my age keeping me young."

I steer us toward an empty table, asking Maya to spill the latest gossip happening around the F1 paddock. Maya and I eat lunch, chatting about how she plans on vlogging during her travels with the team. She tells me how Santiago Alatorre is her brother. Lucky me, I didn't know Bandini's newest driver came with a sister as a bonus.

Maya and I spend the day together before the big gala meant to honor all the F1 racers—a soirée rivaling Jay Gatsby's. Maya gives me the rundown on everything Bandini while we hang out in her hotel room and get ready for the event.

After a few hours together, I declare us friends because I get a good feeling with these types of things. F1 rarely has young females hanging around, so I'll take what I can get.

"What's your living situation like during your time here?" She looks at me while she blows on her wet nails.

"My dad has his own room because of his crazy schedule. I'd rather not be woken up at the crack of dawn. He tried to make sure our rooms are on the same floor since he likes to keep an eye on me, but conveniently there were none available."

She lets out a breathy laugh. "He's protective of you?"

I snort. "That's an understatement. My dad sent me to an all-girls school growing up to prevent me from getting close to any guys. College was the first time I had a co-ed classroom."

She offers me a wobbly smile. "That's kind of sweet of him."

"He never let me date in high school which meant I didn't have my first kiss until eighteen years old. It was awful, and I couldn't even use braces as an excuse for it being so bad."

Maya curls over laughing. "Tell me more. *Please.*"

"It was sloppy, wet, with his teeth chewing on my lip while his tongue waged an unwanted World War against mine. So much went wrong. He even copped a feel despite it being our first date." I try not to laugh at the memory.

Maya giggles enough for the two of us. "Stop. He felt you up? That's awful when everyone knows that's second-date material."

"Nope. I was the unlucky victim of too much tongue and not enough common sense."

Maya wipes away a tear that escaped her eye. "I can't believe this happened to you."

"You're telling me. I think he may have licked a drop of blood that fell from my lip after he bit into me. How very Dracula of him."

She looks at me with wide eyes. "What did you do then?"

"I kneed him in the balls and walked away, only looking back to catch him curled up in a fetal position. My dad didn't raise a fool. He made me take self-defense classes as part of the deal for living on campus instead of at home. Thanks to him, I can kick a dummy's ass into tomorrow. Just ask my sensei."

She seals her nail polish bottle. "Please tell me you at least lost your virginity in a normal way."

I throw myself on the sectional, covering my eyes with my arm. "Ugh, I wish. If only life was that easy or fair. Truly I've had one disappointing, anti-climactic romantic encounter after another. Losing my V-card was nothing extraordinary. Everything went downhill once the guy asked me which hole he was supposed to stick his dick inside. He couldn't find my vagina on his own, let alone my G-spot."

Maya cackles, the sound of her laugh bouncing off the walls, making me join her despite my less-than-ideal stories. Glad my tragedies bring someone happiness. It's a sort of Shakespearean masterpiece if I do say so myself.

Her eyes glimmer under the hotel lights. "You have a way with words. Keep going, do *not* leave me hanging like this."

I sit, tucking my legs under me. "If you insist. Well, I liked the guy I was interested in losing it to. Paul, from my Intro to Statistics class, which should have been a warning bell because his name alone sounds basic and ordinary. Anyway, I knew I wasn't holding out for Prince Charming. I needed someone who could get the job over with and who I felt a semblance of a connection. After a couple of dates, we decided to give it a go in the bedroom. But he didn't tell me he also was a virgin. So, on top of everything, the whole experience was awkward with him coming first, unable to last more than two minutes. There was no happy ending for me. I think my brain represses most of that night to save me from embarrassment and bad memories. A kind of self-induced blackout minus the alcohol."

"Oh, no. Are you serious?" She covers her heart with her hand. "You didn't even have your first orgasm after you gave up your virginity?"

"Dead serious. Paul was a five-minute man, foreplay included. After eighteen years of hype, I had a no go for the O. What a letdown."

"Any better experiences?" She looks hopeful, but unfortunately, I have nothing good to report. This is the exact reason I created my list in the first place.

I shake my head. "Some situations here and there. But honestly, I've been with a total of three guys, none of whom knew what they were doing. I blame my small university with a limited pool of eligible bachelors who can balance a checkbook quicker than they can make me come."

"You'd definitely know if you have, so I'm going to go with no, which makes my heart ache for you. This must be rectified." She claps her hands excitedly.

I grin at her, not ready to tell her my secret. She doesn't need to worry because I've got big plans. Just me, my list, and months of adventure.

CHAPTER FIVE

Liam

My F1 season starts strong, with me finishing within the top three for the last two races with nineteen more to go. The whole season makes up about ten months of the year with a summer and winter break worth a month each.

A racer lifestyle keeps me conveniently busy, making it hard to relax, let alone settle down. My schedule limits my time with family to a few visits per year, like during my home race and short holidays.

It's not like I try to stay away. Distance numbs the dull throb taking up residence in my chest whenever I see my nieces. Time fails to ease the emotional distance between Lukas and me, adding to our strained relationship, along with missed calls and limited brother time.

In short, I've married my job because it's a hell of a lot easier than dealing with my family.

Sounds of popping champagne bottles and laughter emanate throughout the ballroom. Whoever plans these parties sets the mood with soft lighting and low music, along with hot women and A-list celebrities. It's the usual assortment of people. Drinks flow all night long, probably in the hopes that sponsors open up their checkbooks in the name of love and racing.

Don't hate the racer, hate the sport where wealth funds the opulent lifestyle notorious with F1 racing. The F1 Corp showers us in hundred-dollar bottles of champagne for the hell of it, our sport not sparing a single expense. The events I attend are snazzy and excessive, with outrageous decor, Michelin-star food, and top-shelf alcohol.

My hiatus keeps me in check, my self-proclaimed dry spell holding me back from inviting any woman back to my hotel room. I should hang an *out of commission* sign around my neck because three women offer a classic "get to know each other more" that pains me to decline. My efforts deserve a medal of valor for not thinking with my dick for once.

My previous pride dissipates once the ultimate temptation shimmies up next to me. The smell of her hits me first, like the ocean on a summer day, a fucking intoxicating smell of coconuts and the beach.

I do a double take to make sure I'm seeing things right. Her hair reflects a golden hue, looking unreasonably soft, the same color I remember with a hundred shades of blonde woven together. My hands shake at the craving to run my fingers through her thick locks. A healthy glow radiates from her, her cheeks turning a soft pink color at my appraisal.

I withhold a groan. "Sophie, I haven't seen you in years." And those years have done her really fucking well.

Her green eyes widen in recognition, the two spheres reminding me of the rich forests surrounding my home in Germany.

Sophie is no longer an eighteen-year-old I met three years ago. Legal enough to drink and legal enough to fuck—and yes, I'd like to fuck. One look at her gains my interest, my dick twitching against the zipper of my pants.

With her standing next to me now, the age gap seems less daunting than before.

"Liam." Sophie's withdrawn voice makes me grin. She remembers me too, and shit, I like the way my name rolls off her tongue.

My dick may be abstaining like a priest, but my brain fucks like the devil. I may be all jokes and smiles, but I sure as shit love to fuck dirty, edgy, and rough. That's what happens when you drive the fastest cars in the world. The idea of boring sex—vanilla and mundane—irks me. I don't have time for shitty sex in a missionary position with a slow pace and sweet pecks. If sex isn't desperate, crazed, and frantic, then people are doing it wrong.

I withhold a deep sigh when my eyes roam across her body. The silk material clings to her small curves and accentuates her waist. The fabric drapes low across her chest, revealing the upper swells of her breasts and delicate collarbone. I want to run my tongue across her skin, kissing the sensitive area before moving onto other places.

Fuck.

Maya coughs, bringing my attention toward her for the

first time this evening. She looks nice, but I'm not interested in Santiago's sister. Fat chance seeing as my dick throbs in my pants at the sight of Sophie in front of me after a few years.

A look Sophie and Maya share tell me they've become acquainted, with Maya eyeing me disapprovingly when she catches me staring at Sophie again.

I pull it together and remember my manners. "What can I get you two fine ladies?"

Sophie lifts a brow. "Isn't it an open bar?"

Blood rushes to my dick at the sound of her husky voice, sounding like she smokes a pack of cigs a day. It's nothing I'd expect from someone who looks innocent and cute like her, a petite little thing who smirks at me.

"Doesn't mean I can't order it for you. Make a man feel useful." I pout my lip for extra points. Sophie's eyes narrow when they land on me before darting off in another direction.

We engage in casual back and forth before Noah and Jax show up. I can't tear my eyes away from Sophie's pink lips sucking on the straw of her drink. My dick pulses, ready for attention, unaware of how the evening can't go down how I want. And fuck do I want to go down on Sophie.

Reforming my ways and staying out of trouble takes a lot of work. My brain wins, running through everything that can go wrong if I hook up with someone like Sophie. She's the daughter of a powerful team principal who wouldn't appreciate me trying to seduce his daughter, no matter how friendly I am with Noah.

Thoughts about losing my contract and risking my career make my dick deflate because nothing kills a hard-on quite like the thought of losing everything I care about.

I look at Sophie, committing her to memory, possibly for my nefarious plans with my right hand later. Everything about her appeals to me, from the way she laughs at Maya's jokes to how her green eyes narrow when she catches me staring too long.

Sophie happens to be a temptress with shit timing. The whole situation seems like a joke from God, my penance for being a dick to women before. Getting shafted by my team wasn't enough punishment. There's nothing worse than denying myself the hottest chick.

I mentally pat my dick.

Just you and me for now, pal.

Tension in the pit garage chokes me. The Chinese Grand Prix, a usually fun-as-fuck race, feels tainted by my nerves. I drink water to combat nausea and the dryness in my throat.

Jax pats me on the back with a bronzed hand, pulling me away from my negativity as he passes me my helmet. We match, wearing similar flame-retardant gear while looking distinct with customized helmets.

"Try to not let the pressure get to you. As much as I want to kick your arse into next week, I'd rather do it with your head in the race." He runs a hand through his short curls.

I tug on the zipper of my suit. "Says the guy who spends twenty minutes in the bathroom before every race. What are you doing in there? Deep breathing exercises?"

He cracks his neck, drawing my attention to his tattoos starkly contrasting against his pristine white race suit. "Wouldn't you like to know."

"No shit. I know you don't have a chick in there so it's probably something weird and kinky you do by yourself."

"Fuck you very much, arsehole. I happen to like relaxing before a race."

"With all the partying you do on the side, I don't blame you. I don't know how you function half the time."

He shoots me a mischievous grin. "Probably because I have you to clean up my messes for me. Nothing says a good night's rest quite like you tucking me into bed."

Through everything, we remain as tight as teammates can be, not compromising our friendship for competitiveness. Any time he needs me, I'm there for him. A random call at 2 a.m. to pick him up from some seedy side of town while he sports a new shiner? *No problem.* He needs me to help him get out of bed after a complete binger the night before, including removing women from his hotel room? *I got it.* Random last-minute request for my private jet? *Let me call that in.* That's how it is between us, no questions asked.

I struggle to hide my smile. "God, you're fifty shades of fucked up. You know that, right?"

"My issue is that I know it all too well." He walks off toward his race car.

My gloved hand pats the hood of my race car before I slide into the cockpit, the tight space welcoming me back. The steel-gray color glistens from the sun and pit lights while the steering wheel blinks back at me in a silent hello. I take a deep breath, welcoming the scents of oil and rubber.

I pop on my helmet and flip down my visor, ready to get this shit on the road.

Honey, I'm home.

Do you know what happens when you race cars at two hundred plus miles an hour? Adrenaline. I crave a cold beer and a good fuck after a race, except I can't do anything like that until my recent headlines blow over.

New season, new me. What an affirmation.

The adrenaline high from winning the Grand Prix makes it difficult to contain my excitement during the latest press conference. I sit with Jax and Noah as we answer F1-related questions from reporters. No use complaining about these boring parts when I get to live my dream every damn day.

What more can I ask for? Well, maybe the removal of my newly acquired purity ring, but fuckers can't be choosers.

I school my features when a reporter asks about my upcoming contract agreement. "I love the team at McCoy, and they've been great with me over the past few years. The company knows what they're doing, so I'm holding out to see what happens. Call me an optimist."

"How is your relationship with McCoy after everything that occurred in the media this winter break?"

"Things couldn't be better, and the team is ready to win this season. McCoy is my priority and my race car is the only woman in my life."

Noah holds back a laugh next to me. His blue eyes and dark, wavy hair shine from the bright lights. The asshole knows things with McCoy are rocky, ever since Claudia threw a heel at my head when I pulled the plug on our brief sex-capade. Thank fuck for fast reflexes. Sadly for her, her tantrum didn't have the desired effect of rough makeup sex because vindictive women don't do it for me.

The rest of the conference feels mundane once reporters move on to someone else.

Noah pulls me aside once the F1 Corp member announces the end of the conference. He tugs me in for a hug and a smack on the back before letting go. "You need to figure out something to fix this relationship thing. You're going to end up getting screwed out of a contract if McCoy can't trust you to not screw up again. Other teams are probably wondering what you'll do next. You've created a media shitstorm that reporters can rave about."

"And what exactly do you suggest I do? I can't help how Claudia keeps spreading rumors about whatever we did." I find the process of defending myself exhausting.

He smirks at me. "Keep your dick out of any girls for a while. Think you can handle that?"

"Or I can do what you do, hook up one time and call it a night? I don't hear you complaining about needy women and missed calls."

Noah chuckles. "It's worked out for me over the years. You messed up by getting together with women multiple times because that no-strings-attached lifestyle is bullshit. They always expect more time and attention. The thing with Claudia lasted way too long, and now she's obsessed with either getting you back or driving you crazy."

"Hey, to be fair, I didn't think hooking up for a week was too long. It was only supposed to be a winter break thing. I warn the ladies before. The moment they start hinting at labels or long-term situations, I cut it off. Claudia didn't get the memo because she's never told no. Life hack: spoiled rich girls come with a private jet worth of baggage."

He offers a weak smile. "Figure something out. But until then, keep to yourself, at least with the McCoy team. I tell you not to fuck around where you work. I actually want to compete against you, preferably while you're on a comparable team. It would be no fun racing with guys who don't know my every move like you do."

"Shucks, you're making me blush." I press a palm to my cheek.

"Asshole. You'll keep me sane now that I have an idiot for a teammate. Santiago joining Bandini is further proof of how there'll always be someone faster and younger than us vying for our positions. So pull your shit together."

"No need to harp on it. Let's grab lunch because I'm starving." I make my way toward the exit of the press building. This topic has overstayed its welcome.

"That's the best idea you've had all day."

Fans tune in for Saturdays and Sundays, watching our qualifiers and races. But guess what? They miss all the fun behind the scenes, like how I get to meet with Chris and Jax for an exhilarating pre-race debriefing inside McCoy's headquarters.

"All right, boys. It's time for our post-race check-in. Before we begin, any comments on the new cars now that you've raced a few times?" Chris's Russian accent carries words with a guttural sound. He gives off mobster vibes, with black gelled hair, thick brows, and a stocky frame.

"This one rides smoother than my most recent fuck." Jax smiles, his hazel eyes gleaming.

Leave it to Jax to break up our shitty routine. His hair looks wild today, curls unkempt. He traded in his usual black attire for the team propaganda. Black tattoos peek out from the collar of his white McCoy shirt, trailing from his neck to his knuckles, the design intricately woven.

"Thank you for details no one wants to hear. And you, Liam?" Chris's brown eyes land on me.

"I think I need less understeering because the balance feels off. With those changes, it'll be perfect."

"Okay, we can get those adjusted for you before the next practice round." Chris writes his notes on his tablet. "Also, McCoy added extra PR training to your schedule since reporters keep bringing up the Claudia shit."

Jax and I grunt. We hate PR reps because they're a bunch of nosy men telling us what to do and what to say.

Chris holds up his arms. "Hey, I didn't put my dick in a hole it didn't belong in. Let this be a lesson for both of you."

"I don't get why I have to be wrapped up in this torture experience. No offense, Liam, but you fucked up." Jax's British accent makes the words less offensive.

"Last time I checked, there was a picture of you drunk and throwing up outside of a club in England. Not your best look." I sip from an imaginary teacup.

"What can I say, sometimes whiskey hits you the wrong way. At least I made it outside before getting sick." Jax gives me a sly grin.

"Was that before you took a nap in the bush?" I rub my chin.

"One man's nap is another man's blacking out." Jax grins.

"Then enjoy being part of the fun. I'm sure you can use a PR tip or two." My comment gets me an up-close look at a tattooed middle finger.

It's safe to say we both made some careless mistakes over the break, including Jax chewing out an American reporter who made a racist comment. After he fucked with the guy's camera, we can assume no one else on the grid will fuck with him for having a white mom and a black dad anymore.

"And for my shitty sanity and yours, please behave. Play nice with others, keep your hands to yourself, and don't swap spit with someone who can get you in trouble with the media. I don't give a shit what you do behind closed doors, just don't come crying to me when shit hits the fan. My job description doesn't include dealing with blubbering men and drama. James Mitchell has enough dirt on our team to last him a lifetime." Chris dismisses us with a wave of his hand.

Jax and I shoot each other our classic fuckboy grins as we leave the conference room. The very same one we save for parties, pussy, and the Prix.

CHAPTER SIX

Sophie

"I have an idea. But hear me out first before you say no." Maya's words do little to relax me despite her soothing voice.

I look into her warm eyes. "That's what they say in every bad serial killer movie. No question about it, you'd be the first to die. The pretty ones always go first."

She offers me a blank stare. "We're going to a karaoke bar tonight. Please come?"

Well, I didn't expect to cross off an item from my Fuck It list so fast. Look at Maya, making herself useful during my first weekend. "Sure. Sounds like fun."

She clutches my hand as she lets out a squeal of approval. "Yes! It *will* be fun! Santi invited us since he had such a bad race. Noah chewed him out for crashing into him, so he wants to let loose with a little singing and a lot of alcohol."

"I won't lie, I didn't expect Santi to choose karaoke as his destressing activity. Now that I'm thinking about it, do they even have English karaoke songs here? You know, like Backstreet Boys and N*SYNC because I don't want to sing a Korean pop song."

Maya looks taken aback. "Of course. Didn't you know?"

"Do I know what?"

"They *love* karaoke here." Her Cheshire grin says it all. A sane person would take one look at her and run for the Great Wall of China.

"All right, sounds like a plan."

Maya claps her hands and rushes to hug me. "I knew you'd say yes. Think of it as a best friend's initiation ritual."

"More like a ritualistic sacrifice." I smile at her.

We finish getting ready for the night. I choose ripped jeans, a slogan T-shirt I knot at the bottom to look cute, and a pair of booties. The outfit is a nod to my inner rock star. Since my singing skills are limited to shower concerts, I'll fake it till I make it.

Santi introduces himself in the lobby. I get hit with a whopping six-foot-something Spanish man who could moonlight as a model with dark hair and a strong body accentuated by a T-shirt and jeans. His brown eyes assess mine, his olive skin wrinkling at the corners as he introduces himself. He drops his serious brother front once I ask him if he plans on singing better than he drives.

Maya, Santi, and I walk into a dingy Shanghai bar twenty minutes later. Speakers rumble, making it hard to distinguish singing from backtrack music. My shoes stick to the floor while warm air hangs around us.

Santi passes us each a shot glass. "*Salud*. To a fun night and future memories."

"And to new countries, friends, and success." Maya clinks her glass against ours.

We knock back our shots. My eyes water as the liquid burns my throat.

Maya shoots me a shy smile as she passes me a glass of water. I never gravitated toward girls in school, not liking how catty they got about grades and gossip, but Maya acts differently. Although very new, our friendship seems off to a good start.

Our trust continues to grow through the night. After a few drinks, Maya confesses how she finds Noah hot. She whispers her declaration in my ear while Santi grabs more drinks.

Drinks keep coming, a steady buzz making me feel less self-conscious about singing in front of a crowd. I get up on the stage and sing "Don't Stop Believin'" with Maya and Santi.

As the night progresses, I discover two types of people who do karaoke.

The first group of individuals takes their singing very seriously. They choose songs to serenade to, either of the sultry R&B variety or heart-wrenching country songs. The second type chooses to sing songs from an era of nineties boy bands. Performances include a dance number with poorly executed attempts at synchronized moves after one too many tequila shots.

I fall into the second group, becoming a combo of Baby Spice and Justin Timberlake. Maya and I let loose and dance around the stage while we sing into a shared microphone. Never will I underestimate the power of alcohol again. After tonight, I will bow down to the bottle of tequila, claiming José as my master.

And clearly, we have a mixed assortment of people tonight. When we discussed the plan earlier, Maya failed to mention how her brother invited a bunch of people to come sing and drink with us, including Jax and Liam.

Cue the DJ record scratch.

Liam Zander. Prim signature blonde hair, glacial blue eyes rivaling my art class pastels, and a brilliant smile that blinds me worse than a strobe light—a deadly temptation for my self-restraint. He has a beard he trims close to the skin, giving him a bit of an edge while framing sensual lips. His sweet looks hide how dirty and wicked he is on the inside. He's a misleading man who suffers from a permanent allergy to relationships, graced with a reputation of being all seduction and heartbreak.

Exhibit A: Claudia McCoy

Exhibit B through Z: everyone else he's hooked up with over the years

Nothing could've prepared me for how I felt seeing him at the gala the other day. One look from him had my heart racing like I had finished a 5K marathon a minute before seeing him. I don't even run 5Ks, but the pace of my heart was alarming. That's how much of an effect he has on me.

He flashes me a smile across the bar.

Ovaries, please settle down.

I shoot him a scowl in hopes of cloaking my true feelings, but his grin expands, undeterred by my attitude. He screams trouble in the worst kind of ways. His reputation is shit with women, and he struggles to keep his dick in check. I'd know, seeing as my Twitter feed's filled with the latest F1 drama.

I cling to Maya's side like a child afraid to let go. She becomes my protector without even knowing it, saving me from someone who promises nothing but trouble.

A few minutes later, Maya decides to sing a duet with her brother, abandoning me without a backward glance. Her disappearance prompts Liam to sit next to me on a leather couch better suited for Barbie's dream house. That says something coming from me, a pixie whose feet rarely reach the floor while sitting. Liam's presence overwhelms me as his body takes up a majority of the seat. I scoot closer to the side, desperate for some space between us, edgy about how my body responds to his closeness.

He widens his legs, and his thigh brushes against mine. My skin heats at the contact, attraction flooding through me, his smoldering gaze intimidating me.

"I didn't expect you to be such a screamer." His husky voice sends goosebumps up my arms, his accent heavier from yelling over the music.

I choke on my drink. A lazy grin reaches his eyes and hints at smile lines at the corners. *Look, something not perfect about him.*

"Dirty little mind you have there." His eyes flicker over my face. "The microphone really picks up on everything." He points at the stage with his beer bottle.

I take him in. His white shirt clings to his sculpted chest, muscles pressing against the fabric, highlighting lean yet fit arms. Ones he can wrap around me.

Dammit, Sophie, resist.

"Mm, it's hard to sing and dance at the same time. I have a new appreciation for performers. It's a lot of work, and it makes you sweaty." I take another sip of my drink, the refreshing liquid soothing my sore throat.

"You know what else makes you sweaty?" His words pull my

attention back to him. Light blue irises fall on my lips before his body scoots closer to mine, his warmth pressing into my side as my body becomes highly aware of him.

"Lots of things. The gym, the great outdoors, a busted AC unit. The options are endless."

He chuckles, the sound making his chest vibrate against my arm. "Racing does. You look a little flushed, and your eyes have a wild look to them. Are you thinking of something else? Penny for your thoughts?" The low and rough tone of his voice runs against my skin like a caress.

Nope. Not touching his first question with a ten-foot checkered flag.

"Right, racing. And honestly, you're a millionaire. You can spare more than a couple of pennies for what goes on in my mind." I tap on my temple.

He laughs as he lifts his drink to his lips. His throat bobs while he chugs the last bit of beer, his eyes remaining on me the entire time. I hate the way I notice everything about him. Like how good his lips look wrapped around the rim of his beer bottle or the tiniest bump in his nose hinting at a previous injury. I especially dislike the way he looks at me right now, like he doesn't know which way he wants to fuck me first. And most of all, I hate how much I love every second of his attention.

His eyes lazily trace over my face before they fall on my chest. The audacity of this man.

"Cute shirt." His lips twitch.

Like an idiot, I glance down. The sweet *Free Hugs* saying mocks me, pressing against my bust with the words centered above a prickly cactus. That's me: a woman who has an affection level comparable to a desert plant.

"Thanks. I love graphic tees." That sounds as stupid in my head as it does when it leaves my lips. I cringe at my inability to play it cool around Liam.

"Do I make you nervous?" Liam takes advantage of my flustered state. The contact of his hand grasping mine sparks excitement from me, an involuntary reaction I want to control. His fingers brush against my knuckles and leave behind a trail of heat. Safe to say, our stint of attraction still burns strong, unwavering with time.

I never thought holding hands could be such a sensory experience. But my mind takes control, not wanting to go there with someone like him, prompting me to pull my hand away from his.

He laughs, a full throaty sound tugging at my restraint. "You don't need to be scared. Have a little fun."

"I think we both have two different definitions of fun." My version includes a laminated list of items, while his includes screwing around until he gets bored or detached.

On paper, Liam seems like a good option to help me complete my Fuck It list. But in reality, Liam would be the worst choice—too good-looking, too accessible, too risky. Not to mention, he drives for a rival team, which could result in extra unwanted press for both of us.

And to be extra honest, courtesy of tequila, completing items with Liam scares me. I thought I'd cross them off with random guys from different countries, not with one I have to see every week. Avoiding Liam will be damn near impossible, so why bother making things awkward?

Sirens sound off in my head despite an alcohol-induced haziness, warning me why being with him is not worth it. I stand, my head swimming. My body finds balance and a fragment of mental clarity again as I grab my purse off the table. A ride-share sounds like a great idea.

I avoid direct eye contact with Liam as I fumble through the items in my purse, grabbing things left and right. He sits and watches me with a smirk on his face. Unable to find my phone, I curse to myself. My hands sift through the contents again. My fingertips brush against the rough texture of my phone case at the bottom. As I pull it out, I find my list attached to the back of my case, stuck together by static or voodoo. I watch with horror as the laminated paper flutters to the ground.

Liam grabs it off the cement floor before I have a chance to pick it up. "What's this?"

Unlike movies where horrific moments are slowed down, my heart speeds up and I attempt to snatch the paper with lightning speed. "Let me have that. It's nothing, just a shopping list." My voice fails to hide how horrified I feel.

Liam grips the paper harder as he sends me a devilish grin that liquefies my insides. "Tsk, tsk. How rude of you to grab something from my hands. You greedy little thing." He pulls the paper toward his eyes as he attempts to make out the letters in the dimly lit bar. I barely breathe, taking in enough oxygen to not pass out. Although a medical scare sounds like a great diversion.

He holds back a laugh. "A Fuck It list? I'm curious about what type of things you're shopping for here."

"I hate groceries, so fuck it. Right?" I dash for the list again. My fingers grasp the slick plastic coating before Liam lifts himself from the couch.

Liam has to be a foot taller than me, my list no longer in reaching distance. A growl of frustration escapes my lips as I stomp my foot. He smiles down at me like he finds my irritated display cute.

I teeter on my feet, my hands grabbing onto his arms for stability. The warm skin of his biceps heats my fingers. His rigid muscles tense under my hands, teasing me to feel him up like a creep.

I look up at him as I step away, putting some room between us. He offers me a toothy grin as he pulls out his phone and turns on the flashlight to assess my items. I want to die right here, right now, in some dingy Chinese bar to an Asian rendition of Elvis Presley.

"You even color-coded it?" Liam's surprised voice comes off sincere.

My eyes hold his steady, facing my fate. "I like to be organized and detail-oriented. Why make a list if it isn't perfect? Now give it back." I hold my palm out and tap my foot.

Liam childishly waves it above my head. His height makes the task of snatching my list impossible. I bounce up and down to no avail, unable to reach his hand. My body rubs against his firm chest. The contact makes me jump back a foot and nearly twist an ankle.

His chuckle sounds more like a rumble. "You're making it hard to read. Cut it out."

"Well, excuse me for the inconvenience. Didn't your mom teach you that it's not nice to take things from others?"

"Must have missed that lecture. But my mama taught

me how sharing is caring, so maybe you need a lesson or two yourself." His smirk and the alcohol I've consumed override my senses. That and the way he pronounces *mama*, hinting at his accent and boyishness.

"My, my, Miss Mitchell, what a dirty mind you have. I've clearly underestimated you." Liam shakes his head as his flashlight illuminates the page.

I rub my eyes, attempting to rid myself of this nightmare.

Nope, didn't work. Liam is still here, in his sexy glory, illuminating my list with his phone.

He reads my list, ignoring my state of distress. "*Go skinny-dipping. Buy a vibrator. Try foreplay with ice*, now that is quite bold. You're in luck, wanting to *kiss a foreigner*, because turns out you have one at your disposal right here. *Do karaoke while drinking*, completed. *Try new food, go skydiving, watch porn, play strip poker, kiss someone in front of the Eiffel Tower*. Ah, now you're talking. *Get tied up* and *be blindfolded*."

I attempt to rip the list from his hands, but he holds strong, continuing my torture.

"No need to get rough. *Come from oral sex* and *experience multiple orgasms in one night*. Basic, but I like it. *Mirror sex* sounds hot as fuck, you secret voyeur. *Have sex in public, have sex against a wall, have a quickie, and get high*. And last but most certainly not least, *have outdoor sex*. I have to say, I'm impressed by your level of creativity and boldness."

If I had a drink in my hand, I wonder if I would've thrown it in Liam's face. His smirk tempts me to go to the bar and fulfill my fantasy.

He taps my scrunched nose. "You know what we have to do

now, right?"

"I'm sure you'll tell me whether I ask or not."

"Smart girl. I'm making it my project to help you with this. It'll be our secret." His words make my skin break out in goosebumps. Liam has a way of screwing me without ever getting me in bed.

Mindfucked. Every damn time.

CHAPTER SEVEN

Liam

J ax and I spend our free time relaxing in the McCoy motorhome suite area. I lie on a gray leather couch, scrolling through my phone, passing the time before the Russian Grand Prix practice round. Shanghai finished on a high note. The weekend went by fast with a bonus of spending time with Sophie.

Sweet Sophie with lips meant for kissing and a body made for fucking. The girl who looks at me with wide eyes whenever I flirt with her, tempting me to give up on my dry spell. The same one who's popped into my mind over the last week more times than I care to admit.

My phone vibrates. A new text from Claudia lights up my phone, disgust sitting heavy in my stomach as I open another unwelcome message.

"Claudia sent me another nude." I delete the picture before it saves onto one of the clouds.

Jax grunts before taking a swig of his water. "Mate, she's obsessed with you. I thought she would let go of it by now. It's been two months already."

A groan escapes my lips as I try to wipe away the mental image of Claudia lying down in bed without clothes. My life has become a recurring nightmare of unsolicited photos, trashy articles, and ridiculous press releases.

"I didn't want to block her number, but I don't have a choice. I pray she doesn't come to any races because I can't handle that type of crazy."

Jax winces as he runs a tattooed hand through his hair. "Sucks how you can't tell McCoy about it with her being Peter's niece and all."

"I've told my agent, but he tells me not to cause waves during a signing year. He wants to make sure I get the best contract deal out of this. So, it's just me and my right hand, till death do us part." I wiggle my hand at Jax.

He barks out a laugh as he throws a pillow at me. "Keep that shit to yourself. No one needs to know about your sad masturbation schedule."

"This is my life now. Oh, how the mighty have fallen."

"Either you're amazing in bed, or she's plain crazy." Jax cracks up at my frustration. *Asshole.*

"I don't see why it can't be both." I smother my head with a pillow to tune out Jax's roar of laughter.

The sponsor gala for the Russian Grand Prix keeps the vodka flowing, therefore supplying me with a buzz to make it through the night. Small talk sucks. I schmooze for a good hour before I itch for fresh air.

I walk out onto the venue's balcony, taking in a panoramic view of the Sochi mountain ranges. My head snaps toward the sound of ice clinking against a glass.

I stroll toward the woman, recognizing whom the blonde head of hair belongs to. The dimly lit patio basks Sophie in a soft glow and emphasizes how her dress clings to her silhouette. Like a beacon of light enticing me with her back displayed, she teases me with the sparkling material dipping low and hugging her ass. My fingers yearn to drag themselves across every bump in her spine. I tuck my hands in my pockets to resist the urge. Lately, I've exercised enough self-control to rival a monk.

As if Sophie senses my gaze, she looks over her shoulder, hitting me with an expressionless face. She acts like an ice queen with no readable emotions. I let out a low laugh when she knocks back the remaining contents of her drink—her only fucking tell. She abandons the empty cup on a nearby table before she leans against the balcony's railing and looks toward the sky.

"What are you doing out here?" I walk over to her, eliminating the space between us. Just because I can't touch her doesn't mean I can't get close.

"One of my favorite things is to stargaze. I love to see the moon and stars, but it's hard out here with all the light pollution. Did you know some towns are creating lighting restrictions to protect the nighttime environment and prevent the issue?"

"Can't say I knew that. I would've never pegged you as a night lover."

Her laugh has an airiness to it. I wouldn't mind making her laugh again, liking the sound almost as much as her voice. "I am, but I've made myself into a morning person. I've got a schedule to keep and whatnot with school and studying. These events are way past my bedtime."

"Ah. So, let me guess. You like to wake up at the ass-crack of dawn, follow a tightly bound schedule, and go to sleep before midnight. Like clockwork. Rigid, high-strung, and sex-free. That type of thing," I half joke.

"Routines aren't always a bad thing. It's the unknown we have to watch out for." She eyes me curiously, as if she wants to get a read on me. "But during the summer, I love staying up late and laying out by the pool in my backyard sometimes. I stare into the dark, thinking about my day, like what went right or wrong. Maybe an occasional wish whispered up to whoever listens." Her wistfulness stirs up something in me.

My limited attention span focuses on other things she may do under the night sky. I might be suffering from a temporary lapse of judgment.

She shifts her body to face me, giving me a full view of her as her eyes roam over my body. I stand taller at her perusal, my lips lifting at the corners. A beaming smile graces her face when she catches the sneakers I wear with my suit. I tend to be a boy at heart, ditching classic shoes for white sneakers with a snake embossed design on the side.

"They let you wear shoes like that?" Her voice rasps.

"I copied the look from a girl who preferred sneakers with dresses over heels and gowns." I lean on the railing and stare at her.

She laughs as she pulls up the hem of her long gown to reveal a pair of white leather sneakers with embroidered stars. Fuck me. While all the women inside limp from too-tight shoes, she wears comfortable sneakers hidden from the world. And for the first time, I don't prefer fuck-me heels. I want a pair of tan legs and silver starred sneakers wrapped around my waist instead.

"I may have traded kid costumes for ball gowns, but I never gave up on the sneaker trend." She drops the hem of her dress again, my eyes lingering on her hidden legs before meeting her gaze.

Damn, I enjoy her presence way too much. My reaction to her is screwing with me because I can't remember the last time I had this easygoingness with a girl.

Like a knee-jerk reaction, the memory of Johanna draws a sharp pain straight to my chest. Fuck that. Not going there.

I ignore the sensation, pushing away the idea of Sophie reminding me of Johanna. "Quite the pair, you and I."

She scoffs. *Fucking hell, no charms work on her.*

"Are you always such a flirt?" Her eyes twinkle, light reflecting off them like she stole the stars she loves so damn much.

"Usually, but I've been keeping myself locked up this season. This is my no-no square. No girls can touch me here." I gesture toward the lower half of my body while shaking my finger at her.

Sophie drops her head back and laughs. She's a beautiful sight, her cautiousness abandoned, the curve of her throat gaining my attention. Shame I can't see more of her out here. I rely on my other senses, breathing in her scent of coconuts. *Is it her lotion? Her perfume? And why the fuck does it turn me on?*

"You should wear a sign, so everyone knows you're not up for grabs. It'll get the message across better for unsuspecting women. You know, because you're..." She waves over my body like that explains everything.

"Are you trying to hint at how you find me good-looking?"

Her face snaps forward as she shakes her head. "Uh, no. You're not my type."

"So, you're not into handsome men?"

She snorts. *Fucking snorts.* I can't believe I find it cute. It's unlike any other woman who hangs around me, groomed to perfection and putting on a show.

"No, I am. But I also like good guys." Her hands fidget before she grips the handrail.

I can be a good guy when I want, and compared to Noah, I classify myself as a saint. Well, a saint who sins, but a saint nonetheless.

"You know what they say about nice guys is a lie, right?" I enjoy the look of surprise on her face a little too much.

Her eyes enlarge and her lips part as her ice queen façade melts away. "What do you mean?"

"Unlike nice guys, bad boys always finish last. Every. Single. Time. And there are plenty of repeats." My hand has a mind of its own, running down her arm and leaving goosebumps behind.

Her breath catches at my words, encouraging me to get more responses from her. Fuck the repercussions. Touching isn't fucking, so I'm not breaking my deal yet. My skin buzzes when my knuckles graze her face.

A sigh escapes her lips, tempting me to kiss her, to put our connection to the test. Uncertainty bubbles inside of me, not quite sure what to make of my attraction toward her. I'm dancing on a fine line between giving into my desires and holding true to my promise of behaving.

I pull away to avoid kissing her.

"Bad boys are overrated." She rolls her eyes, clearly ignoring her response toward me.

"But I thought you wanted to branch out. Especially with your list and all."

Her fucking list. My dick stirs at the thought of some of the items.

Sophie has the innocent look down, all dimples and almond-shaped eyes, but her list tells a different story I want to know better. I want to feed my craving to explore her body. To learn more about the woman who loves the night sky, who stares up at the stars and makes wishes, unfortunately very aware of things lurking in the night. Bastards like me who want to seduce her and bring her to the dark side. I'd fuck her under her precious sky, making sure the only thing she wishes for is my cock and multiple orgasms.

My mind runs faster than my race car. I miss half of whatever comes out of Sophie's mouth.

"...No one else knows about it, so you need to keep quiet. Do *not* tell anyone. You weren't even supposed to find out, but since you're too damn nosey for your own good, now you know." She shifts her weight about, showing how flustered she is about her error. What a fantastic mess she made.

A grin crosses my face. "I'm going to enjoy this little secret between us."

"You really aren't going to let my list go, are you?"

"Nope. Now tell me, why did you create this dirty list of

yours? Did you get tired of fingering yourself at night, hoping for a better tomorrow?"

She laughs and pinches my arm, the throaty sound hitting me straight between the legs. My cock stirring at a modest touch sets off a bunch of alarms I choose to ignore.

"Who says I do that to begin with?" Her dimples pop as she smiles at me.

I give her a pointed look, silently telling her not to insult my intelligence. "A man like me senses these things. You being a single woman in your early twenties with no boyfriend means you gets off somehow."

"One: how do you know I don't have a boyfriend?"

"I think your list gives you away. If you did have a boyfriend, please dump him because if he can't make you come from oral sex, he's not worthy."

Sophie laughs to the point of coughing. "Okay. Good point. Well, I created my list because I got tired of university boys disappointing me and barely living my life outside of the library. I saw some bucket lists, got drunk while writing mine, and here I am."

What really sticks out to me and my dick is how she mentions university idiots. "What type of guys did you date in college?"

"None since I wouldn't count a few dates as 'dating' really." She sighs.

Sounds like a sore subject for Little Miss Perfect over here.

"Please tell me they got the job done, at least?" I clench my hands while I wait for her answer, battling between wanting to know and not all at the same time. *What the fuck is going on with me?*

Her sudden intake of breath tells me that she knows what I mean. "Nope."

"I must apologize for men everywhere and make it up to you with multiple orgasms and kisses that leave you breathless. Say the words and I'll be your humble servant who makes it my job to help you." I give her a little bow before popping back up again. The ice around my heart chips away at the small smile she sends my way, breathtaking yet cautious, reaching her alluring eyes.

Alluring eyes? Damn, Liam, go get your balls back.

"As enticing as your offer sounds, you need to keep your no-no square to itself. Thanks, though."

Of course, I should listen and keep to myself, but my brain enjoys the tug-of-war going on inside of me. I battle between not becoming another sleazy gossip headline while wanting to spend more time with Sophie.

Maybe I'm lonelier than I realize. A potentially terrible idea hits me out of nowhere, but it seems like a decent plan.

"I want to add something to your list." I bet she has it on her, stuffed away in her purse, her dirty secret following her wherever she goes.

Her eyes blink back at me a few times.

"Go on a date with a bad boy." I shoot her a wide smile.

"No way. We're not messing up the list. It's already typed, so no can do. Better luck next time. Maybe with someone else who wants your help." She shakes her head rather aggressively.

I intertwine my fingers with hers on the handrail. Warmth trails up my arm to my chest, an unrecognizable sensation possibly due to a few too many vodka straights clouding my head and my judgment. My thumb runs over her knuckles in a mindless pattern matching her shallow breathing.

"Seems like you're scared of going on a date. Are you not sure you'll be able to control yourself around me?" I want to poke the rebel inside of her. For whatever reason, I'm not sure. Maybe for the fun of it or maybe to see what happens once she finally lets loose.

My hand squeezes hers before letting go. I turn toward her, my hand retreating into my suit's pocket.

Her eyes narrow. "No, I'm not scared of you. Some people happen to be immune to your charms. Shocker, I know. I should consider myself lucky, unable to be moved by the ultimate heartbreaker."

Shit, I'd like to kiss the smirk right off her face. Immune, my ass. "Heartbreaker, huh? Are you reading articles about me? Don't tell me you've been obsessed with me since we first met. I'm not into stalkers, but I could make an exception for you."

She presses a palm against her chest, batting her lashes. "You caught me. I was biding my time, hoping we'd run into each other years later. I thought we'd walk off into the sunset by now, but maybe Disney was off with the timing. Their wooing period for romances usually lasts a weekend, tops."

Damn, my face hurts from smiling so hard. "Say yes to a date, and maybe our timeline will move up. But let's skip the romance and go straight to the fantasy suite."

What the hell am I doing? I wish I could understand my motives, but I tend to be a *shoot first, ask questions later* kind of guy.

"I hope you know the fantasy suite is from *The Bachelor*, not Walt Disney. And nope, we can't happen."

Time to revise and revisit because I don't take no for an

answer. I take yeses breathlessly moaned into my ear as I pound into a woman. My favorite kind of affirmatives.

My lips tip. "Fine, then let's make a bet. You have nothing to lose if you win."

It appears that I found Sophie's weakness, with the look on her face at the word *bet* telling me she likes to win almost as much as I do. She licks her lips at the notion of getting the upper hand on me.

Un-fucking-likely.

"You go on a date with me if I place on the Russian GP's podium." I have a complete crash and burn past with the track, but the one thing I love more than a race is a challenge.

I don't think things out because I don't care. At least not when I have an innocent interest in spending more time with her. It's not a big deal.

She shrugs. "Since you never make it on that podium to begin with, I'll agree."

"There you go again making me wonder if you've been keeping tabs on me over the past couple of years."

"More like my dad sends me pictures of the Bandini racers winning every time. Last time I checked, I don't remember a certain blonde German ever placing in Sochi. But of course, your ego is insufferable." She fights a smile.

"If you want pictures of me on podiums, all you have to do is ask."

She waves me away. "One date. No more than that."

"Give me the list."

"Can't we just have a verbal agreement? Why ruin the perfectly typed paper?"

"You're going on a date with a bad boy, whether it's me or someone else, so you might as well add it." Okay, I'm bluffing because her date is definitely going to be with me.

She pulls out the list from her clutch. "I hate that you need to write on it."

I grunt as I grab the sharpie from her hand and solidify our deal. My handwriting contrasts against the practical font she picked out, marking the bottom of the page.

I smirk at the symbolic evidence of my corruption. It doesn't take a genius to know Sophie's history in the bedroom, or lack thereof, is the reason she started this crazy list in the first place. Her life has been plagued with shitty sex and shittier fake orgasms.

I make it my duty to do right by Sophie in the name of orgasms and perfectionists everywhere. The list she holds in her small hand hints at her rebelliousness, and I want to draw it out. Fuck, this racing season will be a hell of a lot more fun with her around.

The next day, I attend all my pre-race meetings with the utmost enthusiasm. I have a bounce in my step, my previous annoyance with the team disregarded as I get ready to take on the Sochi circuit like the Champ I can be. My bet with Sophie pushes me to succeed.

After our agreement, I spent hours reviewing tapes of my practice rounds and team notes of ways to improve. An embarrassing fact I'll keep to myself.

My car lands a P3 spot after my impressive qualifier on Saturday. I act like a brand-new man in the pit, no longer nervous about impressing the team, choosing to check in with engineers about my demands with the car. There's no time for my self-conscious shit when I have an end goal in mind.

Unfortunately for the other teams, the better the car, the better you race. McCoy has one of the fastest cars in the whole organization, which means I'm set for success.

On Sunday, I'm pumped and ready to perform my best. I thrum my gloved fingers against the steering wheel of my car as mechanics push me toward the grid, the crowds cheering as they set me up. Energy hums around me while mountain views greet me.

Crew members assist the rest of the racers throughout the grid, creating a crisscross pattern of twenty multicolored cars. Mechanics scatter once they get the all-clear.

Lights illuminate above us before they cut off. The engine roars as my foot presses against the throttle, my gloved hands clicking corresponding buttons on my steering wheel to change gears. My car surges down the runway and hits the first straight in a rush. A buzz runs through my body, unlike any high, adrenaline coursing through me as my heart beats against my chest. It's a feeling I want to chase for the rest of my life.

The car runs smoothly against the curves of the track. I tend to be a slick asshole on the road, pushing myself to the limit for a win, both physically and mentally.

Jax stays ahead of me by a few seconds. I push my car forward, my front wing inching toward Jax's rear wing. We turn in a synchronized move before I use the loss of speed to my advantage. My car zooms past his before I cut in front of him, the dirty air messing with his speed, pushing him into third place.

I keep alert as I hold on to my newly secured second-place position. A podium finish never sounded as good as it does today, especially with a bet on the line.

Once I drive into the pit, the team controls my fate with their speed of tire changes. Crew members complete their job in two seconds flat, and I speed down the pit lane, not wanting many drivers to get in front of me.

I catch up to Noah soon after, regaining my second-place spot. Noah and I dance around each other in a messed-up salsa, dangerously close as we hit a straight section in unison before heading toward the next turn. Neither one of us is willing to pull behind the other. His tire clips mine at one of the turns, nearly causing me to spin out. *Fucking bastard.* I pull my car back as I flip him off with a gloved finger.

"Liam, any damage?" Chris's voice sounds off in my earpiece.

"Let me pull over and check it out." My voice drips with sarcasm.

"I don't know what lit a fire under your ass but keep it up. You may redeem your Sochi shittiness." Chris mutes himself.

"Fucking better." Labored breaths escape my mouth. People underestimate the physical exhaustion that comes with driving these cars, with racers sweating worse than a husband filing for a divorce without a prenup.

The crowd screams over the howls of the car engines. By lap fifty-two, I have a podium finish in the bag. The thought of winning the bet makes me grin behind my helmet.

I raise a fist in the air as my car crosses the finish line. Looks like I secured a date with the hottest girl in Bandini and landed myself on the podium—two wins worth chugging champagne.

I take the stage with Santiago and Noah. Maya and Sophie hang out in the VIP area off to the side of the stage, watching us from afar. Podium ceremonies include a few of my favorite things: winners, exploding champagne bottles, and fans. Music booms from the stage speakers, drowning out screams from the crowd.

A few F1 attendants pass us massive bottles of champagne. Noah, Santi, and I shake the bottles before the resounding *pop* fills the air. We spray the crowds and each other with the contents before we chug any remaining liquid.

From across the event, I point the tip of my bottle at Sophie. My jaw hurts from smiling so damn much. Screw ramifications. Abstinence deserves a small reward, and I'm ready to claim my prize.

CHAPTER EIGHT

Sophie

It's been a few days since Liam's win in Russia, which means my time for avoiding our date is over. Unfortunately for him, I change his original plan into a double date by inviting Maya and Jax. Some call it cowardice, but I prefer cleverness. Poor Liam doesn't know me well enough to anticipate my usual tricks, but he should've been more specific about the logistics of his bet.

After I begged Maya to join me on a double date, I decided to repay the favor by taking her out to lunch and telling her about my Fuck It list. My secret lasted a total of one month between Shanghai and Barcelona. Damn Liam and his performance in Sochi, pushing me to reveal my plan because I needed to convince Maya to come with me.

"Who would've thought Sweet Sophie made a naughty list." She smiles behind her water glass.

"Screw being sweet. I want to be called sexy and seductive."

She laughs as she shakes her head. "Okay, naughty Sophie. Just to be clear, this is one date, right? And you won't ditch me in the end? I need to make sure you won't run off with Liam into the night."

"Of course not, don't be ridiculous. I'll even take you out tomorrow for brunch as a thank you. Think of all the sangria I can supply you with—all that bottomless, sugary goodness can count as your daily serving of fruit."

"I'll never say no to brunch. But seriously, do you even think Liam's cute?" She tilts her head at me.

"Of course, I do. Hence the problem! Liam is funny, charismatic, handsome, and his usual philosophy aligns with everything I crave."

"So how is he not a good fit to help you with your list?"

"To start, he drives for the enemy, and I think I'd die of embarrassment seeing him all the time after doing half my items. Imagine me running into him and blurting out: 'Hi, Liam, remember the time you tied me up in bed and made me come? Good times, right?'"

Maya smiles. "You can always ask him about the weather."

"'Feels pretty cold outside today, kind of like the time you licked my body with an ice cube!'"

Maya lets out a laugh that gains the attention of other restaurant goers. "You need to work on your small talk. But jokes aside, I'm curious about what your dad will say about this double date then?"

I wave her off. "He's not going to find out. He's old and goes to sleep by 8 p.m. anyway."

Maya bringing up my dad reminds me of his expectations, shrouding me with guilt and mistrustfulness. His rules sound like a sad sort of three commandments holding me hostage from getting intimate with someone like Liam. I don't want to disappoint my dad, especially when he does so much for me.

We visit different shops in Barcelona to purchase a new outfit. I may not want to go on this date, but it doesn't mean I can't look the part.

"Really, I don't know why you can't go out by yourselves. It's one date and you're both adults." Maya exits her dressing room, showing off a sexy red dress.

Innocent Maya. Unaware of Liam's seductive nature.

I toy with the satin dress in front of me. "You know what happens when you go on one date? It ends with two dates, and then three, and next thing I know, TMZ is featuring an ugly picture of me leaving a hotel claiming I'm pregnant with Liam's love child."

Watching him last week as he stood on the Sochi podium solidified how I need help because a moment of weakness hit me. I couldn't take my eyes off him, all smiles and sexiness, teaching me how temptation and self-doubt pairs nicely with a race suit and fuck-me smile.

Her eyes dance with humor. "*Ay, dios mío.* You've really thought this out?"

"Duh. Have you seen Liam? His looks alone could get me pregnant."

Maya throws her head back and lets out a melodic laugh. "You know, there's a first time for everything. That's one hell of a conception story that your dad might believe."

I give her a pointed look. "No thank you. Let's go on this one date and call it quits before anything begins."

"Mm, sounds like you're worried about wanting to do more with him than only one date."

"You're underestimating the power of a strong-willed woman with enough restraint to challenge a chastity belt."

We wrap up shopping and head back to our respective hotel rooms, needing time to get ready for the night.

Sadly, a few hours later, my self-control is nearly thrown out the window when Liam and Jax pick us up from Bandini's hotel.

Liam strolls up to me, his expensive leather shoes clicking against the lobby tile. His muscular legs strain against the material of his tailored pants. My eyes land on his golden arms, accentuated by the rolled-up sleeves of his button-down shirt. He shoots me a wink when my eyes meet his. They're the same blue as the sky on the brightest day of the year, shining as he assesses me from head to toe.

I step back, but he moves closer to me, not allowing for any space. Liam's a sneaky man who keeps learning my tricks. My brain cells run amuck inside my head at his clean and fresh scent, not interpreting my desire as dangerous.

"You look lovely tonight. Did you do all this for me?" He motions toward my outfit before he grabs my hand and twirls me in a circle.

I let out a laugh as my dress swirls around me, dark chiffon material whooshing before falling flat once he lets go. "No, I thought I'd dress up for Maya. See, I want to sway her to the other side, but she claims her parents wouldn't agree. She describes them as a religious bunch."

"Here I thought I could sway you toward me, but it turns out you're playing for the other team. Now tell me, have you ever been with a man? Because if not, one night with me will make you change your mind."

I groan. His lips tug into a smile before they brush up against my temple, giving me the faintest kiss. One so soft, I almost think I made it up.

I push away, ending our exchange. It's the only moment of weakness I'll allow.

Good luck with that, Sophie.

Jax and Liam show us fine wining and dining at its best. They rent a fancy car to drive us to a trendy Barcelona restaurant, ordering us an expensive wine bottle once we're seated. The hostess situates us in a back corner hidden away from other diners, shrouding us in low lighting and privacy, a deadly combination with the man seated in front of me.

"They don't have chicken tenders for you, but I can ask for the kid's menu." Liam beams at me.

I softly kick his leg under the table, making him laugh. "As tempting as that sounds, I'll pass. I was thinking about a salad because I'm trying to watch my figure. You?"

"What?" He barely hides his distaste.

"I'm joking. No need to look like I asked you to retire from racing."

Liam rubs his stubbled chin. "I would've been disappointed. Here I thought you were perfect, but then you'd ruin it with ordering a salad when they have steak on the menu. With me paying, I thought you'd consider ordering a fifty-dollar plate to give me a run for my money."

"You think I'm perfect?" I put down my menu and stare into his eyes.

His bright smile hits me straight in the chest, my heartbeat quickening while blood rushes toward my cheeks. "More like someone sent from the gates of heaven to tempt me," he grumbles under his breath, low enough for only me to hear.

"Don't let anyone in on my secret. I'm trying to hide in plain sight." I sip wine to give my hands something to do.

"You can't hide from me, no matter how hard you try, but obviously, you enjoy the chase. Good thing for us, I don't mind our company tonight because I told Jax to distract Maya. A double date can't ruin what I have planned for us." He speaks with the utmost confidence.

I engage in diversions fit for war, pulling Maya into a conversation despite Liam's attempts to have Jax occupy her. That's how it is between Liam and me. A battle of wills, of two headstrong people fighting for control of one another.

Liam whispers wicked things in my ear all night whenever he can. The way Maya glances at us with sweet eyes makes me think he looks adorable. But no, Liam isn't one for cuteness.

Everything is going fine until the double date becomes some weird pissing contest between Jax and Noah, who randomly joins us before our food comes out. Noah pulls up a chair, acting wounded about not being invited. I have a feeling his appearance has everything to do with my Spanish *amiga* here who keeps blushing and hiding behind her menu.

I can't help feeling a sense of relief when Noah crashes the date despite how Liam's jaw ticks whenever he looks at Noah.

Maya's frazzled state amuses me until she spills her glass of water, the cold liquid pouring all over Jax. Her clumsiness distracts the three of them and gives Liam full access to me.

Liam closes the distance, occupying my personal space, the smell of him invading my brain. I fan my face with a menu the waiter left behind.

"Are you hot? I can ask them to lower the thermostat?" Liam's mischievous grin screams everything but kind and thoughtful.

I pull my glass of water to my lips, eager to cool down.

"Did you buy a vibrator yet? If not, I thought about having a company create a copy of my dick for you. I googled it and found a website that seems legit. You can even pick the color, although I'm partial to Caribbean blue."

I choke on my water. My eyes cloud as I fight for air, all while Liam stares at me, his eyes darkening and his grin expanding.

"Who invents these types of things, and why are you even googling this in the first place?"

He places a hand against his heart. "I'm committed to helping you. Count it as my good deed for the year, a noble cause in the name of helping you live a little."

"And your plan somehow includes a replica of your cock?" My eyes bulge.

He winks. "As much as I love hearing that word from your mouth, behave for our guests."

My cheeks flame at the reminder of Maya, Jax, and Noah sitting less than a yard away. "I'd end up selling your little toy on eBay and cashing out."

"I can assure you it would be anything but little. But why don't you find out for yourself? You do have a love for thorough research."

I scoff, hiding how much his words affect me.

He dares to put his arms up, attempting to look innocent, his eyes twinkling under the faint lighting of the restaurant. "I didn't create the list. I'm only trying to help you complete the items."

"Next, you're going to offer to help me use your *big* toy." I use my thumb and index finger to show an invisible gap of about three inches.

"Is that option on the table?"

I smack him with my cloth napkin. "No. Neither is a 3D copy of your cock. Keep that to yourself because that's even worse than a dick pic."

"You haven't been getting the right kind of dick pics if that's your thought on them."

What kind does he send to random women in the middle of the night?

His hand grasps mine, sending a current of energy up my arm, some foreign sensation I frown at. I'm scared of how other things would feel with him if this is how my body responds to hand-holding.

I blame the fact that I've had all but three partners who, when combined, don't have nearly half the sexual energy Liam gives off. It oozes out of him, all baby blues and ridiculous one-liners. Not to mention a six-pack I may or may not have checked out on the internet. He even smells fantastic. Men like Liam lure you in for a night and next thing you know, you're so fucked you don't know which way is up.

I stare at our joined hands, trying to understand the connection between us. It must be the confidence Liam exudes. It's such a different experience when compared to the guys I've been around before, with those sexual encounters being subpar at best.

I somehow break away from his hold, dropping back into the group's conversations. Liam lets me get away with avoiding one-on-one conversations for the rest of the night. Like the gentleman he pretends to be, he pays for dinner, putting an end to our bizarre date.

Outside of the restaurant, I strategically insert myself into Noah's offer to take Maya back to the Bandini team's hotel. Liam doesn't look the least bit pleased based on the clenching of his jaw and the way his eyes narrow at his fuckboy friend.

You win some, you lose some. And I don't want to be the one to lose anything.

The car ride back with Noah and Maya is filled with sexual tension, with me unable to escape them since my body is wedged between them.

I decide to break the awkward silence after a few minutes. "Did you know some versions of paella include mussels in them? Remind me to order mine without them when we have dinner tomorrow."

"Hmm." Maya stares out the window, leaving no room for a back and forth. No worries, I can talk enough for the two of us.

"And we can visit the beach while the guys practice tomorrow. What do you say? Me, you, sangria, and shirtless Spanish boys?"

Noah turns his head toward me. His deep blue eyes assess me before moving onto Maya, lingering on her face. "Just what she needs. More men hanging around her, wanting to fuck around."

Alrighty then. I'll take Sore Subject for two hundred, please.

Maya turns toward me and mouths a silent apology. I

instantly regret joining these two for a car ride because the whole situation is awkward as fuck. My lips remain sealed for the rest of the trip, no longer in the mood to deal with a brooding Noah.

Once we arrive at the hotel, I crawl over Maya's lap, desperate to get out of the backseat as soon as the driver parks the town car. Their kind of sexual tension makes it difficult to breathe without a rescue inhaler.

"See you later, Maya. And Noah, grow a pair or drop the grumpy attitude." I throw them a peace sign for good effort, hoping to send some positive Gandhi vibes their way.

My plain hotel room greets me. I unlace my sneakers and tug them off, abandoning them at the entryway. A knock at the door surprises me. Maybe Maya left something in my room earlier?

I open the door without checking the peephole. "You should fuck Noah and get it over—" Nope. Definitely not Maya. The same blue eyes I spent the night staring into look back at me.

Liam's smile makes my insides feel mushy and hot, a simple look disarming me. "Tempting, but I'd rather not."

"I'm going to go out on a limb here and guess you paid the concierge to find out my room number."

"Not to creep you out, but it was almost too easy to get your information." He leans against the doorframe.

"If the concierge was a woman then that would explain it." My eyes linger on his face, memorizing his soft-looking lips surrounded by weeks-old stubble. He has a faint scar running down one of his eyebrows, another hint of his mischievous past. He's a knockout in every sense of the word—in looks, in personality, and in knocking the air out of my lungs.

"Are you going to keep staring or are you going to invite me in?" His husky laugh sparks some functioning brain cells.

"I like you right where you are."

Letting Liam into my room would be the worst idea of all ideas. No matter how much my body wants me to say yes, my mind wins, solidifying my defenses.

He sends me an irresistible cocky grin. "I'd like you much more in bed, but I can compromise."

My jaw pops open.

He doesn't give me a chance to speak, thank God because I don't know how to respond. "I didn't like how tonight ended."

"So, you decided to come here because…?" My eyebrows lift.

"We have to plan a redo of our date."

"Yeah, that's not happening."

"If you don't, then I get to choose something from your list." He dares to smirk at me, the creator of said list.

"Also not happening. Pretend the list never existed." I cross my arms.

He steps toward me. "Impossible."

"I'm sure you're bound to move onto something more entertaining soon enough. Men tend to have limited attention spans."

"You're such a naughty girl when you want to be."

"How do you make something innocent sound sexual?" I stare into his beautiful eyes, framed with dark lashes that put women's falsies to shame. His eyes remain focused on my lips.

"Add it to my list of talents. You know, all three of them."

Whoa. He remembers how I told him he had two talents three years ago? His attention to detail catches me off guard. Enough so, that Liam surprisingly tugs me into his body as one of his hands wraps around the base of my neck. His thumb rubs against the sensitive skin there, making my skin pebble.

He leans forward, closing his eyes, while mine remain wide open and not ready.

"Wait." My hands push against his chest. His eyes snap open, his lips agape.

I pull out the power card, ready to slap a label on our attraction that no guy likes to hear. At least not a man who offers to make me a custom vibrator and looks at me like he wants to taste me, fuck me, and mark me for the night.

"I want to be friends. Just friends." Words pour from my mouth as defenses get thrown up left and right, protecting me from the one person I can't control.

Liam hits me with a pained look, his eyes wide as they flash with an unknown emotion. His body stills as he catches his breath. *Weird.* He leans in once more as his thumb brushes across my neck. His refreshing smell overwhelms me, playing with my senses and my mental control.

I pull my hands away from his warm chest. He plants a kiss on the top of my head, his lips pressing a second longer than necessary. Two whole seconds leave my body buzzing and my head swimming. My heart squeezes at the tender notion, unable to believe someone like him is capable of something like that.

"If that's what makes you happy. I can be friends." He hesitates on the last word.

"I hope so because I'm not going anywhere, and you don't want to make things weird between us. You have enough haters this season." I smile up at him.

I can't help questioning why his eyes look sad. He pulls away from the door, his fists tightening at his sides.

"Have a good night, Sophie. Thanks for a night I'll never forget."

You and me both.

He recovers from his odd behavior, sending me a signature wink over his shoulder before he enters a waiting elevator. I let out a sigh as he disappears behind closed doors, sealing me off from the seduction trap that is Liam Zander. I may be willing to compromise on my list, but I can't with my heart.

CHAPTER NINE

Liam

Friend-zoned. Me. Liam Zander.

I agreed to Sophie's ridiculous notion last week because I wasn't sure what to do. She caught me at a moment of weakness, hitting me with too many emotions. My last friend experience with the opposite gender didn't end well and left a gaping hole. My reaction to Sophie's request surprised me, damn nearly disabling me for the night with memories of Johanna.

Memories of us biking around our town. Of her creating fake tests to help me study for subjects I couldn't care less about. Of her teaching me to change Elyse's diaper, which led to me nearly throwing up in her nursery.

After one night of restless sleep, I shoved those memories so far away I hope they never come back.

I was tempted to forget about Sophie's idea of friends. I'm an idiot to agree to something platonic when I want to fuck Sophie into next month. How the hell am I going to be friends with her? Shit like this has never happened to me before because I pull the brakes every time, quick to call things off before emotions get too hot and heavy.

The word *rejection* doesn't exist in my dictionary, at least not since I asked out 8th grader Siena Weber to my 6th grade prom. Once my good looks kicked in and the braces came off, there wasn't a woman I met who I couldn't charm.

I stare at the cause of my problems from my seat at the press conference table for the Monaco race. Reporters drone on. Being one of the oldest races in F1 history, the Monaco Grand Prix has a reputation of extravagance, with celebrities coming to drink and party. Hence the overtime spent at press conferences and parties.

The whole crew gets hit with a long-winded question.

"Can you repeat that, sir?"

The entire table groans at Santiago's request. Noah looks like he could strangle his teammate on the spot, his fists balled in front of him to prevent a different kind of show.

Maya and Sophie try to hold back their laughs but fail. A leering reporter shushes them rudely, staring a moment too long. Maya's chest shakes while Sophie tries to swipe away some tears from laughing too hard.

Sophie stuns me, truly one of the most natural beauties I've encountered, not caring about much makeup or dressing up in seductive outfits to gain attention. She doesn't have a single fuck to give, with slogan tees becoming her uniform.

I bite my lip to suppress a groan as she tips her head back and laughs, the move exposing her golden skin. My eyes run down her body, checking out her legs on show for everyone with her jean skirt, paired with white Nike Air Force Ones. I fidget in my seat, thinking of her shoes on my bedroom floor while she lies in my bed.

Shit, Liam, it's not going to happen.

Sophie catches me staring at her. She grins as she wiggles her fingers at me. Only she could make that ridiculous hello look cute, her two dimples popping, making me want to kiss each of them. This is the exact reason I know I'm screwed right up the ass. I find things Sophie does adorable, a new idea to my own ears. But right there, gawking at her across the room, I concede to her ridiculous demand of staying friends. I won't pursue her sexually. For now, at least.

Searing pain shoots through my chest, a bizarre sensation I can't put my finger on. Either I had a bad lunch or I'm becoming weak for dimples and green eyes.

The reporters carry on, but my mind remains elsewhere, wrapped up in the idea of staying friends. I'll do it for her as much as I'll do it for my precarious position with McCoy. The team deserves me staying out of trouble, including the good kind I could have with Sophie in my bed.

My eyes drift away from her and solidify the need to keep things casual between us. I can do it without losing my shit, shoving away the guilt sitting heavy in my gut about becoming friends with another woman besides Johanna. Sophie doesn't seem like she'll settle for being held at arm's length, so I ignore the weird sense of foreboding because I want my past to remain where it belongs.

Reporters wrap up their questions soon after. I say my goodbyes to the guys before walking toward Sophie and Maya, my eyes narrowing when I find two "best of the rest" drivers talking to them. It's not like I want to sound like a total douche right now, but that's what they call themselves because it's hard to compete with the top teams of Bandini and McCoy. These two racers drive for a French-based company called Sauvage. The assholes stand there, all their bravado jam-packed into their race suits, as they make a pass at Maya and Sophie.

My skin prickles as the sight. I'm on a new task to interrupt their exchange, with Sophie playing into my hand without knowing it.

"Oh, hey, you guys know Liam, right?" Sophie's eyes find mine.

I have no fucking clue what to make of this new wave of protectiveness. Sophie pinches my side, silently demanding me to behave when I smile smugly at the two racers. My skin craves more contact from her because a simple squeeze makes my dick stir.

I close the distance, wanting to stake my claim at the same time as wanting to take a deep breath of Sophie's shampoo. Like everything related to her, I can't help myself.

Maya tugs on her ponytail. "So Ricardo and Max invited us to a boat party tonight."

Sophie's list pops up in my head. Does she want to try some items out with these guys? They look like their balls dropped a month ago—a sad display of manhood. They barely fill out their race suits as their arms flex enough to pop a vein. They'll sure as fuck not know what to do with half of the things she wants.

I interrupt their conversation. "Actually, you forgot we have plans tonight."

Sophie and Maya look at me confused. Hell, I'm not sure what I'm pulling out of my ass. But I don't want them to go out with these guys.

"We're going to the casino. It's a classic thing you have to do when you're in Monaco. But maybe next time, guys." I wrap my arms around Maya and Sophie's shoulders and pull them away from the two racers. I grin at the drivers over my shoulder, catching their glares before completing my "fuck off" message with two middle fingers behind the girls' backs.

It looks like I'm about to give Sophie and Maya the full Monte Carlo experience. I text Jax to meet us at a casino while we walk down the line of motorhomes, and he agrees without question.

I feel like a man on death row, unable to do anything with Sophie because she gave me the ultimate capital punishment—friends or nothing. Plus my scheduled programming of a drama-free lifestyle puts a damper on things. I haven't hooked up with anyone, and my two-month break makes my head crazy and my dick angry.

If it weren't for my body's reaction to Sophie, I'd wonder if my dick still works. But whenever she gets near me, half the blood rushes from my brain to my cock like a fucked-up cycle.

I find myself totally screwed, the idea of being just friends seeming like a foreign concept. Google Translate can't help me for shit with this one.

CHAPTER TEN

Sophie

Maya likes to vlog all of our adventures, from Shanghai to Monaco. She plans different vlog segments for each day before the race.

She begs me to make my vlog debut, and who am I to say no? Her *Fan versus F1 Racer* idea convinced me in a heartbeat. I'll compete against Santi in a series of games Maya planned, where the winner gets street cred and a gift card to Starbucks because Maya lives life on a budget. I don't need the money because I prefer gloating rights. Santi makes easy competition because he tends to have poor impulse control.

"Okay, so today you're both going to compete in three rounds of games. Whoever has the most points by the end wins the entire competition." Maya flips her ponytail over her shoulder. She looks all professional in her Bandini polo and jeans, with a clipboard to keep track of points.

Santi grins at me. My body fails to feel anything when he shakes my hand.

"The first round will include a scavenger hunt where you're allowed to pick one person to help you. Here are the lists." Maya passes us each a sealed envelope like a secret spy mission. "Choose your person wisely. Send me your pictures and videos as you take them because whoever finishes first wins a point for this round. Be careful because some items can get you in trouble."

Santi tears at his envelope. "I want to say in advance that I'm sorry for your loss."

"Let the best person win. I hope you're okay with runner-up. I'm sure you're used to it with Noah anyway."

Santi barks out a laugh as he walks away. After reading through the list, I text the only other person I've befriended during my time here, hoping he can help me out.

A few minutes later, I get the all-clear to visit the McCoy garage. I tread carefully into enemy territory. The crew fumbles around, passing tools and tires to different workers while others spend time clicking away at computers. Liam's car is parked smack dab in the middle of the garage. The chrome paint gleams, shining bright and standing out against the plain white walls.

"Look who finally decided to join the dark side." Liam's voice sends a current of energy up my spine.

"Help me, Liam Zander. You're my only hope." I attempt my best Princess Leia voice.

Liam's eyes light up. "Are you a secret nerd?"

"It takes one to know one." I shoot him a cheeky grin. "My dad dressed me up as Princess Leia for three Halloweens in a row.

He claims she's the one princess he respects, and I can't disagree."

"We think alike." He winks at me.

I ignore the way one wink makes me feel because it seems safer than going up and kissing him.

"So, I have a list." I dangle the envelope in front of him.

"We already discussed it. Are you here to knock off an item?"

I shake my head. "No. This one's different. You said you're free, right?"

He nods.

I pass him the envelope. "Perfect! You've officially volunteered yourself to help me with a scavenger hunt. I'm competing against Santi. There are seven items, and we can do them out of order, but we have to finish first."

"All right, read them to me."

I open up the paper. "*Take a video with the checkered flag on the Monaco finish line. Steal a security officer's golf cart. Play flip-cup with a rival racer. Hijack someone's Instagram live video. Steal a tire from a "best of the rest" team. Roll the tire across the pit lane (video or it didn't happen). Take a picture in a non-Bandini car.*"

Liam and I strategize for a few minutes, coming up with the best way to tackle the items.

"Let's hit *take a picture in a non-Bandini car* first. That's easy. Hop in." He walks to the cockpit of his car.

I attempt to get in, except these guys make it look way easier because my legs can't make it over the side without me falling over. Liam laughs before he lifts me and places me in the car. His hands press up against my stomach, and my skin buzzes from the heat of his touch. Stupid skin-on-skin contact.

He pulls out his phone and snaps a picture of me. "Do a

funny one. You never know when you'll have the opportunity to sit in a World Champion's car."

"It takes a special man to get a hard-on from his own Championship title." I throw my legs over the side as I pull my sunglasses down my nose, puckering my lips. "Eat your heart out, Marilyn Monroe."

Liam shakes his head as he snaps a picture, his throaty laugh making me feel all types of things. Hopefully, I come off way more seductive than I feel. Solely for the photo of course.

He coughs as I struggle to get out of the cockpit. No doubt my ass is on display from my jean shorts, a poor choice for today's activities.

Liam and I walk through the pit lane before I snag an unsuspecting Albrecht crew member.

"Hi. Can I borrow you for a few minutes? It'll be quick, I swear." I drag our new helper toward a small pit table away from any watchful eyes.

The poor gentleman attempts to protest as his alarmed brown eyes scan Liam and me.

"I'd go along with it. She's kind of stubborn." Liam passes us ten plastic cups and a couple beers.

"Well, excuse me," I scoff. "You know how to play flip-cup?" I look at my new competition.

The stranger nods. We set up the game, except since it's only two of us, I have to chug multiple cups myself.

By the last one, I'm gagging from lukewarm beer.

"You're shaming my culture." Liam laughs as I cough into the camera.

"Sorry, my bad. I didn't know Bud Light came from Germany.

Forgive me for my expensive taste buds."

Liam laughs as he turns off the video.

"Okay… I'm going to head out now. Thanks for the beer." The Albrecht crew member practically runs away without me saying goodbye.

I nod in the direction he left in. "Shy guy. He barely looked at me."

"I think that's because he was too busy watching your lips wrapped around the rim of the cup."

"That explains his terrible performance. He barely got past the second cup. I didn't think I was that distracting, but I'll take it." I purse my lips.

"So fucking distracting." He huffs under his breath. "That and the way your throat bobs from chugging beer like a champ." Liam winks at me.

My cheeks heat on command. Do I distract Liam, too? I ignore my impulse to ask him. "Quit flirting with me. You're sidetracking me, and we have other items to complete."

We snag an unintended golf cart from a random security officer. Liam drives it toward the Bandini pit so we can show Maya our completed item.

I stop recording the short video of Liam driving. "You know, we don't make a bad team."

"If only you'd agree to working together on a different set of items."

"Ha. Ha. Hilarious. Have you been saving that all day?"

"Yes. I can't help it when you chose a list that I can't get out of my head."

While his tidbit is interesting, I carry on. "If you had to

choose a few items for your own bucket list, what would you pick?"

"Is time travel on the table?" His eyes darken as he stares straight ahead, focusing on our destination.

"I think bucket lists usually have to include items you can actually accomplish." I hide my surprise at his question.

"Then I don't think I have anything I want to do."

"Oh, bullshit. There has to be something you want." My question is interrupted by Liam's phone ringing.

He tugs it out of his pocket. I catch the name *Lukas* before Liam presses the ignore button, shoving it back into his jeans.

"Who's Lukas?"

"No one," he half growls.

Whoa, where did that attitude come from? "Um, okay then."

Liam drives us silently for a minute. "I'm sorry for talking to you like that. Lukas is my brother. I don't talk to him too often, and I'd much rather spend time with you, to be honest." Liam stops the cart and looks at me with an unfamiliar expression, almost as if in pain.

Something about his sad eyes makes me drop the topic of his brother. "You're forgiven if you tell me five facts about yourself that I can't google." I tap the wheel for him to keep going.

Liam lets out a relieved sigh. "If I find these online later, I know who to blame. I'm currently rereading *It* by Stephen King for the second time. Don't ask me why, I just want to. I like to sleep naked. And yes, before your jaw drops, I mean completely naked. The *one* older woman I helped cross the street berated me about feminism and how men think women always need help. Fourth, I walked in on my parents having sex once, and

I'm surprised I can still appreciate doggy-style after seeing them. And lastly, I still play Pokémon Go even though probably only two other people in the world play it."

I don't know why the last fact has me throwing my head back and laughing to the point of my lungs burning, but it does.

Liam looks at me as if he's seen an alien.

"What?" I attempt to regain air to my lungs.

He shakes his head. "Nothing. Let's finish up this list."

I'm actually having a good time with Liam. No sex, no complications. Just time spent getting to know one another.

Can Liam have a few flaws, please? Anything besides his part-time job of screwing women.

We take a break to grab a water back in Bandini's garage.

"Okay, I have to say this. I'm a little disappointed at how oddly normal you are," I blurt out.

"I won't lie to you. That's possibly the best compliment I've heard in a while."

I let out a laugh. "That's kind of sad. But really, no offense, but your reputation sucks. I was a bit afraid to be your friend."

"Your level of honesty is refreshing. Please boost my ego a little more while you're at it."

"Well, you're nothing like the guy I expected based on what everyone says about you." Being around him makes me question what I've read and the truths I've put stock in because he comes off sweet and interested. I regret jumping to conclusions about him because he acts like a model citizen, paying his taxes on time and walking grandmas across the road.

"For once, I really don't want to know what people say about me." He runs an agitated hand through his hair.

"I don't blame you. But at least I'm willing to stay friends despite everything."

"Wow. Thank you for your service." He gives me a half-assed salute.

We finish up our break. Time flies while we hang out, and with one more item to complete, I text Maya to check in on Santi's progress. She says he still needs to steal a golf cart.

"Last one. We need to sneak a picture with the checkered flag on the Prix finish line." I read off Maya's hardest item.

"Let's grab a flag and hit the line. But we have to be quiet and not draw attention to ourselves because I can get in trouble. F1 tends to be protective of their course before a race day." He smirks at me.

"I can be quiet, no need to tell me twice."

We make our way toward the Grandstand overlooking the finish line. It turns out a ton of security officers and F1 personnel hang around the grid area overseeing the finish line.

I push all my blonde hair under the Bandini cap and pull it low on my face. "Do I look like a guy? Maybe a scrawny pit crew member by chance?"

"Is the sky green? What type of question is that? Last time I checked, guys don't wear scraps of material like yours for shorts, let alone a shirt like that." He lets out an exasperated sigh as his eyes trail down my body.

My head lowers to check out my T-shirt, laughing at the *I like big boats and I cannot lie* saying. I bought it specifically for Monaco. His glance makes my heart beat faster, unable to contain my excitement about him checking me out.

Friends, Sophie. Friends.

I don't miss the way his eyes close after they land on mine. But I pretend I did, saving us the trouble and awkwardness. "Well. Can't change anything now. Bitches get stitches."

"You do understand this isn't where you apply that saying, right?" He rubs a hand across his face.

"Duh. But where's the fun in that? We're already rebelling." I step toward the stand housing the different colored flags.

Liam strolls past me, climbing the ladder like he does this all the time. He grabs the flag and tosses it to me. I miss because Liam smiles at me, looking like some kind of German god, screwing with my coordination. The pole clatters to the ground and draws the attention of surrounding crew members.

"Quick. Hurry up!" His yelling snaps me out of my impromptu spell.

I look up from the pavement to find his feet planted back on the ground, his phone filming me. My hand grabs the flag and I wave it around while Liam takes a video. He laughs along with me as I throw the flag in the air and catch it this time. A guard runs toward us, so I ditch the flag as Liam grabs my hand, sending another rush of energy up my arm.

We run toward the McCoy garage, not stopping until we both collapse by the wheels of Liam's car. Our heavy breathing fills the silent garage.

I turn my head to find Liam staring at me, the blue shade of his eyes darker than usual. A look shouldn't make me feel how it does, happy and excited all at once, craving him in ways I'm unaccustomed to. An uneasiness runs down my spine at the idea of feeling something more than friendship for this man.

A McCoy mechanic interrupts our moment when he asks

us to move.

We head toward the Bandini pit area.

Maya hangs around the garage, fiddling with her camera. "Looks like you're the winner of this round. But unfortunately, we have to cancel the Championship because Santi got in trouble." She frowns at me.

"What? No." My lower lip juts out.

"I'm sorry. Santi chose to steal a cart from a twenty-year-old security officer who used to be on the Junior Olympics for track or something. His old teammate from Kulikov slipped by without getting caught."

"Either Santi has terrible luck or an undeveloped frontal lobe," I mutter under my breath.

Liam clears his throat. "What if I step in for Santi?"

Maya and I both snap our heads toward Liam.

"I have nothing better to do. Plus, I'm a better match for Sophie than Santiago." His words hit me like a sucker punch to the chest.

I recover before bouncing up and down, loving the idea. "Yes. Perfect! Let's do it."

Maya grabs her camera and introduces the change of plans. Liam pulls me into the shot as if it's the most natural thing for him to wrap his arm around me. I suck in a breath as his body leans against mine, placing his firm hand on my hip.

"Next round is a race. And no, before Sophie complains and Liam gloats, neither one has an advantage here. I'm all about being fair and square. Well, to a certain extent." She turns the camera toward Liam and me while flashing us a secretive grin.

Maya pulls out two remotes from her bag and leads us toward

the back alley of the Bandini pit area. I have to give it to her. She goes all out with her vlogging because she set up a mini Grand Prix with a plastic racetrack and two remote control F1 race cars.

"Whoever has all four tires off the racetrack loses. Anything goes because what's the fun in playing by the rules. So let this be the dirtiest race you've ever done. You have ten laps to make it happen." She winks at us both.

"I hope your ego can handle a blow here and there because I plan on winning." I gaze into Liam's eyes.

"There are few things I like blown, and that's not one of them." Liam grins while Maya cracks up. I roll my eyes at the camera before I grab the remote from her.

"Bring it on, pretty boy." I rev the toy car's motor.

Liam shakes his head as he grabs his controller.

The idea seems easy enough, at least until we both start our cars and race them. Remote control cars pose a challenge to control. They jerk and swerve, making it hard to keep the wheels on the track for the first lap. Liam handles his with greater ease than me. That simply can't do because I don't want him to win.

Our cars complete another lap after what feels like ten minutes. Maya stifles a yawn.

For entertainment value, both of YouTubers and mine alike, I slam my car into Liam's during one of the straights.

"Ah, the kitten has claws. It looks like Sophie's done playing nice." Liam looks into the camera as I slam into his car again, knocking two of his wheels off the track. My laugh comes off way more like a cackle than a cute giggle.

Liam lets me get away with just about everything before he turns the tables on me. I slam into the side of his car again before

I take up most of the racetrack, not allowing him to move past my car without putting his wheels at risk.

His body inches up closer to me, stepping away from Maya and the camera. He leans in so the microphone doesn't pick up on his words. "See Sophie, I drive like I fuck. Slow, then fast, then slow again until you're all out of gas. I treat my car like a lover, stroking her before I enter her, only offering the best kind of foreplay for my girl. I don't recklessly race because I prefer to be attentive. I fuck like I do everything else, with precision and strength—control and care." He distracts me as his car surges past mine, his words hitting me harder than any collision with a remote-control car. Damn him for making race talk into our kind of foreplay.

Maya laughs at us. I glare at her before I pay attention to our cars again. Liam passes my car once more as I pick up the pace, the wheels swerving down the fake runway. Screw him and his dirty air.

"You don't play fair." My car speeds up along with my irritation.

"No, I don't play at all. I fuck, I own, I dominate. Playing is for boys, and I can assure you I'm all man." He smirks down at me.

Has this man ever had a friend of the opposite gender?

"You can't talk to me that way." My teeth grip onto my lower lip.

His car buzzes past mine again, but I try to concentrate this time, not wanting to take the loss.

"I can because I'm here to fight dirty. If you gave in to your desires, you'd know that. I want to learn every inch of you while I map out your body like the night sky you love so damn much.

And fuck it'd be so good between us, with me showing you things you never thought possible." His tongue darts out to lick his bottom lip.

Everything in me wants to agree except for the two brain cells working together, telling me how bad of an idea this is. I don't have a moment to think about it because Liam's hands find mine and he flips a switch on my controller. My car careens off the side of the track.

My jaw drops as my car rolls toward our feet. I narrow my eyes at him, but he grins before giving me a peck on the cheek. His lips move near my ear.

"You make it too easy with your innocent ears unable to handle such bad things like me. I'd love to see the way you blush when I'm balls deep inside of you. Say the words, and I'm yours, no questions asked. I want a night with you and your list." His teeth graze the soft skin of my ear.

Smug fucker bit me!

He steps away, acting like he didn't turn me on and run over my self-control at the same time.

"Okay, you two. I couldn't pick up half of what was happening, but Liam won that round. I wish I could say it was fair and square, but based on the color of Sophie's cheeks and the evil gleam in Liam's eyes, I'm going to go with a no on that." Maya walks over toward us with a huge grin plastered on her face. Glad she finds this whole exchange entertaining and cute because I sure don't.

Liam gloats to the camera, pretending he didn't whisper the naughtiest things I've ever heard. He remains completely oblivious about how he sent feelings from my heart all the way down to my clit from words alone.

"Friends, right?" His eyes slide from the camera to me.

"*Yup.*" I avoid his gaze as I listen to Maya's next game, the drive to compete seeping away from me. Liam leaves me breathless and confused all at once. Uncertainty sits in my stomach while I mull over his words, not sure how I can stay strong around this man when my restraint wavers from a few words and touches.

For the next game, I remain on autopilot because my brain left my body an hour ago, short-circuiting from Liam's wickedness. He wants to change the game and rip control away from me.

I don't like it. Not one bit.

CHAPTER ELEVEN

Sophie

"**S**o, don't kill me, but I decided to plan something for your birthday." Maya throws herself onto my bed.

"I regret telling you I'm a Taurus." I groan.

"Don't be dramatic. You not celebrating today should be a crime, seeing as even Taylor Swift wrote a song about feeling twenty-two."

"My dad wasn't big on celebrating birthdays while I was growing up. I'm much more of a Christmas kind of girl." I flash her a smile.

Maya cringes. "Oh God. That alone proves why you deserve to do something to celebrate. Don't worry. No one else will know it's your special day. You should be happy, seeing as I decided to turn your birthday into a way to knock an item off on your list."

"Now you're talking." I rub my hands together in my best evil genius impression.

She grabs her laptop and places it between us on the bed. "Get ready because we're about to hustle hard." She presses play, showing us a video of someone teaching viewers how to play poker.

"Oh, Maya. You know the way to make me happy."

"Any normal girl would prefer some boozy brunch surrounded by friends."

"Who needs that when we have strip poker? Speaking of, who are our victims? I hope they have thick wallets." I waggle my brows.

Maya giggles as she leaves the bed. She rustles through her backpack before throwing me a gift bag. "Better study those videos and get ready. You're about to clean house at Kulikov. I contacted some of the guys Santi used to race with and they're up to playing with us tonight at 8 p.m. Room 128."

I rip at the tissue paper, revealing a new graphic T-shirt saying *One Casino. Two Casino. Three Casino. Poor.*

"You might be the bestest friend I've ever had." I jump off the bed and squeeze the air straight from her lungs.

"I have to support your healthy shirt obsession. Wear it tonight. They'll already think you lost your money at the Monaco casinos."

Maya leaves me to my own devices. I spend the better part of the next three hours studying everything there is to know about poker. By 8 o'clock, I'm well-versed in Texas hold 'em and ready to kill with the shirt Maya bought me.

If all goes according to plan, I don't intend on losing much clothes.

Maya meets me outside of the guys' hotel room. She flashes

me her clothes under her rain jacket, revealing too many layers of long sleeves under overalls, shorts, a bathing suit, and more. "Are you ready to hustle?"

"Please. I'm ready to eviscerate the competition." I shimmy my shoulders.

"Good God you look mighty evil when you get that glint in your eye."

The guys open the door to us. They're two handsome racers, with broad shoulders and thick dark hair. They introduce themselves as Nikolai and Michail. Both of them speak with a heavy Russian accent.

We settle into our seats at the dining table, where our hosts pour us wine. Some card dealer they hired shuffles the cards.

"So, how many cards do we start with?" I channel my best Elle Woods impression.

"Three. Definitely three." Maya hides her smile.

Nikolai laughs as he flashes us two fingers. "Are you sure you both know how to play? I can't say I'd hate to see you both lose."

Shameless flirt, this one.

"Yes. I heard this was just like Blackjack." I roll my shoulders back, exuding confidence. Honestly, I hope I'm selling myself here.

Meryl Streep better hold on tight to her Oscar at night. I'm coming for it.

The guys break down each step for us as if we need it. Maya and I go along with their efforts, pretending we need further explanation of different hands. I don't come off too strong at first. Some hands I lose on purpose, while others I win with a pretend shocked face.

After an hour, I've lost my T-shirt, sneakers, and funky socks to the pile of clothes.

Much to Nikolai's disappointment, Maya continues stripping layers until she's down to a T-shirt and jean shorts. He keeps staring at her as if her next hand is the last thing between him and catching a glance at her chest. Both men gave up their shirts first, which was a surprise to no one. To be honest, they're rocking some good-looking abs under those race uniforms.

They may be handsome, but they're not exactly my type. An image of Liam pops up in my head, which is unexpected. Unlike these guys, Liam makes my heart race from one look. I brush off the thought because this is no place to get lost in my head.

Slowly my pile of chips grows to a cool two thousand euros thanks to Nikolai and Michail losing too many rounds they were confident in. To be fair, I've also purposefully flashed a bit of cleavage, but God gave me the goods so it's my job to use them.

Maya and Nikolai fold during the next round, leaving Michail and me to battle it out. Michail is the silent type, with plenty of chips to match his poker knowledge. He flashes me a confident smile as he goes all in with the chips he's mainly won from Nikolai.

I'm talking eight thousand euros in. It's hard not to think about what I can do with that kind of money.

A trip to Fiji doesn't sound half bad at the moment. I imagine a cabana boy offering me a Corona as I tan on a beach bed by the ocean.

I look at my cards again. With a seven of spades and a five of clubs, it's a risk. One I can't help wanting to take. Something in me tempts me to call his bet. Label it a birthday intuition.

"I call."

Maya's jaw drops open while Nikolai looks at me with a mix of respect and hesitancy.

"You sure about that, blondie?" Michail looks at me in disbelief. "Although I won't mind checking you out in your underwear."

Men, so easily distracted by the little things. "Sure. Let's see the cards."

The dealer reveals the flop of a six and nine of hearts, along with a king of clubs.

My heart beats rapidly in my chest. Michail lets out something that sounds vaguely like a curse word in Russian. Both of us stare at the deck as if it can reveal the answers. Blood rushes to my ears as my heart rate accelerates past what should be considered normal.

The dealer shows the next card.

"Holy shit." Nikolai whispers as the dealer reveals an eight of hearts.

Maya and I both jump out of our chairs as we rush to hug one another.

"Oh my God, a Straight. You did it! You just won!" Maya squeals.

Michael stands to remove his pants.

I lift my hand. "Don't bother. We're done here, boys. Gotta leave before Lady Luck doesn't want to share her magic anymore."

Maya and I grab our money and clothes off the floor. Maya struggles to put on her layers before she decides to shove most of her clothes in her backpack.

"So that's it? We lost all our money and didn't even get to see you with all your clothes off." Nikolai puts on his pants.

Michail flashes us a smile before he grabs his shirt off the floor. "I'd feel used, except you both were fun to hang around. We'll have to do this again."

As much fun as they've proven themselves, I think Santiago would kill Maya if she hung around these two more often. They scream trouble.

We say our goodbyes. Maya and I exit the hotel room arm in arm, laughing up to the ceiling as we walk back to my suite.

Turns out twenty-two is off to a strong start. I've made a good friend, knocked off a Fuck It list item, and won thousands of euros.

Siri, please cue Taylor Swift's "22."

CHAPTER TWELVE

Liam

"I have a plan for us that involves knocking off one of my list items." Sophie's hoarse voice greets me at the entrance of McCoy's pit garage after my qualifier and press conference.

"Which one?" My voice betrays my excitement.

"It's one I just added." She winks at me, but it comes off as a twitch.

It looks like I tempted the little demon inside of her by challenging her list and adding a new item. A feeling of satisfaction runs through me at the idea of her branching out.

"Should I be worried?" I nudge her in the ribs.

Her eyes shine with mischief and something else I can't place. "Only if you're afraid of *cliff diving*. Think you can handle it?" She shoots me a smile that would make a normal guy run for the nearest exit.

I drive us to the location of the new item on her list. Her hair blows in the wind as she throws her arms up in the air and dances in her seat to music, enjoying the drive in my convertible I snagged from my Monaco flat. Fuck me, Sophie's gorgeous without trying. She abandons her cautiousness, enjoying the moment, singing along to songs while I drive. I fight to keep my eyes on the road and dismiss the tug on my heart at how happy she looks.

When I added the date to Sophie's list, I wasn't expecting her to go ahead and add one of her own. For sure not something as crazy as cliff diving in Monaco. Let this be a lesson for me to not underestimate her because she surprises me every step of the way.

After I park the car, we stroll together along the jagged shore before I tell her to walk in front of me in case she falls back on the slippery rocks. I came up with an idea out of the goodness of my heart. Checking out her ass ends up being an awesome plus.

"Oh God. Why on earth did I agree to do this?" Sophie fails to hide the fear in her voice.

"Is this part of your pep talk? Because you've been doing a shit job at it for the past ten minutes." My eyes land on her tattered shorts. A hint of her ass peeks out from the bottom, tempting me to touch her. She looks like a present wrapped up just for me. The straps of her bikini call my name, begging me to undo the two little bows holding up each side.

She shoots me a glare over her shoulder. "Why did you convince me to go cliff diving? It's so reckless when you have a race tomorrow. What if you get injured?"

I didn't come up with this idea. Do I tell her this? No way. A stupid man would do that.

"Yeah, you know me, always looking for the next adventure."

"This is why you're in trouble with McCoy. You're too rebellious for your own good." She shakes her head.

Her comment doesn't come across as a jab, especially when she has a point. Would she be into me if I didn't fuck up so badly with McCoy? My mistake is probably why Sophie came up with her stupid "just friends" idea in the first place.

I threw a wrench in her plan the moment I flirted with her during Maya's games. I'd feel dejected if it weren't for how she looks at me when she thinks I'm paying attention to something else. She presses the brakes when I want to floor the accelerator.

We finally get to the top of the cliff after a short walk. I spent half the hike watching the view, both of Sophie's ass and the Monaco shore. Even my insanity has its limits, my heart beating in my chest as I check out the thirty-foot jump. Churning water slaps against the ragged edge and creates whitecaps.

I catch Sophie as she trips, stopping her before she falls face-first on the sharp rocks. Her clumsiness has no bounds.

She presses her back against my shirt-clad chest. I wore it at her request because she claims she can't think straight around me when I'm shirtless, giving me an excuse about how abs and muscles are a mental weakness for her.

"Hands off." She laughs as she pulls away from me all too soon.

I chuckle while shaking my head. She acts like nothing phases her, but she can't hide the glint in her eyes or the way she holds her breath when I get close. I'm very aware of the act she puts on. She only fights her attraction better than me.

Her eyes land on mine, reflecting her nervousness and doubt.

"All right. Well, we made it up here. Don't be scared. It'll be over in a second." She lets out a shaky breath.

"Not sure who you're trying to convince more right now." I look down and let out a whistle. "Well, no time like the present. You know you can't cross it off the list until you do it. The power of the Sharpie remains in my hands."

"Fuck it," she murmurs under her breath.

"Atta girl. I'll go first just in case. Who knows what would happen if you jump before me?"

Beating back my nervousness about getting injured, I take a deep breath. I find it hard to say no to Sophie. Every single time she flashes her emerald eyes at me and bats her lashes, I agree mindlessly. Somehow, I'm pussy-whipped without actually getting any.

I don't spend any more time thinking about Sophie or the jump. One minute I stand on the cliff; the next, I slam into the cold water. My body sinks into the depths of the ocean. The saltwater stings my eyes as I swim toward the surface, gasping for air once my head breaches.

Sophie looks at me from over the ledge. "I think I'm going to meet you down by the shore. You have such great form, and I can't compete. I give your jump an eleven out of ten."

I think she's fucking around with me to buy time until she backs away from the edge, her body barely visible from my viewpoint. "Sophie Marie Mitchell! Get your ass in the water!"

She stops moving, and I take the opportunity to check her out. Her golden hair flies behind her like rays of sunshine. The bikini she wears accentuates her full breasts and tight stomach, making her look like a siren calling out to me, fucking with my head and my cock all at once.

"Okay, no need to be pushy." Her voice interrupts my examination. I lick my lips, salt from the ocean coating my tongue.

Sophie takes a few deep breaths before she gets a running start. She screams as she jumps off the cliff, her body making a small splash as she plunges into the water. Her body disappears beneath the dark blue waves. Seconds pass since her jump and she hasn't come up, making me lose count of the time. My heart rate accelerates at the thought of her hitting her head against the side of some rocks. Panic bubbles inside of me as I swim toward the area she jumped into.

Her head pops up out of the water. I let out a shaky breath as I attempt to close the distance between us.

"Stop! Do *not* come any closer." She looks at me with crazy eyes, her cheeks flushing under my gaze.

"What's wrong? Did you get hurt?" I wince at the unfamiliar sound of worry in my voice.

"No. But I can't find my top." She dips underneath the surface to locate her little scrap of material. Her fashion choice was a bad one for something like this, the item no doubt lost to the ocean's current. My dick pulses at the thought of Sophie naked, but I tamper it down when I realize how bad this is.

She pops back up again with no bikini in sight. I can make out her golden skin under the water, fighting everything inside of me that wants to swim closer and take a peek.

"I can't find it." She frowns.

"What do you mean?" I wheeze, afraid of my limited self-control.

"It got loose when I jumped in. Ugh, it's my favorite top."

I try to think of anything but her naked body right now, gliding underneath the water. My dick doesn't mind the idea. The head upstairs calls the shots, explaining why I can look but can't touch.

She wants to stay friends. You want to avoid drama. Her dad manages your main competition, and nothing good can come from that type of situation. Well, except maybe amazing sex based on the way your dick enjoys Sophie's presence.

Fuck, Liam.

Sophie snags my attention again. "Positive of this situation: I think I can count this as two items on the list. This can be considered as skinny-dipping, right?"

My semi turns into a full-blown hard-on at the talk of her list. "I don't think so. Usually that includes tossing everything." I'm going to hell. It's official. *Noah, please save me a spot next to you.*

"Since when are you such a stickler for rules? You're not the one who's half naked right now."

I look down at my light blue T-shirt before my fingers lift the hem over my head. "That's a great idea."

"What are you doing?" Sophie's eyes bounce from my tan chest to my face before returning to my chest.

"I'm giving you my shirt. You can't get out of the water like that." Yes, it's Europe. No, I don't want her topless, at least not in front of random people. I prefer a private show free of interruptions and wandering eyes.

"Oh, good one. Now if you're shirtless at the same time, does it count as skinny-dipping?" She sends me a beautiful smile, showing off her two dimples.

I cover up my groan with a laugh. "No, sorry about that. Maybe another time."

"I'm counting this, and you can't tell me no. I created the list." She grabs my wet T-shirt from my hands. I glance around at the scenery, trying to keep my eyes away from her as she struggles to get the soaked fabric over her head.

I want to be respectful, but I sneak a peek or two at a perfect pair of tits, her pink nipples barely visible underwater. If she asks, I'll deny it.

"Liam, where's the shore? How do we even get back to the car?"

"Now you're thinking of logistics? I expected you to check out a mini-map of the whole Monaco shore before you planned this." I point out the shore, which is a decent swim away.

"I was trying to be spontaneous. In retrospect, I should've told you I'm not a super strong swimmer."

"Yup. You probably should've. Hop on." I turn around, waiting for her to wrap her arms around my neck. I'll swim us over, even though it'll take double the time with her on top of me and my dick pounding in my swim trunks.

"Are you sure? It looks far away."

I nod. A war rages inside of me, making it difficult for words to come out. Part of me craves to pull her in for a kiss and run my hands across her body while the other part of me wants to push her away and keep a safe distance. For her, for me, for our combustible attraction to one another.

By the time she wraps herself around me, I'm not sure about this plan. My shirt does a poor job of covering her pointed nipples. Her body clings to mine and warms my back, my body becoming sensitive to her proximity.

She shudders when I run my hands across her legs. Every detail of her body stands out to me, like the way her breath hitches once I move or how her arms cling to my neck, warming me both inside and out. I'm sure we look dumb as fuck while I drag us through the cold water.

Sophie detaches from me and wades in the water once we approach the beach. I leave her behind in the shallows as I collapse on the sand, worn out from a piggyback ride from hell. My dick salutes me the moment Sophie steps out from the sea. I prop myself up on my elbows to take advantage of the show because I paid my friendship dues tenfold.

The wet material of my shirt plasters to her body and clings to the curves of her breasts. They're bigger than I imagined, and fuck have I fantasized. Her pebbled nipples push against the fabric, enticing me to lift the material and take a look. I bite my lip to hold back a groan at the sight of her. She rings out the bottom of the shirt, causing water droplets to trickle down her toned legs.

Fuck me. I regret our agreement to stay friends. Screw friendship. Who the hell gives a shit about boundaries? Women like her can't be friends with someone like me because it goes against the law of attraction and every damn rule set up by evolution.

A smirk breaks out across her lips as she walks toward me, her eyes remaining on the bulge in my pants. "You look winded. Should I be concerned about your stamina?"

What a little cocktease, playing with her words and my control.

"Why don't we try it out, see if I meet your standards?" My voice croaks.

She sits next to me, sand sticking to her wet skin like a dirty mermaid with untamed blonde hair and green eyes I can disappear in. God, I'm such a horny fucker around her.

Her finger trails from my neck to my chest before running across the ridges of stomach muscle. My skin heats at her touch. I don't say a thing, afraid she'll back out at a moment's notice. She stops above the waistband of my swim trunks. I silently will her to keep going, desperate for her to cross this stupid boundary she set up to torture us both.

"I'd hate for all of this to be just for show." Sophie lets out a hoarse laugh, her eyes glittering under the summer sun as she lies down on the sand.

She fucked with me and it worked. My body responds to her like no other, and it messes me up, unsure about the fine line between friendship and temptation.

"I'll promise you one thing. Being with me will be the best show of your damn life. I wouldn't just fuck you, I'd wreck you for anyone who comes after me." I trail a finger down the T-shirt's soaked material. My fingers run across the curves of her breasts before I stop right above the waistband of her shorts, doing the same shit she did but better. Sophie's cheeks flush. Her nipples push against the fabric, letting me know how she feels about my touch despite her silence.

"Two can play at this friend game you like. Keep trying to deny the pull between us, I like it. I'm a patient man who can wait you out because I know you'll give in to me."

I want her to crave me like I want her—to beg me to slip inside of her and never leave. Well, until I have to. Because in the end, I always do, no matter the girl.

Even with someone as special and unique as her.

CHAPTER THIRTEEN

Sophie

After our Monaco cliff-diving disaster, I establish new boundaries with Liam. I went too far with him on the beach, flirting with disaster and pushing him to his limit. I devise a plan to prevent us from doing something dumb. Well, maybe to stop *me* from doing something stupid, like hooking up with him to satisfy a craving.

The first phase of my plan includes making myself look as unattractive as humanly possible. My ugliest and baggiest clothes protect me. Forget about makeup. Yesterday, Maya asked me if I was feeling all right. I grinned at her, telling her she made my day. All I got in return was a furrowed brow and confused eyes. Maya wouldn't understand the complexity of the situation because I can't, with Liam messing with my mind as much as my lower region. Never in my life did I think I could be led by lust, but here I am, striving to look half dead to deter the sexiest man in F1.

I only plan on doing friendship activities with Liam. Maybe if he sees me sweaty, dirty, and downright boyish, his attraction will end for me. Although the bulge in his swimsuit yesterday showed promise, I need it nowhere near me. And frankly, he can use some time without female companions because his dick has gotten more press coverage than a Kardashian.

This plan needs to work because I enjoy Liam's friendship. I don't want to lose him because of our attraction to each other. I'm very aware of my desires toward him, but I can be mature and not act on them. Liam just needs to get the memo.

Since Maya and I struggle with F1's finest, we get to work together to avoid the objects of our attractions. Noah likes her, that part is obvious, but he doesn't want a serious relationship. To be honest, I was impressed when he asked me to sit with her at the Monaco Grand Prix. His request is the reason I hang out in the stands with her, overlooking the finish line where I danced around with Liam a few days ago. The memory brings a smile to my face.

Maya preps for her vlog while I check out the cars being placed in their grid spots. Liam's team situates his car near the front of the group, his steel-gray car noticeable.

The Monaco Grand Prix is a difficult course, requiring lots of skill and patience. Noah landed the pole position, my dad's favorite spot on the whole grid. This track has many twists and turns, along with tight roads and narrow straights that make it difficult to overtake other drivers without damaging the cars. It's a big challenge for anyone below P1 to win.

Red lights shine above the cars. Mechanics rush to remove the tire warmers from the wheels before running off the track.

Once the lights shut off, the drivers accelerate. The crowd bursts with energy as the drivers careen down the road.

I love the comforting sound of cars rushing by. It reminds me of childhood summers spent with my dad while he worked, with him giving me headphones to listen to some of the best F1 drivers. He would let me talk to the racers for a few minutes on the team radio. It was the coolest thing ever when I was young, with my dad making me a huge fan since day one.

I focus on watching the race, rooting for Bandini and McCoy. Any fan can appreciate both teams continuously trying to one-up each other. Noah, an F1 icon in the making, doesn't give other drivers much of an opportunity to pass him.

With Santiago on the team, it increases Bandini's chances of winning the team's Constructors' Championship, which occurs at the same time as the World Championship. Despite Noah and Santi's rough history, they have a chance of winning. Plus, if Bandini wins the World Championship, then they get the biggest funds to work on their cars. It would be a huge deal for the team because F1 teams spend heaps of money.

McCoy remains in a close second place spot with Liam at the wheel. Jax follows behind, leaving little space between the two McCoy cars. Despite his friendship with Liam, the two drivers compete savagely against one another, not letting up their positions easily.

Cars speed down the track, sounding like jets rushing by. Smoke billows from the tires as cars hit maximum speeds during the straights. Some drivers graze barrier edges before gaining control of their car again, the squealing sounds of tires echoing off the buildings.

Liam's gray car passes us again as he clocks in another fast lap. He remains consistent on the track, his front wing keeping close to Noah's rear as they turn together at another corner.

Sparks fly as his gray car hits a tight corner. The grating sound of crunching metal tearing against pavement makes a cold chill spread across my body. I cringe at the scene glistening under the sun, smoke billowing from the engine. The entire side of Liam's car is totaled with the tire dislodged and rolling away. Liam remains in the cockpit of his car, hitting his helmet with closed fists.

My heart clenches at his defeated state, with me unable to do anything but watch. Drivers tend to be an emotional group of guys. Tensions, adrenaline, and passion fuel negative reactions when confronted with losses and mistakes.

I get up from my seat to get a better look.

"At least he's safe. Poor guy." Maya's sweet voice rings over the crowd.

"He's going to be pissed. That'll be a blow to the World Championship and Constructors'."

Liam has to retire, a hard loss for any racer. His crash will knock his standing for the World Championship, plus he forfeits points for the team's Constructors' Championship.

My hands shake as I grip the plastic chair in front of me, my legs locked in place as Liam is taken away in a safety car. They announce how physically he's all clear. His medical clearance doesn't make the knock to his ego any less powerful, his crash being a bitter pill to swallow with McCoy questioning his value to the team.

I no longer feel up to watching the race now that Liam is out of it. Noah ends up placing first, no shocker there.

For some ridiculous reason, I walk over to McCoy's motorhome after the race.

Liam stands in a nearby hall with his agent and Peter McCoy. Peter sneers at Liam, his bald head gleaming under the overhead lighting while his face barely contains his rage.

My body plasters itself against a wall, trying to look as inconspicuous as possible. Liam looks unfairly sexy in his white race suit. Muscles press against the flameproof fabric, emphasizing a nice ass and strong legs. Most of his sweaty blonde hair sticks to his forehead while a few strands stand up in multiple directions. His lean frame towers over the two men, his spine straight and his jaw ticking under pressure.

"You're not performing to our expectations. I question if you're worth a fifteen-million-dollar contract. Crashes like that beg to differ. It's something we'd expect from a young racer instead of a World Champion." Peter's baritone voice reverberates through the hall.

"I wonder if Bandini told Noah and Santiago the same thing when they crashed into each other in Shanghai. Can you imagine, the great Noah Slade, crashing into a teammate? He's still considered worthy of his contract, and we stand on the same podiums at almost every Prix." Liam's words match his agitated glare.

I don't blame him for being defensive because Peter seems like a total ass. My dad used to tell me how Peter yells at his racers after press conferences, and how he treats the pit crew like shit despite their help. His poor reputation precedes him.

"The thing you don't get is that Noah Slade has won more

titles than you, not to mention he doesn't fuck around with James Mitchell's family. His performance makes him a Champion and you a runner-up." Peter sneers at Liam.

"Let's not react based on strong emotions." Rick attempts to diffuse the situation.

Liam's nostrils flare. "I'd rather be an F1 runner-up than a piece of shit who sits in an office all day acting like a dick instead of using it."

I suck in a breath. Holy shit, Liam's really pissed.

Peter offers a sinister smile. "At least I don't stick my dick where it doesn't belong."

My stomach churns at how crass Peter is when referencing his niece. Does he have any standards?

Liam's agent gets involved. "I'm sure there's a better way to get our feelings out. Peter, you don't want to say things you don't mean when you're angry." Rick pats Peter on the back.

I don't like the way Rick acts around both of them, making me wary of Liam's agent. Managers like him remind me of used car salesmen who want to make a quick buck. They act slick and thoughtful, but their sharp eyes give away how deep their insincerity runs.

"I think you need to re-examine your driving techniques and your attitude. You're clearly too aggressive on and off the track lately." Peter stabs a thick finger at Liam's chest.

That can't be farther from the truth. I hold back a laugh at the idea of Liam being hostile because he tends to be the safest driver out there. Peter holds an obvious grudge against Liam, dangling poor choices in front of him anytime he messes up.

"I'll be sure to do just that." Liam gives him a mock salute before walking away.

Liam's tightly wound body walks in my direction, nearly barreling into me when he turns the corner. His body tenses as his stormy eyes land on me. *Busted.* I give him a pathetic wave and a small smile which he returns with a grimace, not amused by my presence.

"Liam—"

"Not here." His clipped tone shuts me up.

He grabs onto the crook of my elbow and pulls us in a different direction from the entrance. My short legs struggle to keep up with Liam's long strides. McCoy's gray and white color palette lacks the warmth of the Bandini motorhome, cold silver accents gleaming under the bright lights, matching the personality of some of the staff here. We pass the dining room and bar before entering the private suite area. Liam doesn't stop to talk to anyone, ignoring the few people who call his name.

He remains silent until we walk into his suite and he closes the door. I step toward the shelf housing his different helmets and gear, wanting to keep my hands busy with something. The small room becomes charged with energy as I remain turned away from Liam.

"How much of that did you hear?" His sharp voice is unlike his usual self.

"I showed up when Peter mentioned contract agreements." My finger drags across the multiple helmets lined up on the shelf. Shiny plastic coating glistens, showing off Liam's number and the German flag.

"Lovely. So basically everything." Liam strolls up to my side.

I pick up one of his electric-blue helmets, the headgear

weighing more than I imagined, making my arm drop with it. Liam's hand covers mine, warming my skin at his touch. Rough calluses rub against the smooth skin of my knuckles. He looks down at our joined hands like he questions how they got in this position.

Liam lifts his head. I stare into his eyes, the swirling color entrancing me. His eyes lower to my lips before his eyebrows furrow. He puts the helmet back on the shelf while I step away from him, craving space and fresh air.

I fill the silence and palpable tension. "Peter's an asshole. My dad never talks to his guys that way, no matter what they do. I doubt Bandini's owner does either. That guy never gets involved because he's too busy yachting near Greece."

Liam's eyebrows rise at my confession. I'd hardly count my admission as a Bandini secret because everyone knows how my dad takes care of his team.

"I make one mistake, and now it's all about my contribution to the team. It's frustrating and a lot of pressure with every move I make becoming a question of my skills. And Peter treats me like shit despite my efforts to make him happy. Sometimes it feels like Jax and my team principal are the only ones who have my back on this team."

I can't imagine how difficult it is for him to race with crazy expectations, keeping up with the demands of fans and the McCoy team.

Liam settles into one of the gray couches. He runs a hand through his hair, messing it up, abandoning his usual prim and properness.

I sit beside him, patting myself on the back for my bravery to get close. "Seems like a toxic work environment. There's no love lost between you and Peter, that's for sure. Are you sure you want to do this for years?"

"It's the start of the season. I hope Peter gets over it since we still have fifteen races left." He lets out a deep sigh that makes my heart squeeze.

I lean my head back against the couch, mirroring Liam's body posture. We both stare at the white ceiling. Liam's deep breaths even out as his body loosens, no longer stiff from his pent-up agitation.

I don't press him to talk anymore, preferring to sit in comfortable silence. I thought conversations were a big indication of how much two people got along. Sitting here with Liam, saying nothing, makes me consider how silence is underrated.

Liam's hand finds mine again. His finger traces the curves and contours of my hand. My heart rate increases, my body flushing from the mere contact with him. He gives my hand a squeeze before pulling away. I frown, unsure why I feel a loss when he gives me the space I want.

Liam's slowly worming himself into my life. I need to set clear boundaries again, especially when the briefest touch sends goosebumps up my arm. He's not capable of loving someone like me, and I'm not able to tease apart love and lust. We're a lethal combination.

I take a deep breath before ruining our silence. "You know I can come over and visit before races. Protect you from Peter." I put my fists up and punch the air, giving my best boxer impersonation.

Liam chuckles. "I'd like that. If you came over, that is...

Minus the fists, though. Save them for someone about two sizes smaller than you."

"So basically, a toddler." I turn my head to find him looking at me, his eyes shining under the dim lights. My lungs stop working as Liam's smile expands.

He drops his smile, his eyes darkening. "I want to ask you something."

"What?"

His eyes run over my face, lingering on my lips. "Why do you want to be friends?"

I take a whole minute to answer. "Because you're funny. And you're not too bad to look at either, so I guess that's a plus."

"But why do you deny our chemistry?"

I swallow back the rock-sized lump in my throat. "I don't. You're not used to being around a girl who's interested in getting to know you for more than your acrobatic bedroom skills."

He battles a smile. "One day, you're going to submit, and I can't wait to show you how much you'll regret waiting."

I fake gasp. "Are you trying to tell me you're a Dominant?"

Liam and I have a way of screwing around with each other, and it happens to be one of my favorite things about our friendship. I don't want to risk that for a meaningless hookup throughout the season.

"You need to read less of those books you like. I don't need to assert myself since you'll come begging when you're ready." He knocks me back with a telling smile.

I can't help the way my body hums with excitement at his words. But keeping to my usual pattern with everything Liam-related, I brush his comments aside, hiding behind armor that looks an awful lot like cowardice. I'm very aware of my weakness. Sadly, I have enough insight to admit my fear and my incapability of letting loose and taking risks.

I shake my head. "You have an active imagination. I'm glad that hasn't disappeared with age and all."

"It gets me through the weeks." He rubs a palm down his face as he grumbles something about sexual frustration. His cheeks deepen in color.

Oh. *Oh*.

I drop my head back against the couch and laugh. For some reason, my body tingles at the idea of him alone in his room at night, pleasuring himself. Images run through my mind and invade my thoughts.

His hoarse voice cracks my resolve. "You're looking a little red. Does that turn you on? Knowing I go to bed alone, staring at the ceiling while my fist pumps my cock?"

Oh my God. I want to bury myself into the cushions and disappear. My breathing grows heavier, unable to rid his words from my head.

"Ask me what I think about with my cock stiff and aching for the real deal?" His voice drops low, the husky tone lighting me up from the inside out.

I don't dare ask him if he thinks about me.

He eats up the space on the couch as his fingers grip my chin.

"No." My voice squeaks. I try to break away from his grasp, but his eyes hold mine hostage.

My heart beats wildly against my chest while my fingers clutch onto the leather couch. Blue eyes bore into mine, reading me like he always does, sensing my lies with a glance.

"I think about a blonde woman who's too damn afraid to admit she wants to be there with me, sucking me off before letting me fuck her into oblivion. I can't get a particular someone out of my head who hides behind a friendship because she doesn't want to face shit head-on. My cock aches for a woman who acts fearless to others but runs at the first sign of my interest. Tell me why you are so keen on denying what we both crave?"

"I…well…" *That's the best I can come up with?*

He chuckles, his hand moving away from my chin. "I'll be waiting for you to make a move. Like I said, I'm a patient man with nothing to lose."

"Besides friendship?" I grumble under my breath before rising from my seat.

"We both don't want a friendship. Friends don't feel how we do about each other." His nonchalance pisses me off.

"Well, *I* do. Just because we're attracted to each other doesn't mean anything more than that."

"Glad you admitted how you're into me. Was it that hard?" He smiles at me.

Well, shit.

"I didn't mean…"

He tilts his head to the side. "It's okay to let go and have fun."

At what expense? His brand of fun looks a lot like missed calls, other women, and an end-of-season trophy of being the biggest loser.

I straighten my spine and look him straight in the eyes. "If you keep making things weird, I won't hang out with you anymore."

He laughs, his eyes sparkling. "We both know that won't

happen when you like me too much and I find you too fucking irresistible."

I hate how handsome he looks. Almost as much as I hate the way my heartbeat picks up while looking at him, silently acknowledging how much my body craves the things he shared today. I really dislike how his words burn inside of me and eat away at my reasoning.

"I'm leaving now. If I don't answer any of your apology texts, it's because I'm ignoring your ass until Canada."

His laugh is the last thing I hear before I shut the door of his suite. My back presses against the metal frame, my hand clutching onto my star necklace while I gather my thoughts.

Holy shit. What the hell is happening here?

I flip my pillow over, craving the cool side as I toss and turn in bed. My mind won't calm down, my thoughts reeling from my earlier conversation with Liam, wondering if he stays awake thinking of me.

What the hell did he do, opening up Pandora's box, letting out our hidden desires?

Okay…more like *my* hidden desires.

I lie on my back and stare at the ceiling. My eyes close as my fingers trail the hem of my underwear, running across the cotton. Thoughts of Liam take over, of him getting himself off to the idea of me, of him staying up late thinking of me. I dip a finger inside of my underwear and press my thumb against my clit. My other hand rubs against my pebbled nipples, goosebumps breaking out across my skin as I think of Liam touching me. My finger brushes against my entrance before dipping inside of me.

My phone buzzing on the nightstand interrupts me. I ignore it, choosing to focus on my task, but the repeated vibrating disturbs me. The charger rips from the wall as I rush to grab my phone, not looking before answering.

"What?" my hoarse voice croaks.

"I'm sorry for being a dick earlier. I didn't mean to flirt with you... Well, that's a lie. But I didn't mean to make you uncomfortable with me. Don't ignore me. Please?" Liam's voice carries through the speaker.

My cheeks warm as I think of what I was doing minutes before. Here he is apologizing when I'm just as guilty of doing what he admitted earlier, thinking of him while getting myself off. What a messed-up situation.

I groan. "It's okay. Let's pretend it didn't happen."

"But what if I don't want to pretend?"

My heart clenches at his vulnerability. "We aren't pretending in general; we're only ignoring what happened today."

"Just like you want to ignore what you're doing awake at three in the morning, your voice strained and needy?"

No freaking way he knows what I'm up to. He fishes for a response, testing my control. *Don't give in.*

"Liam...stop." My breathy voice fails to hide how I feel.

"Admit it. You were touching yourself. I dare you to lie to me."

"Nope," I say fast. Too freaking fast.

He laughs. A rough, sexy laugh that makes my legs clench together. "You suck at lying."

"Okay, fine. I was touching myself. Happy now? Drop it." I groan in frustration.

"No can do. Bet your greedy fingers crave to sink inside of you. I'm sure it turns you on to think of me getting myself off to the image of your hands on my dick."

"Uh." I will neither confirm nor deny, seeing as Liam can tell when I lie anyway.

"Let's *pretend*, Sophie. Imagine me there with you, my body pressing against yours as my fingers run against your thighs, heat following where my fingers touch. Your needy clit throbbing for my touch while your pussy desires my tongue. Put me on speaker. Now."

"What happened to you waiting for me to give in?"

"You gave in the moment your fingers touched your clit to the image of me. Don't play coy with me."

I dislike his perceptiveness.

He doesn't let me get a word in. "Get this shit going, I'm done being patient today. My dick is throbbing at the idea of you touching yourself."

My fingers rush to press the speaker button, the sounds of sheets rustling on Liam's end echoing in my room.

What the hell are you doing? Having phone sex with him? You're 110% going to regret this one.

"Stop thinking. Close your eyes and fucking feel." His clipped voice fills me with excitement. "Touch yourself while your other hand palms your tit. Imagine my calloused hands running against your skin, lingering where I want to kiss you. Fuck, I wish I could see you. Wish I could taste you."

My hand follows his demand, running across my center

before dipping inside. I fear to talk, of ending the spell, of every freaking thing involving Liam.

"Tell me what you were thinking about before, what gets Little Miss Perfect off."

I swallow back my fear. "You." One word, heavy with meaning and implication, of consequences and obstacles I can't prepare myself for. The phone feels like a barrier, safely hiding me from facing my feelings head-on. Of facing *him* head-on.

He grunts into the phone. "Push two fingers inside of you. Feel how fucking wet you are for me. Because shit, I'm hard from the thought of you pleasuring yourself to the sound of my voice."

My body buzzes at his order. "I was thinking of you in your room, a bead of pre-cum dripping from your tip as you fist your dick, the idea of me on replay in your head as you come." Where my brazenness comes from, I have no freaking clue. I guess phone sex makes me courageous.

"You're on a fucking loop in my head. The same shit replays because I can't get you out no matter how hard I try, no matter how many times you call me a *friend*. I want to fuck friendship out of you, erasing the word from your memory. I think of you begging me to fuck you, with my cock filling you up and making you feel so damn good. You'll scream my name and scratch at my back. I'll make it my mission to have you chanting my name like a goddamn prayer while I explode inside of you."

A tingle starts in my toes and carries up my spine, nerves firing off as I pump two fingers into myself, curling enough to stroke my G-spot. Liam's words rush through my brain and obliterate any doubt. He paints a picture of us that feeds my desire, his dick pumping into me as he pulls my orgasm from me.

"I always want you like a needy asshole. I'm in so fucking deep that you don't even need to say anything to turn me on. Your heavy breathing tells me enough, the idea of you finger-fucking yourself to me making my balls clench and my dick ache. I want in. I want you to drop your defenses and let me take over. Allow me to show you how good it can be with us." He half snarls the last sentence.

"Yes." I moan as my orgasm hits me, my thumb pressing against my clit as my fingers continue to tease me.

"I'm right there with you." Liam's groan rumbles through the speakerphone.

We both come, my chest heaving as Liam moans into the phone. Neither one of us says anything as we gather ourselves.

Uncertainty creeps in the dark and replaces my orgasm-induced high. Realization dawns on me that I came to the sound of Liam's naughty words and of him jacking off.

Oh God. What did I do?

"Stop doubting everything," he growls into the phone.

"I have to go. Look at the time!"

"Don't—"

I click the red button. It's fitting how the red circle reminds me of a self-destruct button because that's what the fuck I did to my perfectly laid plan.

Maya officially made it on my shit list. Well, at least temporarily because I tend to be emotionally weak when it comes to her.

We lie down on my hotel bed, watching TV while catching up on all the gossip.

She looks at me with innocent eyes and a sweet smile despite her plans on abandoning me. And damn her for looking good while she lets me down, telling me she can't come to Canada.

Noah ruins everything with his smolders and sexy nothings because let's be real, there is nothing sweet about that man. I would know since he comes around every Christmas because my dad has a thing for people with shitty parents.

Yesterday, Noah kissed Maya. I can't allow these things to happen anymore, especially since she refuses to fly to North America for the Canadian Grand Prix.

"You have to come. Think of the maple syrup. The Canadian boys. Niagara Falls." I smack the back of my hand into my other palm for emphasis.

She lets out a laugh. "Niagara Falls is hours away. We would never make it via car."

"Are you really not coming because of Noah? I think my dad has an extra chastity belt I can lend you. I wouldn't put it past him to have packed one in his carry-on luggage."

"I'm sorry. I really wish I could."

"Don't lie. It's unbecoming of you." I still love her.

"Your word choice is something else." She chuckles. "Sometimes, I wonder if you're some posh princess hiding out in F1."

"Please, if I was married to Prince Harry, I wouldn't be hanging out on this bed with you. I'd be popping out little ginger babies that rival the queen."

Her laugh fills the hotel room. "Truly, I'm sorry. I'll make it up to you."

"Fine. I forgive you. But you're coming to the next race. Think of your vlog and the fans. You can't leave them hanging like that."

She shakes her head against the crisp sheets. "You'll have Liam. Don't act like that's not enough."

"It's more than I can handle," I groan while avoiding her eyes.

"If my friends looked at me like he looks at you, I think I would have ditched the friend zone a long time ago. Take me to the end zone. Multiple times, *por favor*."

Technically, his voice scored me a touchdown yesterday. But I remain quiet.

"I keep warning you about him. He's nice and sexy, which is a deadly combo. Liam's got this little twinkle in his eye that matches yours when you get a plan going."

I roll over and bury my face into the comforter, unable to escape from her wisdom.

"With someone like Liam...one day you wake up wondering how everything changed between you two. Mark my words."

"Seeing as Liam has an aversion for serious relationships, I highly doubt I'm some type of anecdote."

She hops out of bed, not content with my words. "I call bullshit. Plus you've been acting weird all day, ignoring his texts to hang out. Mind you, he messaged me an hour ago asking where *you* are. What gives?"

"I did something I probably shouldn't have." I sit and pull at a loose thread on my shirt.

"Like?"

"Like phone sex with Liam." I take a peek at her.

She gasps. "No way!"

I cringe. "Yes, and I don't know how to face him, let alone

talk about it. I want to act like it never happened."

"Why?"

My eyebrows rise. "What do you mean *why*? Haven't you listened to me over the past month?"

"Sure, I have. I've heard you say nothing but nice things about him. You can't say one complaint except for his bad history, which he can't change if he tried. All he can do is work toward a better future. But you're stubborn about staying friends, but clearly coming to the sound of his voice is anything but platonic."

Her level of insight unnerves me.

I hide my face in my hands. "He admitted he jacks off while thinking about me."

She lets out a laugh. "Okay, and?"

"*And*? Why are you acting so casual about all of this!"

She throws her hands out to the side. "Because you keep coming up with every reason not to, while all I hear are reasons to go for it. You both are friends who have the hots for one another. So what?"

"Says the girl running away from her problems," I mutter.

Maya frowns, making me instantly feel shitty for what I said. "I may be hiding, but Noah and I aren't friends like you and Liam. Let's say you hook up with him. Do you really think he'll dump you and never speak to you again? You have a foundation there that won't crumble."

"But what if I end up liking him for more?"

She lifts a brow. "What if he ends up liking you for more?"

Well, when she puts it like that.

"I hope you know this sounds like a terrible idea."

She offers me a sly grin. "You know what they say? Fuck it."

CHAPTER FOURTEEN

Sophie

"**T**he pit crew is gossiping about you spending time with Maya and the McCoy boys." My dad would've made a great detective in another life. He has a nose for anything out of the ordinary, making me cautious about how I should answer him.

I look up from my brunch menu and meet my dad's questioning eyes. He starts off our breakfast in an irritable mood, bringing up Liam without any type of lead-in, making my spine stand straight. Not even Canada's maple syrup can cheer him up based on his frown.

"Yeah, I like Santi's sister. She's been a lot of fun to be around."

"And those guys?"

I roll my eyes behind my menu. "Also friends. You know,

it may be very modern of me, but boys and girls can be friends without dating." I drop my menu, giving him my best fake surprise face.

My dad glares at me. "I was a guy once, and when men hang around a pretty girl like you, it's usually for one reason."

I can do without my dad talking about his old hookup days. "Thanks, Dad. You're ruining me. Here I thought my bright personality brought all the boys to the yard." I jiggle my shoulders and pucker my lips.

"Please don't compare yourself to anything in a yard. Like ever. I'm familiar with that song and would rather not hear anyone needing your milkshakes." He rubs his face.

I crack up, enjoying how he gets all riled up. At least he comes from a good place.

"You sound really uncool right now. No one under seventy even talks like that." I pat his hand to ease his anxiety. "It's going to be okay. I promise. I've defined very clear boundaries." I draw an invisible line in front of me.

I exclude how I think Liam is the hottest guy in F1. That would go against everything I set up so far, including our line in the sand that we've tiptoed around for two months.

"Anyway, tell me about this lady the gossip mags report you've been seeing."

My dad has never quieted down as fast as he does. Ladies and gentlemen, my evasion technique comes off flawless, one so good lawyers would clap about it. His eyes dart across the menu, engrossed in whatever breakfast choice he needs to make.

Bingo. My dad's totally dating again, and I want to know who.

"Don't believe everything you read or hear for that matter." His eyes catch mine.

Interesting words coming from him. I give him a pointed look.

He puts his hands up in surrender. "All right, I understand."

"Lay off the inquisition, would you? I'm twenty-two going on fifty since I have the personality of a grandma. You don't need to worry about me so much."

"You'll always be my baby girl. But I'll work on it, just for you." My dad gives me one of his classic goofy smiles.

We clink our mimosas together.

I offer a genuine smile. "I'll toast to that."

We laugh together when I knock over my glass.

"I'm glad some things never change." Dad cleans up my spiked juice with a cloth napkin.

"Did you know Niagara Falls isn't close to here? Maya told me, and I'm disappointed I missed that tiny detail."

"You missed a six-hour driving detail? I'm shocked." Liam mockingly scoffs as he covers his heart.

He looks rather normal in jeans and a T-shirt. Dare I say he appears domestic, all barefoot while reading a book in a chair off to the side of his bed. I lie on his comfy mattress, pretending to scroll through my phone while I sneak glances here and there. Somehow, he makes reading look sexy.

"Why are you reading *A Game of Thrones*? Can't you just watch the TV show like everyone else?"

Liam turns to the next page. "I'm going to pretend you didn't say that."

"What's so wrong with what I said?" I continue, wanting to distract myself from him licking his finger before flipping the page.

Liam stares at me like I asked if I could have his first-born child. "Everyone knows the books are better than the movies or TV shows."

"Says who?"

"Says everyone who reads books!"

I feel some sense of relief as Liam and I fall into our usual casualness. We both ignore last week's late-night phone call. Well, more like I've ignored Liam every time he mentioned it until he eventually gave up. Turns out, I can evade topics like he overtakes cars. Thank God he can't read my mind. Liam keeps to himself, acting like a perfect gentleman and friend. He gives me exactly what I want. Except I know his dirty secrets, like how his voice sounded when he came while getting me off.

I snap back into the conversation. "Okay, so you really love books. Got it. So, Niagara Falls is really that far away? I'm still disappointed."

"Whoa. You lasted a whole minute without bringing up your failed plan again. I'm surprised because you're usually so well-versed in your little ideas." Liam's playful smile pulls at my heart. *Stupid, stupid heart. I thought we were in this together. You fickle bitch, acting all excited after one incident of phone sex.*

"I think Google lied to me. It's the only explanation. Maybe someone on Reddit hacked my feed and messed with my head. You know, kind of like how our phones show ads about stuff we talk about aloud but never search for. Talk about freaky." Call me a nut, but the one time I talk about kayaks to a friend, ads popped up on my phone for a sporting store all week.

"The conspiracies. Do you think they accessed your Pinterest boards? That would be a total breach of secrecy and the worst kind of hack."

My eyes bug out of my head. I sit, searching for my phone somewhere within the thick comforter. "What do you know about Pinterest?" I whisper. My Pinterest is my diary, not meant for the eyes of people like him.

"The secrets are in the boards." His attention turns back to his book as he avoids eye contact with me, a smug smile displayed on his face. I want to wipe it right off of him.

"How do you know these things? Who is giving you inside information? Tell me now." I hit him with my best glare.

Liam's lazy grin expands as I drag my finger across my throat. "I'm not above offing whoever has loose lips around here."

He gets up from his chair and sits next to me, the mattress dipping beneath him. His weight makes me sink closer to him. The scent of him wreaks havoc on my body and gives me limited mental clarity to deal with the situation at hand.

"Pinterest her interests." He chuckles.

I glance at him, my eyebrows pinching together. "You either missed two-thirds of a haiku or you just made a terrible joke."

He shrugs, not telling me anything.

"Have you seen my boards?" I go from avoiding his touch to clutching his shirt like a cheesy 1950s movie because I need direct eye contact to differentiate the truth from jokes. My Pinterest includes boards of my future wedding, my dream house, and pins of random babies dressed up for Halloween. Basically, all my deepest desires.

We both look at my hands touching his golden chest. A zing of energy spreads across my fingers, the same feeling I ignore daily. His eyes snap back to mine as he licks his bottom lip. I lean into him, tempted to brush my lips against his.

No. This is a bad idea in all capital letters.

I let go of him, putting a foot of distance between us, just in case.

"I will neither confirm nor deny." He shakes his head.

My heart beats faster. I need to change my account name and update my passwords. Either I have a hacker on my hands or an inquisitive man who doesn't believe in standard rules of privacy. Or maybe both because I wouldn't put much past Liam, seeing as he bribes kids and doesn't follow the status quo.

He scoots in close again. "You look like you're about to pee your pants any second." *Charming, Sophie.* "Relax and watch."

I take another deep breath of his cologne because I enjoy a steady state of punishment.

He plays a video on his phone of a guy talking about Millennial Boyfriend School. The man reveals trade secrets about women and how men should have wine and chocolate stocked at home. Damn right they should.

By the end of the video, I'm crying from laughing too hard. It's a habit I've long given up on stopping.

"I'm deceased, so please forward all ten cents of my will." I throw myself back on the bed. My body sinks into the plush comforter that feels way better than my own. Liam definitely gets the upgrades, experiencing perks from being a monster on the track.

He chuckles as he bends over to wipe away some stray tears from my cheeks. How sweet of him. The gesture makes me painfully aware of the rough pads of his thumbs swiping across my face slowly, with him taking his sweet time. I allow this physical rarity between us because I like his attention.

We both play our own game of poker and wonder who will fold first. Unfortunately for him, I have a hell of a poker face if I do say so myself. The concept of folding my cards doesn't register in my vocabulary with my will stronger than a shitty hand.

"Do girls really hate being told to relax?" he asks me earnestly, pulling me from my thoughts.

"The last boyfriend who told me that ended up in a shallow grave in my backyard. My dad helped me cover it up because he said I'm too pretty for prison." I keep my voice steady.

He freezes. His eyes run over my face, gauging my seriousness.

I smack his arm. "I'm joking! But yeah, I personally can't stand it. Maybe you need to go to boyfriend school. Wait, have you ever been a boyfriend before?"

"Nope. I was never good at classes anyway. Teachers would find me roaming around the school or the library." His cheeks blush, catching me off guard.

"You know hooky sounds less badass when you tell people you hung out in the library."

The look he gives me makes me wonder if he'd smack my ass with a book if he could.

"What if I told you I snuck in because I invited a few girls to hook up between the stacks."

My mouth drops open. "I don't know whether to be scared or impressed by your love for literature and female company."

"I can show you how much I love the second." He beams at me.

Liam stares at me as a roar of laughter escapes my lips. His eyebrows lower like he thinks too hard, while his hands ball up next to him. Baby blues focus their attention on my lips before they roam across my body. My skin prickles at his assessment. I wish I could take things further with him, to test out his lips against mine, or to feel his skin under my fingertips. But I don't at the same time.

Confusing as hell, I know.

Ever since our phone call a week ago, I can't get him out of my head. The ideas that cross my mind are everything but friendly. I like us as friends, but I can't help but wonder if I'd like us as more.

CHAPTER FIFTEEN

Liam

"**Y**ou know, when I suggested working out, this isn't quite what I had in mind," Sophie says between labored breaths. Her chest heaves and her cheeks flush. She tied her hair back in a ponytail, bobbing whenever she moves with light bouncing off the golden strands.

Now that she mentions it, this wasn't what I had in mind either. I regret my decision to invite her to come with me. My idea of an outdoor workout before the Canadian Grand Prix is biting me in the ass because Sophie looks fuckable.

The past hour has been an endless cycle of me silently cursing up to the sky every five minutes, wondering how I ended up in this position in the first place. My head surpassed the gutter and ended up in the sewer, thinking about how she'd sound with me fucking her.

Yesterday was a close call in my hotel room. I almost messed up, kissing her on my bed. I wasn't thinking straight, distracted by the way she was laughing and looking at me. She's so damn unaware of how alluring she is.

I don't understand Sophie's stubbornness in denying what we both want, so I follow her plan because I'd rather not push her at the risk of losing her as a friend. It's laughable how months ago I was scared to have her as anything more than a hookup. I didn't want to open myself up to another friendship like I had with Johanna, but with Sophie everything feels so damn easy. She dug her heels in and took up a spot in my life, not giving me a chance to push her away despite my creeping anxiety at becoming dependent on her.

I find it hard to ignore how my dick pushes against the fabric of my workout shorts. It's payback for my stupid plan. She had suggested outdoor yoga by the track, but instead, I convinced her to hit some trails near Montreal. I have little control over my body's reactions to her when she stands in front of me, ass on display in those tight bubble-gum pink leggings. On anyone else, her Barbie getup wouldn't work, but on Sophie, everything goes. Don't get me started on the matching sports bra. What the fuck type of support is that? She calls it fashion while I say it's torture.

I tuck my dick into the waistband of my shorts to prevent her from catching my hard-on. She remains oblivious to my dilemma as she stares at the view of the city.

I wipe my palm down my face. "You look indecent."

She flashes her dimples, hitting me with a stunning image of her. "It's a look. Athleisure is all the rage now." She throws her arms out and does a circle, giving me a view of everything I want to touch, lick, and fuck. In no specific order.

Athleisure isn't the only thing raging right now.

"Seriously, where is your shirt? Here. Take mine." I start to pull my shirt off, desperate for some type of visual protection. Her breasts rise up and down every time she breathes for fuck's sake. I've tried to not look but it gets harder the higher we climb because the more exhausted she gets, the heavier she breathes.

Her winded voice catches when she glances at me removing my shirt, her eyes widening when they land on my stomach.

"No! Put your abs away. No one needs to see that." She covers her eyes.

Her reactions make me want to say *fuck you* to friendship. Especially when she peeks at my body through the gaps of her fingers, catching a hint of exposed skin.

Her eyes meet mine before she becomes engrossed in the landscape views. "Oh look, I think I see a squirrel climbing up a tree. I'm going to go check it out."

My eyes fall back to her butt as she walks away. I consider writing a personal letter of complaint to this legging company she drones on about. Athletic wear my ass. Who can work out in that? More importantly, who can ever get work done in a gym *next* to someone looking like that?

We climb to the top of the trail after another ten minutes of hiking, getting a great view overlooking the city. I'm thankful to be done climbing because I no longer feel tempted to smack Sophie's ass while she walks ahead of me.

Sophie collapses on the grass. "I'm done for the day."

"We still have to get back down."

She fiddles with her necklace. "I'm pooped. Why don't you even look winded?"

"Because I work out like an animal every day?" I smile at her. My body looms over her, casting a shadow and blocking her from getting any light.

She groans. "How could I forget?"

I like getting under her skin, pulling for the reactions she saves for me. She keeps me interested by the faces and quips she sends my way.

"Well, I could show you. Then you'll never forget, I can promise you that," I tease her.

She responds by throwing a rock about five feet away from me.

"You missed." I grin at her.

"Next time I'll aim for the head. It's inflated enough to make for an easier target."

I let out a loud laugh. "You feed my ego more than anyone else. That wild look you get in your eyes when I wear a suit is enough for me. No need to try so hard to avoid me."

She coughs to cover up a gasp. "You really need to get laid because you're starting to see things that aren't there."

Ah, so this is how she wants to play it.

"Is that an offer?" I drop my voice low.

A pebble lands a few feet away from me with a soft thud. She didn't even try with that one.

I lie on the grass next to her. We stare at the sky, comfortable with our silence, no pressure to fill the quiet with useless words. My body brushes up against her as I readjust myself and get comfortable.

Sophie brings out things in me I don't recognize. It's different than what I had with Johanna, with that friendship being solely platonic from the start. My thing with Sophie is damn near flammable, waiting for one of us to set a match to this waiting game, setting our relationship ablaze.

She squints at the sky. "It sucks that Maya skipped out this week. I miss her."

"Now you're stuck with me. I have you all to myself, just how I want you." My voice drops into a husky tone.

"You take up half of my time as it is already."

I have no shame admitting how I like keeping her around and doing stuff together. It helps me pass the time when I don't need to race or do McCoy-related activities.

"How's the list coming along?" I'm curious to know what she's done, or what she hasn't.

"It's not looking too hot. I was supposed to do at least one thing per week to complete it in time, but I'm falling behind." She twirls a lock of hair around her finger.

The grass crunches beneath me as I turn my body toward her. Her eyes land on mine, making me want to kiss her senseless against the grass, fucking up her pink ensemble with dirt stains and greedy hands.

Holy fuck, what is happening with me lately?

I fight my internal war of acting like a caveman or a gentleman. "How unlike you. You're usually on task."

Sophie is the most organized person I've ever met. She sure as fuck has her life together, and even though I have a job and I can be responsible, she takes it to a whole new level.

"I know." She swipes a few blonde strands out of her face. "But I've been so busy. Look, I'm working out. That's not exactly on my list but it might as well be. I mean, I probably lost a pound from our climb alone."

I grumble, "Not that you need it." She's a petite little thing. If she loses any weight, she'll fly away. "But being busy is good. Which ones have you done then?"

I don't reveal to Sophie how I hang around her whenever I have free time, passing on club nights with the boys because I prefer to spend time with her. For purely selfish reasons because I don't want her to cross off those items. At least not with someone who isn't me.

She sits and pulls out her laminated list from her mini backpack. I've never met someone as Type A as her.

"All right. So far, we have…five items completed."

One of my eyebrows rises. She doesn't notice how she dropped *we* instead of *I*.

"What did you complete without me?" I hope nothing too scandalous for her sake and mine.

"I watched porn for the first time. And played strip poker with a group of people. Plus tried new food and drank while doing karaoke in Shanghai. And no matter what you say I count Monaco's cliff-diving episode as skinny-dipping." She sticks her chin out defiantly.

Who the fuck does she hang around beside Maya and me?

I hold back a growl. "With whom?" I'm not used to the possessiveness coursing through me at her crossing off items with someone else.

"Well, Maya set up a strip poker game with some guys from Kulikov she knows from back when Santi drove with them. It was a low-key celebration for my birthday."

A birthday I had no idea about. Lovely. I clench my fists

together in frustration. "How fun. Who won the game?" My jealous ass knows the person who wins wears the most clothes.

"Ugh, I came in dead last. I was down to nothing." She fucking shrugs at me.

My molars grind painfully, my jaw clenching to the point of popping. I take a deep breath. Sophie jabs me in my side with her elbow, her breathy laugh filling me with warmth and calm.

She turns toward me. My eyes land on her bright ones, the evergreen shade easily becoming one of my favorite colors. "Relax. I'm joking. I watched about three hours' worth of YouTube videos before playing that night. You're looking at the proud winner of eight-thousand euros." She swipes her hand across her palm, making invisible money fly away. "It wasn't the full strip-poker experience, but I made it down to my bra. I can't say the same about the boys though because Maya and I hustled."

I bark out a laugh, letting go of my previous annoyance. "I wouldn't expect anything less from you. And the porn experience? I should be offended about not having an invite to that one."

She rolls her eyes while fighting a smile. "That one was just me and Maya after we had a few too many glasses of wine."

"What type of porn did you watch? Girl on girl? Girl on boy on girl? Maybe you're into soft-core porn with a riveting storyline?"

Her laughing into the sky makes my heart beat faster in my chest. I sit, wanting to take a deep breath of fresh air to calm my body down. Except now I get a full visual of Sophie with her soft lips parted slightly, luring me in, her eyes shifting from me to the sky.

My hands move on their own, brushing away some loose

strands of hair that escaped her ponytail and trail down her face.

She takes a deep breath. Her eyes close for the briefest second before they open again. "Liam…"

One word sobers me because her eyes tell me she needs more time. She likes our friendship, and shit, I do too.

I didn't think I would. When she turned me down in Barcelona, I wasn't sure I could be her friend. The idea made me nauseous, reminding me of memories I wanted to keep hidden forever. But the more time I spend around Sophie, the more addicted I get. It's impossible to ignore the pull I have toward her, both physically and emotionally, something I thought was long gone from my life. She pushes me in every way and meets me stride for stride. And fuck if my relationship with her doesn't terrify me as much as it excites me.

"All right, let's get this show on the road." Sophie tugs me away from two girls who look annoyed at the intrusion. I follow her through the event for the Canadian Grand Prix, ignoring sponsors calling my name. F1 put on a nice dinner with music, dancing, and decent alcohol. Candles flicker around the room, shrouding us in darkness except for shadows moving across the walls.

I've barely seen Sophie tonight. We've both been busy since she needs to hang with her dad while I schmooze. Earlier, Rick found me and gave me bleak news about no offers from teams, leaving me disappointed and irritable. But the smile on Sophie's face knocks my bad mood right out of me.

"I was in the middle of something." I really wasn't because girls like those are only after one thing and I've been on a body-wide lockdown for everyone who isn't Sophie. But I'm curious why she feels the need to pull me away.

"I have a favor to ask of you."

"I'm going to start logging all these favors you owe me. First, you wanted me to distract Noah from Maya, then it's to help with your list. Next, you're going to ask me for money." I add the last one to get a stir out of her.

"First of all, you imposed yourself on my list. Second, I don't want or need money from you! Don't insult me."

Sophie has good intentions and never tries to go after the wrong things. She's the perfect girl if I were looking for that kind of thing, but I'm not, so I digress.

She huffs as she drags me away from any prying eyes. "Anyway, I need help. I want to get high once."

I can't help the snort-laugh that comes out of me. "You can't be serious. Now?"

The look she gives me tells me that she is.

"I know you can't smoke because of racing and drug tests. But Maya isn't here and it's legal to do it recreationally in good ol' Canada. So, it has to be done tomorrow because I'm falling behind on items. And I need your help getting the goods and stuff." She rambles while I grin like an idiot.

"All right. Your wish is my command." I extend my elbow to her, craving the feel of her arm wrapped around mine.

I can't help the smile that crosses my face as we ditch the gala without a backward glance. Corrupting Sophie has become my favorite hobby, right up there with racing and reading.

A few hours later, Sophie and I lie on a blanket in some empty park near Montreal, our sides pressed together with a couple of pillows I stole from my hotel propping our heads up. It's quite the setup, coming off unintentionally romantic.

I no longer think drunk Sophie is the funniest one to see. She's high as a kite, giggling at nothing. Earlier while purchasing the goods, she promised this was the first and last time she'd ever do it. She wants to see what the hype is about and I'm happy to deliver it under my supervision. Plus, I get to reap the benefits of her without reservations.

"This list is such a dumb idea, right?" She turns her head toward me. The moonlight shines off her face, her bright smile beaming at me.

I could be out doing something with Jax, but instead, I'm content hanging out with Sophie under the stars. Her and her fucking stars. She tells me how she loves to sit outside and differentiate the bright ones from planes in the sky like Galileo or some shit. Every time I get one wrong, she laughs, and fuck if I don't love the sound of it. I like her laugh so damn much I purposefully confused the little dipper with Orion's belt. That blunder got me a giggle I felt straight to my cock.

Somewhere between the first and second months of the F1 season, she became one of my good friends despite my physical attraction to her. I'm shocked we lasted this long without sex. Sophie denies our chemistry while I've had enough opportunities to make a move or ten.

She taps my hand, bringing me back into the conversation. Her light touch makes my body hum with desire.

Right, the list. "Nah, it's not. You want to live a little and have a good time. There's nothing wrong with that."

She sighs. "I know. My dad is tough, though. I love him. But he's focused on making sure I'm nothing like my mom with all these rules and five-year plans. And I've tried everything to avoid being like her too. So, I'm stuck in this bad cycle of wanting to be perfect while missing out on life."

My chest tightens at her admission, connecting with her more than she knows. "It sucks when we let everyone's expectations for us rule our lives. I'm dealing with that shit and it sucks. What's your mom like?"

She fidgets, trying to get comfortable. Her body curves into mine as she lays her head against my chest. Darkness hides my surprise. I wrap my arm around her, keeping my body loose. No way in hell do I want to discourage her sudden display of closeness. Even though I haven't held her like this, it feels right, and it scares the living shit out of me. I hate being scared. Fucking despise feeling out of control, like I can't get a handle on the swirling shitstorm brewing in my chest whenever I get near Sophie.

"She's probably also high right now, hanging out in some jungle in Africa while saving the world." She giggles, the movement vibrating against my chest. "She left us when I was a baby, claiming she didn't want to be a mom. She'd rather go off and be a fake mom for all the kids in poor towns. I know I sound jealous and I feel terrible about it. It's so selfish of me to be envious of kids who have nothing, but I am because she dumped me. My parents were never married, so her leaving wasn't an issue in that sense. It was a clean break."

No matter how easy a break, the idea of a mom abandoning

their child hurts. The sadness in her voice makes my chest ache.

My fingers run through her hair to ease her discomfort. "You're not selfish for wanting to have a mom who cares for you. I'm sorry to hear that she left. I can't imagine how hard it is to grow up without a mom around."

Her shitty mom reminds me of how I should call mine when I have a chance. I may be a dick at times by ignoring my brother's calls, but my mom isn't someone I actively avoid.

"Yeah, there're some things you need a mom for. So my dad was stuck filling both roles, making sure I didn't get into trouble. At least as much as he could with the F1 lifestyle of constant traveling. I'll never forget the time I got my first period." She groans, hiding her face in my chest.

"What happened?" Her comment makes me wonder about a young Sophie during those times, like when she had her first kiss or her first crush. My mind starts to drift off to other firsts before I snap out of it.

"I asked him for pads. He came back from the local store with adult diapers."

"What did you end up doing?" I fight a laugh.

"He took me with him after I slammed my bedroom door in his face. I cried in the pharmacy as we picked out the right stuff, becoming a blubbering mess while my dad paced the aisle and googled info. He bought me every candy bar to make up for it and pretty much offered anything to get me to stop. I was so emotional about not having my mom around to help me and I felt so embarrassed with my dad. But I've never seen him that uncomfortable. Can you imagine? *Adult diapers.* There was even a picture of a grandma on them. I had no clue what he was thinking. Those are the types of moments I wish I could call my mom and ask her about stuff." She shakes her head, giving me a fresh inhale of her shampoo.

"Do you talk to your mom?"

Another sigh from her. "Yeah, occasionally, maybe like once every two months whenever she gets service. She's still my mom so I've long since let go of that grudge. Some people aren't meant to be parents."

"That's really mature of you." I mean every word.

That's the thing about Sophie. On paper, she may be twenty-two, but she holds herself to a higher standard, coming across older than her age. It makes me feel less guilty about our age gap because I can't see her with a college fuckboy who barely has his shit together. She doesn't deserve that.

"If you knew her, you'd understand. I can't hold it against her anymore because she's so happy doing what she does. She's whacky like a hippie. I'm lucky she didn't name me Rainbow Moon or something scary."

We both laugh at that idea. Being around her knocks me off-kilter because I don't know whether I want to kiss her, protect her, or fuck her. My hand lazily rubs against her back. She tries to shimmy off my chest, but I hold her there.

"Anyway, my list is all types of crazy. It's my way of experiencing new things since I've been held with a tight leash all my life. And not the sexual kind either if your perverted mind is jumping to that conclusion."

An image of Sophie tied up runs through my mind, making my pants uncomfortably tight.

"That's a lot of pressure to put on yourself. But the list is a cool idea. Nothing like trying out a bunch of new things while traveling to all these different places."

"If you could do anything in the world besides F1, what would you do?" Her question throws me for a loop. Where the fuck did she pull that one from?

I think about it for a good two minutes while Sophie lies on my chest, her head pressed against my beating heart while she waits.

"You like heavy-hitting questions. If I wasn't racing, I'd probably go to school for something. Maybe to study architecture. I've loved checking out the buildings we visit in different cities and learning their stories." The nerd in me shines through.

"Wow. A man who appreciates old-world history."

"Have you always wanted to be an accountant?" I don't get the appeal for someone like her because I can't envision her sitting in an office all day long crunching numbers.

"Eh, no." She giggles to the point of snorting. Damn, I got her some good weed.

"Then what would you do if you weren't studying to become an office junkie?"

She lets out a nervous laugh. Has anyone asked her this before?

"I love art." She says the three words in the faintest whisper like she is sharing a secret, adding it to our growing list.

I give her a squeeze. "What kind of art?"

"I do all types. Painting, drawing, but I especially love charcoal because I like to get my hands all dirty and smudge the lines." Her voice betrays her excitement.

"Do you still do it? I haven't seen you with any art supplies this summer."

"Not as much anymore. Once I got busy with school, I stopped, except for a few classes I did on the side for elective credits. Plus, my dad appreciates respectable careers if he's going to finance my degree. If I told him I was switching my major, I think he'd have a heart attack." She sounds wistful and sad at once.

My heart pinches, an unfamiliar feeling for me. She won't follow her own interests because of her dad?

"It's never too late to follow your dreams and see where they take you. Look at me. You're lying down with one of the best drivers in F1."

"Your humbleness never ceases to amaze me. I mean, I can try while on the road."

I stare into the darkness, avoiding everything inside of me telling me to make a move on Sophie. It's a torturous experience. "You should. If you're creative, take advantage. I lack any of that shit." My arms tighten around her, loving the feeling of her lying across my chest.

What the hell is happening to me?

"Tell me a secret of yours. I feel like I always share while you barely do. So what gives?" She taps a finger against my chest.

I take a few deep breaths, regulating my heart rate. She tempts me to share everything with her.

Sophie lets out a deep exhale. "I was joking. You don't have to share something if you don't want to."

She gives me an out, making me feel something I can't label for the life of me. Her selflessness and her ability to not push me gives me the strength to put myself out there because if I can't trust her, is she really my friend? *God, I'm really a sucker for her.*

"People think they know me, but they don't."

"Which people?" she says plainly, not an ounce of judgment in her voice.

"Friends, fans, my team. The person they know is far from the person I really am. I've mastered an image they want to see."

She takes a moment, crickets sounding off in the dark woods surrounding us. "What's your reasoning for doing that? Is it to protect your privacy?"

"No." I swallow, holding back the growing anxiety building inside of me.

"Then?" She lifts off my chest and sits.

"It's stupid," I grumble, running a hand down my face.

"If it means something to you, then it can't be stupid. But you should know that it's okay to hide parts of yourself from the public. For you and your sanity."

She makes my confession easier by being so damn non-judgmental. It's a complete change of pace compared to Peter and the public, all attempting to tear me down in hopes of some sick sort of redemption story.

"I live a lie. It's a far cry from hiding parts."

"I'll let you in on a secret." She looks me in the eyes as she speaks in a hoarse whisper. "We all live lies. Some are just better at disguising them. Others hide and never acknowledge them, instead flinching at shadows looming in the corners because they know what lurks there. You're aware of what you're doing. You consciously embrace your secrets, becoming one with the issues haunting you."

"You wouldn't understand," I groan.

"You're right. I wouldn't. But it doesn't mean I can't empathize and feel for you. Life is about learning to share the burden of your problems with others. It might feel all good and dandy now to hide, but secrets have a way of getting to us all. And sometimes the greatest lies aren't the ones we tell ourselves; they're the ones we believe time and time again despite all the evidence proving us wrong. So share your secrets or keep them inside. The choice is yours. But just know that shit will eat away at you until you're shrinking at your own shadow too."

Silence cloaks us. Her words sit against my chest like a weight, pressing against the ache near my heart. Minutes pass by, neither one of us talking as we mull over our own thoughts. She lies back down on my chest. I feel relieved at the lack of eye contact.

I don't know where I find the courage to share, but fuck I do. Blame the perceptive blonde lying on top of me who builds me up without threatening to tear me down. "My brother married my best friend."

Sophie stills, not saying a word. Her silence encourages me to continue.

"Her name was Johanna." I didn't expect to choke on her name, but my voice betrays my hurt.

Sophie grabs my hand and intertwines her fingers with mine. She gives me an encouraging squeeze. It takes me another minute before I continue because I want to think out my words and make this whole process as painless as possible. Sophie stays silent, her thumb brushing against my hand, soothing me in more ways than one.

"She was my partner for my freshman year science class. I

chose her because I knew she was smart, and I thought she could help me pass. And I did just that, all thanks to her. But we started hanging out a lot together. She and my brother met, and they had this connection I can't explain. But Lukas is a few years older than me, so he didn't want to make a move on a freshman when he was about to graduate. Johanna and I got really close—me because she wasn't interested in hooking up and Johanna because she enjoyed my company. So we can fast-forward through years of friendship. Once Johanna and I graduated, my brother made his move and they dated before getting married. They eventually had Elyse, my oldest niece. Those two couldn't help getting pregnant with Kaia right after Elyse. But during the labor process..." I swallow back the bile rising in my throat. "There were a shit ton of complications that happened and she didn't make it." Wetness pools in my eyes, but I blink back the looming tears.

"Oh, Liam. I'm so sorry. I can't imagine how tough that was and how heartbreaking it is to lose someone you care for in such a sudden way. You and your family have been through so much." Sophie wraps herself around me.

"I feel disgusted with myself that I can't move on. My brother is doing fine, and my parents are always strong, but me... I hate parts of myself. So instead of embracing all of me, I don't. I lost my best friend that night. But also, I forfeited part of myself to survive the pain."

"You can always fight to get it back. You're not a quitter, and one day you'll wear your hurt like a badge of honor. That's when you know you can heal and move on. Everyone handles their pain and sadness differently so those who don't accept you don't matter because acceptance includes all the parts, not only the desirable ones."

"Easy for you to say. I admitted I deceive others and you're here boosting my ego." I'd laugh if my throat didn't feel constricted.

"That's because you're the only one losing when you deflect and hide. If you decide not to get close to others, that's your choice. I'll keep living my life with the bits and pieces you share. But the real question is, can you live with your ruse for the rest of your life? If you can, then you're the most beautiful liar I know because the prettiest lies are the ones we tell ourselves."

Damn. Sophie, despite her limited life experiences, has a shit ton of wisdom packed in such a small body.

She keeps going. "But remember this. I want to get to know all of you, including the parts you're too scared to share. I want to learn about the man no one else knows. So give me every part of you because I'm not here to piece you back together. I like you too much, just the way you are, broken parts and all."

Fuck. Her words fill me with hope I didn't think was possible.

"I suck at getting close to people."

She squeezes my hand, sending an electric current up my arm, replacing my sadness with lust. "You're already getting close to me, you fool."

Well, shit. I totally am, and I'm not the slightest bit sorry. Spending time with Sophie has been the best damn part of this season.

I rub my thumb across her knuckles, craving her touch like a junkie craving his next hit, eliciting a sigh from her. "Not to deflect or anything, but why do you keep ignoring our chemistry?"

"Because I don't want to ruin something good for something temporary." She pushes herself up and away from me. Her hand lingers on my chest, the warmth from her palm radiating through my shirt.

"I'll take anything from you." It's sad to admit how I'm not joking.

"That's my fear with someone like you. You take and take until I have nothing left to give. You'd be easy to fall in love with until you walk away, breaking my heart in the process." She whispers the words like saying them lower makes them less scary.

Her dropping the *L*-word fills me with dread.

"I can't promise anything close to love, but I can promise you endless orgasms, friendship, and mindless sex that'll leave you buzzing from your head to the tips of your toes." I offer her a sly grin, propping myself up on my elbows.

Like always, Sophie does something shocking. She leans in and presses her lips against mine. The kiss feels soft at first, her wariness evident.

Holy shit, Sophie is kissing me.

My instincts take over as I kiss her back, no longer in shock at her move. One of my hands wraps around the back of her neck and holds her steady. My body sings at the contact, my tongue darting out to feel her plump lips.

I pull her on top of me while her tongue—that fucking tongue—probes mine and gives me access to her mouth. I could combust at her touch. An embarrassing yet truthful admission nonetheless because kissing Sophie makes me question what the fuck I've been doing before. Scratch that—kissing Sophie feels like everything.

She gasps as my teeth tug on her bottom lip. My dick throbs in my pants, clearly not getting the memo that this is just a kiss. I find controlling myself around Sophie a hopeless cause. Our tongues test each other while my hand wraps itself around her soft hair, tugging on the strands I've wanted wrapped around my hands for months.

A rush of desire nearly knocks me out. Sophie gains the confidence to explore my body, the feeling of her hands dragging against my chest and arms nearly doing me in.

I roll us, pushing her back against the grass as my body splays atop of hers. Our lips never break contact. Fuck, I love the taste of her, the pressure of her body against me, the whole damn thing. Her fingers graze my stubble before she places her hand on my face.

My body pushes into hers, her moan making my dick pulse as it rubs against her center. I love the sound of her heavy breathing, showing me she feels as affected and helpless as I do from our connection—both victims of our stupid game.

I break away from the kiss to get a look at her. Regret fills me instantly as the haziness in her eyes dissipates and her mind turns back on.

She coughs before recovering. "Uh, we better get going. It's late."

I groan as I roll off of her, standing before helping her up. We both pretend nothing happened and return back to normal as we gather our belongings. Well, we act as normal as friends who kiss like lovers and share the same desperation for one another. Sophie and I put on the best damn show with us pretending to fight our attraction for no good reason except for her thinking she'll catch feelings instead of orgasms.

Fuck feelings. They leave a bad taste in my mouth. Sophie needs to be convinced how feelings are meant for good boys who will cherish her for everything she's worth. I can only promise what I can offer with my career and my past. A future isn't guaranteed, but I swear the only one she'll think of is me doing every naughty item on that list to her.

It's enough for me. But the real question is if it's enough for her.

CHAPTER SIXTEEN

Liam

E ven after winning the Canadian Grand Prix, the press conference sucks. I get hit with a couple questions I don't want to answer. Cameras focus on me, their bright lights causing my skin to flush. For once, I don't appreciate the limelight, the surrounding reporters stifling me as I aim to keep my composure.

A sleazy reporter eagerly moves up to the front of the group. His slicked-back hair and beady eyes send some creepy vibes as he licks his lips. "Liam, several sources claim your McCoy contract is on the fritz. Your performance is competitive, yet you're struggling to beat Noah this year."

"Is there a question somewhere in there?" I rub the back of my neck with my hand, despising how uncomfortable I feel under the intense scrutiny from everyone in the room. Jax and Santiago shift in their chairs.

"Uh, right." He licks his lips again. "So, is it worth putting your contract on the line for Claudia McCoy?"

This shit again. New race, new reporter, same crappy questions.

"The status of my contract is not contingent on my relationship, or lack thereof, with Claudia McCoy. I'd appreciate if it's no longer brought up during these press conferences. I'm here to race, not discuss my private life."

McCoy's PR agent will have a field day with this one. I see another meeting with Peter in my future because he hates when we sass reporters. But fuck all this shit. I've been staying out of the headlines and playing nice with others. Plus I'm a role model for abstinence. Sophie's probably to thank for keeping me in line, to be honest. I haven't slept with anyone for almost three months already. My free time is spent constructively as of late, no longer plagued with bad mistakes and easy women.

Another reporter speaks. "Liam, there's talk that you may switch over to Kulikov's racing team at the end of the season. Would you like to share more about that?"

"No comment." My response garners some hushed whispers.

The reporters process my response. I have no idea where they get their information from, but their sleuthing skills suck.

"Can you tell us more about your relationship with Miss Mitchell? Are you looking to join Bandini next year?" The same slimy reporter from earlier speaks up.

Where the fuck did that come from?

"My friendship with Sophie Mitchell is of no one's concern. Not everything in life revolves around contracts and signing deals." I smirk at the reporter, hoping he shuts up.

He slyly grins. "As of an hour ago, a source reported you're sleeping with Miss Mitchell to climb the career ladder."

My fingers clench in front of me. "Seeing as you mentioned Claudia a moment ago, I'd double-check with your sources about their reliability. Whoever I decide to sleep with, whether it's Miss Mitchell or not, is no one's business. I'd rather commit career suicide than sleep with someone to get ahead in this sport. I'd advise you to find better stories that don't involve the latest scoop inside my bedroom."

The reporter settles back into his seat, his shoulders held high.

The press conference wraps up in record time. My mood darkens despite a Prix win, tainted by tactless questions and untrue stories.

My day goes from bad to worse when I get a call from my agent about Peter wanting to meet with us. I grace them with my lovely presence, my foul attitude from earlier following me around like a dark cloud.

McCoy's motorhome palace greets me, the cold gray aesthetic no longer filling me with a sense of pride. I step into a conference room to find an agitated Peter and my agent seated.

"When I said to stay away from women, I didn't expect you to befriend James Mitchell's daughter. How stupid can you be?" Peter's meaty fists bang on the table.

The notion has me shaking in my sneakers.

Not.

Unnecessary politics need to stop. I show up to drive, place on podiums, and schmooze with sponsors. My contract doesn't include discussing my bedfellow schedule.

"You should've been more specific. You told me to respect your niece and I did that. Sophie and I are friends. It's not my problem if reporters twist our friendship to fit their agenda." I flick a piece of invisible dust off my jeans.

"For the love of God, I appreciate your skills as a racer, but you need to control your private life. I hate hearing reporters talk about you like that and I don't enjoy having McCoy associated with Bandini." Peter comes off genuine for the first time all season. He reminds me of the old him, of the guy who took me under his wing when I was lost.

"I think what Peter means to say is how hanging around someone from Bandini may not be the best choice, especially the team principal's daughter. What if this blows up again? Let's say you have your fun with her and then leave her behind. She can't go away because she's always around." Rick assesses me.

My agent's words make my blood run hot. He should be on my side rather than sucking Peter's cock and appeasing him.

"No, it won't. You two are acting like I'm fucking around behind her back. You'll have to trust me. If you believe I can drive a million-dollar car and win, then you can count on me to not mess up."

Despite my confidence, I know they're right to question me. That's the thing about trust. Once you break it, the journey to get it back tends to be long and tedious. I want to put in the work for my team.

Peter wraps up the meeting with a warning glance and a grumbled apology about losing his temper. Look at that. Billionaires: they're just like us.

Rick stays behind per my request. Clearly, I need to give him direction about what I want.

"I need you to find out what McCoy's plan is for me next season. Ask if they want to keep me or not. If yes, then find out the cost and an estimated timeframe of how long it'll take Peter to get over his dislike for me. My patience is thinning because his attitude changes more than my car shifts gears. If McCoy doesn't plan on offering, I want to see a report about bids from other teams."

"And if McCoy doesn't agree to any terms?" He taps away at his phone.

"Then do your job. It's what you take a chunk of my signing bonus for, isn't it?"

Rick triggers my angry side, with him continuously giving me a hard time about my relationship with Sophie and my image with McCoy. I don't pay him as much as I do to bitch and moan about me. He earns his million dollars by putting up with my shit and finding solutions. He likes money, and I like racing. It's a win-win situation when he motivates himself.

His dark eyes remain on mine. "I'll get right on it. But you know McCoy is your best bet. I've been working Peter down, trying to keep your payout worth you staying with the team. These deals take time so give me a few more weeks."

Everyone and their goddamn mother know McCoy rules F1 with Bandini. But I won't compromise myself and limit opportunities for a sick race car and a best friend for a teammate. At least not unless there is a promise that Peter will relax and let me do what I do best.

"Be careful with Miss Mitchell. As much fun as she probably is, you need to think about your career. This is the very thing you've been working toward since you were a kid. If you keep pissing Peter off, I don't know if I can help you. I can't save you from every mistake."

His words make my stomach twist. With one last glance, I step outside of the conference room to find Jax leaning against the wall.

He glances at me with wary eyes. "Hey, I thought you could use a break from this place."

"Let's go." I follow him out of the McCoy motorhome, leaving behind my shitty mood.

Jax and I make our way to a local pub, hiding in a corner booth far from potential fans. We order food and drinks.

"So, what happened?"

"They got pissed about Sophie and my reputation. Blah blah, same old shit." I tear at the label on my beer bottle while Jax watches me.

"Is there a reason for them to be worried?" His raised brow doesn't sit well with me. I'm tired of people questioning my shit, making me second-guess every move I make.

"Why the hell should they? I can fuck whomever I want without their approval, as long as it isn't Peter's niece."

"So, you and Sophie are hooking up now?"

I take a sip of my beer. "No. But it shouldn't matter either way. I promised to be good and to not draw attention to myself. Never did I say I would be a damn monk for months."

"And how's the not drawing attention to yourself working out for you?" He tilts his head and smirks.

"Screw you. How was I supposed to know some reporter would mention me hanging out with a *friend* at a press conference?"

"The same way you should have guessed they would wonder if you're using your *friend* to get ahead with Bandini."

"Seeing as they already offered Santiago a two-year contract, that shit is irrelevant. And Noah will probably race with Bandini until he retires."

He shakes his head. "Seriously, though. What do you plan on doing about your friendship? Please tell me all this hassle and drama is worth it. Are you at least getting some?"

"No. But not because I don't try."

"Tell me more. Open up to Dr. Kingston." He folds his hands in front of him.

"I pushed her before she was ready. The furthest we've gone is phone sex and kissing."

"Phone sex? What are you, a fifteen-year-old boy lusting after his first girlfriend?"

I grind my molars together. "Fuck off. She kissed me a few nights ago, thank you very much."

"Okay, I'll stop being a dick. But really, you need to do something about your situation."

"And what exactly do you suggest, seeing as the closest female friend you've had is our fifty-year-old massage therapist."

"I can give good advice when I want to. And don't hate on my relationship with Ms. Jenkins when you're only jealous she gives me a lollipop after our sessions."

I rub my temples with my fingers. "You do understand you're all over the place, right?"

"That's what keeps life interesting. You never know what you're going to get with me. But anyway, I reckon that you need to give Sophie what she desires if you want any chance of hooking up with her."

"Feelings?" I choke on the word.

"I mean, do you really not feel anything for her?" Jax lifts a brow.

"I didn't say that. I just don't feel the extreme kind of love she might end up wanting." I take a swig of my beer to soothe my aching throat.

"You can care about someone without wanting to marry them and love them forever. Girls love thoughtful shit. Someone like her won't have sex with someone with your past if you don't show her you like her for more than good looks."

"But we're friends. What else more can I do?"

"Besides terrible phone sex?" He fights a smile.

I shoot him a pointed glare.

"Show her you care and won't dump her after hooking up a few times. Of course, she doesn't want to be another conquest in your long list, especially if it puts your friendship at risk."

What the fuck have I gotten myself into? I know shit is going to hit the fan when Jax starts making sense.

CHAPTER SEVENTEEN

Sophie

After the Canadian press conference from hell, I imagined riots in the Bandini motorhome with signs declaring a traitor in our camp. I thought about crew members wanting to burn me on a pillar while my dad struggles to give me up, stuck between appeasing the fan base and saving me. Realistically, the only one who truly could give me the third degree sits across from me with his jaw ticking.

My dad and I take up shop in the Bandini motorhome, prepping for the European Grand Prix. I have no shame admitting how I've avoided him ever since Liam's press conference in Canada. We conveniently booked separate flights to Baku months ago, allowing me to evade him for two days. The jig was up once he asked me to visit him in his office. He makes me sit and take his glares and growls while he answers inopportune phone calls.

"Please tell me why the hell my daughter is featured in the latest trashy magazine? Because I can't fucking wrap my head around why your name is being associated with Liam Zander and his bedroom."

Okay. Sadly, the few days of distance have done little to ease his anger.

"I swear I didn't mean for any of this to happen."

"Why don't you be clearer?" He takes a deep breath.

I fidget in my chair under his examination, bouncing my leg to the beat of my heart. "I didn't mean to develop a best friendship with Liam. It caught me off guard."

"If it's a friendship, why are the reporters suggesting you're sleeping together?"

"I don't know. They're bored and not good at their jobs?" My laugh sounds more like a wheeze.

"I'm not going to have you embarrass yourself and the team." His words sting.

"But we're just friends." Friends who kiss each other with more heat than a burning Bandini engine, but friends nonetheless.

"If I catch one more bad story about you two, you're going home. No arguments and no begging to stay."

"You're not being fair. I didn't do anything wrong and I can't control what other people say about me. Maybe you're mad my name is being mentioned with Liam specifically?" I raise my chin.

"No. I'm mad because I warned you what would happen if you got involved with a racer. My reaction would've been the same whether it was Santiago or Noah."

"Liam and I are just friends. I swear!" I cross my index finger over my heart.

"You couldn't befriend anyone else? He's a racer for an opposing team and our main adversary. Of course, reporters are going to talk." His eyes soften at my frown before they harden again.

"I know. It's like Romeo and Juliet." My idea sounds credible.

"They both die in the end. And they're lovers, not friends."

I brush him off. Classic stories are more Liam's thing while I prefer smuttier romantic retellings. "Semantics. Anyway…that's not the point. You should be happy for me. I met someone who's my best friend. Everyone needs companionship and I get lonely while you're busy." I'm not opposed to pouting my lip while throwing his packed schedule back at him.

"If he does one thing out of line, I'll make sure his next contract is on an F2 team."

I shudder because nothing is worse than leaving F1. It's a low move, but my dad looks serious with his gray brows bunched together and his lips pressed in a tight line. His wariness puts me on edge.

"What are you so afraid of? We're having a good time, hanging out and stuff."

"Besides the fact that you gained Liam's attention? His reputation and your friendship are a recipe for disaster." He clasps his hands in front of him and stares at me. His concern makes my stomach roll because the idea of getting hurt terrifies me.

I overlook his concerns and my growing doubts. "You worry too much. It's not like that between Liam and me. We have a tight bond, like Bonnie and Clyde."

"You really love using iconic examples of couples to describe you two." One of his eyebrows lifts. My bad. My dad catches me on an off day because I mean nothing by it.

"You can't protect me from everything. You made mistakes and survived."

He sits in front of the best consolation prize of being with my mom.

"Listen, I want what's best for you. You always had a soft heart, forgiving others for everything to the point of putting your happiness on hold. Just be careful, smart, and safe. But I mean it, another incident like this and you'll earn a one-way ticket back home." His knuckles knock on his desk before he gets up from his chair. He comes around to my side and pulls me in for a hug before he leaves his office.

Well...that went better than expected.

I decide to spend the afternoon lounging on the grassy area next to the Grand Prix track. My body curls up on a blanket under the sun, basking in the somewhat cool weather and blue sky. After yesterday's conversation with my dad, my head still reels at his ultimatum, uncertainty eating away at my sense of calmness. Our conversation means I need to be more careful around Liam and how people interpret our relationship.

Speaking of the man who never leaves my mind, Liam finds me, carrying a book and something else. I take him in from my position lying down. The sun hits him at the perfect angle, basking his muscular form in a golden glow. My throat bobs at the sight of him with his arms on display and thick legs within touching distance.

I divert my naughty thoughts. "I think that book is larger than my head."

Liam prefers big paperbacks instead of an e-reader. He got insulted when I asked him why he doesn't pack one for his long travels. If I didn't think Liam was a secret nerd before, the fact that he travels with three different books in his carry-on backpack should've sealed the deal. While some people read BuzzFeed articles and take online quizzes when bored, Liam reads book blogs and watches YouTube videos analyzing literature and film adaptations. Even I, a *Star Wars* fan since childhood, can't keep up with his crazy theory videos surrounding the cinematic universe.

"Want to see what else is larger than your head?" His voice rasps as his shadow hangs over me, blocking the light from my eyes.

I roll my eyes. "You're losing your touch. That was a weak one, like a negative two out of ten."

He situates himself next to me, his clean scent halting my working brain cells. My vision sucks because what I thought was another large book is actually a wrapped-up rectangle.

I look at him warily, pointing to the galaxy wrapping paper. "And what's that?"

"I bought you a present. I saw it in a store and thought of you." A pink tinge creeps from his neck to his cheeks.

My heart constricts at the idea of him buying something for me. *How…friendly…of him.* Not to mention he bought special wrapping paper. Part of my heart melts under the sun's rays, unable to cope with Liam being this kind.

"Okay, gimme gimme." I sit and make grabby hands, bringing a smile to his face, his shyness no longer an issue.

He passes me the large package. My fingers find a crease in the paper but I hesitate to rip the beautiful paper. Stars scatter across swirls of blue, purple, and black. His thoughtfulness confuses me, unlike any friend I've had before, testing my idea to keep things casual between us.

"You're killing me with suspense. It's only wrapping paper." He taps my stilled fingers.

Oh, Liam. So unaware of my conflicting decision between jumping your bones and keeping you as a forever friend.

No longer needing encouragement, I rip at the paper, the dark wrapping giving way to a sketchbook. My eyes water. I run shaky fingers across the rough textured cover, loving Liam's sweet and unexpected gesture. It's like everything between us, both unpredictable and indescribable, creating a friendship that doesn't fit in a checked box.

A dimple-inducing smile crosses my face when Liam tosses a pack of charcoal onto my lap. I stare at my favorite medium, emotional at how Liam remembered my weed-induced confession.

"If I get a smile like that with something simple, I'll have to get you stuff all the time." He beams at me, filling me with happiness and gratitude. My heart has officially reached its sweetness capacity.

"This is so special. I can't even believe you thought of this. Thank you so much." I wrap my arms around his neck and pull him in for a hug. He stills before wrapping his arms around me, his head finding the hollow of my neck. I get a good whiff of his cologne because when I torture myself, I make sure to really take it all the way.

I let go after a few more seconds and end our moment.

His eyes flit to the side, hinting at his bashfulness. "I hope you use it. No more excuses about not having time or being scared. We all know you have bigger balls than half the men on the grid."

This man flatters me and disarms me all in one sitting.

"I'm touched you own up to your faults. I like a man who isn't afraid to let a woman know about his shortcomings."

He jokingly tugs on the sketchbook, but I smack his hands away. I fall onto my back and laugh into the sky. My hands clutch my gift to my chest, still shocked Liam did something so considerate.

Liam cracks open his book and lies down on the blanket. I want to hold on to this moment forever, so I sit and flip my sketchbook to the first page, opening the pack of fancy charcoal he bought. The rest of the afternoon is spent with me sketching a picture of Liam reading his book. I never want to forget the feeling of him buying into my passion and believing in me.

He doesn't ask to see my drawing, giving me privacy I didn't realize I needed. We hang out together for hours on the grass.

While sketching, my mind takes off, thinking of my major and resenting how constrained I feel. Some of my fingers cramp but I continue because I crave the burning sensation in my chest. My passion grows from an ember into a flame, tiny yet tangible, requiring further exploration and discovery.

I forgot how much art fuels me. How running my fingers across the gritty textured paper and smudging perfectly drawn charcoal reminds me of finding beauty in imperfection.

My hand lingers on my drawing of a handsome Liam. Unlike me, he doesn't seek an unattainable goal of perfectionism. We both carry different burdens. Liam strives for success with his team and proving others wrong while letting go of a past haunting him. I'm burdened by both my expectations and the ones set by my father, unachievable and sucking the life from me slowly.

I flip the page, looking at the blank paper behind the drawing of Liam. It's symbolic of how I feel about my life's direction, of the pressure placed on me, of how empty I feel when I think of my future. It reminds me of my distaste for pursuing a degree I have no interest in because I struggle to be perfect, responsible, and making others happy. With those unreasonable expectations comes a numbness I've grown accustomed to.

My fingers twitch, and before I know what I'm doing, I swipe my dirty hands all over the clean sheet. Marking it, smudging it, making it flawed.

It's everything I want to be while being everything I fear becoming.

When we go to pack up the blanket, I give Liam another hug. "Thank you for believing in me and reminding me of something I thought was long forgotten. I can't express what that means to me." My throat closes up.

He says nothing because he doesn't need to. The way his arms tighten around me and the kiss he leaves on the top of my head say everything.

CHAPTER EIGHTEEN

Sophie

The summer break left as quickly as it came. I spent a whole month without F1 activities, drama, and friends. Liam kept himself busy with sucking up to McCoy while I checked in with school. After multiple ripped up pros and cons lists, I decided to continue my course work through the fall semester since I've already committed three years of my life to stupid numbers and a lack of fulfillment. My dad takes the news of online classes well. He buys into my reason of wanting to expose myself to different countries while studying.

Call me cultured AF.

This semester includes classes on business law and accounting information systems. I can't wait to hit the snooze button on my life for another year because my degree sounds less appealing by the week.

I passed the time during the summer break drawing in the sketchbook Liam bought me, chipping away at my fears while telling stories through pictures. The whole process inspired me to grow a pair and live a little.

Over the break, I decided I need to work harder to achieve the Fuck It List items because it's part of my mission. I have my work cut out for me with a total of eight items crossed off and thirteen more to go.

Lately my plans haven't exactly been working out how I like, and although I wish I could blame Liam, I can't. I like his teasing and pushing my limits. Time didn't help eliminate those feelings, especially when he called me during his free time or facetimed me some nights. We never went a day without a text or phone call.

The idea of us unnerves me, so I thrust myself into helping Maya stay away from Noah. It's an evasion tactic with less than altruistic motives.

Did I travel to Spain to visit Maya? Yes.

Did I also visit her because I wanted to create a game plan where we both can forget about the two men who invade our thoughts? Hell freaking yes.

We travel together to the next stop in the Prix. After a month-long break, everyone returns, ready to get back in the swing of things. The first post-summer break Prix stop was too hectic for me to see Liam or the other guys, with them having mid-season tests and endless meetings.

During the next Grand Prix weekend in Milan, I plan a double date for Maya. I personally can't resist a date with a promise for pasta. Our dates are two McCoy engineers named

Daniel and John who choose a swanky restaurant in the heart of the city.

Despite their best efforts, the evening turns out to be a bust for Maya, probably because Noah found her and defiled her in some backlit corner of the restaurant. Guilt from her actions settles right next to my pasta dinner. My shame forces me to agree to another date with my guy, John. I'm not thrilled, but at least he seems like a potential match to knock off a few of my items.

That's how, a day later, I end up standing around the McCoy motorhome waiting for John. A lunch date comes off slightly friendshippy. Since John has limited availability before the race tomorrow, he wanted to take advantage of his free time.

I smell Liam before I hear him.

"Look who finally came to visit me after a month apart. I feel honored." Liam pulls me in for a hug, his arms tightening as he holds on to me.

"Says the guy who's been too busy to do anything." I catch my breath once he lets me go.

"What are you doing here in the opposing camp? Trying to wage war?" His goofy smile makes my chest tighten.

I smile at his disheveled blonde hair, the sweaty strands peeking out from under his backward ball cap. It gives him a boyish look I like a lot. His cheeks remain flushed from the high temperatures of his car. He did a great job today during his qualifying round, landing the coveted pole position.

"I'm trying to understand the enemy while plotting my takeover. It all starts with you, in case you weren't already aware."

His smile grows larger, and I wish I had Maya's camera to

snap a picture of it. "I knew there was something about you that would destroy me."

"Hmm. Well at least you face your demise head-on. How bold. I tried to warn you about how I plot because I'm the worst kind of control freak." I rub my hands together and cackle like an evil genius.

His chest shakes from laughter, bringing my attention to the way his shirt presses against the muscles of his torso. *Bad Sophie.*

Liam toys with the end of my French braid. "I'd face the consequences. Especially when I'd bring out another type of freak in you. All you need to do is admit defeat." His eyes smolder.

My skin heats at his unspoken promises.

"Hey, Sophie, sorry for keeping you waiting. I had some last adjustments to make to the car. Are you ready? Oh, hey, Liam."

I look over at John, a decent-looking guy with a mop of brown hair and kind eyes. Nothing I'd write home about if I did that sort of thing, but at least he comes off genuine. He's the type of guy my dad would expect me to hang out with. Not the brooding man in front of me, baby blues and pouting lips on full display.

Liam scoots closer to my side, his neck pulsing. "Hey, Joe. How's it going?"

"John." I hiss under my breath.

Liam sends me a shit-eating grin, showing me he knows exactly whom he is speaking to. My poor date doesn't stand a chance against the territorial man next to me.

John shifts his weight from foot to foot, ignoring Liam's mistake. "Pretty good. Going to take Sophie out before we get busy again for the race."

"Oh, I had no idea Sophie was making other friends besides me and Maya. Are you trying to make me jealous?" Liam's eyes narrow at me. He runs a hand down my back, my breath hitching at his touch. His large palm lands in the dip of my back above my ass.

I step away from him and closer to John, wanting to avoid the way I want more of Liam's touch. "Don't be silly. I have plenty of time for all my *friends*."

Liam's nostrils flare. John's confused eyes flick between Liam and me, unable to solve the mystery of us. Call me a shitty Sherlock because I can't either.

"Well, it's nice catching up. Text you later, Liam." I drag John away from Liam.

A glance over my shoulder reveals a ticked-off Liam, his boyish charm discarded along with his easygoing smile.

I push aside the image of an angry Liam as John leads me out of McCoy's motorhome. John's hand remains respectfully in the middle of my back, nowhere near the spot where Liam's was. His touch doesn't rile me up like Liam's does. I frown at the revelation.

Our date goes fine, and for some reason, it disappoints me. We walk through Milan's side streets with my hand in his. My body remains numb, not a flutter in my stomach or a hint of chemistry when John grabs my hand. Even my heart keeps to the same pace while my skin remains unflushed, like my body won't recognize John.

I chalk up my limited reaction to needing an emotional connection to someone else. Liam and I developed a friendship first, so maybe I need the same with John. It seems legit enough to make sense.

The idea eats away at me for the rest of the day, even after John drops me off at my hotel. I can't ignore the tiny voice in my head telling me how maybe I like Liam for more. If I wasn't scared at the notion of being attracted to Liam, then the idea of wanting more from him besides a meaningless physical connection and friendship makes me want to throw up.

I don't want to ruin a good friendship over being another conquest in his list of contacts. That thing probably takes up four gigs of memory on his phone.

You know what is more unfortunate than falling for your friend?

Falling for a friend who has no intention of catching you before you face-plant.

A cool breeze brushes over my skin, causing one of the pages of my magazine to flip on its own. I can't resist the hidden rooftop deck the F1 Corporate office has. Their motorhome remains the sleekest, with smooth lines and chill spaces. I lie down on one of the couches with my back pressed up against the pillows.

"How's the list going?"

I smile at the sound of Liam's voice. He's typically inquisitive about the status of my checked boxes.

"Want me to make you one? You always wonder about mine, which makes me think you need one of your own." I stare at him like a weirdo, taking in his gray McCoy polo and backward hat.

He grins at me as I close my magazine. His hands lift my

legs before he sits, placing them back on his thighs. Every time Liam gets near me, my body becomes aware of his closeness, betraying me with goosebumps and an elevated heart rate. I regret the shorts I picked out this morning. They expose my legs to his arms, skin against skin.

"No, I enjoy knocking off items on yours much more. There's nothing like your first time." His sensual tone does things to me.

I squeeze my thighs together. His eyes dance with mischief, looking bright and beautiful as they roam over my face. My body sucks at this active ignoring thing, having a mind of its own, leaning into Liam's body.

"Hmm. And how did you find me here?"

"Find My Friends location." He hides his smile.

"I regret adding you back in Canada. I didn't think you'd use it again. Should I be concerned?"

I almost miss the confirmatory mumble under his breath. He tips his head back on the couch cushions, the sun emphasizing the contours of his straight nose and full lips.

My fingers run across the glossy magazine cover. "How are you getting ready for the race tomorrow?"

"Just checking over my car, making sure everything is up to my standards and running smoothly. Speaking of, I saw Jim in the engineering room. Did your date end early? That bad, huh?"

Liam is the type to fish for information with a spear gun.

I chew on the inside of my cheek. "Oh, it went fine. Jim's a nice guy." Nice, thoughtful, and too good for me.

"You mean John?"

Shit. He tried to confuse me, and it worked. Liam's presence makes it difficult for me to produce smart sentences. His hand brushes up against the smooth skin of my legs. My body jolts at his caress, unaccustomed to his recent touchiness.

Where were these reactions two hours ago with John?

I gather myself. "*John* is a sweet guy. He asked me on another date since he got called in early for some engineering problem."

Liam gives me a tight smile. "That's nice of him. I'm sure it gets busier for engineers as we get closer to race day, with car issues and whatnot. Hopefully, he'll have enough time to balance taking you out again."

Did Liam have something to do with John's early return? I find his smirk questionable, and his tone sounds a bit off.

"Does that mean you'll be around less too? What a shame."

He bites down on his lip. "I'll always make time for you. But what if I don't want you to go on a date with him or anyone else?" He grabs my hand, abandoning his attention to my legs. His touch sends a shock wave up my arm.

I look at our joined hands, unsure where to go with this.

Will I ever be ready for someone like Liam? The idea of us together feels like a collision. Something I can't prepare for, no matter how much I want to. Instant, hard, and painful with metal crunching and sparks flying. Part of me wonders if we are already halfway there, losing control of our cars before either one of us has a chance to fix things.

"I'd say you're acting like a possessive brother." I drop the *B*-word, hoping it'll push him away, except he does the unexpected.

He laughs. "You sure try your hardest to deny everything between us. I know you're attracted to me or else you wouldn't have kissed me in Canada or come to the sound of my voice."

He trails a single finger up my leg. My skin heats wherever his finger lingers before he stops at my upper thigh and leaves his hand there.

I stare at his hand, willing it to move. Higher? Lower? Anywhere but right next to the place begging for his attention?

"You can give in, you know. I won't judge you for it. Hell, I'll reward you, congratulating you for your efforts at lasting this long." He abandons my thigh as he grasps my hand in his again. His thumb traces mindless circles across the thin bones in my hand.

Earth to Sophie. Pull it together. "Uh, well, I should get going." I pull my legs off Liam's lap, not waiting for him to respond. His throaty laugh runs across my spine as I hightail it out of there.

I walk into the Italian Grand Prix gala with my dad, the snazzy affair welcoming us with golden lights glistening off the chandeliers hanging above our heads. A live band plays on the stage while servers offer us alcohol.

My eyes go straight to the food table. "There's a pasta buffet. I repeat, a pasta buffet."

My dad snorts and leads me toward my paradise. "For such a tiny person, you sure do eat a lot."

I pile my plate with pasta and bread. "Don't give me a complex."

He follows me to an empty table and sits with me, giving me a solid twenty minutes of his time between chatting with sponsors and coworkers.

He looks stunned at how I shovel pasta into my mouth. "I'm weirdly impressed. If there was any question of you being my daughter, this definitely rules it out."

I glare at him and drag my fork across my throat. It fails to have the desired effect, instead making my dad laugh loud and robustly.

He offers me a bite of his veggies after he regains his composure.

"I'd rather die than eat a piece of lettuce." I stare at his salad like it offends me.

"You know green food is meant to be good for you." He stabs his food while longingly staring at my pasta. He chose a lean piece of chicken, passing over the pasta bar without looking back. Like he really needs to keep his figure in check. The man works out more than half the guys in my university, probably out lifting them.

"That's good because my cereal has enough green food coloring to carry me through the day."

"One day you'll end up having kids of your own. Then I'll be laughing when you shove broccoli into your mouth while trying to convince them to eat their own, with your eyes watering from trying not to gag. I didn't eat veggies until you came around. Honestly, I thought me eating them would win you over but here I am twenty-two years later."

"Joke's on you." I stick my tongue out at him.

My dad chuckles, his young appearance shining through. He has a youthfulness to him that never went away with age. When he works in the Bandini pit, he shoves jokes aside because he has to be the big guy in charge, making sure Santiago and Noah don't screw up.

"Looks like someone found you." My dad catches Liam's gaze across the room.

I sigh, which gets me a heavy dose of side-eye from my dad. He remains quiet as Liam makes his way toward us, one hand carrying two champagne flutes while the other holds a bottle of Dom Pérignon.

A man after my heart.

Okay, let me stomp on that thought about fifty times.

"Mr. Mitchell, nice to see you." Liam pulls out a chair next to me as he nods to my dad.

"Liam." My dad eyes him curiously.

"Long time, no see." Liam wraps his arm around the back of my chair.

"I saw you yesterday. Should McCoy be concerned about your memory?"

His smile softens my already weak resolve, acting like a seduction trap with free alcohol. He needs to put those shiny bad boys away because the light bouncing off them blinds me.

Ever since my date with John, Liam lays his flirting on extra thick, like a new wave of possessiveness took over his lightheartedness.

My dad kisses me on my temple before excusing himself. No one misses the daggers he shoots at Liam, his skepticism evident for all to see. Too bad he didn't include his shovel-and-shotgun speech. It's a classic.

"I brought reinforcements." He pours us two healthy glasses of bubbly.

"I knew I liked you for a reason. Match made in heaven." The words flow from my lips before I realize what I said.

"I didn't know you felt that way for me." He hits me with another wink that goes straight to my clit because he has a way with making me feel all types of things.

"I was talking to the champagne bottle so get your head out of the pit lane. You and I are destined for hell." My eyebrow rises on command.

Liam breaks out into a deep laugh he saves for me. "Matches made in heaven are overrated anyway, being all saintly and shit. Doggy-style is the devil's work."

I clench my thighs together as I chug my champagne and nearly drain the glass of all the fizzy liquid. A trickle escapes the rim of the glass and trails down my lips. Before I have a chance to lick the droplet, Liam leans in, his tongue lapping up the drop before tracing across the seam of my mouth. My lips buzz at the contact, my lungs burning as I take in a sharp inhale.

What the actual hell.

Butterflies be damned because Liam is too naughty for that. Being around him feels more like hornets wreaking havoc inside of me as they try to escape.

"What are you doing?" I whisper.

"Things I should have done a long time ago."

My eyes look everywhere but at him. "Why?"

"Because I'm ending the game."

"What game?" I can't tell what's gotten into him. He tears me up inside, my rules disappearing along with my self-control.

"The one we both already lost. Fuck ignoring how we feel because we're both too chickenshit to do anything about it."

Does he like me for real? Or is it only about something physical?

"What kind of feelings?" I leave things open-ended, despite how my brain begs to ask a different question.

"The ones that make me want to rip that dress off you and fuck you with your sparkly sneakers wrapped around my waist. I want them pressed against my ass while I come inside of you, your fingers clawing at my back because you can't get enough."

So, the physical kind of feelings. Got it. I can't deny how my heart squeezes, awareness flooding me about how Liam wants nothing past our friendship and fuckship.

I pretend his words don't bother me. "You're only horny after not getting with anyone for months."

"You're shit at trying to ignore my advances. I'd almost believe you were unphased if you didn't squeeze your legs every time I flirted with you."

My cheeks flame. Cheeky bastard, this one.

A new voice breaks our staring contest. "Oh look. Liam and a new tart."

I'm going to use context clues and guess that I'm the tart. My lips purse at the shrill voice ringing across the table, a British accent lacking the usual allure.

Liam's body goes ramrod straight in his chair. Gone is flirty Liam, replaced by stormy eyes and a clenched jaw. It's a much scarier version of himself.

"This tart's name is Sophie. Nice to meet you." I put my hand out, but it remains in the air unshaken. Liam pulls my hand away and holds on to it.

"Claudia." She leers at me.

I strangely feel like the other woman based on how she treats me. Claudia looks beautiful, but her scowl and rough personality make her unattractive to me. She's all long legs with pale skin, dark hair, and sharp cheekbones.

"What do you want?" Liam's voice sends a chill across my skin. He puts a possessive hand on my thigh, drawing Claudia's eyes to them. His thumb traces slow circles across my skin, a calming gesture I desperately need once Claudia sits in a chair next to me.

"Oh, Liam. I thought we were giving up on these games." She lazily assesses me. It doesn't make me feel too great to be honest, not that I'm the one to put myself down, but damn her intimidating stare unnerves me. Screw her for making me feel less than. But she looks like she walks runways on the weekends so it's no wonder why Liam had a thing for her.

"There are no games. We're over." Liam's hand continues its slow torture on my leg.

Claudia taps her heel against the marble floor. "And you think being with someone like her is really going to improve your chances at a McCoy contract? Think about your future. Do you really want to be a has-been driver with only two World Championship wins?" She looks at me the same way I check out a salad.

"Why don't you leave the contract deals to those who actually work for a living." Liam squeezes my leg reassuringly.

"It's hard to not offer a word of advice."

"Yet I didn't remember asking. Next time I need some help, I'll be sure to ask someone who can reference something other than *People Magazine* as their reliable source of information."

I fidget in my seat, beyond uncomfortable by their exchange and the toxicity throwing off my positive vibes. No champagne buzz can cure this.

"For someone keen on not ending up in another magazine, you sure are okay with tempting tabloids to talk about you and the daughter of Bandini's team principal. How interesting. That sure is one way to secure a contract, I'll give you that." Her lips purse together like she ate a lemon.

Her assumptions can't be further from the truth. I take a deep breath, pissed about sitting next to this manipulative woman who looks at me like I have the personality of a houseplant.

A wave of possessiveness controls me. "Are you usually this much of a bitch? If Liam and I fuck around, it's none of your business. Quit acting like a sad cliché because the *scorned woman desperately clinging to a man* storyline is overused. Feel free to leave whenever you want; this conversation is a bit dull."

Liam's wide eyes make me worry I went too far. My heart pumps fast, the rhythm drumming in my chest while my emotions run amuck inside of me. If I wasn't a classy lady, I'd shift my weight from foot to foot with my fists up, ready to pounce. Verbal sparring will have to do for now.

"Liam may not want my advice, but I'll give you a piece of my mind anyway." She pats my arm like she has the sweetest intentions. Her touch makes me frown, fighting back the urge to shake her off. "This man uses women until they have nothing left to give. Then he'll disregard you like you mean nothing. He did it to me, and he'll do it to you. You know how many women he's played with? He's not like Noah, who sleeps around. No, Liam is the worst kind of guy who fucks around with you until you think he wants you back. That is, until you aren't convenient anymore." Mary freaking Poppins glares at me.

"Enough, Claudia. You're embarrassing yourself, acting like we were anything more than a casual fuck. Get over it. God knows I have." Liam doesn't give us a chance to engage in another back and forth. He grabs my hand and pulls me away from the Wicked Witch of Racing.

CHAPTER NINETEEN

Liam

Sophie looks like she wants to mull over what Claudia said. There goes my plan to ease her into the idea of us slowly, hoping she'd be open to the idea if I gave her all the good reasons.

I pull her away from the gala into a private hallway far away from anyone potentially finding us. It's dark and empty. Perfect because I don't need any more exes of races past ruining any chance we have at something good.

"I'm sorry about that. She won't leave me alone. I blocked her so she'd stop texting me every week, sometimes with photos or messages. Peter finally let up on the issue, so I don't want to cause drama by bringing her up again."

"Mm." Sophie's dazed eyes look off into the distance.

"Are you upset about what she said?"

"No, don't be silly. She's just plain rude. Do you really need so many ex-girlfriends? What were you creating, your own army?" The old Sophie comes back to the surface.

I let out a breath I didn't notice I was holding in, relieved when her eyes land on my face. "I thought about it, but I didn't like how much upkeep they needed."

She laughs at my poor joke.

My shitty history makes another comeback. I don't want it around, fucking up my chances with Sophie. Before I can stop myself, I brush my knuckles up against her cheek, her smooth skin running against the bones of my hand. I enjoy the feel of her. The way my body begs for more contact, or the feeling of electricity running through me when she gives me all her attention.

I'm a fucked-up guy, giving into our attraction while screwing over my plan to remain sexless and drama-free for the season.

Sophie takes a deep breath, holding it in as she looks at me with big eyes. I do things without thinking because my plan has already gone to shit. Since I've lived my whole life like that, why stop now? Fuck it.

One of my arms loops around her body while the other grips her chin, holding her where I want her. My lips find hers as her body loosens in my arms. I forgot how much I loved the feel of her lips against mine, the sweet taste of her invading my mouth.

Our kiss feels sweet at first, with her soft lips pressing against mine. I crave more from her. Something inside of me wants her to be as desperate for me as I am for her. My body buzzes as her fingers clasp together around my neck and her lips part, giving me access to her mouth.

Screw platonic, I want catastrophic. I stroke her tongue with mine, the taste of champagne flooding my mouth. Kissing her is addictive as hell. It's like chasing an adrenaline high for hours.

My hands follow the curve of her back, testing the limits she'll allow, finding the tight globes of her ass and giving them a squeeze. Her body is fucking fantastic. I feel her gasp straight to my dick, stiff and ready for her, wondering about the hold-up. A four-month prohibition makes me needy.

Our tongues mingle and the taste of her overrides my ability to think. The connection is mind-numbing perfection, making my brain muddled as we devour each other.

Kissing her is the best fucking thing, like all feels right in the world. Her tongue, first tentative, now teases mine. Sweet Sophie is replaced by the seductress inside of her. My fallen angel, tempted away from the gates of heaven to join me in the pits of hell. Her teeth grip onto my lower lip, pulling and sucking, taking control of our kiss. Fuck, it makes my body hum with encouragement while my dick throbs in my pants.

Her hands run down the front of my tux, groping me without a single fuck given. I roll my erection into her because I long to hear the noises she makes. Fuck, I crave to thrust inside of her. To pull all types of moans and groans from her as I bring her toward ecstasy.

When I push my dick toward her, her body tenses, probably realizing where we are, who we are, and what we're doing. The switch flips and the old Sophie comes back. She lightly presses against my chest, and I sigh as I pull my lips apart from hers.

The last thing I want is for her to shy away in fear and stop us before we have a chance. She's the best kiss I've ever had, and I need to see where this goes.

People tend to manage others like glass. With caution, in fear of breaking the person and shattering their heart. But with Sophie, I handle that shit like a bomb, as if she can explode any second. She's a ticking clock with a fuck ton of complicated wires. Once detonated, shrapnel and crap flies everywhere, piercing you from all directions, fucking you up from the inside out. Both explosive and disastrous.

I come up with ideas faster than my brain can process them, creating a plan to compete with Sophie's. "Let's be friends with benefits?"

Yup. That's my genius idea. All five words of it.

CHAPTER TWENTY

Sophie

My hand moves to my lips, running my fingers along the swollen area Liam's tongue licked and nipped.

Liam acts like the ocean, erasing my carefully drawn line in the sand, similar to a rolling tide flooding my ability to think of reasons to disagree.

There's no use denying my desires anymore. I drop my excuses, ditch the denial, and nod my head along to his idea. Because, shit, I have to see what happens. His lips, our kisses, the whole thing blows my mind. My brain works double-time to get things up and running.

I mean, friends with benefits seems plausible, right? Obviously, we can't put our chemistry aside anymore. Not when he kisses me stupid.

Liam paces the hall, his blonde hair no longer slicked back. Did I do that?

"But what about feelings?" Go me for thinking ahead. I don't want benefits to change anything between us because I enjoy spending time with him.

"Don't worry about that. We like each other, so we can fuck around without developing anything more than friendship. But you can't ignore this thing between us anymore. I know I can't. Nor do I want to."

Despite the risk of developing more for Liam, I definitely can't pretend I'm not attracted to him anymore. Kissing him feels like my entire life has been robbed of good kisses. I was able to hide after Canada, but things keep changing between us, developing into more whether we want it or not.

Liam stares at me like he wants to kiss me again. He inches closer while I step back, my butt hitting the back of a wall.

"Okay. But secretly because my dad will kill me if some gossip article posts something about us hooking up. He's fine with us being friends, but no more defiling me in some poorly lit corner." My brain catches up to my body. About damn time. "I made late-night plans with Maya, so I better go."

"Your dad won't find out. Hell, neither will McCoy." He closes the gap, his cologne conducting torture on my senses. His hand softly grasps my face before he pulls me in for another kiss. His lips press against mine, leaving behind the faintest peck.

He breaks away, his eyes gazing into mine. "It's a shame I can't corrupt you in corners though. I think I'd like it."

My body buzzes from the mental image. "It would defeat the purpose of appearances around F1 crew. You know, because friends don't do that."

Liam steps back and gives me space. "You'll be so busy

moaning my name, you won't have time to regret this. I'm so beyond fucking ready to reap the rewards of our cat-and-mouse game. Enjoy your last night of freedom because tomorrow you're all mine."

He flashes me a mischievous smile before walking away, leaving me panting in a dark hallway.

After collecting myself both physically and mentally, I hop into a waiting town car and head back to my hotel. Maya answers my emergency text and tells me she'll come after running to the store. I slide out of my dress the minute I get inside my room, desperate to take a shower and get into comfy PJs.

I process the day's events while I wash my hair, wrapping my head around my agreement to Liam's plan. Worries dance inside my head while the pros and cons weigh themselves. But unlike times before, I push them away because I don't want to fight our attraction. It's a losing battle not worth another day.

Maya comes to my hotel room with reinforcements in hand. We sit on the couch in our PJs and fuzzy socks, the epitome of attractiveness. The only two men we can count on during this lifetime are Ben and Jerry. Before diving into our individual pints, we clink our spoons together in a mock toast.

From the looks of her, Maya has seen better days as well. Her sad eyes burrow into mine as she shares her recent issues with Noah. My beautiful best friend deserves the world, so he needs to wake up and smell the gasoline because time is ticking away, his window of opportunity narrowing.

"I'll avenge your honor. I can mess around with his radio, making them play annoying pop songs the whole fifty laps. That'll drive him crazy, I know it."

She lets out a sad laugh.

I rub my hands together like a villain. "Never fear. I've come up with the perfect plan to help you."

She skeptically checks me out while failing to respond.

"I've commissioned Liam and Jax to help this time. We are all going to bond and spend time together, away from Noah and the racetrack."

Maya shakes her head. "You're too good to me." She dives into her ice cream, filling Noah's void with frozen goodness.

"I have a confession to make." I take a bite of ice cream for courage.

"I have a priest for you." Maya looks at me seriously.

I snort. "Speaking from experience?"

"I felt guilty lying to myself for weeks about Noah. Then there was that sunscreen application incident in Monaco that was our personal foreplay. I needed to vent to someone, so a priest seemed like a good idea. My mom still raves about my commitment to the church. We went to mass every week during the summer break."

I fail to hide my look of horror.

"Anyway, tell me your confession." Maya gestures for me to continue with her spoon.

"Well, I met Claudia."

Maya's inhale of breath says it all. "Tell me all about her. I'm assuming it went terrible based on your frown."

"Yup. She's as vile as they describe her. She called me a tart like she's from the nineteen hundreds or something. And then she tried to give me some womanly advice."

"Oh, no." She groans. My feeling exactly, wrapped up in one grunt.

"Oh, yes!" I stab my ice cream with my spoon.

Maya's eyes twinkle. She finds amusement in the worst things, and although I love that kind of optimism, it does little to ease my growing irritation.

"But that's not the worst part."

Maya stops her spoon midway to her mouth, chocolate ice cream dripping onto her pants as she waits. "Okay. Don't leave me hanging here…"

"Liam kissed me." I evade her eyes.

"He what?" Maya screeches, making my ears ring.

"I know. And even worse, it wasn't terrible." I peek at her from the corner of my eye.

"You're not stamping his kiss with a glowing recommendation here."

My cheeks heat at the memory. "No, it was amazing. That's the problem. And now I can say with certainty that it's not a fluke because I actually kissed him in Canada."

"And you didn't tell me?" Maya pouts.

"I was afraid to admit it while stupidly denying my attraction toward him. It didn't die down during summer break. Instead, everything feels more intense. How is it possible?"

"You both have this magnetic energy with one another. Everyone sees it except for you two."

All right, Maya, the ever-observant one. If only she applied these skills to herself.

I sit in silence, unsure how to approach the conversation.

Maya turns her whole body toward me. "Okay, and then what happened after he kissed you tonight?"

"I kissed him back. Duh. And then he asked me to be friends with benefits."

Maya's eyebrows draw together, the pinched look adding a couple temporary wrinkles to her forehead. "Are you sure that's what you want?"

"What do you mean? Nothing else can happen besides that. And nothing will change between us because we're adults who can separate feelings from sexy time."

Maya laughs wholeheartedly. "Oh my God. Please never say that again. Like *ever*."

"Is it a bad idea?" Doubt seeps into my head.

"Probably. But you're committed to the plan and Liam doesn't look like the type to give up. What's your aversion to developing something serious with him anyway?"

I spend a minute thinking it over. Maya sits comfortably in the silence and eats her ice cream.

"His past, his future. Because no one, including him, knows what he'll be doing next year. And I'll be back in uni finishing up my degree."

"You can't predict the future, no matter how hard you try to control everything in your life. Sometimes the best changes aren't the ones you plan for. And with school, you've told me a few times you don't really love it. Do you really want to keep pursuing something that doesn't make you happy?"

"I never imagined making my dad happy would cause as much suffering as it has. I don't know right from wrong, smart from dumb, or pro from con anymore. My brain feels more confused than ever before and I can't exactly blame a kiss for it."

Instead of giving me comfort, following my dad's plan suffocates me and holds me back, providing an illusion of a safety net. In reality, I've created a shiny cage, hiding myself in the name of not wanting to disappoint my dad.

I want to live my life to the fullest. Rather than taking risks, I've spent my life blaming my dad for locking me up in a tower and setting unrealistic expectations. Part of me wonders if I've been just as willing to never test myself and break free from what's expected of me.

It looks like it's time to find out.

CHAPTER TWENTY-ONE

Liam

McCoy kept quiet after I performed well in Milan. I should've been wary of their silence, because before the French Grand Prix, they share how they hired a new PR person to help me with my image.

Hence the reason for Jax and me to be trapped in a McCoy conference room.

Thanks to Claudia's lack of discretion and delusions of grandeur, McCoy hired a new PR rep from Mexico named Elena. McCoy welcomed her to the team because I'm an idiot and Jax because he got caught with his pants down, quite literally. Jax is on a one-way trip to fuckboy town if he keeps up with his latest antics.

I give her a rundown on the shitstorm that has become my life. Safe to say, yesterday's drama article about me reconciling with Claudia at the Italian gala put a damper on my mood. Why does Claudia continue to tell absurd stories to the press? She needs to find a new hobby or a new rich boy to fuck because her attitude has gotten out of hand.

Jax sneaks looks at Elena throughout our meeting. I spend my time checking him out, holding back a laugh at how he fidgets in his seat and taps his hands against the table. His reactions are questionable, to say the least.

Jax rarely gets rattled by a woman. I mean, Elena looks nice and all with hair framing her face like a dark halo, brown eyes with dark lashes, and skin with a healthy tan. There's not a blip of interest on my end. But Jax looks intrigued, and I catch Elena eyeing him a couple times as she runs through the new PR questions and standards. She keeps professional by never looking too long. Props to her for withstanding Britain's finest who has enough secrets to fill an F1 motorhome.

Jax fails to answer a question she asked, choosing to look at her with a confused face and an apologetic smile. I'm dumbfounded by his reaction.

"Did you listen to a word I said?" Her accent has a melodic rhythm to it. She stares at both of us, awareness dawning on her of how we barely paid attention, both of us caught up in our thoughts.

Jax licks his lips. "Not really. Mind repeating it, love?" He shoots her a grin that usually works on women he picks up, except Elena frowns and shakes her head. Not even Jax's British accent can save him this time.

"Okay, you two. This is the last time I'll go through this. Liam, you have to deny everything regarding Sophie Mitchell and Claudia McCoy. For the sake of your career, you don't want to be seen as a ladder climber who sleeps around with women to get what you want. And Jax, you need to keep away from women for the unforeseeable future until this drama blows over. No more late nights at clubs after that last incident." She looks at us with an evident distaste.

I withhold the urge to snap at Elena. "I'm not using Sophie. And Claudia throws shit around to stir up trouble. Why doesn't McCoy deal with her instead of hounding me down, forcing me into these types of meetings? I don't need to sell stories to tabloids to make money."

Elena's eyes show a hint of warmth, breaking away from her professional demeanor.

"Listen, I don't think you're a bad guy. I want to help save your career, which may or may not involve a contract with McCoy. And I want to help shine the brand in a more positive light. I'm a fixer, with these types of projects being my specialty, especially in sports like F1."

I let out a deep breath, willing to work with her. "Well, to start, I'm going to be sleeping around with Sophie. Just in case that secret gets out."

"No shit. When did this happen?" Jax bounces in his chair, hitting me with a big smile.

"I asked her to be friends with benefits after Claudia terrorized the gala and said a bunch of shit."

Jax's smile dims. "Whoa. Are you sure that's a good idea? What if she catches feelings?"

"You know that feelings aren't an illness, right?" Elena blurts out.

Jax glances at her, the shine in his eyes replaced with darkness I notice from time to time. "To me, they might as well be. Worse than a plague."

Elena laughs and rolls her eyes. Jax raises his eyebrow, something indiscernible flashing across his face before he returns his attention to me.

I tilt my head at him. "She's down to have fun, and so am I."

"Look at you and Noah, acting like a pair of lovesick twats chasing after the two friends. I'll be spending the rest of my days in the club, tears dripping into my liquor." His eyes assess Elena shaking her head. "Well, once your shit blows over."

"No one said anything about love. Relax." Part of me hates Jax for pointing out my biggest insecurity as of late. It's not that I don't care for Sophie, but the idea of love freaks me the fuck out.

"Ay, no need to get pissy. It's only a matter of time before your relationship with her explodes in your face. But you can see where this takes you. I mean, you're already shit out of luck with McCoy, so what else could go wrong?"

I smack him across the head, hoping my hit knocks the stupidity out of him. The way he checks out Elena after tells me it may take more than one hit to cure him.

After another half an hour of Elena's assistance, we wrap up the meeting because Jax and I have a limited attention span.

I call my agent when I step out of the conference room.

Rick picks up on the second ring. "Hey, man. Just who I wanted to talk to." His chipper attitude boosts my mood.

"I take it you have good news?"

"The very best. You've impressed McCoy with your podium placements for twelve out of the fourteen races so far. They want to extend another contract deal to you."

"That's amazing." A wave of happiness takes over me. "What are we looking at?"

"Well, the contract has a slight pay increase because of your performance this year, with a yearly salary of 20 million for another two years. You're looking at 40 million total. Congratulations!"

"Fuck yes." I let out a relieved laugh. It's the exact deal I've been waiting half the season for.

"But they did have a few comments before you can agree."

Dread sits heavy against my chest, replacing my elated mood. "What comments?"

"You have to stay away from Sophie and anyone from Bandini who isn't Noah. McCoy doesn't want to be associated with their rival, no matter how friendly you are with the girl. Obviously, you don't need to be rude to the Mitchells, but the gossip about a relationship needs to end."

"I need to think about this. Can we counter-offer about this? I don't like the idea of cutting off friends for brand purposes."

"Of course. Whatever you want. Think it out and get back to me next week. McCoy said they can wait you out." Rick hangs up once I say my goodbyes.

I should be kissing the ground he and Peter walk on, thankful for another chance with my team. Instead, new rules and regulations choke me, ruining my good mood. Like Sophie, my brain needs time to process and assess the pros and cons of signing with their set of demands. Decisions like this take time, especially when I could risk blowing up a relationship I've grown to care about.

No one warned me about the consequences related to being

friends with the daughter of an opposing team. I didn't think having Sophie in my life would put me at risk in more ways than one. Because in the end, can I sacrifice my dream team for a relationship with so many boundaries I can't see past them?

Years ago, I told Sophie about how she should do the saving in her story. But I didn't realize she was saving herself from me because I'm the real villain in this messed-up fairy tale.

Because unfortunately for us, everything in my life is temporary.

CHAPTER TWENTY-TWO

Sophie

My phone buzzes in my bag. I pull it out after searching around for a good minute, my purse an endless pit of loose gum strips, old receipts, and plane ticket stubs.

> **Liam:** I have a plan for tomorrow. Meet me at the McCoy motorhome at 3 p.m.
> **Me:** What if I have plans?
> **Liam:** Do you?
> **Me:** No. But thanks for asking. Meet you there.

He responds with a middle finger emoji. I laugh, loving how he doesn't try to overly impress me, choosing to be true to himself.

When Liam told me he made plans, I didn't think he meant something like this. He tugs me along behind him toward the grassy area near the Eiffel Tower with a picnic basket in hand, which would probably look ridiculous on someone else. When I question his masculinity, he does a quick twirl, absurdly comfortable with himself.

Liam finds a perfect spot, the green grass lush beneath our feet and the sun hitting us with golden-hour rays. He pulls out a blanket and situates it on the grass. I follow along when he gestures for me to sit. If he were someone else, he would be perfect. But I don't want to read into this too much, putting labels and ideas where they don't belong. I stomp all over my rapidly beating heart.

He makes it hard to resist him, especially when he pulls out a bottle of wine and a cheese plate.

"I thought this would be fun before the next Prix."

"Do you do this for all your French girls?"

His cheeks blush. A bashful Liam tends to be one of my favorites. "Nope. Only sassy little Americans."

"I'm not little." My bottom lip juts out. He swipes his thumb across it, the brush of his finger sparking something within me.

"You can fit in my carry-on bag if we tried." His eyes smolder as they roam over me, taking in my loose blonde hair and mascara-coated lashes framing my eyes.

Did I put effort into my appearance for Liam? Yes.

I'm so screwed.

"I don't think I want to fly private jets in a carry-on. I didn't peg you for such a cheapo who wasn't willing to share his life of luxury."

Liam barks out a laugh I've grown to love. *Uh, like.* He pours the wine like a pro, cloth included for wiping off any excess drips.

We look like classy people using real glasses instead of plastic ones.

"Cheers to another city and another race." He smiles.

I clink my glass with his and take a sip. The liquid cools me down from the heat of an August day and Liam's nearness.

I scan the perfectly manicured lawn. "Can you believe people propose here? I don't think I would ever want something so public."

We already saw one proposal while walking over to our picnic spot with the sounds of a crowd cheering ringing through the quad.

"Are you a hidden romantic? Do you want some private proposal instead?" His eyes dance, the sun's rays reflecting off his irises.

"Maybe. I don't know. I never thought about it before, especially with my parents and their failed attempt at love."

His eyebrows tip down, his lips matching the movement. "Oh, come on. Every girl thinks of it."

"Not this girl. Don't be so quick to jump to conclusions because not every female dreams of a three-bedroom house with a dog."

"Of course not. Girls dream of fancy mansions with Bandini cars instead of dogs."

His crazy picture of love makes me laugh up into the sky.

"For someone who talks about how in love his parents are, you sure have a dark outlook on life."

Realization dawns on me when his eyes dart away from me. I try to backpedal. "I didn't mean to bring that up."

He focuses on the Eiffel Tower in front of us. "I know. But

it happens. It's not like I want to be some irritable asshole who lets one comment taint my mood. But in the end, you're right. I shouldn't be like this, but I am. Because, sure, my parents have the best marriage, but they have a son with the worst. So it doesn't matter what we grew up with when Lukas lives a daily nightmare."

"Have you talked to your brother about this? Based on what you've told me, it seems like he loved Johanna. I wouldn't count that as the worst marriage." I can't help but wonder if Liam paints a worse picture in his mind about how his brother copes.

"Even if it wasn't the worst, it didn't have a good ending. Hell, it shouldn't have ended, period. And no, I don't talk to my brother as much anymore. At least not like before."

"Then who are you to assume he lives this terrible life? He has two beautiful daughters from the photos you've shown me. Johanna may not be alive, but the memory of her continues in her kids."

Liam's eyes appear glassy as he turns his head toward me. "I don't know…"

"You're right. You don't know." I clutch his hand in mine and look him in the eyes. "It's okay to stop torturing yourself over an idea of how he's living. Maybe you should ask him instead of hiding."

"It's easy for someone to give advice when they haven't experienced it."

I scoff. "It's anything but easy to confront you about this. Easy would be to not mention anything. To sit back, enjoy our limited time together, and take off into the Italian sunset when all is said and done."

"Then, why do it?" His eyes hold mine captive.

I swallow back my nerves, wanting to say the words before I lose the courage. "Because I care about you. Whenever you mention your brother, you get this wounded look in your eyes. The tragedy in Johanna's death wasn't only her dying. It was also you losing part of yourself to compensate for the emptiness of losing a best friend."

"I think you missed your calling in psychology," Liam grumbles.

I let out a soft laugh. "Nope. My calling was to end up here all along, ready to kick your ass into gear. You've been on more podiums with me around than last year. You're welcome, by the way."

Liam shoots me a beaming smile that I feel all the way to the deepest parts of my heart. "You, Sophie Marie Mitchell, are right where you belong. Screw accounting, you're too hot to sit in a cubicle all day."

Leave it to Liam to go from somber to humorous in one sitting. I let him get away with his diversion, content on enjoying our happy hour together.

We sit together and people-watch, making up ridiculous stories about tourists and locals alike. He sips his wine, bringing my attention to his lips wrapped around the rim of the glass. The same lips I want kissing me again.

I drain the remaining contents of my glass in a couple of swallows.

"Easy there." His gravelly voice makes me clench my thighs.

And then I remember my saving grace. The whole reason Liam and I got into this mess together, the start of a relationship

I could never prepare for.

I pull out the Fuck It list from my pocket and assess the deeds I can do. "I want to plan what to do next."

His eyes darken. I review some of the items, wondering what I can choose by myself.

Liam grabs the list from my hands yet again. "The whole point isn't to plan every little detail. I think I'll choose this time."

Goodbye control, catch you later.

"Found one. *Kiss in front of the Eiffel Tower.*" Liam clasps my hand, pulling me in flush against his body while strong hands hold me close.

I push away from his chest to look him in the eyes. "What are you doing? We can't kiss here. We're in public! That's not what friends with benefits do. They keep it exclusive to specific domains like friends in the outside world and benefits in the bedroom."

His lips twitch at my rambling. "If you keep benefits to the bedroom, then you're doing it all wrong." His deep voice goes straight to my core, a dull throb betraying how much I want him.

"We need clear rules and expectations of what friends-with-benefits means. I think we both have different ideas."

"Fuck rules and plans. Stop thinking so damn much."

Liam doesn't give me a second more to mull over our status because his lips find mine while his hand cups my face. The fresh taste of white wine raids my mouth and runs across my tongue as his lips claim mine. His lips possess me and control my brain and body, bending me to his will as I become putty in his hands.

Tongues clash, sending a shiver down my spine. My toes curl inside of my sneakers at the sensation building inside of me. A soft moan escapes as his hands run across my back, initiating another round of sparks across my skin.

I get lost in the taste of him. Liam claims me piece by piece with a kiss alone, owning my heart and my lips. My arms lock behind his neck and pull him in closer. I nip at his bottom lip. He lets out a groan as my tongue teases his, giving me back a small bit of control.

The sounds of people clapping brings me back to the present moment. Heat floods up my neck to my cheeks while Liam readjusts his pants and puts his hat back on, the brim sitting low enough to hide his face.

"The city of love strikes again." An innocent bystander smiles at us.

No, sir, there's no love here.

"Bring out the list."

My hand fumbles at Liam's request. I grab the list from my purse and place it on the table of his hotel room. His suite looks like an upgraded version of mine, with a sitting room, dining area, and a huge bedroom.

"Where's the Sharpie?"

I find a pen after removing two lip balms, hand cream, and a brush. "Are we checking something off? I don't see anything on here we can do." My voice betrays my excitement.

He grabs the Sharpie from me and writes at the bottom of the paper, next to his last addition.

Have a friend with lots of benefits.

His written words have a sense of finality to them. "Now that we added that, I wonder where to start... Oh, I know." His voice drops down to a husky whisper, making sirens go off in my head. "I forgot what a dirty mind you had making this."

My cheeks burn. Liam rises from his chair and runs one finger down my shirt-clad spine, goosebumps breaking out where his finger trails. He grabs me and carries me toward his bedroom without a backward glance. I'm thrown onto the bed as if I weigh nothing, my body landing in a mangled heap with Liam staring at me from above. The room has enough lighting to make out important details like the way he smiles with mischief.

His gaze lingers on my chest before meeting my eyes. "See, I worry you're going to back out of our deal. You tend to get all worked up, and as much fun as that is, I'd rather have you unwinding."

Liam sees through me effortlessly. His words cause a bubble of something to build up in my chest. I stay silent, wondering where this will go.

"So, I think it's a great idea for us to work out some of the kinks in our arrangement. In the name of making this work between us. So, I have an idea of what we can do to set the record straight."

I feel afraid yet weirdly excited about which number he chose. "Something from the list?"

"Right. You're a good girl. You like to be very thorough with everything you do, right?"

I nod my head along to his words.

He snickers. "You don't want to give up on your list after all this time, right?"

"No." I lie there like a sacrificial lamb while his eyes gaze over my body, taking in my jean shorts and black T-shirt.

"So, let me help you."

Liam drops down in front of me once I nod in agreement. What a sexy sight, him with his knees planted on the bed. I lick my lips as he crawls toward me.

My heart thrums in my chest. Liam's lips find mine, shutting my brain off and dismissing concerns. This kiss doesn't compare to our previous ones. From the get-go, intensity rolls off him, his lips pushing against mine. Our fingers intertwine as he traps my arms next to my head. Fuck, it feels good.

Liam's tongue licks across my lips, tempting my mouth to open for him. His teeth pull on my bottom lip as he rolls his body into mine. Emotions and sensations cloud my judgment and apprehension. I already screwed our friendship to hell with a simple kiss, so I might as well enjoy the ride.

He releases my hands, now more interested in exploring my body. His rough hands run across my curves. Despite the material separating his calloused fingers from my skin, I feel him everywhere. On my body, in my head, under my skin. There's no dismissing the way he owns me, making my body desperate from a few kisses and touches alone. He lets out a moan when I nip and tug on his bottom lip.

My hands embarrassingly grope him like a horny TSA agent, testing out the corded muscles of his arms and back. *Jacked* doesn't begin to describe him. Taut muscles press against his shirt, tensing wherever my fingers linger.

I pushed him away before, never wanting to look too close, afraid of my own self-control breaking. Everything about our chemistry makes me question my sanity for denying our connection.

Liam's teeth graze my bottom lip before they break away from mine. His lips follow the curve of my neck. I sigh at the sensation of his stubble running against my skin, loving every second of his attention.

Our attraction makes me panic, hoping I didn't ruin anything between us. *Will Liam talk to me tomorrow? Am I ruining something between us?*

Like Liam can sense my doubts, he tugs on my hair and draws me back into the moment. He erases my concerns with his lips. This man kisses me like it may be our last, branding himself, so I never forget him. And God, I'll never.

How did I say no to this for so long? And why?

"I've wanted to kiss you like that for months." Liam's voice strains as he places soft kisses down my neck.

His words seep into my heart and occupy a permanent space, an unwelcome invasion holding me hostage. Silly me for putting feelings where they don't belong. He runs his thumb across my swollen lips, his eyes assessing mine.

He places another quick kiss on my lips, his stubble brushing against my face. "Say you've wanted me just as much?"

My heart squeezes at his vulnerability, catching the way his eyes widen and his eyebrows lower.

I lift my back off the bed and give him a chaste kiss, which shouldn't mean as much as it does. He pulls away, giving me a huge smile that warms my heart.

"You're a hard man to resist. You're easily becoming my weakness." I drag a finger down his chest before I cup his prominent bulge, thick and hard beneath my palm. My body pulses with excitement at touching him. A mischievous smile spreads across my face as he groans, his body responding to my hand rubbing up and down his length. A welcome surge of pride takes over at making him crave me.

"Fuck, that feels so good." His head drops to the crook of my neck. "I'd rather not come from your hand alone." He softly tugs my hand away from his pants. His hands grab the hem of my shirt and pulls it off, chucking it somewhere over his shoulder. My shorts come off next, revealing most of me to him.

"And you wax? Shit." His voice rasps.

"Yup. Makes me feel sexy." Screw waxing myself for a guy. I don't go through that kind of pain for anything but boosting my self-esteem.

"Shit, Sophie, you're my naughty girl." Liam's eyes remain glued to my lavender lace bra.

I mentally high five myself for wearing a fancy bra and matching underwear. His lips return to mine as his hands squeeze my breasts, the lace fabric brushing against my sensitive nipples. My clit throbs at his touch.

Liam pulls away from me. "It's not too late to stop now. We can go back to normal. Are you sure about this?" He catches me by surprise with his *get out of bed free* card.

My throat wells up at his sincerity. Instead of shying away, I tug his lips back to mine, giving in to him and the desire circling around us for months. One of Liam's arms wraps around me and snaps off my bra while the other pulls at my topknot to unleash my hair. He proves himself a man of many multitasking talents.

Our kisses go from intense and needy to soft and sweet.

Almost like unspoken words between us, our kisses say things our brains can't make out. I grind myself against his cock, creating marvelous friction, going from hesitant to begging in a moment. How quickly everything changes.

His lips break away from mine. "We're going to play a game to knock off an item."

"And what are the rules?" My husky voice sounds foreign to my own ears.

Liam presses his bulge into my sensitive area. "No rules except for you to orgasm. You asked to *experience multiple orgasms in one night*." *Oh*. "Let's see how many I can pull from you. I bet three, at least."

I nearly choke on my sharp inhale of air. "Is that even a real thing? I thought that was something movies and books made up."

His lips find the hollow of my neck, trailing kisses across the curve. "I can promise you everything with us is the real thing. Even when you feel like you're seeing stars from me fucking you." His hot breath runs against my skin.

I shake when he brushes a finger down my body to the top of my thong. "Then do your absolute worst. I expect no less from someone who promises so many wicked things. More show, less tell."

His head snaps up at me, a promising grin crossing his face, reaching his eyes. I have no clue where my brazenness comes from, but I'm here for it.

It appears I tempted the demon inside of Liam because he shuts me up with a searing kiss that leaves me breathless and mindless. The kiss kindly tells me to shut the fuck up.

With one last peck on the lips, he rolls out of bed. His knees hit the floor before he grabs my thighs and pulls me toward the end.

His fingers find the edge of my panties and tug them down. Another garment of mine gets lost to the floor of Liam's hotel room, leaving me exposed and waiting for him. He lifts my legs from the bed and lays them over his shoulders.

He leaves a light kiss on the inside of my thigh. "Remind me again what your list said about oral sex?"

"*Come from oral sex?*" My body flames at the reminder of my intimate yet simple request. It's a stupid idea now that Liam kneels before me, looking handsome and oh-so fuckable with my legs parted for him.

Liam kisses my center while his eyes remain glued to mine. My back arches off the bed, embarrassingly so, from the new sensation.

"Let me help you out. Has a man ever eaten you out and worshipped you like the goddamn queen you are?" His husky voice sends a warm feeling up my spine.

I shake my head side to side because words take brainpower, and I tapped out about five kisses ago.

He chuckles, sexy and rough, as hot air brushes against my exposed skin. "I'm more than happy to welcome you to the best night of your life."

No more warnings and no more words as Liam's mouth lowers. And fuck, once his tongue darts out, I'm knocked out mentally while my body thrives. He really knows what to do because my legs shake as they grip onto his shoulders like a lifeline.

My fingers claw at the sheets in search of anything to ground me. A million nerves fire off in my body, buzzing with arousal and excitement at Liam's torment. Never in my life have I experienced something as amazing as this. My toes curl and my core throbs.

Tonight is an essential lesson of distinguishing men from boys. Liam's hands grip my ass, holding me in place as his tongue brands me.

My body disconnects from my brain, entranced by Liam's dedication to his task. His tongue brings my imposing orgasm to life. He looks at me, hitting me with a look of hunger and satisfaction as his lips wrap around my clit. The sight of him, combined with his synergistic torture, pushes me over. He promised I'd be seeing stars, and damn, the universe has never looked or felt so damn good.

My body quakes as he continues lapping at me, never stopping until my body calms once more.

I blink at the ceiling. Liam gives my sensitive area one last kiss before he places my legs back on the edge of the bed. He leaves behind a few kisses on my thighs before rocking back on his heels, leaving me panting and waiting. I prop myself up on my elbows.

Liam sends me a satisfied smile.

I bite on my swollen lip. "I think the list is going to break me."

How can I complete all the items with him when a few set me on fire?

"No. *I'm* going to break you. But I'll put you back together to watch you fall apart all over again around my cock. What fun we'll have together." He gets up and strips out of his jeans, giving me a view of his muscular legs. His hands pull off his shirt. I suck in a breath at the sight of him standing in front of me. Golden skin and ridges of muscle from his traps to his toes greet me, along with his stiff dick pushing against the fabric of his boxer briefs.

Basically, to put it short, Liam is fine as fuck. Screw looking like a Ken doll when he fits the expectations of a G.I. Joe action figure reporting for Operation O.

With two more orgasms to go before he breaks his own bet, I struggle to withhold my enthusiasm. Liam returns to the bed and crawls over my body.

"I've wanted to do this since I saw you in Shanghai." He traces a line of kisses across my collarbone, my skin pebbling when his tongue darts out and traces the delicate bone. Liam's lips never leave my skin, moving onto my breasts. His lips wrap around one nipple while his other hand squeezes and plays with the other. I can die from the happiness and desire flowing inside of me, never doubting his skills again.

Liam's eyes meet mine every so often, his icy-blue gaze resembling a summer storm, brewing with swirls of blue.

I push myself into him because I want more. Liam's tongue runs across the valley of my chest before finding my other pointed nipple. He licks and teases me, bringing me closer to the edge again. His unoccupied hand moves down my stomach.

His fingers pump into me while he teases my breasts, his lips sucking at the soft flesh above my nipple, marking me for no one but him to see. The bite of pain mixed with his steady pumping sets me off again, my brain soaring away from me without a glance back.

He gives me time to come back to the present moment.

"Look at that, you have more than one in you."

This man gives the devil a run for his money. Liam gets up from the bed, opening up the side drawer and pulling out a condom. He pushes his boxer briefs down, revealing his thick cock, looking smooth and ready.

I crawl toward the edge of the bed, my fingers grabbing the package from his hand and ripping the foil. He takes a deep breath as I roll the condom down his shaft. One of my fingers runs up his length once I finish. My knees wobble, but I stay steady.

Liam gets on the bed, tugging me along with him. My head falls against his chest, and his fingers run along the ridges of my spine, his touch searing itself into my memory.

"Ever ridden someone's cock before?" His husky voice rings through the room.

"Nope."

"Now's your turn to show me you want this with us. Make me believe you because I'm afraid you'll walk out that room and avoid me once everything is done." He whispers in my ear before his tongue traces the sensitive skin.

His task weighs between us. He wants to give me control because he doubts my commitment to trying. My heart hammers in my chest, afraid of doing something wrong.

"You're sexy as fuck. Stop doubting yourself." He grabs my hand and presses it against his cock. "Feel that? There's no denying I want you to fuck me. You should be confident in yourself, and in trying this out with us."

My chest tightens at his thoughtfulness to build my confidence. It confuses me. Everything about him sets me off, in good and bad ways, making me uncertain of where to go from here.

I lean into him, pressing my lips against his. My tongue teases his, stealing his groan as my hand runs down his chest. I climb on top of him, kissing him without caution, not giving a damn about something swirling in my chest.

I slowly guide him inside of me, sucking in a sharp breath at the feel of him in this position. My hands press against his chest to stabilize me. Anything to keep me from drifting away, the feel of him overriding every nerve inside of me.

We both sit in silence, our breathing growing heavy as we stare into each other's eyes, officially breaking the last seal of our friendship. There's no going back as his cock fills me, an unforgettable sensation I feel all the way to my toes.

"Fuck, you're so damn tight." He readjusts himself and presses his back up higher against the pillows. His eyes bore into mine, churning with unreadable emotions.

I banish any thought of wanting to know how he feels. Instead, I decide to live in the moment, done with excuses.

I sluggishly rise before pushing down again. "Oh my God."

"Sophie. Shit." His voice strains as his fingers dig into my hips.

His words from earlier about showing him how much I want him run through my mind. I want him so fucking badly. For months I've craved him, despite hiding behind friendship and fears. Stupid to think I could avoid our connection.

He guides me up and down, showing me a tempo that makes my head drop back. "You're so hot. Riding me like you're desperate for my cock. Show me how much you need me."

A tingling sensation runs up my spine as I continue to ride him, instinct taking over. Liam's fingers find my clit, pressing against the sensitive area, helping my orgasm build. I find an amazing rhythm, unable to keep my eyes away from his as I move.

Screw time standing still. It feels like everything rushes by me, with emotions making my chest pinch as I continue to ride Liam's cock. Liam's eyes remain half open, his lids heavy from lust. I love the sight of him at my mercy.

"Let go." His fingers sink into my hipbones, taking control, letting me find my release as he changes the pace.

Everything fades as the pleasure builds inside of me. I moan as I fall apart, giving into temptation and the way he makes me feel: strong, sexy, and so fucking scared.

Liam flips us over, my back sinking into the fluffy comforter as he rams into me. A relentless surge of pleasure takes over my body as he rides through my orgasm.

"You've got one more in you. I've got enough stamina to fuck you until you give me what I want." He brands me with a possessive kiss before moving onto my neck, sucking and nibbling the delicate flesh.

"Yes." I groan and push into his body.

He continues his pace, grabbing a nearby pillow and shoving it under my ass, changing his angle. His dick brushes against my most sensitive place as the pad of his thumb pushes against my clit. The sensation sends heat through my veins as my body pulses with need, the blood rushing through my ears matching my heavy breathing.

"That's it. Give me everything you have. I want it all. Fuck, I want to steal every last thing from you." His words and touch push me over, my eyes closing before he tugs on my hair. My eyes snap back open, catching his soft blue irises and prideful smirk as he watches me detonate.

His pumps become erratic as he drops his head to the side, hitting me with an image of him coming undone. "My beautiful angel. Too wicked for heaven, too good for hell."

I may be his beautiful angel, but he's my masked devil—too naughty for my heart, too irresistible for my body.

Liam's body drops onto mine, our bodies pressing against each other as we regulate our breathing. He holds on to me, not moving, the feel of his hand intertwining with mine bringing a smile to my face. My heart squeezes at the simplest gesture.

If I didn't feel betrayed earlier about my growing feelings toward Liam, this evening sealed the deal.

Seems like I got fucked in more than one way.

CHAPTER TWENTY-THREE

Liam

I spend the week before the Hungarian Grand Prix collaborating with the team, testing my car, working out, and spending time with Sophie. The latter ditched me when her dad asked her to spend a few hours with him.

Jax and I hang out in the McCoy gym. It's an athlete's playground housing all types of equipment, reflex trainers, and the best F1 simulation system. The smell of cleaning supplies and sweat welcomes us as we get a workout in between our packed schedules.

"I've barely seen you all week. You're going to ditch me, leaving me to make friends with Santiago and that silent and brooding asshole from Vitus. You know the guy. He looks like some Michelangelo statue with the personality of one too. Stiff wanker." Jax's muscles flex as he lifts a dumbbell.

I withhold my chuckle. "Well, Noah and Maya aren't a thing. And I've been busy doing my job."

"Those two might as well be. Noah stares after her all the time, and Maya avoids him like he has an STD."

I clutch the weight in my hand. "Eh, I don't know about them. Noah's not one for commitment."

"And what? You're a commitment advocate all of a sudden?"

I shrug, trying to come off more nonchalant than I feel.

"Oh shit, is the mighty Liam thinking about a real relationship? Is the sex that good with your Bandini princess?"

It's easy to forget how effortlessly he reads me. I increase the speed of my reps. "Again, it's not like that. We're just having fun. I don't want to talk about what we do in private with you."

He looks at me stunned. "Since when do you not care to share info about whatever girl you're shagging?"

I grit my teeth together. "Starting now. Stop making a big deal out of nothing."

Jax leans his head against the workout bench, his chest shaking from laughing. "Shit. Relax, I was fucking with you. I wanted to see how serious you are about her, but I guess it's nothing but sex between you two."

My chest tightens. "Did you forget to take your meds today? I forgot if being a total dick was a withdrawal symptom."

He howls from another laugh. Jax doesn't find my low blow the least bit hurtful, pissing me off more. I hate his words because they hit true. I have no idea what the hell I'm doing, with Sophie agreeing to my terms because I'm a selfish shit who wants her and our friendship.

I distract myself with jumping rope. Jax grunts as he switches to the cardio machine. He discards his T-shirt, revealing most of his tattoos. A badass motherfucker, going through that kind of pain for a body full of tattoos.

"And you're not the slightest bit concerned of her wanting more than friendship from you?" His gaze sizes me up.

"No, we added benefits, not vows. Stop being such a shit friend right now, looking to get a rise out of me." I'm glad I never shared Sophie's list with him because he'd give me crap all day about it.

He whistles at me. "All right. I'm sorry. I'll drop it so don't get your knickers in a twist. But just so you know, this will never turn out well."

I shake my head as I wrap up the last set of jumps. "I don't know why you keep making such a huge deal about this thing with Sophie."

He fiddles with the treadmill's buttons. "I'm warning you that you might not like the end result if you don't face your shit."

Guilt sits heavy in my gut at the ramifications of a new contract with McCoy. I never told Jax about Rick's call, afraid to face the truth. But the truth has a funny way of catching up to me whether I like it or not.

Crew members work around the garage, checking on the cars while my engineers talk to me about logistics. I tell them the different issues I found while practicing. People underestimate the amount of time racers spend with the crew, testing out new theories and working through problems. Besides racing and attending parties, I spend a shit ton of time in business meetings.

I crave winning this race. Even though Peter offered me a contract extension, I don't want to feel a false sense of hope since he hasn't gotten back to me about my counteroffer regarding the anti-Sophie clause.

Claudia hasn't attended any other events since the gala where she met Sophie, thank fuck. Her absence helped me repair my relationship with the team and Peter. He seems in better spirits, even going as far as giving me a clap on the back after a McCoy press conference.

Despite Peter's good mood, I won't close myself off from other teams, no matter how much I like McCoy. They need to revisit their deal and come back with a better offer, preferably one that doesn't include giving up someone I care about for racing.

Peter shows up out of nowhere, gracing the garage with his presence. The fancy suit he wears sticks out against the crews' fire suits and headgear. "You've been doing amazing this season, Liam. Place in the top three for us, why don't you?" He grins at me.

"I plan on it." I continue with my pre-race checks, killing an hour before the race. I'm man enough to admit I get pre-race jitters and whatever fucker says different is a liar.

I head on up to my suite, ready to hop into my race gear. My phone buzzes from a new message.

> **Naughty Sophie:** Word on the street is that you do pretty well here. I don't want to inflate your ego any more, but good luck and hope you don't suck too badly.

I laugh as I type out my message.

> **Me:** Want to make a bet?
> **Naughty Sophie:** Those never end well for all parties involved.
> **Me:** Says who?
> **Naughty Sophie:** Says the party of one who loses every time.
> **Me:** This one will end better. If I end up on the podium, you hang around McCoy garage for the German Grand Prix.

Seeing as Peter needs to attend some McCoy board meeting in London that weekend, I don't see his presence being a problem. Chris could give zero fucks about who hangs around his garage as long as I perform my best.

The three dots appear on my screen once before disappearing. Minutes pass and I call it a loss, zipping up my race suit. I can't help wanting Sophie to spend time with me and my family during my home race, a part of me wishing to stake a claim and show her off. Another part of me invites her for the purely selfish reason of being afraid to face my brother alone. Sophie keeps me sane enough to not do something stupid, like avoiding my family while booking them VIP seats far away from the action.

I smile when my phone vibrates against the coffee table.

> **Naughty Sophie:** Sounds like a benefit for you.
> **Me:** No. We both win from a quickie in my suite. You hanging around is an added bonus.

Disappearing dots taunt me. It's a stupid bet to get her to

hang around me instead of the Bandini garage for once. And to be honest, I wouldn't say no to a pre-race fuck.

> **Naughty Sophie:** You need to up the ante if you're going to be sending me messages like that. You get me in all of your McCoy glory if you get P1. I prefer winners.

I beam at her sassy words. She throws me off yet keeps me centered all at once.

> **Me:** We can both be winners if you agree. Podiums and Orgasms. You're turning me into a modern-day poet.
> **Naughty Sophie:** Good luck. I'm leaving before my phone combusts. Bye!

Talking to Sophie puts me in a much better mood. I like hedging bets with her, especially when it breaks up the usual expectations to succeed and place on the podium.

I leave my suite and head back to the pit garage. I situate myself in the cockpit, adjusting my neck brace and steering wheel as the crew pulls me toward my third-place position on the grid. Sophie wants me to place first, which means I have to overtake both Santiago and Noah and keep the lead within seventy laps.

There's a slim chance I can pass Noah, the leader of the race and a damn good defender. But screw it, I'll give viewers quite the show, all for the blonde-haired, green-eyed woman invading my brain every single day.

Lights flash one at a time before they all shut off. My foot pushes against the throttle and my car speeds down the track before I rapidly approach the first turn.

Bandini cars rush in front of me, the two scarlet red vehicles competing against one another. My race car lingers behind them. The front wing of my car nearly brushes against Santiago's as I close the distance between us.

The blur of the crowd flashes by me as our cars pass another lap. My car vibrates as I press down on the accelerator, the rushing sound of the car bringing a smile to my lips. Sweat clings to my suit as we go around the track for the next twenty laps. I keep my P3 position, defending myself against Jax as he hangs behind my car.

"Liam, Noah and Santiago are going to have to pit soon. We have a strategy that can help you win, but you have to trust us. We're going to have you pit three times this race and use soft tires." Chris's voice echoes through my earpiece.

It's a risky move that will give me greater speed than the standard medium tires, but more pit stops mean less control of my overall time. I could still win, but I'd have to race like my car's on fire.

"How certain are you that the crew can complete the stops in under two seconds?"

"I'd give it a fifty-fifty chance." *Shit*.

I clench my gloved hands. "All right. Let's do this."

"Box after this next lap." Chris mutes himself.

My car shudders, the grip of my tires slowly becoming less stable as I continue to drive down the track. After another lap, I pit and my team absolutely smashes it, completing the stop in under one point seven seconds—a new F1 record.

"Nice work, Chris. Good call." I eat up the distance between the Bandini boys and my car, leaving little room for error if they do anything rash. The three of us move in tandem and conduct a beautifully executed turn. Noah and Santiago drive side by side at the next straight, their red paint glossy under the afternoon sun. Their front wings remain parallel to one another as Noah tries to inch up ahead of his teammate.

The next turn approaches quickly. Noah remains concentrated on Santiago and not letting him overtake at the corner to the point that he forgets about me.

I rush by the two of them, leaving them behind in my side mirror. My soft tires push me faster than theirs. The team goes ballistic in my earpiece, screaming as I solidify my first-place spot. I smile at the crowd's roars competing with the rumbling of my engine.

I aggressively hold on to my first-place position because I don't want Bandini to gain confidence. Like an addict, I live for this high, becoming a lifetime junkie for adrenaline.

"Liam, you're an absolute animal today. Good work." Chris congratulates me while I run my last lap.

I lift my fist up into the air the moment I pass the checkered flag. Chris plays one of my favorites as I race down the track once more for a victory lap, the sounds of The Killers' "Mr. Brightside" crooning through my earpiece.

I hope Sophie likes the color gray because she'll look killer in my number. She should blame herself for my plans. After all, I learned from the best.

CHAPTER TWENTY-FOUR

Sophie

Maya and I keep up our tradition of Wine Wednesdays. We sip from white wine a la box, which is a classy affair when paired with our plastic wine glasses, two pounds of fried chicken, and French fries. The whole girls' night wouldn't be complete without a grand finale of Hershey's chocolate.

"This is American dining at its finest." I groan at the best chicken I've had on this side of Europe.

Maya nods along with me. "I only get the best for us."

"What do you think of the wine? I'm getting a good one-year-old vibe here." I swish around the contents in my glass and sniff like I know what to smell for.

She picks up the box and analyzes the contents. "It tastes like a bad hangover in the making. Why did you suggest this anyway? There are way better options."

"I felt like it symbolized being young, dumb, and broke. But now I'm not so sure."

"Except you're not dumb, or even broke for that matter."

I roll my eyes. "Because 8,000 euros will get me really far in life."

She taps her glass to mine. "So, catch me up on everything between you and Liam."

"Besides the fact that we did the dirty?"

Maya faces me. "You've been holding out on me again!"

"You've been busy with your vlog and avoiding Noah, so I didn't want to make it worse for you. But we had sex and I orgasmed multiple times. The whole thing was amazing so I hope my heart doesn't get hurt in the process because that would suck." I tend to suffer from word vomit around Maya.

I take a few sips from my glass of wine while she processes everything. Some people need liquid courage, but I need liquid wisdom because I suck at making decisions lately.

She tilts her head at me. "Why do you think you'll get hurt?"

"Because I did exactly what you warned me about and started liking him for real?"

Maya shakes her head. Her look of pity reminds me how deep I'm falling, proving how I'm no better than any of the other girls Liam's been with. I sympathize with them. Okay, more like everyone except Claudia.

"When did you figure this out?"

I think back to last week after he won the Hungarian Prix. "Probably around the fifth time we had sex. It took everything in me to leave his bed and go back to my hotel room. My heart hurt at the idea of him not caring if I left."

"Oh, no. And did he let you go?"

"No, he cuddles better than a weighted blanket. Snug, warm, and secure." I hug my glass of wine to demonstrate.

"Have you tried to tell him how you feel?"

My eyes narrow at her. "No way in hell because I've learned from Liam's exes of past and present. Claudia was the biggest exposure therapy, showing me exactly what happens to women who fall into Liam's love-nest trap. They become bitter and sad while begging for scraps."

"Well, I know what you need to do." She puts down her wine glass and clasps her hands together.

"Free therapy and wine, what more can I ask for?"

She offers me a small smile. "You need to be yourself and enjoy the time you have together."

"How can you count that as advice? That doesn't exactly help me once it's over."

"You're assuming it may end between you two. What if he feels the same?" Maya looks at me with hopeful brown eyes.

"He doesn't. Liam never fails to voice his love for his career and how busy he gets. There's not a week that goes by when he doesn't mention how little time he has to commit to anything more than a basic intimate relationship. So, all naughty things must come to an end."

Maya laughs into her wine glass. I don't want to ruin our girls' night, so I swallow my feelings and chase them down with wine and chicken tenders.

"Do you understand how disappointed I feel not attending Oktoberfest this year? I'm only young once," I whine.

The German Grand Prix occurs in July, which means my dreams of beers and Liam in a lederhosen outfit are squashed. Liam and Jax chuckle like I'm cheeky and adorable. Maya bounces around the McCoy garage as she prepares to film another vlog interview with Jax. Liam and I stand off to the side so they have space to work, not bothering them with our usual shenanigans.

"You act like I'm not from here. We could go to Oktoberfest whenever." Liam mentions the future casually like we will still be friends. Why does the thought make my heart beat against my chest like a speaker at a techno club?

"But I wanted to go this year. I want to buy an outfit, chug a beer, and drunkenly sing German songs I don't understand."

Liam roars with laughter, causing Maya and Jax's heads to snap in our direction.

His eyes sparkle. "You can always save the outfit for me. Let's buy one today and do a little role play."

I let out a soft laugh. "Cut it out. You're distracting the talent."

"Hey, I'm half the talent around here." His waggled brows and boyish grin add to his allure, hitting me with a sense of dizziness.

"Do you typically lay the charm on this thick? I'm wondering if I'm becoming immune to your advances."

"I don't know, want to test it out?" He brushes his knuckles across my cheeks. "My room tonight. I have another item for us to complete."

Blush moves from my chest to my cheeks, my body blending into my Bandini T-shirt.

"All right, you two. Quiet on the set." Maya's words kill our conversation.

Maya and Jax film the interview. Jax gives an exclusive peek at his McCoy car, minus the secretive steering wheel. Maya asks lots of professional questions while Liam and I watch from the sidelines. Liam tries to distract me multiple times with a few soft kisses, but I push him away once Jax laughs at us. After twenty minutes, Maya wraps up.

"Don't forget about my party tomorrow. Be at my parents' house around 7 p.m." Liam rubs the back of his neck.

"How can we forget. It's the big boy's twenty-ninth birthday celebration." Maya claps her hands together.

Liam tilts his head at Maya. "Yeah. Noah and Santi told me they can't make it because of some exclusive Bandini boy's social event. So, no excuse for you."

"How come I don't get threatened?" I look straight into Liam's eyes.

"It's already a given that you're going. My family won't stop talking about meeting my new friend."

That *F* word is becoming my least favorite. The way my chest pinches at the sound of it reminds me how I really need to get myself in check.

Maya drags me to the pre-race press conference since Santi is on the panel. Liam sits straighter now that I stand in a corner, prompting me to send him a GIF of Leslie Knope fake laughing during a press meeting. I dangle my phone in front and tap the screen to get his attention.

He peeks at his phone while a reporter asks a question to Santi, hiding his laugh behind a cough. I don't know how they spend an hour up there, having question after question hammered at them.

"Noah, you've been fighting to remain at the top of the Championship ranking. Any reason behind some of the slipups? It looks like Liam is catching up to your points."

Maya gives me a heavy dose of side-eye.

Noah rolls his eyes. "Liam's been my competition since we drank juice boxes instead of champagne bottles. So, I'm not surprised he's been closing in on me."

Another reporter jumps in. "Liam, any concerns with this Grand Prix being your home race?"

"Concerns? Not really, no. At least nothing more than the usual pre-race nerves, but I'm confident I can win. I have to watch out for these two, though." He makes a fist before spreading out his fingers and making a soft explosion sound.

I cover my mouth with my hand to muffle my laugh.

"Liam, another one for you. It's been brought to the public's attention that you're dating a woman inside of the F1 organization. How does McCoy feel about you dating someone in the industry after everything that happened with Claudia?"

With everything in me, I resist escaping the room. At least they keep my name out of the question because my dad would murder me before sending my body bag on a flight back to Milan.

"It's not polite to bring up people's exes, so no comment. I would've hoped your mom had taught you better than that."

"How do reporters get these inside stories?" I whisper to Maya.

She lifts her shoulders. "No idea. I mean there's nothing

wrong with dating someone here, but I'm guessing for him it's not a good look."

I swallow back my nerves. The reporter smooths over his comb-over before fidgeting with his mic. A few reporters around him shake their heads, trying to discourage him.

"I'm wondering if McCoy's worried you have an opposing team insider warming your bed."

Earth, I wouldn't mind falling into a sinkhole. I fidget with a loose thread on my shorts, tugging on the strings to hide my shaking fingers.

"I don't need to sleep with someone to do my job well or negotiate a contract. I'm done commenting on these types of questions so leave my personal life out of this." Liam's eyes find mine once I glance up. I don't think he likes what he sees based on how his frown deepens.

I stick it out for the rest of the conference because I don't need to show my embarrassment or guilt. Liam and I aren't serious, so it'll all disappear after the season's over and he finds someone else.

The idea eats away at me as I head to my favorite spot. Liam finds me soon after the conference, knowing my preference for the F1 Corp's deck spot.

"I'm sorry. Thank fuck they didn't say your name." He tucks a stray curl of my hair behind my ear, a sweet gesture I've come to love.

Like. Come to *like*.

"It's okay. That's probably the most action that reporter's gotten all year." I scrunch my nose.

Liam lets out a rare nervous laugh. "Right. But seriously,

you're okay with this?"

"Sure. But we need to be more careful because my dad is already annoyed with me. Eventually you'll get a new contract and I'll go home, and everyone will move on to other stories once the season ends. There'll be no more warming beds for this insider."

He fails to grin, lacking any humor in his eyes, giving me absolutely nothing to go on. I don't want to overthink anything about us because it usually gets me into some sort of trouble. But could Liam want more too? I can't decide between optimism and skepticism.

Hopefulness is like smoke, dissipating at a moment's notice. No matter how hard I clutch onto the idea of Liam and me, there'll always be someone waiting in the shadows, biding their time before ripping away my faith.

I accepted heartbreak the moment Liam threw me on his bed, grinning at me like I was part of his world. Stupid me for adding an invisible item when I handed over my list to Liam.

Get my heart broken.

My heart thumps along with my knuckles as I knock on Liam's hotel room door. He opens up in nothing more than a white towel around his waist with water dripping down the ridges of his abs, tempting my tongue to lick the droplets.

Liam smirks at me as he opens the door wider, giving me room to enter. He grabs the list from a nearby table before I have a chance to make myself at home.

"I've been thinking about this all day." He drags me toward the bedroom, anticipation eating away my nervousness.

My chest feels tight and hot. "I wonder if you're worth the millions they pay you. If only fans knew how much you daydream."

"At least I get to turn my dreams into a reality." He shoots me a dazzling smile before he disappears into his walk-in closet.

"Well. Shit." Yup. At least I got two words out.

Liam comes out of the closet carrying a tie. I walk up to him. He starts to protest, but I brush my index fingers against his mouth.

"Nope. I get to call the shots now." I take my confidence and run with it.

His eyes expand a fraction before his lips tug into a smile and he throws the tie onto the bed. My hands explore the stiff muscles on his stomach, his skin feeling smooth and warm beneath my palms. Liam's chest tremors at my touch. I smile, enjoying the reactions I pull from him.

My hands work to undo his towel, the damp material falling to the carpet with a thud. Liam's dick springs free, tempting me as I run my hand across the smooth flesh. I lick my lips as I lower myself to the ground. The sound of Liam's ragged breathing sends a rush of excitement through me, feeding my courage. He brings out a seductress in me I fail to recognize.

A bead of pre-cum escapes his tip. Liam groans as I lick him, with power coursing through me from making him weak. Men like him don't bend often, but when they do, it's glorious and thrilling.

"Are you going to stare at my dick or suck it?"

I look up at him, finding humor in his eyes as he winks at

me. Our eyes stay connected as I pull him into my mouth. His lips form an *O*, which is all the reinforcement I need to get going. I lick him from base to tip in a zigzag pattern, his salty taste coating my tongue as I switch between sucking and licking.

"Fuck. You have a wicked mouth."

I smile around his dick. He's a man of few yet meaningful words.

One of my hands massages his balls while I suck. I'm addicted to the taste of him and the sounds coming from his mouth, of the labored breaths he lets out when I softly graze my teeth against his shaft. It invigorates me to make someone like Liam helpless to lust.

"Fuck. Do that again."

I tease him with my tongue, keeping to a lazy pace, in no rush to have him come because I enjoy hearing his occasional groans all too much.

Liam is practically panting minutes later. "Sophie, if you don't want me to come in your mouth, stop now. But really, I don't want you to. Just so you know."

I laugh at his warning, my throat vibrating around his dick. Despite never swallowing before, I have no interest in stopping, instead choosing to lock eyes with the man who makes me feel all sorts of emotions.

Liam's last resolve snaps as he takes control. His hand finds my hair and he tugs my head up and down his cock, fucking my mouth with reckless abandon. My eyes prick with tears and I love every second, his desperation for release fueling my willingness to comply. A groan of pleasure escapes his mouth as his head falls back.

His cock twitches as I suck down his release. I welcome it, craving more, high on lust and happiness because I want anything and everything Liam gives me. His fingers let go of my head once he finishes pumping into me.

He pulls me up and kisses me relentlessly, branding me from the inside out, stamping a hot iron to my heart with his initials. And like hot metal, it hurts like a bitch to know I want what I can't have.

Liam gives me no time to collect myself as he pushes me toward the bed. I collapse onto it, enthusiastic and ready for anything. A smug smile crosses his lips as he stares down at me.

I tap my lips with my index finger. "Are you just going to stare at me all night or...?"

His nostrils flare at my taunt. "I'm deciding what item I'm going to knock off first."

"This evening got a whole lot more interesting."

"I know you're an eager woman who wants to mark off many items in a short amount of time. So, I have some plans."

Blood rushes to my ears, my heartbeat posing as a temporary hearing problem. "Should I be embarrassed that it turns me on to hear you talking about plans?"

He lets out the softest laugh. "First, let's get rid of your clothes."

Liam doesn't need to ask me twice. One sandal flies toward a corner of the room while the other lands on the dresser. He chuckles at my enthusiasm but doesn't lift a finger, watching me with crossed arms. My dress goes flying somewhere while my bra and panties find the same fate, lost somewhere in the dark. I lie against the pillows and wait. I'm not exactly sure where I found my confidence, but I'm not opposed to it.

He smiles while shaking his head. "Is someone excited?"

I bob my head up and down. He turns his back toward me as he pulls out something silky from the nightstand.

"Ah, *be blindfolded.* This is exciting," my voice rasps.

"We both know you get just as excited about crossing off items on your list as you do about completing them."

No use disagreeing because I love the idea of knocking off items with Liam. It's our type of foreplay. "I'd like to thank my horny, lonely self for getting drunk and exploring sexy bucket lists at 2 a.m. on a Saturday. My pending orgasms are forever grateful."

"I'm seriously wondering why I didn't buy a gag too."

"Shut up. You love my ramblings."

Ugh, Sophie. Not the L-word again.

Liam's penetrating gaze is the last thing I see before he covers my eyes with the blindfold. If I die today, what a final sight to remember. I'm willing to sacrifice myself for the cause. The search for the best orgasm sounds like an epic way to go, possibly becoming my tombstone statement.

Liam pushes my head back on the pillows. "Senses are a funny thing. You take out two, it heightens the rest." He grabs my wrists and wraps them up with what I assume is the tie he threw on the bed earlier. The knot is tight enough for my hands to not get loose, but not enough to hurt me. Looks like Liam wants to knock out *get tied up*, as well.

I test it once and am met with resistance. "Were you a Boy Scout before? That's one good knot."

"Nope. I preferred the kids' book club."

I sigh. "Only you could make being a member of a book club sound sexy."

He closes the gap, his familiar scent enveloping me. Something makes a metallic clanking noise off to the side before Liam's body slides down mine, tracing the contours of my body with warm kisses. When he reaches the area begging for his attention, I get hit with an ice-cold kiss.

Literally, ice cold.

Damn, I nearly forgot about *Try foreplay with ice.* With any other man, I wouldn't find this sexy, the chilly feeling prompting my ass to lift off the bed. But somehow everything with Liam feels good. Warm fingers reach my aching places, giving way to some relief before his cold tongue finds my clit. It pulses with want as he sucks. His tongue brushes against me, lazily tracing circles.

"Holy shit. Are you for real right now?" My words morph into a moan.

The heat from my body melts the ice cube as Liam licks me with ruthlessness. His tongue is built for sin, running over my entrance before plunging inside of me. Pressure builds within me like a ticking bomb to the beat of my heart. Not being able to see or touch anything makes me attuned to everything else: my breathing, his touch, the coolness where his tongue lingers.

"I'll take that as a good thing." His rumble of a laugh vibrates against my clit, my spine prickling at the pressure swirling inside of me.

"I'm not even jealous of the girls you've been with before. I should send them thank-you cards."

He slaps my core with the palm of his hand. My clit throbs, leaving me a needy mess at the sensation.

"Don't bring anyone up. While you're traveling with us, you're mine. The fucking end. Do you have a problem with that?"

The blindfold blocks me from seeing his face, but the edginess in his voice tells me enough. I struggle to come to terms with his words. They remind me of our expiration date, of him slowly becoming my everything while I'm his temporary distraction. But like with everything, Liam doesn't let me off easy, running the pad of his thumb against my clit, applying the slightest pressure. And like that, he banishes the negative thoughts as he pulls me back into the moment.

"Last time I checked, I blindfolded you, not gagged you. What do you have to say?"

Another brush of his icy tongue has me rising off the bed, leaving me panting for more. His hand holds me down while he waits for an answer.

"Whatever you want. Anything, everything. Past, present, future. Please." I can't think, let alone form the coherent sentences he wants. My hips shimmy and beg for his touch again.

Liam laughs, dismissing his agitation as his tongue plunges inside of me. Calloused hands part my legs more, opening me up to him. The sensations overwhelm me. His hands brush against my thighs, making my skin flush. The blindfold blocks me from seeing him touch me, lick me, fucking own me. He teases me like I'm the best fucking thing, and damn if I don't feel that way around him.

"If these are the benefits friends have, I wish I had signed up months ago."

"I told you, but you're too stubborn." He returns back to his task.

I wouldn't change what we did for the world—our closeness, the way he makes my heart clench and race all at once, the foundation we've built over time. My orgasm rips through me. Shudders course through my body at his caring touch.

My body crashes and burns, simmering down once my high disappears. An ice cube makes a return appearance. Liam trails wet kisses up my stomach, goosebumps breaking out. His tongue traces meaningless lines around my breast before his cold tongue flicks across one of my nipples. My back arches at the touch.

"It's too much." Three breathy words leave my lips in a hoarse whisper.

His mouth pulls away from my nipple. "Want me to stop?" He traces his fingers down my body.

"No! Finish what you started. I didn't peg you for a quitter."

Liam chuckles as he continues his torment on my body. He fails to leave an area untouched, unkissed, or unlicked as he maps out my body like he promised all those months ago. His lips return to mine as he rocks his hard length into me. The smoothness of his dick brushing against my naked center pulls another moan from me, prompting my hips to grind into him.

"Fuck, Sophie. No one knows how naughty you really are behind those braids and dimples. I love the sounds you make. But I especially love knowing they're just for me."

My heart throbs at his use of the *L*-word. I ignore it, afraid to inquire more about his feelings. "Are you a possessive type?" My voice croaks as his fingers grip my waist tightly.

"With you? Yes."

I moan as he rolls his hips into me again. His lips find my neck and he sucks and nibbles on the sensitive area.

I laugh as I shake my head side to side. "Stop. You're going to give me a hickey. I don't want to meet your parents like that."

"Doubt they'd mind." He grazes his teeth against the hollow part and my body shakes at the sensation. I push at him with my body since my hands still remain attached to the headboard, useless when all I want to do is touch him back. His lips pull away from my neck.

His hand cup my cheeks and I smile in the general direction of him.

"You're so beautiful." His simple sentence means the world to me. And it scares me to death, the way his words wrap around my heart and grip onto me.

Liam tugs the blindfold off, revealing his wicked grin. I smile and wiggle my tied-up fingers at him.

He shakes his head side to side. "As much as I'd love your hands all over me, I think tonight will play out differently."

I nod along. With expert agility, Liam flips me over. My head sinks into a pillow before I turn my face and watch him sheath himself with a condom. He settles behind my spread legs. Blood rushes through my body, courtesy of my racing heart. His fingers grip my stomach and lift me onto my knees. My elbows support some of my weight while Liam carries most of it, his hands pressing into my skin.

"Are you ready to fall?"

I freeze, not sure if he means the same thing.

He brushes my hair to the side, hitting me with a stunning smile. "I'm ready to drag you to hell before returning you back to heaven where you belong."

Right. Not the same falling. He kisses the base of my spine, tracing some of the bones with his tongue.

Liam runs the tip of his cock across the seam of my center. "God. Look how sexy you are, waiting for me. Tied up like a present for me to unwrap." He pulls me closer to him, causing the tie to tug against the headboard. My neck turns, giving me a better look at him, his blue eyes finding mine. We remain entranced as he sinks into me. My teeth bite down on my bottom lip to suppress a moan, the feel of him one I have yet to get used to.

Liam groans once he completely sits inside of me, his hands gripping my hips in a stronghold. My heart melts when he leans over and places a kiss on my shoulder. I want to relive this moment on repeat, the look of him tipping his head back as he thrusts in and out of me. His groans mix with my moans of pleasure.

This thing between us isn't only a benefit. It's not some cheap label placed on a growing relationship out of fear of the consequences. Not for me, at least. So, I show him with my body instead of words, giving him every part of me.

One of Liam's hands leaves my hip to wrap around my hair, the blonde strands running through his tight grip. I keep my eyes on him.

"Fuck. You feel so good, Sophie."

Why do things that feel amazing hurt us the most? I don't have time to answer my own question. Liam increases his pace, bringing him and me to the brink of pleasure, my climax exploding along with any last defense I have against him.

CHAPTER TWENTY-FIVE

Liam

My parents are disgustingly in love. They experience a life of daily sex, breakfast in bed, cute nicknames, and lustful looks. It was all very gag-worthy while growing up. Their type of love challenges any movie or book, a nauseating display resulting in me finding them in multiple compromising positions over the years.

I spent a week worrying about bringing Sophie over to their house because my parents can sniff out love like a shark smells blood. They've been curious to meet the girl I've spoken about for months, wondering who captured my attention while helping me stay out of trouble.

They put together a small outdoor birthday party for me in the house I grew up in. In a few days, I turn twenty-nine, which means I'm one year closer to the dirty thirties with Noah. My parents set up a makeshift dance floor because they love to dance together. Thanks to their endless dancing at parties, I was the victim of one too many lessons.

I mingle for a while with some old friends. Jax comes soon after and catches up with my parents, knocking back a beer with my dad while my mom fusses over him and his recent PR disasters. Despite Jax's terrible decisions, my parents treat him like a son. They ignore his public blunders because he'll close himself off like a vault.

Maya and Sophie get to the party last. I'd know, seeing as I scanned the patio every five minutes, waiting for them to arrive.

"Fashionably late. A timeless excuse no one ever questions." Sophie stands on the tips of her toes and gives me an innocent kiss on the cheek. It shouldn't make my heart beat faster in my chest, but it does.

Her curled blonde hair frames her face, ditching her usual braids or messy buns for my special occasion. She dresses up in a light pink cocktail dress with fluffy layers.

I bend over to check out her glitter Vans. "Beautifully late. No excuse needed." I grab her hand and twirl her in a circle, spinning her around as she laughs and the material swirls.

"You flatter me. Give Maya a spin so she doesn't get jealous." Sophie lets go of my hand and pulls away.

I offer an extended hand to Maya, but she smiles while shaking her head side to side. Maya walks off to say hi to a McCoy employee she knows.

"So if this isn't the girl we've heard so much about?" My mom comes up to us with my dad following behind her like the lovesick puppy he is.

Sophie pushes her hair behind her ear. "Hopefully all good things. Although, I wouldn't put it past Liam to say embarrassing stories about me. We get arrested one time..."

My mom's eyebrows shoot up as her head snaps in my direction.

"She's joking. Good God, you actually thought I got arrested? I don't know if I should be insulted. Sophie, these are my parents, Jakob and Lily." I look at my parents.

My dad fights a smile as he tugs Sophie into a hug, shocking us both. "I knew I'd like you from the moment Liam said a girl wouldn't give him the time of day."

Sophie's widened eyes find mine once my dad lets go. "Well, someone had to take a needle and deflate his head. His ego was so inflated I'm surprised he didn't suffer from a brain aneurysm."

My parents both laugh.

I roll my eyes while fighting a grin. "Please ignore her. Sophie's jokes get worse the more nervous she gets."

Sophie hits me with an icy glare I want to kiss away.

"Please don't be nervous. We wish we could spend all night getting to know you, but it's a busy one with everyone coming to visit Liam. Maybe we can spend time with you both before you leave. Liam's always too busy to visit during his breaks, so we need to take advantage." My mom sends me a heavy dose of side-eye.

"I visit when I can. You know, like Christmas?" I try to hide my annoyance.

Sophie's eye bounce between me and my parents. "I heard Christmas in Germany beats every Hallmark movie combined."

"You're always welcome to come and visit. Christmas is

amazing. And don't get me started about New Year's. Our town has a huge firework show to celebrate. Maybe if you come, it would give Liam a reason to stay." My dad's telling glance is enough to set off alarms in my head.

Sophie blinks up at me. "Oh, yeah. Maybe depending on school and if Liam and I…" Her voice trails off as she taps her sneaker nervously.

"Liam's welcome to bring a friend for the holidays." My mom smiles at Sophie.

Fuck, she really is bringing her A-game today. Never in my life have my parents been so obvious.

"Right, his friend. Well, I'm going to go grab drinks to make it through the night. Be right back!" Sophie glides through the backyard, leaving in a rush of pink and glitter.

My dad grins at me. "So, she's nice."

"A real gem, that girl." My mom nods along.

"And you got that in the few minutes you spoke with her? I'm surprised you could speak with all your Cupid-level scheming."

My mom pinches my cheek. "You'll thank me for it later. You used to love coming home for the holidays."

"Yeah, things change." I take a chug of my beer.

My dad excuses himself with a wary glance, leaving me alone with my mom.

She nudges me in the ribs. "Lukas told me you planned a day with him at the track tomorrow."

Blame Sophie and her fake therapy sessions for my bravery. I can't deny my fear of spending time alone with him after years of circling around each other, never talking about Johanna or spending more than the necessary amount of time with him and my nieces.

"My brother duties are long overdue. He's going to love what I planned."

"He told me about it multiple times this week. I haven't heard him sound this excited to spend time with you in a while. And we'll all be there on Sunday to cheer you on. Your dad tried on his old shirt to make sure it fit over his recent weight gain, but I told him beer bodies are still in." She waves at my dad across the patio. His eyes follow her everywhere, still obsessing over her after thirty-one years together.

I lift a brow. "I think you mean dad bods. You know I can send you all new gear."

"We don't like to fuss over those kinds of things, especially if you may not be there for much longer. Any news about next year?"

I'd rank her transition as smooth as driving an F3 car.

"Some news." I leave it simple, not sure if now is a good time to talk about it.

My mom tugs on my earlobe like I'm three years old again. "Spit it out."

"Ay. No need to get physical. McCoy offered me an extension with similar pay." I battle between a smile and a scowl.

"Then why don't you look happy?"

"Because the stipulations include staying away from Sophie." I let out a deep breath, the heavy weight of my secret sitting against my lungs, accompanied by guilt.

My mom looks at me with wide eyes and pursed lips, making soft wrinkles on her face more apparent. "Didn't you tell me she's going to go back to school anyway?"

I don't know what to make of the burn in my chest when I think of Sophie leaving. Spending time with her has kept me sane this season, providing me with a steady friendship and a fuck ton of laughs.

"Right. She is. But…I mean, I don't know. I can't help feeling bad about signing a deal with that type of expectation. Sophie isn't some dirty secret, she's my friend…"

"And more." My mom says it like a statement rather than a question.

"I don't know. Maybe? I have no idea what to make of the feelings I'm experiencing. But Rick hasn't mentioned anything about other teams, so it looks like McCoy or bust for the next season."

"Sounds like you need to speak to your agent and keep an open mind. You still have plenty of races left, so teams can contact you and offer better deals if you hold on a bit longer. McCoy can wait. You're one of the best out there, and you need to remember that. Maybe you need to follow your heart rather than a paycheck." My mom wraps her small arms around me, tugging me in for a hug.

That's the problem. I don't understand my heart enough to follow it blindly.

She goes back to drinking in a corner with my dad, giggling at things he whispers in her ears. Both recently turned sixty and they still act like teenagers.

I stare at Sophie like a creeper across the yard. She dances around with Maya, switching between old eighties dance moves that should be long forgotten. Her terrible running man makes her shoes sparkle under the string lights.

I go up to them and ask Sophie to dance. She looks over at Maya for saving, but her best friend walks off toward Jax, leaving us alone. Next time I see Noah, I need to smack him because Maya's a cool chick who takes our shit with a smile.

"Just so you know, I have two left feet. Seriously. There's a reason I don't dance at the galas."

"All 100 pounds of you can step on my toes. Doubt I'd feel it."

"One: I love pasta way too much to weigh 100 pounds. And two: you asked for it." She grabs my stretched-out hand.

A familiar buzz runs through me as I grip her hand. It's unlike anything I've experienced before, accompanied by a constant itch to be near Sophie. I wrap my other arm around her. She doesn't take me up on my offer to step on my feet, but she lets me lead her around the dance floor. We sway to the melody playing from the speakers.

"You're not too terrible. Maybe you had bad dance partners, kind of like with everything else."

Sophie looks up at me. "Don't tell my dad that. He thinks he's got moves like Michael Jackson."

I surprise her with a turn. She releases a throaty laugh that hits my dick at the same time. It's how things are between us, with her turning me on at the simplest things, cursing me with a permanent semi around her.

I'm not surprised when my mom changes the song to Coldplay's "Yellow." My parents like to meddle because they think life is all one big movie, with happy endings and fairy-tale stories. Sophie's head tilts up at me when she recognizes the lyrics. I shrug because I didn't pick a perfect song about stars, love, and a color that reminds me of her and that damn bikini she wore all those months ago in Monaco. My mom clearly listens to my stories a little too closely.

I pull her in closer, prompting her to lean her head on my chest.

"This isn't how the young ones dance at parties." She stifles her laugh.

"Keep cracking jokes about my age. You won't like what happens."

"Will you hold good on the threat? Because I bought you a birthday present that may or may not include a subscription to a life-alert necklace."

I chuckle into her hair, taking in a fresh inhale of her coconut shampoo. "When a clumsy person buys you a necklace about falling over…"

We break away from one another after a few songs. She scurries away toward Maya, claiming she needs to tell her something. Soon after, my parents bring out a ridiculous cake with a photo of me aged about thirty years. Sophie cackles at the sight and mouths something about my life-alert present.

I stand behind the table with no one by my side. For the first time, I notice how empty it feels, unlike my brother who has his kids or my parents who have each other. It pisses me off how my gloomy thoughts color my mood, awareness running through me at how isolated I've made myself over the years. Instead of feeling proud of being untouchable, it fills me with disappointment.

My eyes connect with the one person who ripped at my mental walls. Her green eyes assess me, reading me like no other.

Everyone sings "Happy Birthday," but I remain enthralled

by Sophie. I find it difficult to ignore the growing sense of guilt at hiding McCoy's deal from her. After my parents sing their German rendition, I blow out the candles and make a wish about my contract. I regret it a second later. I'm pathetic to wish for something minuscule and small in the grand scheme of things. Some people wish for love or good health, but selfish fucks like me wish for better career choices because I dislike choosing between two things I want.

I can't help resenting part of myself. Here I am getting older, and I'm still as self-centered as ever. But I can't change the course of my life no matter how much I want to.

And man, I'm really starting to want to.

I wake up the next morning to my dad cooking breakfast. We chat, catching up on the past few weeks since our last call.

"Son, I don't mean to pry about the girl."

"Of course, you do. I'm shocked you lasted five minutes without bringing her up."

He runs a hand through his blonde hair, looking like an older version of me, except he ditched the short beard about ten years ago. "What the hell are you waiting for with Sophie? Girls like her don't come around often."

"We're just friends." I clench my teeth together.

"Right. Who believes that lie more? You or her?" A smile tugs at my dad's lips.

I don't like his level of insight into my problem. He passes me a plate of food before leaning against the counter.

"It's not a lie. We're friends who happen to hook up on the side exclusively. There's nothing more to it. I took her out on a double date, and she slapped a label on it when the night was over."

"You're that bad of a date, huh?" My dad's chest shakes from laughing.

"No. It looks like my reputation and the standards I set with women precede me. So, we've ended up doing everything as friends."

"And how's that working out for you?"

"We upped the relationship to friends with benefits a month ago." No use withholding information when he used to be an absolute asshole back in his day before he met my mom.

"You know, that has to be the stupidest decision I've heard you make."

My eyes narrow at him. "Gee, thanks."

"Let me give you some advice. This thing with Sophie may happen once in your life. If you keep burying your shit deep inside of you, then you'll have to deal with her leaving you in the end. For your own good, you need to let go of the negativity you have about your brother and Johanna. If you don't, you're going to be so stuck living in the past that you won't be able to see your future. I watched how you and Sophie look at and act around each other. I sure don't act like that around my friends. Your mother would hang me by the balls like a Christmas tree decoration if I did. So you need to ask yourself if you can deal with her walking away."

"Who says she will?"

"You accept that contract with McCoy, and you might as

well pay for her flight back home."

"Ma told you?"

He tilts his head at me. "You bet she did." Leave it to my mom to tell my dad about Rick's deal. They're tight like that, never having a secret between them.

I ignore the way my throat closes up. "I think they'll agree to my exclusion of the Bandini clause. It's ridiculous and archaic."

"And if they don't?"

"I don't know…"

"Your mom's supportive of your career and the decisions you make. But I think you're a fucking idiot if you agree to a stupid term like that."

My lungs burn at the thought of losing everything I've labored over for decades. Ever since I was a young kid, karting at three years old before moving up the Formula phases. It's all I've known. Can I really risk my livelihood for another person, despite how she makes me feel, whether it's lust or love?

Lukas shows up at the track at 10 a.m., ready to spend some bro time together. I'm not sure who was more shocked about the invitation, him or me. Since I keep my visits to Germany short, I rarely spend one-on-one time with him and his two little minions, Kaia and Elyse.

I ignore the sharp pain in my chest at the sight of them, happy and laughing while my brother chases them down the pit lane.

I hate to think I was wrong all this time, putting my brother in a category of widowed and depressed when he really was coping the best he could. In other words, I'm scared to admit I've been a shitty brother who distanced myself to save me from the pain of our past. Admitting I'm a coward doesn't sit well with me.

Sophie's words of wisdom bounce around my head, accompanied by self-doubt. Maybe she was right after all when she told me the only person losing from my lies is myself.

My nieces run around the garage, blonde ponytails bobbing while they pick up random tools. They don't listen for shit. It reminds me of Lukas and myself, getting into trouble during our younger days.

"The sitter couldn't come and help today so I don't have anyone to watch the girls if we go out on the track." He chases after his mini-monsters and wraps an arm around each of them, securing their tiny bodies to his side.

I planned for us to race two older F1 cars. Lukas loved karting when we were younger, and he remains an avid fan of my racing career despite my crappy evading techniques. A lack of a sitter throws a kink in my plan. The McCoy crew can't watch two kids below the age of five because it's a safety hazard and all.

I text the next best thing, knowing she'll save my ass. A few minutes later, Sophie barrels into the pit garage, rocking a *beers not tears* shirt with ripped jeans and Nikes. Her blonde hair hangs loosely around her, layers framing her flushed face. Stunning without trying.

God, I need to get a handle on myself.

"I heard someone needs a babysitter." She drops a huge bag on the garage floor. A few loose crayons and snacks roll out.

My brother glares at Sophie. "What qualifications do you have with kids?"

I run a palm down my face at my brother's formalities because his touch with females is long gone. "Would it kill you to start with a 'Hi, who are you?'"

Sophie takes his gruff attitude with grace. "Besides the fact that I'm cool and am two feet taller than them? Nothing. But I think the kids will love me."

Her personality brings a grin to my face.

"Oh, and I brought snacks because I know bribes work well." She flashes me a telling smile.

I laugh. Kaia eyes Sophie curiously while Elyse goes up to her and runs a chubby hand across the ripped holes in Sophie's jeans.

"You have holes. Are you homeless? We take her home, Daddy?"

My eyes widen. Not hard to guess where Elyse gets her bluntness from.

Sophie lets out a cackle. "No, tiny human. It's called fashion. And what about you?" Sophie kneels next to Kaia on the floor. Elyse follows behind, staring with wide eyes.

"*Prinzessin* Rapunzel?"

I erupt from laughter at Kaia's question. Since I've been a grade-A dick with my nieces, I forgot how funny and honest kids are.

"It doesn't take a genius to guess what she said." Sophie smiles.

"*Sie spricht kein Deutsch*" I shake my head at Kaia who switches to English as she talks to Elyse. Sophie looks at me with wonder, and I can't help smiling at her.

"I haven't heard you speak German before."

I raise my brows. "You think it's sexy?"

"I refuse to answer that." She hides her laugh with a cough before addressing the kids. "Anyway, I'm not Rapunzel but we can watch her on YouTube. Your daddy is going to go have some fun while we hang out together. Don't tell him, but we're going to have a better time."

Kaia and Elyse each grab one of Sophie's hands and they spread out on the McCoy floor, no longer paying us any attention.

I can't help the way my heart clenches at watching Sophie with my nieces. An unsolicited image of her hanging out with a kid who looks like me flashes through my mind. It's a complete mindfuck out of nowhere. Since I don't know what the hell to make of it, I pretend the thought never happened.

Seems easier than admitting I'm growing attached to Sophie.

I show my brother the two cars I picked out for us to drive, leaving behind Sophie and the girls, wanting to put some distance between us.

Lukas runs a hand across the glossy paint, smiling at the attendant who passes him the flame-retardant gear and a helmet. "I'm surprised you invited me here. You've been so busy over the past two years; I didn't think you'd have time."

"I thought some sibling time was overdue. It's been a long time." I take a good look at my brother, facing him head-on for the first time in too long. Lukas looks healthy, his eyes no longer sunken in or his skin uncharacteristically pale. His smiles reach his eyes. They have a sheen to them I haven't seen in some time, no longer plagued with the hauntings of his past.

I'm envious of him. For the first time, I'm the one being held back while he moves forward in life. It's a sick cosmic joke.

"I miss you. You can call me every now and then, you know?

It's not like I do much besides work and take care of the girls."

Guilt scratches away at my nonchalance. "I should. I've been an idiot, and I'm sorry."

"No need for apologies. Just be better. You've skipped out on Kaia's birthday for the past two years and it's so obvious to everyone why you do it. I'm not mad at you, I'm just concerned."

"I'm fine. You and our parents always worry, but I love my life."

"That's good. I sure hope you do with all the sacrifices you make. I don't know how you handle all the traveling and snooty people. You couldn't pay me enough to trade in my family and my home because life on the road sounds like my personal hell."

I hate the way his words pick at my doubts. Seeing as I've done enough self-reflection this season to last me a lifetime, I brush aside his comments. "Why don't you stop talking and hop in the cockpit? I'll show you how great life is behind the wheel."

"Let's go, hotshot. You always did talk a big game."

"At least I back it up with trophies." I shoot him a goofy grin.

We both hop into our cars. I show Lukas how it feels to live my life, how the adrenaline high I chase beats nothing else.

I can't help questioning my life choices while driving around the track. The kernel of something growing in my chest is tough to ignore. Lukas commenting on my life on the road adds to my rising distress about my contract next year.

It's difficult to fight the urge I have to return to the pit, hug Sophie, and save her all for myself. I want to seal us off from the world and the screwed-up people in it trying to keep us apart. How the hell am I supposed to pretend I don't want to keep her after the season and not let her go back to Milan?

And damn if that thought doesn't scare me more than anything else.

CHAPTER TWENTY-SIX

Sophie

never spent time hanging out with little kids. Being an only child limited my exposure to their endless ideas and unfiltered mouths. Babysitting Liam's nieces taught me how I freaking love kids, which was a total mindfuck out of nowhere.

No, I don't have baby fever. But I love talking to them while coloring on the cement floor of the McCoy garage. We spend an hour together while Liam and Lukas race around the track.

They draw me pictures of their house. Elyse colors a ten-thousand-square-foot addition in the backyard for me (*pool and convertible included*) while Kaia draws a picture of me and her dad with a heart (*sorry little lady, I have the hots for your uncle*). They share stories about their mom (*I shed a tear or ten for them*) and how their dad makes the best mac and cheese (*who knew Kraft could be considered gourmet*). In an hour, these two blonde babies captured my heart and attention. Time flies by and I love every second of it.

I draw each of them a portrait to take home. Coloring opened them up to me, allowing them to tell me stories, both good and bad. An idea hits me to research more about art and kids once I head back to my hotel room later.

Kaia and Elyse look sad when their dad shows up with *Onkel Niam*.

"I should feel insulted at their frowns. Turns out you're pretty good with kids after all." Lukas shakes his head in disbelief.

"I know my beer shirt doesn't portray me in the best light, but Liam gave me no time to change. Honestly, I loved them so much that I'd offer you money to keep them for a week, but I'm broke." I already checked my bank account. A few shopping trips with Maya and booking a trip to Bora Bora sucked up the last bit of money I made during my strip poker night.

"Will you work for beer because this can be arranged?" Lukas smiles at me.

Liam smacks him across the back of his head. "Quit flirting with my girl."

Two words make my heart clench. *My girl.*

Lukas looks at me sheepishly, a blush creeping up his neck. "Well…you can join us for whatever else Liam has planned." He offers an invite before Liam says anything.

Liam shoots me a toothy grin that reaches his eyes. "What a good idea. I think Sophie will *love* what I planned next."

Liam leads us out of the garage, telling us about his race day for the kids. He traded F1 cars for karts, which look like they came straight from a Mario Kart game, costumes included. My heart can't catch a break as his nieces hug each of his legs.

Liam grabs a Bowser onesie while Lukas picks a Mario costume minus the mustache. I choose the green Yoshi onesie because both girls eye the Princess Peach and Daisy costumes, not that they'd fit my body anyway.

"Baby Zanders. What are the rules?" Liam gets into character, looking ridiculous yet amazing all at once.

I really like him. Like really, *really* like him.

"Have fun!" Kaia claps her hands. Liam holds up a finger, waiting for the other two answers.

"No hitting each other." Another finger in the air when Elyse answers.

"And *Onkel* Niam no win." Kaia raises her chubby fist.

Kaia officially became my favorite, repeating the rule I whispered in her ear a few minutes ago. What a quick learner. Liam glares at me as I hold back a laugh. He lifts a finger, conveniently flashing me the middle one. I curl over from escaped giggles.

He lets out his own rough laugh. "Last one."

"Watch out for bananas and smells." Elyse can't pronounce her *sh* sound clearly yet.

Liam set up the track with a crew from McCoy throwing fake shells and bananas at the adults' karts like a real game. Where he found the time to plan all of this beats me. Words can't describe how proud I am of him trying with them.

We each hop in our karts and give Elyse a head start. Lukas has a special kid carrier for Kaia since she's still too young for racing on her own. Liam and Lukas declare a rematch after Liam won the F1 car round, proposing whoever wins buys a round of beers.

Our karts take off down the track, rumbling and chugging along. I somehow get in front of Liam and fling a banana peel in his way. He narrowly misses. His laugh can be heard over the vrooming sound of the tiny engine in my kart, his deep rumble running against my spine in a caress.

"You're going to have to try better than that. You throw like a girl." His voice carries loud and clear despite the muffling of his helmet.

I push down on the pedal hard, my height not exactly giving me an advantage here.

"Told you I could get you a booster seat." He drives next to me.

"Over my dead body would I use a booster seat."

"Then enjoy being in last place." Liam pushes down on his accelerator and surges past me.

We go around and around the track, avoiding banana peels and shells. The girls enjoy themselves, with Kaia tossing peels and Elyse driving through grass patches.

Turns out Elyse, the little cherub, gets the checkered flag much to Lukas's shock. We may have the very first female F1 racer here.

Liam carries his niece on his shoulder, tugging at every single heartstring inside of me like a pull-apart piñata. Weeks ago, he told me how he and Kaia have never been close. I would have never believed it. Seriously, I can't breathe at the sight of him tickling her and throwing her up in the air. Kids are amazing and forgiving because the two baby Zanders accept Liam wholeheartedly.

Lukas grabs the hand of his tiny clone and leads us toward the podium where Liam hopes to place first on Sunday.

This time, Liam trades champagne for sparkling apple juice.

The girls get showered in the sticky substance while Liam and Lukas dance around them to a Disney song. I keep a safe distance away until Liam drags me onto the stage and sprays a fresh bottle on me, liquid spraying on my face and body. The sickly sweet smell invades my nose.

Liam gets down on one knee and chugs straight from the bottle.

"You look ridiculous." I fail at holding back my smile.

He pulls the bottle away from his lips. "Well, I'd prefer you on your knees, but I'll compromise."

I release a loud laugh. "You can't talk like that in front of kids."

Liam glances over at Lukas washing the girls down with a hose. "Seeing as they're about to knock out from a sugar high, I think we are safe. Plus, I can't help myself, with what you stir up inside of me."

"Erections don't count."

"God, I love your mouth." He shoots me a smile that has my knees shaking.

Somewhere between Shanghai and Germany, this happy yet noncommittal man wrapped his hands around my heart and owned me. I memorize his every detail, from the hidden scar at his hairline to the razor cut he got on his neck yesterday from a fresh blade.

I love him from his head to his toes. For his quick wit, boyish charm, and back scratches in the middle of the night. Our story fits a tragedy. It's ironic how, while exploring myself and learning who I am, I discovered someone else who brought out the absolute best and the downright worst in me. Falling in love is ugly like that.

And damn if ours turns out to be the ugliest of them all.

CHAPTER TWENTY-SEVEN

Sophie

"I never pegged you as a narcissist, but now I'm second-guessing myself." I stare at the custom shirt Liam had made for me with his number and name.

"What gave me away? My stiff cock at seeing you wear my name or how I fucked you in front of a mirror this morning?"

"Here I was thinking you were staring at me in the mirror." My cheeks sear at the memory of Liam pulling me into his suite bathroom, claiming we needed to cross off *try mirror sex* from our list. *Our* list like we made it together.

Never in a million years would I have thought mirror sex could be one of the most erotic experiences of my life. Leave it to Liam to tear down all my beliefs, challenging my expectations at every turn. He does it so well with everything else in my life.

"I couldn't take my eyes off you, let alone check myself out..

But we can go for round two and give me some equal attention. What do you think?" He tugs me in for a kiss. We stand in an empty hall next to his suite, no onlookers present for our display of affection. Or lust.

Does affection imply loving feelings Liam lacks for me?

"You two can't keep to your respectable room? I want to hear about your sex life almost as much as I want to hear about the latest stock market updates." Jax's voice reverberates off the walls.

I break apart from Liam, putting a good foot of distance between us.

Liam winks at me. "Is that a challenge? I can make the Dow sound sexy as fuck too."

"You've stooped to new lows. The pit called us down, so let's get a move on, mate."

"Duty calls." Liam brushes his lips against my temple before we go down the stairs toward the garage.

"You're hanging with my fam. Hope you can handle them because they tend to be a lively bunch." Liam's eyes shine, looking lighter than ever at the mention of his family.

"What's the worst that can happen?" I fight down the nerves clawing at my chest. His parents are kind, but it doesn't mean I'm not scared to spend a couple hours alone with them.

"Besides the fact that they'll become as obsessed with you as I am? I'm guessing by the 30th lap, they'll offer you a home and a car if you move to Germany."

"I'd say yes to a BMW convertible."

Liam covers my mouth. "We don't speak of that company here. McCoy or bust."

I shrug once he drops his hand. "Guess Germany's not in my cards then."

He laughs as he drags me toward his waiting family. With a quick goodbye, the crew shuffles him and his car toward the track.

"So, Sophie, we've heard so much about you. We didn't have a chance to chat much at Liam's birthday party with him hogging you." His mother, a strikingly beautiful woman with hair rivaling gold, tilts her head at me.

"He tends to monopolize my time." Isn't that the truth. Liam prefers to spend his free time with me or in me.

"We see. He sends us pictures of his new friend. We loved the one of you two in Paris." Her smile fails to warm the chill running through my blood.

Stupid *F*-word. I hate myself for labeling us because it looks like Liam describes our relationship the same with his family. Seeing as I came up with the stupid plan, I don't have a right to be sad. Instead, I take whatever he gives me, willing to live in the moment and suffer the consequences later.

Look at me living life on the edge.

"Yup. We get along well." *I'm so awkward.*

Liam's dad walks over to us, leaving his grandkids painting on the floor. I'd totally trade spots with them. "Funny, I was friends with his mother before we dated."

I see what Liam meant. These two play matchmakers better than the producers on *Bachelor in Paradise*.

"How nice. What happened?" Call me curious to find out how they got out of the friend-zone. Not for my own personal research, per se.

"His father pulled his head out of his ass after I went on a date with another man. He showed up at the restaurant, drenched after standing in the rain watching us. Best date crasher ever." Liam's mom smiles at her husband.

Looks like I'm out of luck, seeing as I already went on multiple dates with John. Liam's head still remains very much implanted where the sun doesn't shine.

"She went on a date with a total douche from a neighboring small town. He sat and sipped his wine like an idiot while I professed my love, not once fighting for her. Further proof he wasn't worthy." Liam's dad grins at me.

I cover my mouth to suppress my laugh. "And then what happened?"

Liam's mom shares a smile that reaches her gray eyes. "We ran off into the rain and never looked back. We got married a year later and had Lukas ten months after. The rest is history."

"Wow, quite the story." I wish I could generate more words but watching them smile at each other hurts my heart as much as my head. A dull throb makes its way through my body. Stupid me for choosing someone with a history of collecting hearts like trophies.

"But less about our story. Tell us about you. What are you going to do in a few months when the season ends?" His mom gives me her full attention.

Besides eating my weight in ice cream after your son shatters my heart? "I'm finishing up my degree, so I'll probably continue my classes."

"And you're studying accounting? How interesting." His dad shoots me a weak smile.

I grimace. "About as interesting as talking about it."

They both laugh at my half joke, half truth.

His mom shows me a genuine smile. "We hear you like art. Any plans with pursuing that on the side?"

"To be honest, I recently got back into painting and drawing. Thanks to Liam, actually."

"Our son has a soft heart and can be thoughtful, even though that's not what the media says about him. He wants the best for people despite his poor executions lately," his dad chimes in.

"Bad decisions are expected in a sport where racers make a living off rash choices. We can't fault him for the habit spilling over into the rest of his life," his mother adds.

Kind of like an impulsive decision of sleeping together despite how it'll ruin our friendship? Sounds about right.

Our conversation continues until sportscasters announce the start of the race. We all watch together inside of the garage, the kids going crazy as Liam speeds around the track. Their screams bounce off the pit walls. His car zooms across the pavement, a blur of gray and black as he holds on to his second-place position.

A home race tends to be a big deal. German fans come in droves, decked out in McCoy gear, flags, and posters with Liam's name on them. Liam has a lot of pressure to perform well, and he does so, holding on to his second-place position throughout the first ten laps. His car inches up on Noah's and leaves little room for error. Screeching tires ring through the overhead televisions as cars run down the straights, with Liam's gray car rushing at high speeds.

I barely pay attention to Bandini's rankings. For once, I want the opposing team to win. This is an important race for Liam, with him needing to prove himself to his German fans and McCoy.

Blurs of colors pass as Bandini and McCoy compete against one another. The crew prep for Liam's pit stop, with the mechanics running around carrying spare parts and wheels. Adrenaline courses through me at the prospect of Liam winning. He flies through another lap, clocking in the fastest time yet.

Liam rides Noah's tail as they race through the track. My body pulses with energy, wishing the best for Bandini while wanting Liam to overtake Noah. The two of them, a haze of red and gray, fight for first place.

Liam's car hums as he takes down the track. With a few laps left, Liam's window of opportunity to overtake Noah is closing. Noah hits top speeds as he drives through the narrow straits of the German track. McCoy's vehicle is best equipped for sharp turns, which makes Noah vulnerable during the next curvy section of the track.

Liam presses on the accelerator early during one of the turns and his car inches ahead of Noah's. He pushes past Noah before cutting in front of him. The move closes Bandini off from the first-place position. Liam's family and I go wild, jumping around as the pit crew whistles and claps.

Liam expertly defends his position against Noah for the final two laps. He passes the finish line, clocking in the fastest lap and the German Grand Prix winner title in one go.

"We're so proud of him. That's our baby boy." His mom pulls me in for a hug. I still in her arms, not used to this type of affection.

Liam's family beams, their smiles bright and their eyes shining as they watch Liam complete his victory lap. They pull me in for a group hug. I'm not accustomed to such a large family unit, but I can't help loving how it feels to be welcomed and included.

The whole Zander experience is another chip at my heart. I accept their affection because, why not, I'm already committed to seeing this through straight to my demise. There's nothing quite like pairing heartache with unattainable wishes. If my relationship with Liam wasn't torture enough, he had to add a sweet family into the mix.

Well, damn. I really screwed myself over this time.

CHAPTER TWENTY-EIGHT

Liam

R ick and I set up a meeting in Brazil to discuss logistics and offers because I rarely hear from him nowadays. It's been weeks since he called me on my birthday. His job keeps him busy as he handles me and a few other clients, instead preferring to discuss contracts once we could meet in person.

We sit together in a McCoy conference room. He scatters papers around the table, some with Excel sheets and others with transcripts of his conversations with other teams.

"Any word on McCoy's thoughts about my counteroffer?"

"He's willing to look past you associating with any Bandini workers."

I only care about one Bandini woman. "And Sophie?"

"He doesn't seem happy about that relationship. There's no guarantee it won't go badly between you both, and I don't think that's a risk he wants to take. He's offering you a ton of money. A higher salary than your previous contract."

"I'll have to think out how to approach this deal. Maybe I accept less money for Peter to drop the Sophie thing? Money always talks."

Rick sighs. "I'd advise you against that, but if you tell me the amount, I can talk to Peter."

"He's not going to get pissy because this is taking so long?"

"These types of deals usually last months. I won't lie to you, your deal has lasted longer than I'm used to, but you're a big deal. The best, right up there with Noah."

"Thanks." I run a nervous palm through my hair. "What about other teams?"

"You received some offers from lower teams, like Albrecht and Sauvage. Due to their smaller budgets, they can't offer anything over eight million."

"Shit, that's less than half of what I make with McCoy." Even though I keep my finances in line by investing rather than overspending, I don't want to compromise millions of dollars and a stellar car.

Rick's jaw clenches. "Unfortunately so."

"And the best of the rest? I don't see any mention of them." I stare into Rick's dark eyes.

He checks the time on his phone. "I really haven't received much word."

"So just McCoy and these two?" The lack of offers hits me harder than I expected. But I get it, with my poor decisions, I'm a risky bet for next year.

"Yeah. And you know which I think is best."

Of course, he does. Who wouldn't like a nice bonus paycheck for brokering a deal with McCoy?

"I'll have to give it some thought." I rub my chin. "I'll reach out to my accountant and get back to you on the price-drop counteroffer."

"We're lucky Peter McCoy is a patient man who's sure you'll accept a deal."

"Peter's patience looks a lot like assholery, but to each their own. I don't know how I feel about a contract offer clearly stating how I need to avoid public relations with Sophie or any other Bandini representative."

Rick gives me a half-assed shrug of his shoulders. "Well, everyone except Noah."

"That's not exactly the issue, and you know it."

"Listen, I want what's best for you. *You*, not my bank account. Shitty cars from the lowest teams don't make World Champions. You'd be kissing your career goodbye."

"Then let's hope Peter accepts my next offer."

He glances at his spreadsheet. "With these crappy offers from other teams, the decision shouldn't be this hard. Get your head in the game, and I'm not talking about the one in your pants. You've spent years climbing up to the top. Sophie may be a good time for the season, but it's only that. For a season."

Rick dismisses himself, claiming he needs to meet with Peter and Chris. I ask if he needs me to join, but he says my time is better spent elsewhere. I couldn't agree more. Meetings and talking shop bore the hell out of me.

I visit my Bandini princess in her motorhome fortress. She hangs out with Maya, who busies herself with prepping for an interview with Sophie's dad. The man looks at me like he can't make up his mind about my intentions, his green eyes following every step I take. Her dad wears a Bandini polo showing off arm muscles that seem like they can knock me out with one punch. He takes my offered hand and shakes it, giving it a warning squeeze before letting go.

"Look who it is. Just in time to keep me from hearing my dad lull me to sleep with his pit talk." Sophie gives me a quick hug. She rocks braids, jean shorts, and a T-shirt that talks about wearing pink on Wednesdays. Damn I love how she dresses.

I don't know where to put my hands with her dad staring at me like I want to kidnap his child. "I heard you needed saving."

Maya looks pointedly at Sophie while rubbing her heart. "Some people appreciate F1. And to think you claim yourself as a fan. You should be revoked of your princess title."

"I raised a warrior, not a princess. She can protect herself." Her dad eyes me instead of his daughter.

"Claims the man who made me wear space buns instead of braids like every other normal girl at school. I distinctly remember how you threatened to take away a girl's glitter lunchbox after she made fun of my hair. Sounds like protecting to me." Sophie misses every unspoken word her dad sends my way, from his clenched fists to the death stare he shoots me like he knows exactly how attracted I am to his daughter.

I shake off the bad feeling and steal Sophie away, the unwavering sensation of James Mitchell's eyes following me with each step I take out of the Bandini garage.

I lead Sophie to the Wrangler I rented, ready to knock off one of her last items. She put it off for long enough and I can't enable her anymore because I prefer to get shit done. Somehow, we crossed off most of her list over the past two months, holding off on a few more because of our limited free time.

"Where are we going?" She buckles her seatbelt.

"I've decided to keep it a surprise until we get there."

Sophie eyes me cautiously but accepts my demand. I drive us through the city as we share the aux cord like a functional couple. She declares my music taste worthy, and I let her play her pop songs.

"Okay. I'm about to hit you with a song that, if you don't know the lyrics, makes me question if we can be a thing anymore."

"Just like that? I didn't think you could be cold, cutting me off like that."

"Don't hate the music player…" She presses play and Mario's "Let Me Love You" streams through the car speakers. Of course, I know this song. Lyrics pour from her lips as she watches Sao Paolo pass us, trees and city streets flying by in a blur of colors.

All I can do is watch her. The way her eyes close and her body moves to the music, not giving a damn if I know the lyrics or not. I join in after a minute because I don't want to disappoint her. We laugh together when she uses her phone as a fake microphone.

While driving down the street, doing absolutely nothing, the realization hits me that I need to spend more time with her. Our time is coming to an end and I have no idea where life will take me. I'm a fucking idiot for not making Rick push McCoy harder about my stipulation.

Fuck, I'm a coward for not talking to Peter myself and laying down the law. I need to handle this situation ASAP before it's too late.

Sophie continues playing songs until I pull the car into the parking lot. I hop out of my seat and go around to her door, opening it for her.

"Oh, no." She clutches onto her seatbelt like a lifeline.

"You only have a few more items. I'll be there for you the whole time." I lean over and unbuckle her seatbelt.

"I'm scared."

"So am I." My honesty sobers her.

Sophie grumbles nonsense while getting out of the car. We walk into a warehouse hand-in-hand because I'm afraid she'll make a run for it.

A secretary greets us. "Welcome to São Paulo Skydiving. We are so appreciative that you decided to fly with us today, Mr. Zander. We're huge fans here. Your plane is waiting, and the trainers are ready to start orientation." She hands us our papers.

Sophie trudges behind me. "I really hate you right now."

"There's a fine line between love and hate."

"There's also a fine line between sanity and insanity. Guess which side you're on."

I laugh as I grab her hand and pull her close. "Just a few more items and then you're all done." It's hard to disregard the way my chest throbs at the notion.

She sticks her chin out and rolls her shoulders back. "We can do this. People skydive all the time."

"That's my girl, fearless after ten pep talks."

We go through the orientation and get set up in our gear. Our plane rushes down the runway, ready to get us going.

In no time, the plane takes off with Sophie and me attached to our two instructors. I eye her partner, sending fuck-off vibes while Sophie mumbles words of encouragement to herself.

I break up her nervous chanting. "Ready to fly, Sunshine?"

It's not my fault she looks and acts like the sun. Like the destructive yellow orb in the sky, she eats away at my protective layer while lighting up my darkest corners.

"I'd jump out of the plane at that nickname alone."

I release a carefree laugh. "Well, here's your chance."

"I'm zero percent ready for this."

How fitting, when I was zero percent ready for her. But here I am, about to jump out of a plane because I like this girl and want to take as many firsts from her as I can.

An attendant opens the door. Sophie and I both waddle with our partners to the open area. My heart beats rapidly in my chest, my throat closing from the restricted airflow to my lungs. I turn toward the girl who captured my attention months ago and never let go.

She shoots me a beaming smile worth this crazy Fuck It list item. "Liam Zander, it was a pleasure knowing you. Please pick up my remains at the orientation table."

"That's it? I expected a declaration of love."

She rolls her eyes, visible through her tinted goggles. "How about a declaration of annoyance?"

"Close enough." I pull her in for a kiss, ignoring the two dudes strapped against our backs. Our kiss is simple and sweet, satiating my lust and our gravitational pull, easing my rapid heart rate.

"Three...two...one," the two men say behind us before Sophie's scream fills the air, shrill enough to hear over the roaring plane's engines.

The wind howls in my ears as we propel through the blue sky. We rush through the air, four people falling, inching closer toward land. Sophie's a black blob with two flailing blonde braids around her, posing for the camera. My heart races in my chest as blood pulses through my ears. It's a different adrenaline rush from my usual race day, free-floating and unlike anything I had experienced before. My stomach clenches as my throat becomes dry.

We push closer to the city, our bodies jerking when the attendants pull on the parachutes. Sophie's smile radiates as she gives me a thumbs up. My kind of girl, trusting me and my insane plans despite being scared out of her mind.

We both drift in the wind. Instead of watching the city below us, I watch her. My eyes stay glued to the way she beams at the experience.

I don't have the slightest clue of how to approach things with her. How can I when I don't even understand what I want? She gets spooked easily, and I don't have a track record worth much, which poses as another hurdle of many for us.

Liking Sophie is kind of like jumping out of a plane. Exhilarating, addicting, and damn near impossible to forget.

My feet land on the grassy patch near the plane hanger. Sophie lands a minute later, hitting me with a genuine smile and bright eyes as her attendant detaches all the straps.

She runs up to me and launches herself into my arms, knocking her head back and laughing into the sky. Her legs wrap around me before she rubs up against my now-stiffening dick. I groan into her neck as her body shakes, enjoying this torture experience all too much.

"Oh my God, that was the best thing ever. Is this what it feels like to race? I feel fan-freaking-tastic."

I laugh into her neck. "Probably. Do you feel edgy? That your heart is pumping so loud, you hear it in your ears?"

She looks at me with wonder. "Yes," she hisses before leaning into my ear. "What do you say? Let's get out of here?"

My body responds to her offer like no other. With Sophie, my dick knows what's up, never settling for anything but her. Our hooking up has been the best thing, keeping me away from destructive patterns for my career while spending more time with her. In her. On her. Next to her.

I place her on her feet, ripping off my tacky flight jumper before grabbing her hand.

"Wait, I need to take mine off too." Her green eyes have a lightness to them I want to memorize.

"Allow me." I rush to tug at the Velcro straps, pulling at the suit like it offends me.

She shakes her head while fighting a smile, helping me by lifting her legs when I push the fabric down. My hands heat wherever they linger on her skin.

Our attendants hand us our belongings and we head toward the Wrangler.

"That was one of the coolest things I've ever done. My heart hasn't calmed down, and my spine's tingling because, holy shit, we just jumped out of a plane!" Sophie opens the passenger door.

I situate myself in the seat. "I hope I didn't turn you into an adrenaline junkie. Hugs, not drugs."

"Doubt you're complaining." Sophie surprises me as she climbs over the center console and places her knees on either side of me. Her body presses right against my dick.

"What are you doing?" I swallow.

"Less talking, more kissing." Her lips press against mine.

I wrap my arms around her and tug her close, her body molding into mine. Our tongues fuse while we nip and play. The kiss is primal like we both can't satisfy this hunger between us no matter how hard we try.

Kissing Sophie became one of my favorite things, right up there with having sex with her, making her come with my tongue, and getting blowjobs from her. Basically anything with her because I like everything we do together, including our friendship outside of the bedroom.

Her lips travel to my neck, sucking and pulling at the sensitive skin.

"Fuck." My teeth grind together to hold back a moan.

My hands roam over her body, grabbing her plump ass and giving it a squeeze. Her tongue darts out to taste my skin before her teeth graze the hollow of my neck.

"You bit me? I've turned you into a little devil."

She breaks away and looks at me with heavy eyes and a lazy smile. I love that look on her, especially when I'm the reason for it in the first place.

Fuck. Love? Really, Liam?

"Didn't you hear? To play with devils, you need to become one." Her lips crash against mine, our teasing nature gone as our tongues stroke one another. Teeth clash and lips swell. It's a whole fucking erotic display, with heavy breathing and groping.

Her fingers undo the button of my pants. "I need you. Now."

"Right now?" The words leave my lips in a wheeze. I haven't

had sex in a car since I was a teen, let alone in a fucking Wrangler where anyone can pass by. I pull away from her and assess the situation, which I probably should've done the moment Sophie planted herself on my lap like a goddamn present. An empty lot greets me like a blessing sent from above.

"Fuck it." My fingers become greedy fuckers, tugging at her jean shorts and underwear, sliding them down her smooth legs. She follows my lead and pulls down my shorts with my help.

"I act like a fucking teenager around you," I grumble into her hair, breathing in her intoxicating smell.

She laughs, the hoarse sound sending a rush of pleasure straight to my dick. I line myself up, pre-cum dripping from my tip, edginess creeping up my spine at the idea of fucking Sophie in a car where anyone can see.

"Wait. Condom!" Her breathy voice echoes in my head.

"Shit!" *Condom? Motherfucking condom!* When in the ever-loving hell have I ever gotten so caught up in fucking someone I forgot a condom.

Holy fucking shit. I stare at my dick in disbelief, wrapping my head around the situation, as if staring at it will solve my distress.

Sophie ignores my panic, shifting away from me to grab her purse as she searches for the solution to our problem.

Rule number one of F1: do not fuck girls without condoms. Racers don't need kids and baby mama drama. No one wants to end up like Noah's dad with a model sinking her claws into him for a monthly check.

But this is Sophie. She wouldn't do that to me, manipulating me for her gain. I've known her for almost a whole F1 season already. We're friends. Sure, with benefits, but friends nonetheless.

And if something were to ever happen, I'd never believe it was intentional on her end.

Right?

Of course, right. I'm a fucking idiot, questioning if she would do that.

"Found it! I should really, really clean out this purse. I think this one was from my university orientation or something but looks good."

She runs her hand down my shaft, my dick pulsing at her caress. Her finger swipes away at the pearly drop at the tip before she sucks on the pad.

"Fuck me." I barely function around her when she gets this way, acting like my hellion through and through.

"That's the plan!" She laughs to herself.

I recognize the brand as she rips at the foil. "That's not going to fit me. Are you trying to cut off my dick's circulation?"

She rolls her eyes. "What do you mean?"

"Don't insult my size, woman."

"If I wanted someone cocky, I could have dated Noah." She taunts me with a mischievous smile.

"I'll show you someone cocky. Right fucking now. You're on birth control, right?"

She bobs her head up and down. "For like the past five years."

"Care to ditch the condom that sure as fuck won't fit me anyway? We're both clean, right?"

What the fuck am I doing? Thinking with my cock, that's for sure.

Sophie denies anything and agrees, and with one swift motion, I plunge myself inside of her. She takes in a sharp breath, her head dropping back, the tips of her blonde hair tickling my thighs.

My eyes shut because, fuck, this feels amazing. Never in my life have I had sex without a condom, the feel of her a motherfucking nirvana. I don't move, let alone think.

Sophie slowly lifts, drawing my attention to my glistening dick. I'm in a trance. Her warmth, her body, every-fucking-thing. My body sings as she lowers herself again. She fucks me up on the inside while she rides my cock, her body arching as her eyes close.

My mind numbs, my spine tingles, and my toes curl. All sensations fire off inside as she fucks me into oblivion. I used to joke with her about breaking her, but at this moment, I realize I'm the one breaking little by little at her hand.

My fingers grip her thighs, strong enough to leave marks, but I can't control myself. I find the curve of her neck and tease her.

"Oh, Liam. Yes," she hisses.

I growl, sucking at her skin, claiming her in ways I can. "Enjoy your ride because your time is almost up."

She lets out the airiest of laughs, so fucking soft as it tugs at my heart. *What is this woman doing to me?*

My instincts take over, one hand clutching her braids together while the other grips her ass. She follows my lead, lifting herself up as I ram into her, no longer interested in soft caresses and slow pumps. I want her right fucking now, coming on my dick while moaning my name.

Her breathing quickens as I push in and out of her, my movements becoming erratic. Wild like my thoughts. Untamed because of the beauty before me.

"You're so fucking hot, taking everything I give you. You feel like heaven. I never want to fucking leave now that I've had a taste." My thumb finds her clit, teasing her as my other hand tugs on her hair.

She groans. "Why does it feel so freaking good with you?"

Damn, if my ego doesn't swell from her words. Her body shakes as I continue my torture, her fingers gripping onto my shoulders as she stares into my eyes. I get lost in the feel of her.

I feel her everywhere. In my body, in my mind, in my goddamn blood, pulsing with need and adrenaline at her coming undone. I hate it as much as I love it because I can't control this thing between us and what it's morphing into. The thought scares me and I slam the brakes, not interested in pursuing that problem right now.

Sophie's eyes glaze over, hooded and so fucking gorgeous. Her body shakes as she explodes. My body tightens as she squeezes my dick, her lips crashing against mine as her tongue owns me. She devours me, banishing my worries with her addicting kisses. I grab onto her hips, controlling her movements as I lift off the seat, desperate for my release.

She stamps herself onto my heart like she fucking belongs there. With wild pumps, I explode, a prickling sensation starting from my toes and ending at the base of my neck. I don't stop moving until I finish.

Sophie collapses against my chest while her arms wrap around my neck. And for once, I don't know what I like more: having sex or having someone to hug me afterward. We stay like that for a few minutes, regaining control of our breathing. Part of me wouldn't mind staying here until the sun sets. I wouldn't be opposed to another round or three, knowing one time with Sophie is never enough.

"We better go." She lifts herself off my dick, my cum seeping out of her.

"Damn, I'm locking away that visual for-fucking-ever."

"You're such a perv." She pulls up her shorts and settles into the passenger seat, shooting me a wicked grin that reminds me of myself. Her braids are a mess with hair sticking out whichever way. Her lips look swollen, and her cheeks have a natural flush to them. I can't help smiling, knowing I did that.

I love how she looks and I want to hold on to these moments before she goes back home in two weeks. My lips turn down in a frown, the tight sensation in my chest becoming familiar ever since Sophie came into the picture.

"Cheer up, Buttercup. I'm not going to get pregnant and we can use a condom next time." Her side-eye unsettles me.

I can't understand why my throat closes up and my lungs burn at her misinterpretation. Is it because I'm an asshole who makes her think I'm grimacing at the idea of getting her pregnant? Or is it because I don't want to use a condom with her again?

I put the car in drive like nothing, my mind drifting off as Sophie plays music.

My phone vibrates as Rick's name flashes across the screen. I click the side button, ignoring his call. Nausea rolls through me at hiding my contract deal from Sophie.

For the first time in my career, I don't want to think about next week, let alone next year. I don't want Sophie to go back home, but I can't stop what I set in motion. Like an F1 fan, I'm helpless while watching a collision. Except this time, I'm the reason, and I get to watch as my car drives straight into a wall.

Because life is funny that way, fucking you over without your consent.

CHAPTER TWENTY-NINE

Sophie

People underestimate the beauty and rawness of Brazil. Even though I love Rio more than Sao Paulo, the electric feeling of the city brings a smile to my face and puts some pep in my step.

It's hard to believe how fast time flies when on the road. There are only two races left before I go back home, which means there are two more before Liam decides where he wants to go. He keeps quiet on the matter, shutting down whenever I ask about it. I let it go because he probably feels nervous about his uncertain future and where he will end up.

I want to tell him I'll be there for him no matter what—whether it's a McCoy contract or not—but the words get stuck in my throat in fear of rejection. Call me a coward, I'm well aware.

When he joked about me loving him when we went skydiving, I nearly confessed my feelings.

Liam and I completed almost every item on the list except for one. With only two more weeks together, I have no idea when or how it'll happen. He took a liking to the list and prefers to plan everything under the guise of spontaneity.

I mull it over while drinking a cocktail. My seat occupies a corner of the bar at the gala with not a single person sitting next to me, probably sensing my mood. Fans keep Liam occupied while Maya busies herself with sucking Noah's face off somewhere in secret.

I drain the contents of my tumbler, the mix of rum and coke not easing my sadness.

The clank of two shot glasses being placed in front of me draws my attention toward my new neighbor. I eye Rick suspiciously. His presence is a rarity since he never speaks to me, instead offering me a withheld sneer and a side-glance every time.

Rick motions for a bartender to pour us each a shot. "Just the person I was looking for."

Amazing how seven words make my skin crawl. The bartender fills our shot glasses with a clear liquid I don't dare ask about, instead choosing to focus on not throwing up at Rick's obvious perusal.

"How can I help you?" I give him a dazzling fake smile.

"I love someone who's willing." Rick tests my gag reflex. "I want to check in with the woman who stirs up more trouble with her pinky than Claudia did with her pussy."

I can't tell if he means to insult or compliment me. Based on his cruel eyes, I'll go with the first option.

"I'm doing great." I pull out my phone. "Oh, wow. I hate to leave this conversation, but I didn't realize the time." My butt lifts off the stool before a cold hand clamps around my wrist. Rick doesn't mean to cause pain, but his unsolicited touch makes my stomach roll all the same.

Did I mention I detest agents?

He continues, ignoring my discomfort. "I think you should stay. After all, don't you want to hear about Liam's predicament? He won't tell you, but he has an important choice to make in the next two weeks."

I say nothing as he reels me in like a nasty fisherman with old bait and a rusty hook. "See, McCoy offered Liam a contract deal despite how he fucked the owner's niece. Can you imagine being that good at racing? Being so powerful that you can screw around with McCoy's niece and still keep your job? Wow." He shakes his head in disbelief. "Anyway, only two other companies offered him a spot, but they're the bottom two teams. The contracts are shit and Liam knows it. Those deals would ruin his career before he had a chance at another World Championship."

"I fail to see what this has to do with me." My patience wavers. I look around for a savior, but I find myself immersed in a wave of unfamiliar suits.

"Everything really. McCoy offered Liam twenty million dollars, but only if he cuts ties with you because of your connection to Bandini. Can you sleep at night knowing he gave up his dream to be your friend or your lover or whatever you kids call it nowadays? I sure as hell wouldn't be able to. And Liam's thinking about it. He's actually considering giving up his best contract for a fling with a hot young thing. He won't agree or disagree to the new contract, instead choosing to sit around with his dick in his hands, waiting for better deals that won't come. His time is running out."

My heart sinks into my stomach, rolling around with acid and alcohol. I want to run away from Rick and this secret Liam kept. But instead, my butt stays planted on the stool.

"People can negotiate deals and stupid conditions." I straighten my spine because I can't let Rick sense my fear. There have to be other options. Companies can't act this way, right?

"Liam's tried. I've tried. But a deal is a deal at the end of the day."

I remain speechless while staring at the shot glass, wishing it could solve my problems.

"I'm telling you early enough to figure it out. To either decide if your relationship—" his eyes roam over me before he licks his lips "—or lack thereof, is really worth that much money. Not to mention his career. The clock is ticking. I wish you the best of luck with this difficult decision. For me, no pussy is worth that much. But hey, if I was as rich as Liam, I guess I'd have the luxury of choices too." He knocks back his shot and tips the glass upside down, leaving me alone with a full glass.

Once he leaves, I swallow my shot despite my queasiness. The burn takes away from the sting in my eyes.

I leave the gala without a backward glance, not in the mood to pretend that Rick didn't rip into my heart and steal a piece. I'm unsure of what to do and who to turn to.

I don't know what to feel. Hurt Liam needs to think about cutting me out of his life? Happy he's considering saying no in the first place? Confusion mixes with alcohol, my head swimming with doubt and insecurity, pain festering inside me like an infected wound.

I make it to my hotel room and land face-first in my bed, hoping alcohol knocks me out quickly.

"I'm concerned with how you're stabbing your pancakes. Have any qualms to share?" My dad looks at me with questioning eyes.

"Only that you talk like someone from a Victorian novel. Who says *qualms* anymore?"

"Well-educated individuals who read lots of books. Speaking of which, how are your classes going?" He loves to check in about school.

"Really smooth transition, Dad. They're rough, especially online." *Lies.*

As of last week after Germany, I dropped my two classes and pushed my graduation back a semester. My palm shook as I pressed the withdraw button after speaking to Liam's parents and researching art with kids. I made one of the rashest decisions of my life all by myself. No one knows about my recent life change. Not even Liam, who has lately become my go-to for all things related to me.

If that doesn't say personal progress, I don't know what does.

My dad tilts his head. "And what do you plan on doing after you graduate?"

"I'm not sure yet." The words barely make it past my lips. I hate lying, but I hate lying to my dad so much more.

"There has to be some internship or something you want to pursue. Either that or get yourself signed up for a master's degree so you can pass your accounting exams."

That idea sounds about as fun as getting a root canal.

"What's the rush?" I avert his gaze.

"You need to start planning your life and getting ready for the next big step. You've had fun traveling with me for months, but it's time to head back home in two weeks."

Home. An idea that used to bring me comfort reminds me of how hollow I feel. Somewhere along the way this year, my heart found a home somewhere else. Particularly with a German man who offers nightly cuddles and toe-curling morning kisses.

The tightness in my chest pushes me to ignore the thought.

Rick's nuclear bomb of a secret makes my chest ache and my stomach churn. I struggle to comprehend how Liam battles cutting me out of his life. It's like a sad re-enactment of some television show deciding whether to cast me out of the island or not. I don't want to be pushed away and forgotten, but I don't want Liam to lose his shot at winning a World Championship.

My dad's voice rumbles. "It's okay to be afraid of your future and what comes next. No one likes failing. But I've taught you to get up, brush the dirt off your knees, and try again."

"What happens if I don't want to get up?" You know, because my heart lies around me in a million pieces.

"I raised you to rise above your challenges. Whether it happens in a minute or a day. You *will* get up. It's not a matter of *if*, but *when*."

My dad, wise beyond his years and about one step away from creating his *TED Talk*.

"Of course, you can say that. You're you. A badass who doesn't take shit from anyone." I grumble as I shove a fluffy piece of pancake in my mouth.

"I've had my fair share of bad days. Hell, I raised you on my own with no parents to help. Only you, me, and a few parenting books to figure out if I was going about things the right way. There's no self-doubt quite as grand as that of parenthood."

My smile wobbles. "You did your best."

"You bet your ass I did. You're the greatest thing that ever happened to me and I wouldn't change a thing. Some dads want a son—someone to create into their prodigy. But you captured my best traits. I wouldn't trade you for anything."

"Glad you put that out there because I checked with the hospital and the return policy is a bit sketchy."

He shakes his head and laughs. "Anyone who hears you wouldn't doubt you're my daughter."

"After all, I did learn from the best." I shoot him a small smile, pushing away my bad mood for later.

I'm still a hot, indecisive mess after Rick's confession yesterday. Emphasis on the hot because the least I can do is boost my self-esteem.

Earlier, Maya asked me to join her with setting up a game for Liam and Jax to play during a vlog. I drag my feet toward the McCoy garage, grumbling under my breath.

"What made you so grumpy?" Maya fumbles with her camera settings while we wait for the guys. McCoy's pit crew works around us, busying themselves with pre-race prep, while we wait outside the garage.

"Nothing. Just tired and didn't sleep well last night."

Probably because Liam's dick of an agent took away my sense of control over my relationship. If I can even call it that, seeing as Liam is struggling between kicking me to the curb and keeping me.

"I'm not used to seeing you this out of it. Hopefully, you can get a good night's rest before the race. Maybe with Liam?" She sends me a sly grin that doesn't take away the empty feeling inside of me.

"I think I'm going to chill without my personal body pillow for a few days." I need air and time to think. Hanging around Liam makes me weak. Part of me wants to ask him about what his agent said while another part of me doesn't because I'm afraid of his answer.

"Any reason?"

Before I have a chance to respond, Liam and Jax make their presence known in the McCoy garage.

"If it isn't our two favorite ladies." Liam brushes a loose strand of hair from my face before planting a kiss on my temple. "You didn't show up last night after the gala. You're not quitting on me, right?" he whispers into my ear.

I turn to find his eyes sparkling. "Nope. I wasn't feeling well and wanted to go to bed early. No reason to hang out if we aren't...you know..."

His smile drops. "That's bullshit. You know we spend time together without fucking. Don't sell me a fake excuse when we're friends first and foremost."

Ah, there's that word again. "Well, okay…"

He eyes me before stepping away, giving me room to breathe again.

"Let's get this show on the road. I have places to be, people to bang." Jax claps his hands together.

"You know, beneath that rough exterior is a boy who cuddles with his pillow at night and dreams of a better tomorrow." Liam holds his palm to his chest.

"The only future I think of is kicking your ass at every race."

"Okay, you two. This is one of our last episodes before the end of the season." Maya breaks up the jokes and gets to work.

Maya interviews the two of them while they play a game. I tune out their conversation because I have no interest in listening, only attending because Maya begged me to film the exchange. I ignore the weird looks Liam sends my way. His omission of his contract deal sits heavy between us, and I can't handle how part of me feels grateful he didn't say yes to McCoy right away.

Despite his inability to decide if he loves me, I still love him with everything inside of me. I'd do just about anything to help him be happy. It looks like I fell in love with someone untouchable and unbreakable, proving to me how shattered people like Liam can't fall apart again.

Welcome to my disaster ever after. Pull up a chair, bust out the popcorn, and enjoy the show.

CHAPTER THIRTY

Liam

I never pegged myself as a thoughtful guy. At least not until Sophie, where we dance on the fine line between friendship and more, never fully submitting to the idea of lovers. With my past and her future, there's no point in thinking about anything but the next two weeks.

Despite telling myself that, I can't help but wonder what it would be like after the season. The idea of returning back to my empty Monaco apartment fills me with sorrow. For some reason, after all these months spending time with her, I don't want her to go.

Is it selfish of me to want her to stay when I'm not willing to commit to a relationship? Of course. So I bottle up my bubbling anxiety and put it on a shelf, instead choosing to make her final item memorable. The last thing on her list—the very one that reminds me of her—took some planning. I spent hours researching because Sophie rubs off on me in more than one way.

I rented an off-roading truck yesterday to prepare for our trip tonight. She has no idea what I planned, thinking I'm taking her to dinner in Abu Dhabi. Sophie seemed distant this week so I wanted to cheer her up. She barely hung around me, choosing to spend time with Maya and her dad instead of me. Every time I asked her if anything was wrong, she shrugged me off, claiming she wants to spend time with everyone before she leaves.

I can't help wondering if she doesn't want to share her nervousness about what will happen after the season ends. I plan on spilling everything to her once the race finishes on Sunday because McCoy promised a final offer by then, with them agreeing to rethink the Bandini clause at my insistence.

Her playlist of songs fills the silence. I let her choose the music, hoping it would boost her mood. The closer we get to our destination, the giddier she gets as she returns to her usual self.

Her smile eases the tightness I've felt in my chest all week.

"Are you planning on burying me out in the desert? Creative, I'll give you that," she sasses me. Grumpy Sophie no longer seems like an issue.

"I considered it, but everyone knows where I'm taking you. So, although effective, I'd be the primary suspect."

"Everyone, huh?" She tilts her head at me.

"Just our friends."

Somewhere along the way, our separate groups of friends merged into one. Santi hangs out with Jax on his own because I've been busy with Sophie. Maya and Noah officially came out as a couple, leaving Sophie to myself this evening.

She hums along to the music as I take us to the spot I researched. The moment I park the truck, she bounds out of the car. I kill the headlights and hop out, shrouding us in darkness, the sky on full display.

"No freaking way." She runs a few feet ahead of me.

I walk up to her and wrap my arms around her as I look up at the bright Milky Way, courtesy of the Al Quaa desert. She listed *have outdoor sex*, and I hope I delivered.

Silence surrounds us—not a single animal or person around, the cool air brushing against our joined bodies. Sophie's skin breaks out in goosebumps and I squeeze her closer.

She gasps. "I don't think I've ever seen anything this amazing." *I have.*

We both stare up at the starry sky. I unwrap myself from her after a few minutes to grab the supplies. Thanks to Maya, I packed enough food to hold us over until tomorrow, along with basic camping necessities. I pull out a telescope I bought and set up a padded blanket with a couple of pillows. A tiny lantern lights up our makeshift bed.

"When I wrote that item, I would've never ever thought this up. I'm impressed because this is straight out of a storybook. Thank you." She pulls me in for a hug.

My arms instinctively wrap around her and tug her flush against me. I love the instantly recognizable smell of her, summertime and ocean waves wrapped up in one. "I'd buy you the whole damn night sky if I could."

Sophie laughs into my chest before she disentangles herself and lies down on a pillow. I busy myself with setting up the telescope.

She watches me, her eyes following every move I make. "Did

you ever hear back from McCoy or any other teams?"

My hand stills on a lever, her question catching me unprepared. "Yeah, but I'm still waiting. You know, just in case."

"So, McCoy offered an extension?" Her eyes shift from me toward the sky.

"Yup. Them and a few others."

She pauses before speaking again. "What's the holdup?"

"Contract deals are complicated. As smart as we both are, I leave that side of the business to my agent."

Her bouncing leg freezes. "If you had a gun to your head and you had to choose a team for next year, out of all the teams except Bandini because they can't offer anyone a seat, who would you choose?"

My heart races in my chest. I run my tongue across my lips, buying time to think up a response.

"Stop thinking and go with your heart," her hoarse voice whispers.

"McCoy. I like the team and Jax, plus Peter finally chilled out," I blurt out.

Her eyes slide from mine to the sky again. "Even with Claudia causing drama?"

I can't tell if her voice sounds sad or annoyed. "She's like Day of the Dead, coming out once a year to wreak havoc, only to return back to the fiery pit she came from."

Sophie laughs, but the sound isn't the same as usual, coming off forced.

I fumble with the telescope. "But there's still time. Other teams can offer deals until the end of the season, and I haven't made up my mind. You know things can be contingent on the final Championship standings."

"Yeah, maybe something happens." She lifts off the blanket, abandoning the conversation and grabbing my extended hand. Thank fuck. My breathing slows down again.

Her blonde hair glows from the lantern as she bends down and stares into the telescope. "Whoa. Just wow. I don't have adjectives for this. You have to see this."

I feel the same about her half the time. "I interpreted outdoor sex as spending a night under a starlit sky. I hope you like it."

"You exceeded my expectations. As per usual." She offers me a sweet smile.

"Do I get a kiss for my good efforts? Well, to be honest, I'll take a kiss or a blowjob. Who am I to discriminate?"

She lets out the softest laugh that I want to record. "We can negotiate a deal of our own." Her lips find mine in the dark. I tug her close, loving the feel of her pressed against me—a high worse than any drug.

Her soft lips kiss mine and her tongue teases my bottom lip. She invades my mouth like she does my life—unforgiving and unapologetic. Not that I want her to be. Shit, being with her brings out parts of me that I never knew were there to begin with. Her tongue caresses mine, our warm breath mingling together, an erotic feeling I don't want to let go of. I crave everything with her.

I want to steal her kisses, leaving her mindless and numb, the only thought playing in her head is of me fucking her until stars dance behind her eyes. With her, I want to kiss and suck at her skin until I leave bruises so no fucker comes near what's mine.

Mine? Shit. More like mine for the season.

My brain shuts off when her teeth graze my bottom lip and her hand cups my dick. I push Sophie into the blanket and crawl over her, the warmth of my body protecting us from the chilly desert breeze. Our lips never move away from each other. The hunger between us burns strong, fueled by our indisputable chemistry.

Her hands find the hem of my hoodie and she tugs it over my head. She traces the ridges of muscle from my shoulders to my stomach before removing my belt and chucking it to the side. I follow suit, removing her sweater and jeans. Not caring for anything between us, I make quick work of her bra and panties, along with my own jeans and boxer briefs.

I hate barriers as much as I hate the way she looks at me with lust and something else I can't place. Something about it is off. It's a look she hasn't given me before, so I have no way to gauge what's happening with her. Her glassy eyes find mine, the bright stars reflecting off them, calling out to me like a lost man finding his way home.

My fingers skim her pussy, finding her ready for me. She pants when I pump two fingers into her, bringing her to the brink of pleasure, kissing her to combat the swirling emotions inside of me. The very ones that creep in the night, tugging at my composure and challenging my rules. This is the very reason I set expectations in the first place. With my life on the road and my past rearing its ugly head time and time again, I don't have the capability of doing more.

Do I?

Like Sophie senses my mind drifting as I kiss her, she pulls me back, her fingers lightly scratching against my back.

"You want to be fucked under the sky?" My words come out mumbled between kisses.

Sophie bobs her head up and down. My lips trail kisses down her neck before I pull one of her nipples into my mouth. She lets out a gasp as my tongue darts out and licks her, sucking the hard tip. Her moans encourage me. I leave a path of lazy kisses across her chest toward her other breast, paying special attention to her.

Everything with her feels so fucking right all the time. Somehow being with Sophie became as essential as eating and sleeping, and that thought alone makes my chest constrict.

She's my star in the dark sky, shining bright and guiding me back from the shadows. But unfortunately, the Prix lights will shut down in a few days, casting us in a cloudy night with no light in sight. Because in the end, us together is like a stormy evening—starless, dark, and destructive.

"I need you right now," her voice croaks.

A stupid man would ignore those words and continue on. I release her from my torture, lining myself at her entrance as I push away the negative thoughts clouding our moment.

"Wait. Condom." She pushes her hand against my chest.

I don't know why the request bothers me. Last week she was all for going bareback, but she's been distant ever since Brazil. Adding a condom to the mix feels like another way she wants to pull away from me. But I can't figure her out, let alone argue with her reasoning for wanting protection. Instead of complaining, I should be thankful because other women would use me during a moment of weakness.

I busy myself with a condom from my wallet, pushing away my uncertainty. Then I return to her. In one move, I bury myself to the hilt inside of her. Her legs wrap around me, her nails running down my back while I smother her cries with my lips. My dick throbs at the pressure of filling her. My eyes close while my body stills, wanting to enjoy the moment.

I regret shitting on the missionary position because with Sophie, it's unreal. Sex with her never feels vanilla or boring. Quite the opposite, always pulling everything out of me, no matter the position. Anything with Sophie feels right.

Control wavers as I move inside of her. She switches between staring at me and the starlit sky, enthralled with us both. I shift my position and brush my dick up against her sensitive spot. Her body shakes at the new sensation, her arms wrapping around my neck as she tugs my lips toward her. My dick continues to pump into her, enjoying how desperate she grows to find her release.

"Fuck yeah, babe. God. It never feels like enough with you. I want you every fucking day, and I don't know what to do about it." My hand palms her breast.

Her body bucks under my torture, unable to handle the different feelings. And I'm right there with her. My brain can't make sense of the emotions running through me. A blend of affection and unrestrained desire.

Sophie climaxes, erupting around my dick while making the best sounds. I slow my movements and milk her orgasm. Her eyes open and a lazy smile crosses her face before she kisses me tenderly.

"You don't know how sexy you are. And you're all mine." I bite on my lip.

Something flashes in her eyes before she closes them, her hands tugging at my hair again. I don't need her words because her body tells me everything.

I shift my position to give myself a better angle. My release is imminent, needing a shove before I topple over the edge. Sophie sighs as I increase my pressure and speed. Her body takes every powerful stroke while my lips suck on the skin at the hollow of her neck, obsessing over marking her in more ways than one. There's no use controlling the wave of possessiveness running through me.

Cries and groans fill the silence of the empty desert, our heavy breathing providing the best soundtrack.

"Oh my...Liam..." Her sultry voice runs against my skin, the heat of her combatting the cold air around us. Sophie's not one for false moans and words to boost my ego. She keeps it simple and sweet—just like her.

A warmth creeps up my spine as I come, my dick pulsing inside of Sophie while I continue to slowly pump over and over again. It's a mind and body fuck all at once.

I collapse on top of her. My lips leave soft kisses on her neck in a silent apology, the dark spots already forming, evidence of our night together. "I apologize in advance for the hickeys."

Her throaty laugh brushes off my comment. I pull out of her slowly, disconnecting our bodies, both of us sighing at the loss. My lips find hers again and leave a lingering kiss before I grab a blanket from the corner of our makeshift bed.

"You spoil me." She runs a hand across the soft quilt.

"Take advantage of me. You won't hear me complaining."

She sighs as she finds her preferred spot against my chest, her body hugging mine while one of my legs wraps around hers.

Sophie hasn't spoken much today. I don't know what to make

of her silence—a rarity for her. I push away a seed of doubt about Sophie leaving next week, about where we stand as friends once the season finishes. About what will happen with McCoy and what I'll do without her by my side next year.

I drift off to the rhythm of her breathing and her fingers brushing across the bare skin of my chest. I'll face my problems tomorrow.

CHAPTER THIRTY-ONE

Sophie

People describe heartbreak as this instantaneous feeling where a heart breaks into a million irreparable pieces, scattering in different directions. Some pieces go missing while others stab you in the foot as you clean up the mess. Heartbreak is a ruthless fucker like that, kicking you while you're already down.

I think those people who describe heartbreak are liars. Every single one of them who talk about a shattering experience, like you can fix a heart with superglue and willpower.

I can safely say heartbreak feels dull and hollow, leaving behind nothing but a husk of an organ. A broken, mangled weight inside of me, clenching and unclenching at the words Liam shares throughout the night. The glances he takes at my body, the feeling of his hands touching me, the way he sets me on fire from a single caress. His actions cut out parts of my heart with a rusty serrated knife.

Hearts don't shatter because that'd be too easy. Hearts get ejected from an airplane, left to fall hard sans parachute.

Liam hiding the issue of his contract with McCoy is a surface-level problem. I know he has pure intentions. The real issue is his love for McCoy and his uneasiness at accepting his contract deal despite a problematic ex, a negative work environment, and the potential sacrifice he'd make giving me up. And for what? Friends with benefits? In the end, we're a shinier upgrade from what he typically prefers.

The black sky with radiant stars brings me comfort amidst my sadness. Liam knocked out hours ago, too content and satiated to stay awake. Despite my grief, I loved every single second of the night.

I should be happy and thrilled with how he cares about me the way he does. And I am. But also I'm not. Selfish, I get it. People can blame the only child in me for wanting my cake and eating it too. The thing is, being an only child meant I had lots of leftovers, so I never had to share my cake, let alone decide between eating it and saving it.

But when Liam wakes up to the desert's sunrise, it's obvious what I have to do. I've thought about it for hours. For the sake of him and his future, I need to make a sacrifice because he won't do it. My test earlier failed, proving to us both how much he wants to continue with McCoy. Somehow I pretended his words didn't faze me when he pulled the trigger, stating his wish to stay with his team while blowing my heart to pieces.

His wish is my command.

Lucky for me, I know the way to get to Liam. Over the months, I've learned everything about him, from the way he preps for races to his preference for cuddling with me on rainy days while he reads a book. What I've learned most of all is how he has very few triggers. With people like him, all I need is one spark to bring his demon to the surface, challenging his life built on illusions and half-truths.

I'm about to blow this shit up like World War III.

"Morning." He looks at me with groggy eyes and a lazy smile. The knife digs deeper inside of me, a clusterfuck of ripped-up tendons, veins, and arteries. A slow bleed invisible to the naked eye.

I sit up and take a few deep gulps of air to gain courage. "I've had a lot of fun. I really can't thank you enough for helping me with the list." I take a breath to steady my voice, the sharp inhale feeling like a thousand piercing needles against my lungs. "But with the end of the race season, we need to call it quits. Friends with benefits has been fun and all—great even—but you have to race, and I need to go back to school."

I wish I could shut my eyes and erase the pain in his eyes. To take the words back and swallow them whole, pretending I don't know about his deal.

"Fun? Fuck fun. What the hell are you even talking about?" The roughness of his voice scrapes against my eardrums. He sits up to meet my eyes, his blue ones hitting me with a reflection of the rising sun behind me.

"We both know feelings aren't your thing. Not to mention we won't see each other after next week. I'm going back home and you're going somewhere."

"Feelings aren't my thing?" Liam says the words with disbelief.

I stare at my hands to avoid his hurt gaze. He makes me weak yet strong because I need to do this for him and his future. "*I love you*. I have for months but you've been too blind to see it, unable to acknowledge me and my feelings. To *see* me." My eyes meet his. "I can't do this to myself anymore. The season is almost over, the list is finished, so we're done. I'm sorry I broke your rule, but we can't be friends anymore. So, let's cut our losses before things get complicated. Before things happen that we both can't take back, no matter how much we may want to." My voice chokes on the last words, my airflow constricted.

"Like this conversation?"

I suck in a breath. The woundedness in his voice makes me want to stop. But he can't give up his career for me—for this weird blend of friendship, sex, and one-sided emotions. My heart thrums against my chest like it wants to tell me it still beats strong for Liam.

Sorry, heart, I apologize in advance for the explosion.

I stand, brushing my shaky palms across the leggings I put on to avoid the desert chill. My legs wobble before I gain control.

He gets up too, closing the distance between us, staring me down. "I don't know why you're ending our friendship. Just get over your feelings and let's go back to normal."

Tears prick at the corner of my eyes. "There's no going back. I can't expect you to understand, seeing as you've never been in a relationship with someone…let alone in love. You have no idea what it takes. Let's be real—you can't even get over your past, let alone look toward your future. We both know I'm not part of it." My vile words disgust me.

His eyebrows scrunch together and his eyes become glassy. I hate myself. I hate myself so fucking much I want to scream at him and myself all at the same time. But I don't. I take a few steps back, my toes curling under the sand, grounding me from floating off into a mental space filled with pain and contempt.

"I can't believe you're really going to end our friendship over something temporary."

My lungs burn from the hot air and imminent tears. "Love shouldn't be temporary. At least not to me. That's exactly why our little imaginary life needs to come to an end. Today. Now. I don't want to love someone who views everything as fleeting." I walk toward the truck. My hand grips the handle, the door creaking open before Liam slams it shut.

He turns me and pushes me against the cool metal. His hand gently—ever so fucking gently it hurts my heart—tips my head up to look him in the eyes.

"I don't want to hurt you." His lips brush against mine, leaving behind a soft kiss. It's comical how the same lips that helped seal my fate still make my insides heat. Just another screwed-up part of Liam and me.

I let out a bitter laugh. "You know, I'm a fool. Thinking you could love someone besides yourself. For believing we could hook up and stay friends while neither one of us gets hurt in the process. I'm an idiot."

"Then stop making things weird. We promised not to fall for one another," he growls.

"No, *you* promised. And I'm not making things weird, I'm making them honest. Can you tell me you love me? That all the words you whisper in my ear at night mean something more? Go ahead, admit how you feel."

Silence greets me, the dull throb in my chest increasing as

Liam stands there, his wild eyes roaming over my face. I prepped myself for this moment all night long, knowing he would never confess to something he can't recognize.

To be honest, no preparation could've helped me handle this.

"Don't do this to us and our arrangement," he rasps.

"That's your problem. For someone so keen on living life to the fullest, you sure trick everyone, including yourself. You throw my rules back in my face when you're the most rigid one of us all, holding on to lies you tell yourself to protect you from the unknown. Funny how you taught me the most important lesson of all. There are some things you can't plan for, no matter how hard you try."

"But we're friends. You can't leave and forget about us."

My eyes narrow. "Yeah, Liam, well this friendship *sucks* right now."

He takes a deep breath, stepping away from me and turning his back. "I can't give you anything more than what we have. I travel as my job for fuck's sake. You're going to go back home, and I'll keep racing. It's not the right moment. Maybe if it were under different circumstances, at another time."

I drop my head against the car door and laugh, the noise grating against my ears. If heartbreak had a sound, that would be it. "Laughable how you told me that almost four years ago when you met me. Yet here we are, years later, with you following the same pathetic lines."

"Please, Sophie. I really like you. Don't ruin something between us for something like love." His eyes plead with mine.

"What does that even mean? There is nothing wrong with love." It takes everything in me to not yell.

Fuck Peter and Rick. Screw Formula 1 and the sucky men who bully women into submission through manipulation and money. I'm so done with it all. Like Dorothy, I want to click my red Nikes together and get the hell home.

"I thought we were on the same page." His look of pity adds to my distress.

"Forget the same page. We're not even reading the same book." Everything hurts inside of me. My body can't cope with Liam's inability to recognize his feelings for me. His wounded face pulls an ounce of pity from me, tugging at my aching heart.

I may be stupid enough to have fallen in love with him, but I'm not blind to the way he looks at me, or how he fucks me, staring into my eyes like he wants to hold on to the moment.

Looks like Liam got his wish because he gets to keep his contract. All at my sacrifice, blowing my friendship to hell, with me along with it.

Liam turns back toward our abandoned campsite. He shakes his head at my offer to help as he grabs everything and shoves it in the trunk. The empty plot of sand mocks me, not a single shred of evidence lingering where I broke my own heart. No bloodshed or shattered pieces are visible to the naked eye.

Absolutely nothing.

A perfect symbolism of the emptiness inside of me.

CHAPTER THIRTY-TWO

Liam

I stroll into the Bandini pit garage, finding Maya and Noah making out while Sophie has her back turned.

"I hope you realize I have better things to do than wait around while Noah shoves his tongue down your throat." Sophie's voice carries over the loud activity of the pit garage.

Maya groans before pushing Noah off her. She heads toward Sophie, who has yet to notice me.

"Hey, man. What's up?" Noah's voice prompts Sophie to turn around.

My chest tightens at the sight of her scowl before she turns back toward Maya.

"I want to steal Sophie away for a moment." I brush off the way Maya looks at me with shocked eyes.

Sophie turns on her heel and exits the garage. I follow as she leads the way, her blonde space buns shining under the sun as she takes up a spot next to the pit wall.

She looks at me with a bored expression. "You needed something?"

"Don't be that way. *Please.*"

"Like what? An ex-lover? Why not, when I fit the role so well, filling Claudia's shoes and then some."

It takes everything in me not to growl. "Do not compare yourself to her. Ever. You know it's not like that between us."

"Last time I checked, it looks very much like that, except I didn't throw a shoe at you because I'm not batshit crazy."

"No, you're not. Like I said, I really like you and I care a lot about you. If you don't want to have sex, fine. But don't pull the plug on our friendship because you're afraid of me."

Her eyes glisten, her only tell of distress. "I'm not afraid of you. I *pity* you. You'll have to live with regret when I move on. And I will, eventually. But love takes time, a concept you don't understand, let alone empathize."

I ignore the burning sensation in my chest at the thought of her with someone else. "Then why are you ignoring my calls and texts? If you're not afraid?"

"Because thinking about you makes my heart ache in ways I didn't think possible. Because I'm weak around you and I'd give in to one last time between us. But most importantly, because I love you and you stomped all over my dream of ever feeling that back from you." Sophie whispers the last sentence, nearly gutting me.

Silence greets us like an unwelcome third party. I don't know what to say, let alone how to express myself. Fear eats away at my strength, aware that I want to be everything for Sophie but knowing I can't.

Sophie scoffs, not giving me a chance to say anything. "You know what? Fuck this. Screw love, screw people controlling me, and screw me for being so fucking gullible."

She storms off toward the Bandini offices, a flustered Maya following behind her.

Noah strolls up to my side. "Maya and I didn't mean to eavesdrop, but she wanted to check on her friend."

I roll my eyes. "Of course, you both did. Did you come here to offer some wise advice now that you're in a happy relationship?"

"Cut your shit, Liam. Don't be a dick to me when I'm offering to help you. I never loved my best friend, and I never thought of having a girl version in the first place. The closest person to a friend is Maya, and we know how that ended up." He fights his smile.

It's an unfamiliar sight on him, his broodiness replaced with a lightness I didn't think he had in him. I despise it because I want that for myself, but I can't because I'm a selfish shit. Losing Sophie while securing a McCoy contract doesn't feel as good as I would've hoped.

Noah ignores my stewing emotions. "Anyway, you went about things differently, like usual. But honestly, man, you're fucking up by not trying out a real relationship. If I could, I'd kick myself in the balls months ago for not giving my relationship with Maya a chance sooner. For not confronting my fears and moving past my self-centered ways. Instead, I caused her pain. All I'm saying is I'm lucky she gave me a fucking chance because now I can't picture ever going back to our old lifestyle."

"Well, if Sophie keeps avoiding me, I guess I'll be ruling next season with Jax by my side."

Noah shakes his head. "Don't be an idiot. What's holding you back? For fucking real this time?"

"To start, she's moving back to Milan once the season ends, and I'm going to commit to a team."

"I'll let you in on a secret Maya told me today about your girl." Noah scans our surroundings before leaning in closer.

"What's that?"

"Sophie dropped out of her program. After Germany, she withdrew from her classes but didn't tell anyone. She and Maya had a sleepover last night, wine included, which made Sophie a chatty one."

"What? Why would she do that? And why didn't she tell me anything about it?" I wheeze.

"That's not for me to answer. But no one knows, so don't say anything. I'm telling you to prove a point and show you how you're making decisions based on old news."

"And my contract deal?"

Noah's brow lifts. "That shit again? Don't you get bored of the drama with your team? I personally wouldn't want to hang around the squad of my ex-fling, but maybe that's me and my prideful self. If a team told me I had to choose between Maya and them, I don't know if I'd be too willing to hang around. And not only because of her. Manipulative fuckers don't do it for me, no matter how shiny their cars are or how enticing the deals look. Maybe you need to reassess your worth."

"I'm not trying to stay without changing the deal."

Noah runs a hand through his hair. "Have you tried talking to your agent?"

"Yes. Obviously. But he keeps telling me to hold on." I let out a frustrated breath.

Noah's eyes thin. "Listen, something doesn't seem right here. I don't know if it's your bullshit about not loving Sophie or the fact that no other team expressed interest in you besides the bottom ones. I recommend figuring out what to do about your feelings and your future because—newsflash—that shit is intertwined whether you want to accept it or not. I suggest finding solutions rather than creating more problems because you might regret it when other people start making decisions for you."

"Thanks for listening." I pull him in for a hug and slap him on the back.

"Don't thank me until you go and get Sophie back. Then I know I did my job right."

Sophie loves me. She went against every goddamn rule and admitted she likes me as more than a friend. I broke us beyond repair, unable to face the emotions brewing inside of me.

My body sinks into the cushions of my hotel room's couch as I call my dad, desperate for someone to talk to.

My dad answers on the third ring. He automatically clicks the FaceTime button, not leaving room for hiding. "Hey, how's it going? We didn't think you'd have time to call us with all that Abu Dhabi partying. What a treat."

I don't miss the *us*. Turns out, I get a two-for-one special of both parents listening to my struggles.

"I need advice." I run a shaky hand through my hair.

"About?" My dad's voice sounds through the speaker.

"I think I fucked up with Sophie."

"Oh, no. Please tell me you didn't," my mom whines, appearing in the camera frame.

"What do you mean?" I choke on the words.

"You broke her heart, didn't you?" my dad grumbles.

"Why don't you assume she broke mine?" It annoys me how they paint me as the bad guy here when Sophie went against our agreement.

My dad gives a *what the fuck* look. "Because yours is surrounded by a block of ice while she displays hers like those graphic tees she loves."

"What the fuck. I didn't call to get my ass handed to me."

"No. You called to have someone validate your decisions. Tell me, why do you think you messed up?" My mom takes up a spot next to my dad on their living room couch.

"To start, she admitted she loves me when I didn't ask her to do that. Second, she canceled our friendship after I didn't admit the same feelings. How the fuck is that okay?" I run an agitated hand down my face.

My dad lets out a low whistle. "How do you expect her to want to spend time with you after she was vulnerable like that?"

I all but growl as I tug on my hair.

"Liam, dear. We sheltered you and ignored your poor decisions. We didn't help you as much as we should have when Johanna died, pretending you were better off than you were. You hide behind your race car and helmet and we let you because we don't want to cause you more pain. There's no point living in sadness anymore, acting like you shouldn't pursue something with someone you care about because you're afraid of losing it. Something's gotta give. Either you give it up now and live with

Sophie needing space, or you pull yourself together and show her how you're worth her love."

I dislike how much her words resonate with my fears.

My dad leaves little room for self-pity. "Tell me what you like about Sophie. Right now, don't stop to think."

"I like how easy everything feels with her. How we can do absolutely nothing together and it still feels fun. How she smiles at me differently than everyone else because I get to take her home at night. I especially like how she hides behind rules and restrictions when she really craves to be reckless and carefree. I like pulling that side out of her."

"And what do you dislike about her?" My mom sighs.

"The way she plans every little thing in her life. How she won't pursue her dreams because she shackled herself to an idea of making her dad happy at her sacrifice. At least she did."

"You do realize that you're about to do the same thing by signing your life to McCoy at the expense of losing your best friend?"

"I've been trying to work out a deal." My hands painfully clench in front of me.

My dad shakes his head. "Then you don't deserve her. Because if I had to choose between your mother and something I really fucking wanted, I would have chosen your mother, hands down."

"Why the hell don't I deserve her?"

My mom takes over. "Besides the fact that you can't admit you love her even though you clearly do? Is there a bigger reason needed?"

Wait, what? "How do you know that's what I feel? You're not me."

"Nope, but I gave birth to you, so I'd say it's pretty close. Friends don't notice those details. No friend wants to make love to his girl under a desert sky because he feels like it. You got pissed at her for falling in love with someone who loves her back. And, Liam, no friend can do fuck buddies without risking love. You both were screwed from the very beginning; she only realized it sooner than you." My mom looks at me with sad eyes and a frown.

"Fuck me."

If someone asked me a week ago if I like surprises, I would've said hell yes. But now, looking at my latest surprise across my hotel room, I could live without any more.

See, after Sophie kicked my ass to the curb, I didn't think things could get worse. With my brother showing up with a six-pack of beer and a carry-on suitcase, I'm not so sure.

Shocked is an understatement to describe how I feel. My brother stares at me, his blue eyes assessing me like those damn sudoku puzzles he loves so much. Leave it to my parents to call in reinforcements less than twenty-four hours after our call.

"So, as interesting as your visit is, I'm not sure why you're here." I break the awkward silence.

Lukas crosses his leg over his other knee. "You're not? Come on, you've always been smart. No need to sell yourself short."

"Well, I'm guessing your impromptu appearance has more to do with Sophie than scoring tickets to the final Prix."

"Bingo. It's time we let it all out. You and me, plus our old friends." He plucks a beer from the cardboard box and passes it to me.

The iconic sound of bottle tops falling to the ground

accompanies our silence. We stare at each other for a few minutes, with me draining half my beer in a few tugs.

Lukas taps his fingers against his thigh. "The first time I was intimate with someone else after Johanna's death, I cried."

Holy shit. This is how Lukas wants to start? I thought he would lead me in easy with useless chatter and reminiscing about the old days.

He doesn't give me room to intervene, thank fuck, because I have no clue how to respond to his confession. "It was only a few months ago. I broke out in sobs in the middle of sex, and it was the most embarrassing thing. But it was also the most human I had felt after so damn long. It was like my heart was breaking while fusing together again, and I could do nothing to ease the ache. I spent years avoiding Johanna, only to have her for less than a decade. The pain her sudden death left behind was torture. But I put on my brave face and faced the world for my daughters because they deserve a father who would help fight their battles. Parenthood does that to you."

"I'm so sorry." I swallow back the lump in my throat, barely able to conjure up words.

"I'm not telling you this to feel guilty. I'm sharing my story because you need to understand. Even though I felt like shit for being with someone else, I *needed* to do it. I had been living for my daughters, thrusting myself into both parenting roles while ignoring my basic needs. I forgot to live for myself. Every day I woke up ready to make it the best day of my girls' lives while denying myself any intimacy or closure. I had been so fucking lonely, and I hated myself for being angry at Johanna for leaving me."

"Sometimes, I hate her. And then I hate that I feel that way, but I can't help it." The words pass my lips in a whisper.

Lukas shakes his head. "I think part of you hates her when you really want to hate yourself."

How can one sentence feel like Lukas dragged an invisible knife down my chest, spilling my secrets?

"Why do you think that?" I let out a deep exhale.

"Because you live a lie while pushing others away. I sure as hell would hate to be you, pretending to be someone I'm not, hiding in plain sight while living an empty life. I embrace my pain while you stuff yours away. Vulnerability isn't a weakness, it's a strength amongst those who are too scared to live. I'm done living in fear, and you should be too. It's time to let go for your mental sanity and your future. Johanna's not coming back, no matter how hard you try to hold on to her memory. She would punch you if she could, knowing you're using her as some excuse to stop living your life to the fullest. She'd be pissed as fuck about you denying yourself love because of some messed-up fear you have of ending up like me. And most of all, she'd be mad at you for abandoning me when I could have used my brother and my best friend."

My eyes dart to the side, focusing on the textured wall instead of my brother's intense gaze. Wetness gathers in my eyes. "I let you down, and I'm sorry. I was a shit brother, disappearing because the pain was too much. I despised how much it hurt to look at Kaia and not think of Johanna. I hated the way it made me feel. Guilty, disgusted, hurt. And I can't stand myself for doing that to you. I'm really fucking sorry." My voice cracks.

"I forgive you. But the way you can help me forget is by not making some shitty mistake because you're afraid. I'll give you one last piece of my mind, for old time's sake." He shoots me a weak smile. "Don't be an idiot. Get the girl because those who have an issue with it shouldn't be the same ones you trust while driving a car at three hundred kilometers per hour. If I could have one last day with Johanna, I would in a heartbeat, despite knowing when she leaves, I would break again. If you don't feel that way about Sophie, then let her go for good. But I have a feeling you're coming to your own realizations about her. So, by all means, pick the contract or pick her. But when you do, please ask yourself: if you let her go, can you look yourself in the mirror in your McCoy race suit without flinching? If so, then you really never loved her to begin with."

And with that, my brother shines a light on my darkest secrets, highlighting the lies I kept hidden from the world. But most importantly, while banishing the darkness, he sparks something inside of me I hadn't realized I was missing.

Hope.

CHAPTER THIRTY-THREE

Sophie

I only agreed to attend a Bandini sponsor event because my dad forced me earlier. He rejected my request to book a flight back home early, claiming no daughter of his will miss the Championship after all this time.

We sit together at an empty table in a dark corner. I shove my food around my plate while my dad stares at me, his watchful eyes narrowing at me after my fork clatters against the fancy plate for the third time this evening.

"What's wrong with you? You love pasta."

I lift a shoulder in a half-assed shrug. "I'm not hungry. Just not feeling well today."

"You said the same thing yesterday and the day before. Ever since you had a sleepover at Maya's." His pointed stare does nothing to me. "You know, being full of bullshit isn't a sickness.

It's an allergic reaction to not sharing your feelings."

Oh, Dad. So perceptive.

"Catch flights, not feelings." Do I make sense anymore? The jury's still out.

I take a sip of wine. My dad grabs the glass once I put it down, holding it hostage. My lip juts out while my eyes plead for him to let go of the subject.

"This has to do with that boy. I refuse to let you whimper around like a kicked dog when I raised you better than this." *Ouch.* "Either you tell me what happened, or I'll go talk to him. Don't put it past me, Sophie Marie Mitchell."

Under no circumstance do I want him to go talk to Liam, so I give in to protect us both.

"I ended up falling for Liam." Those six words take every ounce of courage from me.

"So what? Everyone knows that."

My head snaps from my plate to my dad's face. "What do you mean?"

Either I'm about as transparent as the wine glass he holds, or my dad really is some undercover Interpol agent.

"You're my daughter. Whenever you look at Liam, you get this look in your eye that I've never seen before. Not even when you check out pasta. It's obvious how you feel about him. And he looks at you similarly."

"How are you so nonchalant about this?"

"What do you expect me to do? Yell at you? You're twenty-two now."

"Uh, yeah. Maybe even storm out of the ballroom after we have at it."

My dad sighs. "I've been dealing with enough drama this year with Noah and Santi. You and Liam have kept your own stuff under wraps for the most part, minus the slipup with the press conference."

"So, you're not mad about me breaking your rule?"

"Oh, I'm mad. But I can't exactly say 'I told you so' when you're about one wine glass away from crying into your dinner."

I sigh at my dad's wakeup call. "Wow. You need to work on your delivery. No wonder you don't have a girlfriend."

He chuckles. "Look at you, making a joke. Why don't you talk to me about whatever's going on? Your old man here used to deal with his own lady problems before I married my job and became a single dad. I made plenty of stupid mistakes growing up. But I'll tell you one thing: anyone who earns your love better be worthy because your heart takes up more than half your body. You carry more soul in your pinky than some people have in their whole bodies."

My dad's kind words bring a small smile to my face.

"Well, it all started with a terrible princess costume and a party you forced me to go to."

He rubs a hand across his face. "I better grab us more wine; I have a feeling this is going to be a long one."

I let out a laugh at my dad's retreating form. For the first time in days, I feel relief.

Speaking to my dad yesterday about Liam opened up a whole new set of wounds. I didn't realize how far I had fallen until I shared my story from start to finish, leaving me vulnerable and lost. Despite my confessions, my dad handled it like a champ, offering a few pieces of advice, along with denying my request to fly home early yet again.

Instead of stewing in my sadness on a flight back to Italy, I get an up-close and personal show of my own demise, set up by my beautiful best friend.

> **Maya:** This is your hourly reminder to not bail on me tonight. You won't like what happens if you do. ☺
>
> **Me:** Threats work better when you don't include a smiling emoji.

Maya responds by sending me the same emoji paired with a knife. I get dressed and look my best because I need to. If I'm going to pour my heart out to Maya at the expense of seeing Liam, I better look the part of an uncaring person. Nothing screams *screw love* quite like an open-back dress.

A couple hours later, I find Maya mingling in the gala's crowd, her sparkly dress nabbing my attention. My hand wraps around the stem of her half-full champagne glass.

"Hey, I was drink—" She stops dead in her tracks.

Either I have an amazing poker face that stuns her, or I look as wild as I feel on the inside. I knock back the contents in a couple gulps, the cool liquid trickling down my throat.

I dub this version of myself as post-Liam.

"Remember during our sleepover when you told me to give Liam some time? That maybe he'd come around to accepting his feelings about me?"

She nods along, attempting to smile but deciding on a frown instead.

"Well, nothing has changed. I'm falling deeper and deeper into trouble by the day." I pout my lip to stop it from trembling.

Maya's frown deepens. "What kind of trouble?"

"The *cleanup in aisle ten because my heart exploded on the ice cream section's floor* type."

A passing waiter makes an appearance. My hands grip his sleeve, not letting him go anywhere without hearing my request. "Sir, can we please have another round of champagne? Stat." The man has a nose for heartbreak because he dashes away.

Maya offers me a sincere smile. "I'm sorry. I thought he would wake up and realize how much of an idiot he's been."

"Before we continue, we need alcohol. Lots of alcohol."

Maya nods in understanding.

My dear friend the waiter shows up with not one but two champagne bottles. He'd be a man after my heart—that is, if I still had one.

We each grab the bottle from the tray and take off toward a corner of the gala. I learned nothing from my previous corner experience, but at least this time I have good company. Maya and I take sips straight from the bottle, forgoing the glasses, chugging between my confessions. We're an image of etiquette and grace, sitting on the floor behind a table hiding us from other partygoers. I share everything with Maya, not skimping out on details.

I sip champagne every time I want to laugh or cry, which turns out to be rather often. A few tears escape, and Maya ends up crying with me, proving how I picked a winner for a friend.

By the time I drain half the bottle, I become a giggling mess, running on caloric fumes and poor decisions. I regret not eating a proper dinner because a cupcake doesn't count as an essential part of the food pyramid.

"I hope you know—" I hiccup "—how much I appreciate you."

"You've only told me three times so far. But I love the gratitude." She laughs before taking another sip of champagne.

"How did you know you loved Noah?" Another hiccup escapes my lips.

"When it hurt more to be without him than with him."

"I don't think Liam loves me." I hold back the tears.

"Why do you say that?"

I frown. "Because he didn't exactly proclaim his love for me when I admitted my feelings."

"And it was so brave of you to try. Maybe he has trouble sharing how he loves you, especially with his shitty contract deal and the pressure he's under. He might be afraid of letting you down. But I don't doubt he loves you."

I take another large gulp of champagne. "He needs to drive more than he needs to breathe. That means I'm out of the picture, replaced by a tempting contract and a brand-new season."

"Right. But what's a contract if you can't be with the person you love."

"I told you he doesn't love me."

Maya rolls her eyes. "Really? Because the way he keeps staring at you from his spot by the bar tells me differently."

I look up from the top of the table to find Liam hanging out with Jax and Noah, his eyes finding mine like two magnets. My eyes narrow before I slip back to the floor.

"Do you think if I hide under the table, he won't find me?" The idea has a certain amount of credibility to it.

"You never know. Maybe we can convince Santi to cause a diversion." Maya looks around for her brother.

"Okay, text him." I pass Maya her clutch that houses her phone.

"Never mind, I think the jig is up." She giggles as Noah plops himself next to her.

I point at Noah with a scowl. "You skedaddle. This is our girl time."

Noah ignores me as his face nuzzles Maya's neck.

"Sorry, Sophie. Noah, stop." She pushes him away with little effort. He grabs her bottle of champagne and chugs it, choosing to wipe his mouth with the sleeve of his tux.

"You guys are disgusting. Truly, I'm nauseous from looking at you."

"You're nauseous because you drank your weight in champagne." Noah taps his bottle to mine.

A pair of shoes stops in front of me, my drunken reflection shining off the leather. I look up, thinking I'll find Liam, except Jax's smiling face greets me. His crazy curls are kept down with rows of short braids, and his grin does little to comfort me. A pang of something happens in my chest at seeing Jax instead of Liam, but my brain feels too numb to register the sensation.

"Come on, love. Leave the two of them to get their rocks off." Jax squats down, his hazel eyes leveling with mine. "Let's turn that frown upside down. What do you say? We don't have to tell Liam because the wanker's been in a terrible mood ever since your little romp in the desert."

I grab his extended hand while picking up the champagne bottle, not willing to part ways just yet.

Jax tsks at me like he scorns a child. His tattooed hand wraps around the bottle, faux skeleton fingers pulling at the neck and placing it on a random table. "I think we've had enough of that to last a lifetime."

"Says the man who chugs champagne for a living."

"Hey, I may be a world champion at chugging bubbly for a living, but I place on some podiums too." He winks at me.

I laugh until I start hiccupping again. Jax talks like he doesn't have an F1 World Championship win under his belt.

He leads us through the crowd, going slow since I continuously trip over my sneakers. My eyes land on Liam who stands by himself, dark and gloomy in a corner. I give him a lame wave with wiggling fingers. His frown deepens, not amused by my sudden friendliness.

Jax takes me outside the ballroom. We ride an elevator down to the ground level, the silence between us giving way to confusion at why he wants to help me. I hurt his best friend. His help doesn't make sense unless Liam sent him.

Stop wishing for things that aren't there, Sophie.

I don't get a chance to ask him because once we walk outside and fresh air hits me, my stomach rolls and my head swims. My body teeters.

"Oh no, you don't." Jax grabs my hair before the champagne betrays me, my stomach revolting against me as acid hits my throat.

"Shit, Sophie. I really loved these shoes. You're lucky my best mate loves you enough to buy me a new pair."

I don't remember anything else except for Jax's voice, sounding more concerned than pissed. My world fades to black, a welcome feeling to ease me from the ache in my chest, pain giving in to numbness.

CHAPTER THIRTY-FOUR

Liam

I wish I could confess my feelings to Sophie. But I'm a coward, mulling over our relationship and my future instead of chasing after it. Despite my brother's help and my parents' verbal ass-whooping, I still struggle to come to grips with my wants versus needs.

I'm afraid. I didn't think my family calling me out on my secrets would've fucked with my head this much. But here I am, worried about conceding to Sophie's love.

I'm not scared of loving her. That would be simple and stupid as fuck. I can't help fearing the very worst, like everything that comes after the big *I love you* back. Thoughts of things going wrong between us make my stomach roll.

Until I can come to grips with my emotions, I need to stay away from Sophie, for her sake and mine. Everyone is right. She deserves the world, and until I can guarantee that I can give it to her, I don't deserve to hang in her orbit.

I follow Jax out of the gala, watching him help out a sick Sophie. She passes out in the grass once her legs give out. Pain grips my heart in a chokehold, knowing she's hurting because of me.

"I hate seeing her this way." I grab her from the ground, her body curling into mine like she knows who carries her.

"Because she smells like a podium after a Prix?" Jax winces at his messed-up shoes.

"No, you idiot. Because I'm the reason she drank to the point of blacking out."

A random bulb flashes, my eyes squinting at the unexpected invasion. A few more flashes go off as a few reporters ask questions about Sophie and me. The bright lights affect my vision, my anger surging at their disregard for privacy.

"What the fuck," Jax growls.

"Shit. This isn't good. Grab her purse and call the car. *Now*." I turn my back toward the paparazzi, shielding Sophie while power walking toward the hotel's valet area.

Tomorrow, I'll deal with the fallout of those pictures. I need to get her back to her room before we run into any other vultures looking for a trashy story. She grumbles into my chest, her fist clutching onto the fabric of my tux.

My head throbs with conflicting emotions. I'm happy to be near Sophie again, while distraught and angry at her for getting shit-faced, and downright pissed at myself for hurting us. I want my friend back, but most importantly, I want her back. All of her.

Jax helps me grab a car and walks with me up to Sophie's

room. He hangs around the suite while I help Sophie in her bedroom, wanting to ease her discomfort as much as I can. She wakes up enough to let me brush her teeth, remove her makeup, and get a set of pajamas on.

I place her on her favorite side of the bed and set up a trash can nearby just in case. She looks small with her body curled up. It pains me to watch her while avoiding how much I want to cuddle next to her, banishing away her hurt while easing my desire to be close to her.

Resisting the urge, I head on out to the living room.

"You're in love with her." Jax brushes a finger across his chin.

"Unfortunately."

His eyebrows dart up. "Do you really mean that?"

"No. I'm an idiot who fucks up everything good in my life."

He eyes me skeptically. "Why don't you tell her how you feel?"

"Because I don't know what I'm going to do."

"You need to sort your shit out. It's not fair to her or yourself. Or to me, the guy waiting to know if you'll be my teammate or not. I'll stay here for a couple of hours and make sure she doesn't choke on her vomit, but you need to go because it'll hurt you both if you stay."

I barely recognize this mature version of Jax, offering me advice and a wakeup call at the same time.

I step outside of her room, the hotel door closing her off to me once again.

CHAPTER THIRTY-FIVE

Sophie

I wake up to a pounding sound that I assume is my brain telling me how angry it is at me. Ignoring the ache, I tug a pillow over my head. Pounding ensues again, but it sounds like it's coming from the door instead of my head.

Oh shit.

Memories flood my brain of me getting drunk and throwing up on Jax.

I crawl out of bed, rubbing the sleep away from my eyes as I open my hotel door to a fuming James Mitchell.

"Hi, Dad." My voice croaks.

"Pack your shit," he growls as he enters my room, commandeering the space like it's his garage.

"What?"

"You're going home. Congratulations, you earned yourself a

flight home. A first-class ticket too because they had nothing else left for last-minute flights."

"I don't understand why you're so angry."

He hands me a local newspaper. "I swear to God I told myself I would be understanding when you told me everything about your relationship with Liam. But you've pushed me too far. I expect you to pack your suitcases. I'm waiting here to escort you to the airport."

My eyes water as I read the title of the gossip column. *Bandini Princess Falls from Grace, Escorted by None Other than Liam Zander, F1's Refined Heartbreaker.* My eyes roam over the page, catching phrases like *hidden relationship* and *secret night visits.*

My cheeks flame from embarrassment. I square my shoulders and look up into my dad's stormy gaze. "This article is trash and you know it."

"I don't care. I warned you what would happen if I found another article like this. I can't work with you causing drama, making dumb decisions because you're hurt. You can go home, relax, and head back to school."

I take a deep breath. "No."

"Excuse me?" My dad takes a step backward, hitting me with flared nostrils and narrowed eyes.

My head pounds but I carry on. "I'm not going home."

"Yes, you are. You never defied me before, so don't start now when I'm pissed as fuck."

I shake my head. "I'm sorry, but I can't go home."

"You will because I say so. I'll handle the Liam problem, but I need you to get the hell out of here. Switch your online classes to the real deal and suck it up." My dad grabs the tabloid and tosses it in the garbage can.

"I can't." Words leave my lips in a whisper.

"Why the fuck not?"

"Because I withdrew for the semester." I shut my eyes, cowering from him in the one way I can.

"You what?" My dad speaks in an eerily calm voice, preferring to seethe and stew as opposed to scream.

I open my eyes to find my dad staring at me with anger evident in his gaze. "I'm not happy, and I can't keep doing something to appease you, like leaving here when I need to finish this out. I love you so much, but I chose a major to make you happy, and it's sucked the life out of me. It's my fault for not being honest in the first place. I hate accounting. I detest the classes and the idea of doing that for the rest of my life. Literally, all of it. I did it because you gave up so much for me." Tears break free, running down my face.

My dad looks gutted. "I'm so disappointed in you. I never thought you would lie to me, let alone for years. And to drop out and not tell me? That's not the daughter I raised."

More tears leak from my eyes, uncontrolled, as my dad stares at me in disbelief. "How can I tell you when I'm afraid of letting you down? You hold me to the same standards of those who work for you. I'm so damn afraid of failing or going against your plans that I'd rather hide the truth than tell you."

"I do push you because I care. Because I don't want you to end up lost or depending on me."

"No. You don't want me ending up like *her*."

He sucks in a breath.

I hold his gaze, not backing down. For the first time in my life, I'm willing to go toe to toe with my dad, unafraid of his consequences. He can send me back home or to Timbuktu for all I care.

"Is that really so wrong? So what if I don't want you to end up like some pothead escaping responsibilities for the rest of your life?" He throws his hands in the air.

"If I choose accounting, I wouldn't be evading responsibilities. I'd be escaping my shot at happiness to fulfill yours."

My dad's eyes harden. I've never seen him like this, his rage simmering beneath the surface as his fists ball up at his sides. Without another word, he turns around, my hotel door slamming behind him.

The battle with my dad has drained my last bit of energy. I sit on the couch, put my face in my hands, and let out a sob.

Winning this battle feels insignificant when I already lost the war.

I never thought of myself as a crier. There was no reason to test how I look due to limited opportunities to screw up. But it turns out, when I cry, my face gets bloated and blotchy with not a dimple in sight. My green eyes become bloodshot, contrasting against the red like an ugly Christmas decoration.

So I, in all my puffy glory, knock my fist against my dad's office door. For hours, I thought about our conversation, unable to sleep off my hangover while my dad was angry with me. Guilt made me restless and irritable all morning.

"Come in," my dad's muffled voice carries through the door.

I take a deep breath as I push open the glossy red door, preparing myself for his anger.

Instead, I get hit with my dad's sorrowful eyes. His vulnerability tugs at me, wetness instantly pooling in my tear ducts.

Come on eye ducts, I thought we were in this together.

"I knew you'd show up eventually. I thought you wouldn't last an hour before hounding me down about our fight. Took you long enough." He sends me a wobbly smile.

Was I the type to make apology letters when my teenage hormones got out of hand and I said stupid shit I didn't mean? Yes. But if anyone quotes me, I'll deny it.

"Am I that predictable?" I stand near his desk, eliminating the gap between us.

"If you asked me that question yesterday, I would have said yes. But seeing as you threw me for a loop today, I'm not so sure anymore."

"Well, I thought the season was getting old with Noah winning and you ruling F1 with Bandini, so I figured I'd shake things up."

My dad fights a smile, replacing his sad eyes with warmth. "Safe to say, you did just that."

"I didn't mean to lie to you for all this time. I didn't know how to break the news to you."

"I'm not sure who I'm more disappointed in. You for lying about your dislike of school for years, or me for not noticing how much you hated it. You're my daughter for fuck's sake. I should be able to tell when you're unhappy or distressed."

"You've been busy. It's understandable when you have Bandini and Noah and Santi to deal with."

"Stop making excuses for me." He stands.

"I can't help it." I have the biggest soft spot for my dad.

He pulls me in for a hug. "Why did you hold this back from me? You should have told me you didn't like your major."

"I didn't know how to break it to you. You looked so happy when I talked about the program. I had no clue how to go about telling you I actually disliked it so much. But I'm done with pretending and hiding what I really want. I'm a grown woman, and you can't force me to go home, just like you can't force me to live a life I hate. That's not living, it's surviving. And you taught me to thrive and make the world kiss my sneakers."

My dad holds me at arm's length, looking at me like he's not sure how I grew up in such a short amount of time. "I can't say I regret giving you the tools to become a strong woman. I never expected them to be used against me."

"I'm sorry for getting drunk last night and ending up on some gossip article looking like the walking dead. I shouldn't have done that, but I felt so sad. My chest hurts all the time and I can't look at Liam without wanting to cry." My smile wavers.

"I'll get back at the people who hurt you. I have a plan, but you have to trust me."

"Get who back?" I don't want him to hurt Liam, although a good scolding sounds nice.

"The bastards who made my daughter cry. Let me handle it." He tugs me back into his chest.

I breathe in his woodsy scent. "I don't want to have Liam end up dead or something. Can you be more specific?"

He chuckles before letting me go. I sink into one of his office chairs, my head pulsing and my fingers shaking. My hangover is getting to me, not pairing nicely with the raging emotions happening inside of me, along with my dad's plan.

"He's too good-looking to mess up. Plus, he loves my daughter, whether he admitted it to you or not."

My chest tightens, but I carry on, choosing to ignore his observation. "Feel free to transfer my first-class ticket to two days from now. I'd love to ride in style back home after the World Championship."

"You sure you're past your expiration date for hospital returns?"

"Positive. I double-checked after I dropped out of school because I knew you'd kill me."

"That's my girl, planning her funeral. We'll talk about your school decision at another time when you don't look like you might throw up your liver."

"Sounds like a plan." I shut my eyes, ignoring the ache in my head and my chest. It's a welcome feeling, reminding me how I'm still here, waiting to live through my last round of torture.

CHAPTER THIRTY-SIX

Liam

I performed decently during my qualifier, landing the P3 position for the final race of the season. The positive placement doesn't carry the same excitement despite my runner-up standing for the entire World Championship. Noah and my competition lack the same fun, with another year of us fucking around for the top spot.

Sophie doesn't make it to the press conference, probably due to an intense hangover she undoubtedly suffers from today. Her absence means I can't speak to her before McCoy keeps me busy for the day. With her refusing to answer my texts, I'm left with no way to talk to her, her absence leaving a void in me.

Unfortunately for me, surprises don't stop coming. Not only did a newspaper publish a terrible photo of me carrying a passed-out Sophie, but James Mitchell comes up to me once an

F1 member calls the end of the qualifier conference.

"I need you to come with me." His green eyes, a copy of Sophie's, glare at me. Where Sophie's eyes fill me with warmth, his remind me of a stern parent. And one look from him tells me to not fuck around and give him a hard time.

I follow him to his Bandini office.

"Sit down. Can I get you something to drink?" His cordialness surprises me.

"A water's fine."

He passes me a chilled bottle before taking a seat at his desk. I break out into a smile when I check out his framed photo. A younger Sophie sports a toothy grin and space buns, ignoring how her body is surrounded by bubble wrap. Her little Nike shoes peek out from underneath her.

My head lifts to meet her dad's face, his jaw twitching as he looks at me like I admitted to killing the family pet.

"See, as much as I want to pay you off to never step foot near my daughter again, I know we both have her best intentions in mind. I did some digging. When my daughter comes to me, not eating or smiling, I will do anything to make sure whatever fucker hurt her regrets the day his parents conceived him. Forget being born because nine months in the womb counts as too much freedom."

Holy shit, he's intense as fuck.

He keeps going. "I'm livid about how she got hammered and ended up featured in a gossip article because she was unable to control her rampant emotions about you. It eats me alive, knowing she's upset. So, I found out the man who needs to be held responsible for her crying. I did the heavy lifting because when my baby girl looks at me with tears in her eyes, I stop at *nothing*. Let that be a warning. My rules were meant to prevent this very thing from happening to her. But you slipped in and tore down her defenses, and she fell in love with you. God knows why." He closes his eyes and pinches his nose.

His words hang between us. Is he talking about me? Does he want to kick my ass?

James senses my confusion and opens up a file on his desk while sliding a matching one to me. "Sophie confessed something heart-wrenching to me a few days ago. She shared how your agent told her you had to dump her if you wanted a spot with McCoy. How if you didn't agree to the offer, you'd be demoted to one of the bottom teams. Imagine my daughter receiving this news with her heart of gold. She understands the consequences of a decision like that because she grew up learning about this business. But most importantly, she gets you because she *loves* you. You played right into her fear of you not loving her back, proving to her why her sacrifice was worth it. Because you showed her how you love racing more than you love her. Sophie admitted to me how you'd freak out if she said she loved you. Congratulations, Liam, you won the biggest dumbass award. Sorry, it doesn't come with a champagne shower and a trophy, but hopefully your heart hurts like a bitch because my daughter's sure does."

My hand stills on the manila file, his words tearing into me. *Shit. Fucking shit.* She knew? Why didn't she say anything? Not a word about Rick ever passed her lips. Never did she mention my contract, or how McCoy was threatening our relationship. But why would she when she knew I kept it as a secret?

My mind races, assessing words she threw in my face when

I took her to the desert. Her weird pushiness about the McCoy contract and the answers I gave.

I'm a fucking idiot. A walking, talking dumbass who gave her every reason to do what she did. She set me free so I could keep living my dream. It was a selfless act that crushed us both, me because I'm a coward and afraid of love. And her because she loves me and wants the best for me.

"When did she find this out?" I choke on the words, my hands shaking as I lift the water bottle to my lips. My throat feels like I swallowed acid instead of water.

"Brazil. Your piece of shit agent cornered her and told her all about your current dilemma. I don't know whether to pity you or punch you for taking so long to decide your feelings about my daughter. I know you love her. But her? Not so much. But after everything, why should she?"

My teeth press together painfully at his judgment. I deserve it and everything else he swings my way. "I do love her. I didn't need to decide because I was waiting to hear what McCoy would say about my revisions. I told them to modify the deal or fuck off. But they didn't tell me or Rick anything."

"If I were you, I'd fire your agent and find better representation. Fuck, I'll help you. But I'm getting off-task, and I'm a busy man as you can imagine."

A cold feeling creeps up my spine. I nod along, confused and wanting any answers he can give me. His eyes slide from my face to my squeezed fists and shaking leg.

"You know, I kept my daughter away from this place for years because I love her. I want her to be happy—not caught up in this life of deception and shitty people like Rick. I tried to protect her from a life full of missed dinners, phone calls interrupting important moments, and men who can't commit for shit. All I asked her to do was follow three simple rules. But during this season with you and her, I realize I made mistakes of my own, trying to protect her from making the same errors. She needs to live a life riddled with slipups and learned lessons. Because that's the point. One day when you have kids, you'll understand. You'll want to protect them with everything in you because you've never loved anything as fucking much as them. You'll want to stop time and hold on to the special moments with a death-grip." He taps on the photo of a bubble-wrapped Sophie. "No bubble wrap can save her from you. I know my daughter and you are the one thing I can't shield her from."

I don't know what to say because words don't come easily. The statement he shares affects me in different ways, pulling me apart in multiple directions.

"What you do with this information is your choice, but I thought it was worth sharing with you. If you want to prove to me that you're the man for my daughter, then I suggest you choose what you do next very carefully. You're a fortunate asshole because my daughter forgives easily." His challenging glare doesn't fill me with alarm. Instead, hope floods my veins and takes root.

I flip open the file James made for me. My eyes scan the pages, flipping through information, transcripts, and heaps of dishonesty. If I didn't want to look psychotic in front of him, I'd scream up to the fucking ceiling at the information he found.

Instead, I mumble a thank you to James before taking the file and booking it to my suite. Lukas hangs out on the living room couch, still dressed in his McCoy gear after attending my qualifier. I itch to rip off my own McCoy shirt, but I keep it on, not wanting to waste time.

"I need your help." I toss the file on his lap.

"What's this?" He leaves it unopened as he stares at me.

"I don't even know how to start without losing my shit. I've been a fucking idiot, standing around while two assholes played with my future. They messed with Sophie, my deals, everything. All for money."

"You're losing me."

"McCoy. Peter. Even Rick was in on the plan." I motion toward the file. My hands shake from built-up anger and frustration, begging to unleash on the two people who tried to mess with my life at the expense of a paycheck.

Lukas combs through the papers James gathered from God knows where. "Who gave you all this?"

"Sophie's dad."

"Shit."

I clench my hands. "I'm such an idiot. Sophie told me she loved me, and I said *nothing*. At least nothing worthy of her. She knew about McCoy offering me a contract if I dropped her and our friendship. She fucking knew, and still gave me a chance to prove her wrong."

"What do you mean?"

"She asked me if I wanted to work for a company with drama revolving Claudia and Peter." I take in a sharp breath to ease the panicky feeling growing inside my chest. "I told her yes. I told the girl who loves me that I didn't mind dealing with an ex-fling as long as I got a deal in the end. I'm a fucking moron. I don't know how she can forgive me. Her knowing I kept that secret from her, it changes things."

"Liam, stop being an idiot. It doesn't change anything. You're still in the same position, with her not talking to you. Now you have to work harder to get her back. That's it."

I pull on the collar of my shirt. "I don't know how to go about fixing this. The whole damn thing gives me anxiety."

"Okay, well I have an idea, but it might be crazy."

I settle into the couch across from Lukas. "I have a feeling your version of crazy is pretty tame."

"Hey, you're looking at the man who got arrested for public nudity."

"Does it count if you were busted with Jo because the cop was an asshole who didn't like you hooking up in a car at a local park? You make it seem like you were caught streaking or something cool."

Lukas shows me a rare middle finger. "I had to beg the officer to not arrest us. Jo was crying in the backseat while I was cuffed in my boxers. It was borderline traumatic, with me shaking because I was afraid I ruined my chance at med school. All for a quickie because we couldn't wait to get home."

"Gross. TMI." I fake gag. "What does the crazy, rule-breaker have to offer me as far as plans go?"

My brother flips through a few pages of the file, scanning the content. "You're going to eat shit after you hear what I have planned."

"I'm on a strict diet, but thanks for the offer."

"Fuck off." Lukas smiles at me. A genuine wide smile I haven't seen in some time—at least not directed toward me.

On top of everything I've learned over the past few days, I

realize two more things. One: I'm a dumbass for ignoring my brother and evading his calls. I didn't realize how much I miss him and the easygoingness we have with one another. And two: We talked about Jo without my chest stinging. That thought alone has me holding my head higher.

My brother snaps his fingers to get my attention. "First step: hit them when they least expect it."

"How so?"

"These two seem to love a good story. Why don't you give them a taste of their own medicine?" Lukas shoots me a mischievous grin I didn't know he had in him. I return one, ready for whatever he has planned.

I hope the F1 world is ready for me because I'm about to set fire to the whole fucking thing.

CHAPTER THIRTY-SEVEN

Sophie

I mend my torn-up heart with masking tape because I don't have time to heal before I go back home. Wounds need to be licked in private, preferably under the supervision of Ben and Jerry's and *Parks and Recreation*.

I attend the race because I want to be there. At the end of the day, Liam's my friend. No matter what happened between us or whether he places top or not. He could drive for McCoy or Albrecht and I'd still cheer him on because I love him. There's no use avoiding my feelings because the constant throb in my chest calls me out on my bullshit, reminding me of what I lost.

So, I shelve my pain as Liam gets showered with champagne, standing proudly with Noah, who won the title of the World Champion this year. I hold a smile the whole time and cheer them all on. No matter how much it hurts me to watch him, I clap my hands when they announce Liam as the runner-up.

His eyes catch mine from the stage and he winks at me before tipping his champagne bottle in my direction. It's a repeat of the time he placed in Sochi, reminding me of the domino that started this all. I shake my head and laugh. My eyes cloud with tears, but I hold them back and give Liam a wobbly smile.

My dad finds me in the VIP area and pulls me in for a hug. "You know, kiddo, you've impressed me a lot of times in your short life. But you standing here and facing something that brings you a lot of pain, now that's courage."

I give him a squeeze before he lets go. "How did you deal with everything when my mom left?"

"I woke up one day and realized I can either spend the rest of my life holding on to hope that everything will fall into place... or I can shove two middle fingers at life and make it my bitch. Pardon the language, sweetheart."

Both my dad and I break out into a laugh together.

"I think I prefer the second option." I look into his eyes and smile.

"Of course, you do. Where do you think you get it from?" He sends me a wink I'm sure brought all the ladies to their knees back in the day.

Noah shows up out of nowhere and showers my dad in champagne, a gesture of appreciation for all of his hard work, catching me in the crossfire. My soaked Bandini T-shirt clings to my skin. Somehow, I entered a wet T-shirt contest I did not sign up for.

I let my dad have his fun, taking my sad vibes and newfound confidence with me.

I make my way down the empty pit lane, passing by each team's deserted garage, no longer humming with activity and mechanics. The emptiness matches how I feel inside, mocking me as I say my final goodbyes to F1 because I don't know if I'll ever come back.

My dad warned me about the guys here and the world they live in. But I didn't listen, resulting in getting hurt. But on the flip side, I found bits and pieces of myself, discovering what I love along the way. I found love in art again. And now I appreciate the way life happens naturally, without plans or lists. This season helped me mature whether I wanted to or not, and similar to growing pains, it hurts.

I'm ready to go home and show the world what I'm made of. For real this time. No more hiding behind a degree I hate or a Fuck it list to prove to myself how I can have fun and let go.

"Sophie! Wait!" Liam's voice echoes off the pit walls.

My feet turn on their own to find Liam running toward me in his race suit, looking like a white knight.

He stops in front of me, not the least bit winded. "I need to talk to you."

"About?" I cringe at the roughness in my voice.

"I had no idea you knew about the McCoy deal. Fuck. I tried to change it by getting them to agree to my conditions." He runs a hand through his damp hair, probably wet due to a mix of alcohol and sweat.

"It's okay. I get it."

"Why are you acting casual about this? I'm so sorry. You probably feel betrayed, but I swear I was working with them to secure something better. They didn't tell me anything. And fuck, the fact that Rick talked to you behind my back makes me want to rip him a new asshole to match his personality." Liam's worried eyes run over my face.

"I understand why you didn't. It's really okay. You have to do what you need to for racing because that's your end goal."

He grips my hands in his, a current of energy trailing up my arm. "That's not true. Not anymore. I want you."

I shake my head in a weak attempt to rid his words from my ears. "I can't blame you for struggling to decide between not being my friend anymore or staying with McCoy. Which is so fucked up, but I get this world. I get *you*. But you hurt me, not admitting you loved me despite everyone telling me you do. And I'm tired of people telling me. It's not their job, it's yours."

"I do love you. I swear. I've done a shit job at realizing it, and an even shittier job admitting it to you. I love you more than racing itself. I've been miserable since you started avoiding me, where even spending a week without you is fucking torture. My chest aches, my sleep cycle blows, and my head throbs every fucking day. I can't stand how I feel without you around. And I don't want to anymore."

"After all this time of waiting to hear those words…I feel hollow." I don't recognize my flat voice.

His face crumbles. "What can I do to make it better? Please, I'll do anything."

I nearly give in at his broken voice, but I can't. Not anymore. "Like I said. Everyone wants to tell me how much you love me, including yourself. You know what? Now it's your turn. I want you to prove it."

I turn, heading toward Bandini's suite, leaving behind a distraught Liam.

The prince can't be saved if he's too stubborn about staying locked up in his castle.

CHAPTER THIRTY-EIGHT

Liam

Sophie's dad didn't throw a grenade at me yesterday. He dropped a motherfucking IED and hoped I knew what to do with it. Lukas plotted with me because Sophie taught me plans lead to effectiveness. I privately spoke with different teams, surpassing an agent because fuck Rick the dick very much.

One of the last items on my list is to confront the sly motherfucker and his goon of a sidekick.

Cameras face me as reporters ask questions about the final Prix and my runner-up standing. I'm proud as hell of my performance this year because despite the stacked odds and snakes in the McCoy pit, I placed second against many talented racers.

"Liam, care to comment on the recent article about you and Miss Mitchell?"

"Since you're bringing that up, I'd like to announce some important news. My relationship with Sophie Mitchell will be just that. *My* relationship. I'm tired of you asking me questions about my personal life, or about her. She's off-limits—to you, to paparazzi, and to any other straight male within a one-hundred-mile radius of her. She's mine, the end. I'm a lucky bastard who she for some reason fell in love with. That means I'm not allowing my relationship to go to shit because of vultures who want to tear us down. This is my first and last warning regarding the subject. The next person who brings her up in any way besides complimenting her gets blacklisted from the interview schedule. You guys love to comment how damn replaceable we all are here, so let's turn the tables, shall we?"

Noah's head snaps toward me, his lips fighting a smile. "Damn. I didn't think you had that level of assholery in you. I'm impressed."

Microphones don't pick up on my voice. "I've been watching you be a dick for years. Learned from the best."

I bide my time, aware one of these reporters will ask exactly what I need. They can't help it.

"Liam, have you decided what team you'll be driving for?"

Predictable fuckers. "It's funny you ask. Here's some more breaking news." Camera bulbs flash and reporters seem to scoot in closer, waiting for me to speak. "I will not be competing with McCoy next year. My ex-agent Rick is a con who manipulated me because he wanted me to sign with the team again. Richard Johnson is a fraud and anyone who's hired him should seek new representation. For months, he lied to me and told me how only two other teams besides McCoy were interested in signing me.

He wanted to receive a bigger pay cut from McCoy instead of letting me choose between different offers." I toss my McCoy ball cap toward the side of the stage.

"And where do you plan on going next year?"

"To be determined. But let it be known, whether I come back or not, I drive F1 cars for the love of it. Not for the drama and sure as hell not for dicks in suits telling me what to do."

Noah and Santiago clap at my speech. Jax whistles from the sidelines, standing next to Elena, who stares at me with wonder and shock. *Sorry, dear, no PR rep can fix this.*

I spent the whole season trying to make up for my mistakes with Peter and the team. In the end, my idiocy has no bounds, with me concentrating my energy on a team that didn't matter instead of on people who did.

As far as me competing next year, of course I am. But I can't announce anything until I get the girl. Without her, there's no point.

Jax pulls me aside once the press conference wraps up. "I'll miss you. Now I really have a chance at winning another Championship."

"I'm joining a different team, not dying. Better luck in about seven years when I retire." I pound his fist.

"Nah. It'll be sooner than that once you start popping out little blonde-haired babies with your future wife."

I pull him in for a hug.

"As much as I hate to interrupt this powwow, a little warning would have been nice." Elena's melodic voice greets us.

I turn around, ready to set the record straight.

She interrupts me before my mouth opens. "I could have

helped you devise a better way to say all of that. I'm disappointed you didn't drop an F-bomb to really drive the point home."

Jax needs to pick my jaw up off the floor because I didn't expect her reaction.

I grin at her. "Can I keep you on retainer? I'm bound to fuck up at least once or twice."

"I'll give you my card. Looks like McCoy and I will have our hands full with this one—" Elena points at Jax "—but I can handle multiple projects at once." She passes me a matte business card.

"What's that supposed to mean?" Jax snaps her. I don't know what shocks me more—the way he acts around her, or how she remains professional and ignores him.

She squints her eyes. "Have you picked up a magazine lately? You've got more issues than *Vogue*."

I drop my head back and laugh for the first time in a while. "You have your work cut out for you. Just a tip, he works best after a nap."

Jax stares at Elena with a clenched jaw and crossed arms, a gleam in his eye present for the first time in a long while. If I didn't have any plans, I'd push him for more, wondering what about Elena sets him off. Instead, I say my goodbyes before walking away because I have places to go and people to wreck.

Life comes full circle. Before the season began, Peter and Rick met with me to discuss my issues, cast judgments, and throw jabs at me. Now, I call a meeting with them because I can. Rick squirms in his seat with his gelled hair askew and pinstripe suit wrinkled. Peter remains neutral with a flat smile, clasped hands, and a shining head.

I take a deep breath. "Rick, I wish I could say it was a pleasure to work with you, but I'd be lying. I know honesty isn't a familiar concept for you so let me break it down. You fucked with the wrong man. I suggest you crawl back to whatever American hellhole you came out of because you'll never be hired in this industry again, let alone another sport. I'll make it my personal mission to ensure you never have a chance. I trusted you, and this is how you repay me? Fuck that."

"I don't know what you've been told, but I'm sure we can work something out." Rick's throat bobs.

"Are you really trying to pretend you didn't fuck with my signing?"

"I didn't say that. But I'm sure we can come to an agreement about your contract. Maybe Peter is open to offering you more money." Rick's eyes alternate between Peter and me.

"To make this all go away, I'm willing to add another ten million. With a stipulation that McCoy is kept out of any drama related to Rick." Peter taps his hand against the table.

"Are you both fucking for real right now? This isn't about money, or about a stupid contract for next year."

Rick's look of shock feeds the anger and resentment inside me at him not only messing with me, but with Sophie. For making her cry, for being a crappy agent and an even shittier human being. I can't believe I ever trusted this man.

I continue, staring straight into Rick's panicked eyes. "I hope it was worth cutting a deal with Peter to receive an extra million if I stayed with McCoy without ever finding out. Truly, your greed for an extra six zeros will need to hold you over for the rest of your life because you're done here. Same with you, Peter."

Peter and Rick rotate their heads toward each other. *The jig is up, motherfuckers.*

"Liam, I don't know where you got this misleading information but…" Peter's eyes flare.

If I weren't in such a piss-poor mood, I would laugh at the rattled site of him. I grab two manila folders from my backpack. Peter shuts up as I slide him the folder.

"Oh, I almost forgot a few things. Anger clouds my judgment like that. Peter, I didn't invite you here for a show. I hope you enjoyed that false sense of security because I'm about to rip not only the carpet out from under you, but the whole fucking foundation. I respect the hard-working McCoy team too much to screw with the image of the brand. They don't deserve to suffer from your greed, manipulation, and selfishness."

Peter shifts in his seat. His eyes remain on the dull yellow folder, not bothering to flip a page.

I offer a wicked grin. "You know, all this time I thought Claudia was releasing information about me to the press. I assumed she wanted to get back at me for what I did and the pain I caused. But imagine my surprise when I found out you were the one behind those articles. Because why would I ever assume the man who wanted to defend the brand—who should've wanted to protect me—would do something callous like that? Well-played, I'll give you that. Unfortunately, I can't take the credit for outsmarting you. All I can say is that you messed with the wrong man's daughter. Although you can thank yourself for the bullet wound in your foot, you can thank James Mitchell for the one to your cold, calculating heart."

Peter opens the folder and flips through multiple pages of transcripts with reporters. Everything is documented nowadays, including Peter's use of his personal computer to privately message reporters using a fake account. Peter was no match for James Mitchell, who did something along the lines of tracking IP addresses back to hotels or something. I'm too afraid to ask where he learned his hacking skills, but apparently, he was able to connect Peter to the gossip magazines and paparazzi.

"It doesn't matter what I did when my family owns the company." Peter has the balls to stare me down, alluding to the venom he expertly disguises. I wish I had realized his deception sooner, saving Sophie from experiencing pain at the hands of these two fuckers.

"Is that so? You're a smart man since you tricked me after all. But let's apply some critical-thinking skills here. In the end, you treated me like a pawn in your own game, but unfortunately for you both, you messed with the wrong queen."

Rick's wild eyes gaze upon Peter as realization dawns on him. Took his slimy ass long enough to come to grips with how his time is up, with no Peter McCoy swooping in to save him. How can he when Peter's too busy losing his job?

I stand, the chair's wheels squeaking against the polished floor as I place my hands on the table. "Enjoy the last ten minutes of managing McCoy."

Peter sucks in a breath at the knock on the door.

"Looks like your replacement is here." My footsteps echo off the walls.

Two sets of beady eyes follow me, their bodies frozen.

"Have a nice life." I salute them with a middle finger and walk out the door.

CHAPTER THIRTY-NINE

Sophie

I couldn't help watching Liam's press release on a loop over the past week. Everyone in the racing community talked about his agent's deception, shock waves rippling about how something like that can be done in the first place. Liam kept quiet, not a single message or missed call popping up on my phone. Instead of brooding and gorging myself with ice cream, I used my sadness as motivation, shifting my focus from him to myself.

Over the week, I spent hours researching and making calls, inquiring about my areas of interest. Liam's courage to stand up to his team lit my own fire. It gives me the strength to stand in my dad's office, a library fit for a movie set, while he stares at me. The smell of books calms me before I take a seat in a leather chair across from him.

"You might as well spit out whatever's bugging you." He

takes off his reading glasses and places them on his cherry wood desk.

"Well…I don't know how you're going to take it. But I can't hold it in anymore," I stammer, the words not coming out smoothly.

"Are you pregnant?" he blurts out.

My eyes water as I break out into a fit of coughs. "God, no."

"Good. Now that we got that out of the way, what's bothering you?"

"Whoa, you insinuated I was pregnant, and you segue into something else? Are you trying to tell me I need to lay off the Chunky Monkey? I buy one pint of ice cream…"

"No. You've been a blubbering mess ever since you left Abu Dhabi."

I frown at my dad. "You need to be way less blunt with people."

"Sorry. That was rude."

"Yeah, thank you very much. Now I don't feel so bad about dropping this on you."

He shakes his head at me "I have no idea where you got your sass from."

"Sir, you're looking at the product of your own creation. Anyway… Spending time with kids inspired me to research what I can do with my creativity. I want to go to school for art."

His elbows rest on his desk with his chin pressed against his hands. "Nothing you do with art will ever support you and a family."

"I know that. But I did the math and if you die within the next ten years, your will should be large enough to cover my living expenses for about two hundred years, give or take a century. Until then, there's always stripping."

My dad lets out a husky laugh. I laugh with him, the sound foreign to my ears after a week of sulking.

"Jokes aside, what would you like to do?" His sincere tone touches my heart.

"I want to pursue art therapy. After spending time with Liam's nieces, I realized I want to work with kids. What can I say? They gravitate toward me. I think it's all in the height because they see me as an equal."

"If that's what you want, I'll support you. Anything to bring a smile to your face because I hate seeing you sad and mopey." He frowns.

"I'm not mopey. I'm a bad bitch who enjoys the comfort of pajamas and wine as a food group."

"It's okay to admit you've been sad. I don't blame you after what you went through."

I shake my head side to side. "I don't want to talk about it…"

"Then why don't you tell me more about this program you want. No daughter of mine is going to become a stripper, so I might as well see what I'm paying for."

I pull out my laptop and show my dad the program I want to attend in Milan. The whole conversation with my dad went shockingly easier than I thought. A weight lifts off my shoulders that I didn't know I was carrying around, my future looking brighter by the day.

For the rest of the afternoon, my dad spends time with me. He watches a couple videos on how art therapy helps kids of all ages before pulling me into a hug and telling me how proud he is of me.

Everything finally feels like it'll be okay. Well, almost everything.

I run down the stairs of our house when the doorbell rings. The mailman must be dropping off my new sneakers, a *you go girl* gift from me to me. My order may have been a result of watching Tom Haverford telling me to "treat yo self," but if my dad asks, I'll feign indifference.

I open the door and bend over, expecting a package on the ground. My eyes meet a pair of Gucci sneakers that most definitely do not belong to our delivery guy. My back straightens, and I stare straight into a pair of blue eyes I know well. The same blue eyes I've missed more than I'd like to admit.

"Surprise?" He smiles at me hesitantly.

I freeze, unsure what to do.

"Blink twice if you're still in love with me." His rendition of the first words he said to me warms my heart, a steady thump reminding me how much he means to me.

Damn him, pulling a reaction from me from nothing more than a smile and a simple sentence.

Nothing has changed with his blonde hair perfectly parted, his beard trimmed tight to his skin, and his muscles bulging against his shirt. But his eyes look different and the same all at once. Lit up with happiness, humor, and a bunch of other stuff, creating an emotion rainbow.

I blink twice without thinking.

Liam pulls me into a hug, his arms wrapping around me and

enveloping me with his scent. "I've missed you so damn much, but I didn't want to come before I settled everything. It's been hard as fuck to stay away from you for this long, especially when you are upset because of me. But you deserve my all, so I'm here to deliver."

He lets go of me and pulls out a small jewelry box, snapping me out of my mental holiday.

"Whoa. No. You can't just show up out of the blue and bring a ring box."

He shakes his head from side to side as he stares at the box. "I don't know whether to be amused at your assumption or pissed you look horrified. Here goes nothing," he mumbles under his breath as his cheeks flush.

I love nervous Liam. It's a rare occasion saved especially for me.

"Sophie Marie Mitchell, I would like to announce first and foremost that I have never known someone as incredible as you. When I met you almost four years ago, I had no idea you'd pop back up in my life years later, acting and looking the way you did. I'm not one to believe in fate or destiny for that matter. But seeing you at that gala, fuck if I'd believe in anything for you. Literally anything. When you talked to me about the stars and the sky, I knew I had to spend more time with you. The girl whose eyes twinkle as bright as the very things she loves to watch. And while you were busy staring up at the vast nothingness, I'd watch you while envying a damn sky. A sky for fuck's sake. But at the time, I didn't realize I wanted you to look at me that way. With unconditional love."

My eyes cloud as I stare into Liam's eyes.

He takes a breath and smiles at me again. "The more time I spent with you, the more I fell, but I was too stupid to realize it for what it was. I was scared to let someone in after seeing what my brother went through, but there you were, not taking no for an answer. You challenged me in every way. You gave me all of you while I hid behind a mask, and with that, I let you down. It's something I never want to do again for the rest of my life. At least not without heaps of make-up sex and apologies because I want to be a man you can count on. One who is worthy of your affection, *I love yous*, and orgasms."

"Leave it to you to make me laugh and cry all at once." I swipe away a tear that lost the fight with my tear duct.

"I love you so fucking much. I never want to go another day without saying it or a moment without you knowing it. Fuck friends with benefits. Give me all the damn benefits, love included because I'm a stupid fucker for thinking I could let you walk away from me." He pops open the lid of the jewelry box, revealing a pair of diamond star earrings twinkling under the sunlight.

My eyes betray me, the tear I shed before turning into a waterfall. "You're a little stupid. But that's okay because I still love you."

His smile grows wider at my words. "I researched all about stars. And the funny thing was how I thought you were my star—a bright spot in my life keeping me constant company no matter how dark everything else got. But in reality, we're stars because they are born in pairs. They're created by a big fucking boom of dust and shit, forming into something beautiful and eternal. You're stuck with me for life because we're a duo." He leaves no room for opposition.

"And if I say no?"

"Then too fucking bad. You can't deny a cosmic boom." He pulls me in for a soft kiss with a promise for more.

I cup his cheeks and hold his eyes hostage. "I love you. For meeting me where I was at and helping me grow into who I am. For never giving up no matter how many times I shut you down. And for showing me what it feels like to love someone else and be loved in return in all the ways that count, even when you weren't able to admit it to yourself. When words weren't an option, you showed me with everything in you. I love you from your dirty brain to the tips of your ridiculously expensive sneakers."

His lips find mine again, his tongue invading my mouth, welcoming me back.

Liam breaks away from our kiss. "Before I forget because you're sexy as fuck and I lose my shit around you." He pulls out my little laminated list, showing me every checked item.

"Okay…" I look up at him with confusion until he flips it over.

My eyes mist again, happy tears mixing with shocked ones. Liam wrote a ton of new items. He kisses away the tears streaming down my face while I read, missing a couple that trickle down his Sharpie creation.

Join the mile-high club.

Get married.

Buy our first Christmas tree.

Make a mini Liam.

Design Sophie's art studio.

Spend Christmas in Germany.

Fuck Sophie's backdoor.

Buy the house first (see other).

Make a mini Sophie.

Have a quickie while the kids play outside.

Visit space (ambitious).

Watch our child's first kart race (either gender because feminism rules).

Buy a dog (if you're a cat person it's over).

My eyes blink at the final item. *Move to Italy and join Vitus.* Liam hits me with a goofy smile, warming my heart.

"You're moving to Italy? For Vitus? You forgot to mention that in your little speech!" I wrap my arms around his neck.

"I didn't because that's not the most important thing anymore. What good is racing if I can't spend all my time with the person I love." Liam twirls us in a circle while running his nose against my neck. A couple of my neighbors leave their houses to check on the noise, but I wave them away.

"You're so getting laid." I kiss him softly on the lips.

"Now that's what I like to hear." He plants me back on the ground so we can be face-to-face. I giggle as he pecks my face with a bunch of kisses, leaving no area untouched by his lips.

"I can't believe you're moving here. Like for real."

He sends me a breathtaking smile. "Anything for you."

Heart, please don't melt on the doormat.

"Well, now that you mention it, I did envy your McCoy Menace. You know, the one you drove in Monaco?"

"I offer you the stars and you ask for my car. You truly are a girl after my heart." Liam looks at me with every ounce of love in his eyes.

"Didn't you hear? I already have it."

CHAPTER FORTY

Sophie

One Year Later

Ever seen one of those Christmas movies? Like the Hallmark ones, where the girl travels to a small town filled with holiday cheer and tiny shops decorated to perfection?

Well, multiply that imagination times ten and you'll have yourself a very merry German Christmas.

"I won't lie to you, when you told me we should come to join Liam's family for Christmas, I didn't imagine this," my dad whispers into my ear as we sit together on a couch in Liam's living room. Everyone opened their presents already, leaving behind heaps of wrapping paper. Liam offered for us to change sitting rooms, but I shut down that idea after throwing a wad of wrapping paper at his head.

I mean, multiple sitting rooms? Come on!

My dad's reaction to Liam's mansion yesterday was the same one I had when I first visited months ago. I nearly pushed my dad inside the massive foyer, telling him to act cool. It's hard to not blame my dad, seeing as if it's not exactly normal to have a car garage straight out of a *Batman* movie and enough rooms to house the entire Bandini team.

Liam always told me about his multiple real estate investments, but I didn't expect his home in Germany to compete with his Italian villa. The same one with a personal movie theater, an arcade room, a gym I never step foot in, and a custom art room Liam set up for me. And that's only covering the lower west wing.

Not to mention he shares a backyard with Maya and Noah.

This is the life I live now, with a boyfriend who has enough properties to compete with a season of *House Hunters*.

I break away from my thoughts. "I didn't expect Liam to dress up like Santa Claus for his nieces either."

My dad laughs. "Lord, I hope he always works out because he doesn't look good with that kind of gut. Sorry, sweetie."

"I'm kinda into it. Especially with Kaia and Elyse sitting on his lap. Who can resist a man playing with kids?"

Liam laughing with his nieces fills me with a sense of pride I can't explain. He came a long way from the broken man who avoided his family at his own expense. We've visited Germany multiple times this year, including this visit for the holidays and Kaia's birthday.

Yup. Kaia's birthday. Liam has shown such incredible progress to the point of helping Lukas plan a birthday party for his niece that includes a real-life Rapunzel and a mini inflatable palace.

"I need to lock you up at home. Don't think I'm not aware of your late-night visits and random sleepovers with Zander."

"Are you now a stickler for not sleeping together until marriage?" I mockingly gasp.

"I'm a stickler for you staying with me as long as you can. I don't want you to grow up so fast. I remember when I was the only man in your life. Now look at you." My dad's smile wavers. Something about his eyes makes me pull him into a hug.

"You'll always be my favorite dad."

"Gee, thanks, my favorite daughter. I'm glad I beat the competition for your love." He laughs as he lets go of me.

"Hey, Sophie, can I pull you away for a second?" Lukas interrupts us.

"Sure. Be right back, Dad." I wave at him as I walk behind Lukas toward the kitchen, leaving behind Liam's family in the living room. Baked goods occupy every surface along with my failed gingerbread house attempt.

"So, I wanted to thank you." Lukas looks up at me with blue eyes similar to his brother's.

"For what exactly?" My confusion must be apparent because Lukas lifts his hand at me.

"This will be much easier if I get it all out in one go. I want to say thank you for everything. Really. My brother has grown so much in the past year, and I know you're part of the reason. He spends time with his family more, and he makes an effort with me to connect again. Plus, he actually checks in on my girls and that means the world to me. When Johanna passed, it tore me and Liam apart in different ways. But thanks to you, and the love you showed him while calling him out on his bullshit, he changed for the better. I've never been able to say a proper thank you. You're basically part of the family now." Lukas shoots me a smile. Something glimmers in his eyes, but I can't place it.

He pulls me in for a hug and I let him. I feel like his moment of gratitude is important for him, especially with everything he has lost and gained.

"I warned you about messing with my girl. On Christmas, dude? Sophie, I promise the stomach is only temporary!" Liam barrels into us, squeezing me into his brother in the strangest hug I've ever experienced.

"Speaking of your stomach, it's digging into my back, and it kind of hurts." I laugh as Liam backs up.

"I was just thanking Sophie for how much of a help she's been with Kaia's birthday. Imagine if you went with the pink bounce house instead of the purple one." Lukas pretends our conversation never happened, and I let him.

Liam gasps. "The horror. Who knew Kaia had a sudden allergy to anything pink?"

"I did!" I stick my tongue out at Liam.

"Okay, Miss Know It All. I need to steal you away from my brother. Hope you enjoyed Sophie while it lasted, Lukas. She's all mine. Forever and ever." Liam grabs my hand and drags me down the hall.

"You're such a weirdo." I laugh as he guides the way toward his mega garage. The lights turn on one by one, the noise echoing off the walls. "Also, that totally seems like something from the Bat Cave."

"Why are you obsessed with this garage and *Batman*? I'd be concerned about him if I didn't fuck you against the hood of my

McCoy Menace."

My cheeks flush as I check out the car Liam references. "Har. Har. Hilarious."

"Want to take her for a drive?" He walks to the wall that houses all the keys.

"On Christmas? It's snowing and your family's upstairs."

"So? My parents are going to drink with your dad, and my brother's going to put the girls down for bed. Santa needs to get moving." Liam pats his ridiculous stomach prop.

"Does Santa have a special gift for me?"

He shoots me a smile as he throws me a pair of keys.

I rush to catch them. The key fob has a BMW insignia on them. "Liam, these are the wrong keys. This isn't for the Menace."

"Are they? My bad. Here, catch."

"What?" I screech as I nearly drop the second one he throws at me. This one weighs more. When I check out the fob, I find the loop filled with other keys. "Another BMW one. Are you forgetting what your old logo looked like already?"

Liam closes the gap between us. He brushes a loose strand of hair out of my face, making my skin tingle from his touch. "Nope, I remember it. I wasn't offering for you to drive the McCoy car. I want you to drive this one." He taps on the fob, and a beeping noise sounds off.

I turn to find a BMW convertible with the tiniest bow on the hood. "What's going on?"

"Check out the bow on that sucker. I mean, big things come in small packages, am I right?"

"Did you buy me a car?" I choke on the words.

"Remember when you told me you'd move to Germany if my

parents offered you a BMW convertible?"

My head snaps toward his. "That was over a year ago. How do you even remember that?"

He taps his temple. "With you, I remember it all. Except my parents aren't asking you to move here."

"Are you trying to tell me you're moving to Germany? I'm so confused."

Liam tugs me into him. He leaves behind the faintest kiss before grabbing the key fob from my hand. "Nope. I'm asking you to move in with me. Period. All these keys belong to my different homes. I want you to be by my side every day. In the mornings. In the evenings, and every moment in between. No more sneaking around behind your dad's back and no more uni dorms. Say you'll move in with me?"

"Of course!" I launch myself into Liam's arms. He kisses me to the point of breathlessness, leaving me aching for more.

"Thank fuck because I already had someone come in and customize a closet for your massive sneaker collection. I used to dream of your sneakers around my waist but turns out I really fantasized about keeping them in my house forever."

I laugh as he kisses my neck. "I love you and thank you for the car. You never fail to surprise me."

"Oh, babe. You haven't seen anything yet. No need to wish on stars anymore when I'm here to make your dreams come true."

I groan. "Your pickup game is so weak."

Liam places me lightly on the hood of my new car. "How about my sexy game? Still up to your standards?"

He kisses me without me ever answering his question. There's no point. With Liam, everything is exactly how I want it. He's the man I want to spend all my time with. The man who continues to grow into a better person each day, no longer plagued by his past. The same one I dream of marrying one day.

Liam is right. I don't need to wish on stars when I already have everything I could dream of.

EPILOGUE

Liam

Two Years Later

I always thought F1 was it for me, the idea of being with someone an impossibility. But I ended up finding love in the very place that was supposed to be my everything.

Sophie single-handedly turned me into an emotional fucker over the years. Ever since she came to spend her summer with Bandini years ago, she scratched away at my rough exterior until nothing was left to protect me from her. Her list captured my attention, but her essence stole everything else. Sophie accepted my secrets. She saw past the man on the stage, not taking my fake display of happiness as anything more than a show.

Sophie upgraded her laminated list to Post-its scattered around the house, the colors switching between neon shades depending on the task or mood. It's a game we've played together for years. Pink Post-its have sexy stuff, blue are happy notes, green includes need to-do or buy items, and yellow has sweet messages she finds on Pinterest.

We still keep our famous list hidden away, only marking off items when we complete them. I didn't pick easy-to-knock-off items for a reason. It looks like Sophie's stuck with me forever because she can't resist a good list.

Every time we plan for something, it usually goes wrong before going absolutely right. The day I planned on proposing, I left the ring at home, unable to pop the question on the Monaco cliff where Sophie stepped out of her comfort zone and took a chance on my crazy idea of testing her control. Since home was hundreds of miles away, I couldn't hop in a car and grab it.

I changed the idea at the last minute and proposed smack dab in the middle of our bed. Note to the poor schmucks out there: popping the question in bed is wildly underrated because the sex after that type of commitment will blow anyone's mind.

It stormed on our wedding day, but Sophie insisted we get married outside anyway. We danced in the rain like some old-school movie under the string lights of our backyard. It was one of the most memorable nights of my life, dancing around with my wife, her glitter Vans hidden beneath her wedding gown.

Despite our romantic night under the rainy sky, Sophie got sick after. So, we rescheduled our honeymoon, which was another plan gone amuck in the best way. The doting husband in me tended to her before I caught whatever she had, with her dressing up like a nurse. I can safely say I got the better end of the deal.

I love living in perfect disharmony with her because the best things happen when we're busy focusing on everything else.

Switching to Vitus opened up a whole new F1 journey for me, my career growing as I help a team rise from the "best of the rest" to a top contender with Bandini and McCoy. McCoy's betrayal was a blessing in disguise. It granted me the ability to move on in so many ways, including becoming a better brother, uncle, and lover.

Sophie typically spends the entire F1 season with me, but she left the Prix schedule two weeks ago when she got sick with a bad flu. Her dad and I thought it wouldn't be a good idea for her to travel while throwing up every time she smelled coffee or cigarettes. She pouted all the way home, but I promised to FaceTime her every day until I could come home for summer break to make up for *my betrayal* as she puts it.

I brought her a special present I had custom made to cheer her up. Creativity struck and I delivered. The wheels of my car squeal as I park my McCoy Menace car in our driveway, a smile tugging at my lips at the memory of me fucking Sophie against the hood in this very spot.

I unlock our front door quietly, wanting to surprise Sophie. She thinks my plane lands tomorrow instead of today.

She lounges on the couch and scrolls through her phone. I take a moment to get a look at her, the sickly green color she rocked two weeks ago no longer a problem. Her skin has a golden glow that matches her hair cascading around her.

As if she senses me, she looks up from her phone, sending me a breathtaking smile before she bounds off the couch and jumps into my arms. I nearly drop her present on the floor when I grab her.

"You're back early!" She leaves behind a few kisses on my cheek.

"If this is the welcoming I get, I should stay away longer."

She pinches my arm when I put her back on her feet. "Next time you should let me know if your flight lands sooner. Imagine if I was in bed with our neighbor." She looks at the ceiling and catches a breath. What a faker.

"I didn't think Mrs. Ricci was your type, but grandmas do make good cookies." I pull her in and give her a quick kiss.

"I know. What do you think I found attractive about her in the first place? God, Liam, not everything is about looks."

"I think I learned that when you purposefully tried to look bad three years ago and I still wanted to fuck you into next week."

She smacks me lightly on the shoulder. "It took effort to look that bad. I'm almost disappointed."

She initiates another kiss, our tongues clashing together after a long time apart. The attraction between us never dulls. Instead, it's grown stronger over the years, as we've learned and appreciated more about each other.

The moment you move in with someone, you learn everything. Like how Sophie needs coffee before all else, including sex. I learned my lesson after one too many grumpy sunrise sex sessions. Now every morning, I bring her coffee in bed. Purely selfish of me, but the smile she gives me every damn day makes walking downstairs with a boner well worth it.

I learned how she enjoys trashy American reality television, resulting in us joining a *Bachelor* fantasy league, much to my horror. Or how when a storm comes, she likes to lounge in bed all day drawing while I read. She especially loves lying outside and staring up at the night sky, like she told me all those years ago, but now she gets the added bonus of my kisses.

Three years later and I still love her with everything in me.

"I have something for you. You know what they say: happy wife, happy life." I break away from our kisses.

"That's the most basic phrase, but damn I love hearing it."

"Shit. You're right. Forget happy. I want you to be ecstatic every day of your life, never questioning how you ended up with someone as naughty as I am."

She lets out a soft laugh. "I'd never question your naughtiness. That's one of the best parts."

I grab my present off the couch and place it in her hands. "Well, glad my husband services are working out for you. Here you go."

"Roses? Out of fabric? You shouldn't have."

Even when trying to be nice, she makes the funniest faces. She stares at the present with a confused look, so I help her out with one, grabbing the intricately wrapped rose. I pull it off the detachable stem.

Her smile hits me right in the heart when she reads the words on the shirt.

"What! No way." She grows excited as she detaches another shirt.

I love the way she laughs, both unabashedly and softly at once. What can I say? She turns me into the sappiest motherfucker on the planet.

She unwraps each shirt, a new slogan tee with a funny or sassy statement staring back at her.

"This is such a great idea!" She holds up a shirt to her chest that says *If the love doesn't feel like 90s R&B I don't want it.*

Sophie throws the shirts on our couch and barrels into me

again. She hits me with more kisses and breathless *thank-yous*, her lips making my body hum and my dick harden.

Have I said I'm a lucky man?

She pulls away after showering me with affection. "Now that you're here, I couldn't reach the bin that has all of our spring décor. I wanted to set up the table for dinner with Maya and Noah."

"My dick's hard and ready to go and you're asking me to help you decorate?"

"Yes. Sorry little guy." She pats my pants, eliciting a groan from me.

"I should fuck you right now to remind you how so not little I am."

"Sounds like a plan...after you get the bins." She leaves me with one last kiss before she sits back down on the couch.

"That's my cue to go." I step out of our living room and into the kitchen, craving a water bottle before I locate the bins for her. A green Post-it hangs on the front of the stainless-steel fridge next to a photo of us. *Buy more snacks.* Vague but she knows what she likes. I open up the fridge and find a yellow note dangling near our reusable water bottles, the color standing out against the white interior. *Drink more water. We're all houseplants with more complex emotions.* I laugh at that one.

A green Post-it stuck to the edge of the counter catches my attention. *Get someone to round out the counter corners.* Her clumsiness never ceases to amaze me.

"Getting a little heavy-handed with the Post-its lately. Are you stressed?" My voice carries through the hall.

"Hmm. Maybe," Sophie says from across the house. I walk

through the hall leading to our garage. A yellow Post-it note greets me at the arch, with the saying *Twinkle twinkle little star.* Weird but I don't like to judge.

Another green note hangs off a frame of our gallery wall, starkly contrasting against the black and white photos of us over the years. *Google if stars come in triplets.* I have no clue about that one, but possibly. Maybe I need to call her more and check in if she's feeling anxious.

A pink note catches my attention on the door that opens to the garage. *Save fuel. Ride an F1 racer.* I bark out a laugh as I open the garage door. Just another reason I love her because she never stops putting a smile on my face, from her sassy mouth to the way she looks at me like I snatch the stars for her.

I hurl myself over random items scattered around the floor. My feet nearly trip over an old pair of shoes and a discarded scarecrow that scares the shit out of me. Note to self: I really need to clean out the garage. I make it over to the other side where Sophie keeps her seasonal bins. We're domestic as fuck now, with enough Christmas bins to challenge a small German village.

I look around for the ladder because it isn't in its usual place. Instead, a tarped object occupies the floor with a blue Post-it taped on top. *If you're reading this, bring my dad a beer.* I'm not going to lie; I could totally use a beer right now.

I lift the tarp up to reveal a baby blue kart with a yellow sticky note. *Does this kart make me look like my daddy?*

I inhale a sharp breath as I run out of the garage, tripping over the same pair of shoes before catching myself. Excitement surges through me because no fucking way. My heart beats against my chest, and my lungs can't get enough oxygen.

Sophie beams at me from her spot on the couch, blonde hair everywhere, green eyes shining. The best fucking sight in the damn world. She points down at a shirt she wasn't wearing minutes ago, white block font standing out at me. *Pregnant AF.*

"Surprise!" She raises her arms in the air.

I lift her off the couch and plant kisses everywhere my lips can reach before I place her carefully back on the cushions. My knees sink down onto the hardwood floor as my fingers lift up the hem of her shirt. I place kisses all over her flat stomach.

"Holy shit, we're going to be parents?" I can't believe that question came out of my mouth.

"Turns out the flu wasn't exactly the flu. More like first trimester tummy troubles, kind of like a bad hangover without alcohol."

"You know what this means?" I look at her from my spot on the floor, my face no longer kissing her stomach. "You're protecting the future of F1, the very competitor against Marko Slade."

She sends me a raised eyebrow. "And if we have a girl?"

"Even better. Nothing like getting your ass handed to you by a badass chick. She'd absolutely wipe the track with him."

Sophie drops her head back against the couch and laughs with me.

Damn, I love this girl with everything in me. The girl who captured my heart and never let go. The one who wishes on stars, wears sneakers instead of heels, and kisses me senseless every night. The very woman who gave me a happily ever after. Turns out I was the lost prince and she saved me with glitter Vans and a sword crafted from love and selflessness.

THE END

EXTENDED EPILOGUE

Sophie

Fourteen Years Later

"Looks like Stella might beat Marko this year." Maya clutches onto her homemade sign. Glitter scatters as the wind blows in our faces, the cold weather making me wish the kart race was on another weekend.

I don't do well in the cold. Especially when I don't have Liam to cuddle up to, seeing as he's busy with Noah discussing strategies near the racetrack. They watch the other competitors, writing down their weaknesses while watching our kids race.

"She's spent too many hours practicing with her father. There were times I went to bed and they were still out in the kart park." We're one of those groups of friends, with houses next door to each other and a customized kart park for our kids.

Money can buy a lot of things, but endless memories in a shared backyard? Priceless.

"I heard. Noah goes down there sometimes to see her progress. Do you ever get scared Stella or Leo might want to keep going, like more than a hobby?" Maya grabs her loose dark hair and throws it in a ponytail.

"You mean, as a career? Is it weird we think about our kids' careers? Stella and Leo are only 13."

I think back to earlier this week, with Stella focusing on racing while Leo watched a movie with me. When I asked if he wanted to practice in the backyard, he told me he'd rather be watching Star Wars with me. I raised a winner.

"Probably, but it's their reality. The sports world has been waiting to see what they end up doing. Some scouts are checking out Marko and asking if he's interested in driving for F3."

"But he's only 14!"

Maya shoots me a small smile. "What can I say? He's got his dad's skills. But I don't know if I'm prepared for him to be gone with all that traveling."

"I can't imagine Stella and Leo going off into the world. They're my babies."

"They're growing up so fast. How do we stop it?"

I brush my index finger against my chin. "I don't know. What if we lock them up in their rooms until the end of time?"

"Might work, but I think Marko would enjoy it. He hangs out in his room a lot lately. Just last week, I caught him watching Stella practice with Liam and Noah through his bedroom window."

I laugh at the image of Marko pressed up against the glass, watching my daughter race. "What did you tell him when you found him?"

"If he wants to impress Stella, he's better off going down to the park and giving her some pointers."

"Oh my God. You did not. You're such an embarrassing mom." I let out a loud laugh, causing other parents to stare at me.

"You know it's true. Just last month, when I was doing the laundry, I found a handwritten letter crumpled up in his jean's pocket. I knew it was for Stella because he drew a bunch of stars on it."

"Stop! And what did it say?" My heart races. I always thought Marko had a crush, but hand-drawn letters? I'd call him a young romantic if it weren't for how distant he's been with Stella lately. Enough so that my daughter notices.

"I can't tell you." Maya twirls a piece of her hair. Typical.

I cling onto her arm. "You're not allowed to say your son wrote a letter to my daughter and then cut off right there! You're such a tease! How does Noah put up with you? Better yet, how did you get pregnant again?"

"My lips are sealed." Maya zips her lips before patting her swollen belly. Somehow, Maya and Noah had a miracle baby this late in the game. They tried for years after Marko was born, to no avail. Once they were about to call it quits, boom, positive pregnancy test.

Care to imagine how protective Noah is about her late pregnancy?

I'll give you a hint: if there were a scale, Noah would've broken it about five months ago.

I clutch onto the sleeve of her vintage Bandini sweater. "You're the worst kart mom ever. At least give me a little gossip to get me going through the day."

"Oh, look!" Maya lifts out of her chair shockingly fast for a pregnant woman.

Stella's white kart rushes down the road with Marko's black kart right at her rear bumper. I'd pay attention to the last lap, but my brain can't catch up to Maya's admission. "Now that you've got me thinking up conspiracies, isn't it weird they have opposite kart colors?"

"Hmm, kind of like stars in the dark, right? Interesting how he chose that color when he had the whole rainbow to pick from."

My mouth drops open. "Shut up. How did I not see this before? I'm flabbergasted to say the least."

"You weren't looking close enough." Maya smiles at me.

"Oh my God! She's actually going to beat him. Get out!" I cup my hands over my mouth. "That's my baby girl, you show these boys how it's done!"

Maya and I scream as Stella rushes past the finish line. Marko passes the checkered line a few seconds later, with Leo securing third place. We run down to the road barriers, rushing into Liam and Noah with their clipboards. Well, I rush while Maya waddles, but semantics.

"Our baby did it!" I jump onto Liam's back, my legs wrapping around his waist.

"Yes she did. All by herself." Liam spins me around in a circle as I cling onto his neck.

My voice hits all new levels of high. "And Leo got third. We're sweeping podiums left and right. Go Zanders!"

"Who knew having twins would mean double the wins?" Liam laughs as he puts me back on my feet.

"I still hate you for those stretch marks. They're hideous."

Liam leans into my side, his lips brushing against the shell of my ear as his voice drops. "I think they're sexy as fuck. One look at them gets my cock hard, reminding me how you looked pregnant with our kids. Plus, we both know how much you love when I kiss them." Liam's eyes sparkle with mischief and love. He pulls me in for a kiss, teasing my lips open for him as he shows me exactly why I love him, excessive stretch marks and all.

Some kisses are knee-buckling while others are panty-melting. Lucky me, I get all of them rolled into one, day after day, from the best husband in the whole world.

"Ew! Can you both save this for after my podium party? You're ruining my appetite!" Stella whines. My daughter, with her sweaty blonde braids and a neon pink race suit, stares at us with a huge frown. She places her hands on her hips.

I push Liam off me with little effort.

He lets out a loud laugh as he reaches for Stella. "Come give Daddy a hug. I'm so proud of you."

"You both are so embarrassing!" Stella runs in the opposite direction without looking, barreling straight into Marko. He steadies her before stepping a foot away as if Stella's contagious.

Stella looks back at us with flushed cheeks that weren't pink a few seconds ago.

Interesting. Damn, Maya. I really have been living under a rock.

Marko runs a hand through his wavy onyx hair as he glances at Stella again, eerily reminding me of his father with calculating eyes.

Leo, Stella's protector (because two minutes makes all the difference for twins), slings his arm around our daughter's shoulder. "What's up, kleine schwester. Nice job out there." He rubs his sweaty blonde head against hers, messing up her braids even more.

"Gross! Mom, tell him to stop." Stella tries to shove him off her.

"But I'm only showing my affection. Do you love me?" Leo looks at Liam and me, asking for backup.

"Of course I love you, you big doofus. You're too needy, just like Dad."

"Hey! Take that back." Liam lunges for our two kids, tugging them both into him. They wrap their arms around his waist. He whispers something into their ears, and I can't tear my eyes away.

I sigh, loving my husband more and more each day. He gave me two kids named after the stars, because love is endless, like the dark sky we kiss under every night before bed.

"Marko, why can't you give me hugs like that? Liam's making me jealous." Noah smiles at his son as he inches toward him, rather creepily if I do say so myself.

My eyes gravitate toward Marko, finding him staring at my family, his face neutral except for the smallest twitch of his upper lip. I'm onto you, buddy.

Secret letters? Check.

Staring for a second too long at my daughter before looking away? Hard to miss.

Avoiding her like the plague, just like your dad did with your mom for months? You got it.

Looks like we have a childhood crush on our hands.

This can only go two ways, and based on the way my daughter remains oblivious, it might not turn out to be in Marko Slade's favor.

THANK YOU!

If you enjoyed *COLLIDED*, please consider leaving a review! Support from readers like you means so much to me and helps other readers find books. Join my Bandini Babes Facebook group for all the grid gossip about the Bandini and McCoy racers.

SCAN THE CODE TO JOIN THE GROUP

ALSO BY LAUREN ASHER

Throttled

Read Noah and Maya's forbidden romance.

Wrecked

Don't miss out on Jax's enemies-to-lovers story.

Redeemed

if you like fake relationship romances
with a grumpy hero, check out Santi's story.

SCAN THE CODE TO READ THE BOOKS

ACKNOWLEDGEMENTS

To all my readers — Thank you. Without you, this dream would not be possible.

To the bloggers and Bookstagrammers who support the Dirty Air series, I'd like to say a HUGE thank you. Your reviews, edits, kind words, and love for my characters encourages me to continue writing.

Julie — There aren't enough words to describe my appreciation for everything you do. Your constant support, positivity, and phone calls helped make everything I dream of come true! You've become one of my closest friends throughout this process and I can't wait to see you grow in your own career. The book world is lucky to have someone like you.

Mary and Val at Books and Moods — I think I tell myself weekly I don't know what I would do without you both. You've been the best support system with your cover designs, teasers, formatting, video trailers—well everything!

Erica, my editor — I'll never forget emailing you about beta reading Throttled. I didn't tell you, but your opinion on the book was actually the make it or break it decision for me to pursue the project. I wasn't sure if anyone would like it, but your encouragement and push to work with Amy and Traci helped me publish my first book. Thank you for all your hard work with my projects. Seriously, you are the best editor (Note: this acknowledgements section didn't get her love so don't judge me LOL). I can't wait to continue working together on future projects (*cough *Jax and Santi* cough cough*). You're amazing and I'm thankful for you.

Mr. Smith — You may never read this, but if you ever do, thank you from the bottom of my heart. You're an incredible man who keeps me in check with excel sheets, data tracking, and book updates.

To my beta team (Kenzie, Rose, Andi, Mary, Z, Amy, and Traci) — You ladies are the BEST team I could ask for. Thank you for your time and believing in my characters. Your attention to details, comments, and support helped Collided become what it is today.

To my Street team and ARC team — 1. I can't even believe I have one of these now. 2. THANK YOU. Your dedication to sharing my work with the world is amazing and I can't wait to continue this journey with you all.

Mom — *You'll Be in My Heart*. Sorry for all the Catholic jokes.

Dad — Thanks for everything, including not asking me all about my secret project.

EZ, my little brother — I never considered the impact of my books on you. I hope me pursuing this passion project shows you that you can attempt anything, *especially* the things that scare the shit out of you.

CPSIA information can be obtained
at www.ICGtesting.com
Printed in the USA
LVHW081420200822
726395LV00015B/351